A WHITE CHRISTMAS ON WINTER STREET

Sue Moorcroft writes award-winning contemporary fiction of life and love. *A Summer to Remember* won the Goldsboro Books Contemporary Romantic Novel award, *The Little Village Christmas* and *A Christmas Gift* were *Sunday Times* bestsellers and *The Christmas Promise* went to #1 in the Kindle chart. She also writes short stories, serials, articles, columns, courses and writing 'how to'.

An army child, Sue was born in Germany then lived in Cyprus, Malta and the UK and still loves to travel. Her other loves include writing (the best job in the world), reading, watching Formula 1 on TV and hanging out with friends, dancing, yoga, wine and chocolate.

If you're interested in being part of #TeamSueMoorcroft you can find more information at www.suemoorcroft.com/street-team. If you prefer to sign up to receive news of Sue and her books, go to www.suemoorcroft.com and click on 'Newsletter'. You can follow @SueMoorcroft on Twitter, @suemoorcroftauthor on Instagram, or Facebook.com/sue.moorcroft.3 and Facebook.com/SueMoorcroftAuthor.

700034348127

Sue Moorcroft

A White Christmas on Winter St.

avon.

Published by AVON
A division of HarperCollins*Publishers* Ltd
1 London Bridge Street
London SE1 9GF

www.harpercollins.co.uk

HarperCollins*Publishers*
1st Floor, Watermarque Building, Ringsend Road
Dublin 4, Ireland

A Paperback Original 2022
1
First published in Great Britain by HarperCollins*Publishers* 2022

A catalogue copy of this book is available from the British Library.

ISBN: 978-0-00-852567-5

This novel is entirely a work of fiction. The names, characters and incidents portrayed in it are the work of the author's imagination. Any resemblance to actual persons, living or dead, events or localities is entirely coincidental.

Typeset in Sabon LT Std by Palimpsest Book Production Limited, Falkirk, Stirlingshire

Printed and bound in UK using 100% Renewable Electricity at CPI Group (UK) Ltd

MIX
Paper | Supporting
responsible forestry
FSC
www.fsc.org   FSC™ C007454

This book is produced from independently certified FSC™ paper to ensure responsible forest management.

For more information visit: www.harpercollins.co.uk/green

Acknowledgements

Thank you for reading *A White Christmas on Winter Street*.

In a previous Middledip book, *Christmas Wishes*, we met Nan Heather, who had been a long-time foster mother. My editor agreed with me that it would be great to bring one of her foster children back to the village, and Sky Terran was born.

Of course, I needed a reason for her return to the village that had given her a period of happiness in her childhood. The spark came from the property refurbishment TV show *Homes Under the Hammer*. It featured a large house that had been empty for so long it had almost vanished behind a neglected garden. Much of what I've described in The Corner House was there, including the poignantly empty gardening boots. I was already weaving a story about these in my imagination when the show moved on to the now refurbished house.

All its charm had gone!

The trees had been uprooted and the outside rendered, interior stonework was plastered over, and the wrought iron removed from the windows. It looked disappointingly like a block of vanilla ice cream. I decided that Sky would return to Middledip to save The Corner House from the same fate.

As always, the ideas that wander into my plotty head would never become novels and reach readers without help from a lot of other people. I'd like to thank:

My brother Trevor Moorcroft, who took on the lion's share of research for this book. His fame is spreading as he's helped several of my author friends now.

Mark Lacey, retired detective superintendent and member of the parole board, for helping me construct Lewis Brown's prison experience; and Keith Martin, an old bank colleague, for helping me construct Lewis's fraud.

David and Julia Roberts, who used their nursing experience to provide me with the details of Wilf's accident and injury.

Mark West, who beta reads my books, for always finding something nobody else has noticed and keeping me entertained in the comments column. I'd also like to use this space to remember Graham West, Mark's father, who attended so many of my local events that he must have known my talks by heart, yet always laughed in the right places and had a question ready to get the Q&A segment rolling. The world is a poorer place for Graham's recent passing.

Pia Fenton and Myra Kersner, who their readers know as Christina Courtenay and Maggie Sullivan, for their valuable friendship, sharing of writing retreats and the Sunday evening WhatsApp calls.

Angela Britnell for her help with Marietta, a British woman who married an American man and lived most of her life in the States.

Wonder-agent Juliet Pickering and the team at Blake Friedmann Literary Agency for sprinkling my career with gold dust and being the staunchest of staunch support.

Team Avon HarperCollins, for producing my books to such a fabulous standard and driving my books along with their enthusiasm. Ever friendly and supportive, the team is never fazed.

My publishing teams around the world who take such care of publishing my books in the best way to appeal to their readers.

Team Sue Moorcroft – hooray! A group of wonderful people who joined my street team not just to chat, help choose character names or enter exclusive competitions – such as the competition for the dedication of this book – but because they enjoy my work enough to tell others about it. (Check out www.suemoorcroft.com/street-team if you think you might like to be a member too.)

All my friends and readers who follow me on social media, the fab book bloggers who join my blog tours and invite me to post on their sites, Facebook book groups, bookstagrammers, booktokkers and tweeters. You add sparkle to the love of books and authors.

Anyone who writes a lovely review of one of my books!

And, of course, you, dearest readers. I hope you enjoy meeting characters old and new in *A White Christmas on Winter Street*. I write my books for you.

*To Ann Cooper
a long-time and much-valued member of
Team Sue Moorcroft.
Thank you, Annie!*

Chapter One

Sky ended her call and turned back to her laptop. 'Sounds as if Ramsey will hit his deadline,' she told Freddy.

'Good,' he murmured, without looking up from his computer.

From her place at the third desk in the office, Minnie – Sky's trainee property development manager – chipped in one of her pointed comments. 'On that call you referred to Freddy as your brother, but he's not. He *was* your *foster* brother, that's all.' Several months ago, streetwise Freddy Walker had fallen for Minnie so hard that Sky thought she heard the crash. Upmarket Minnie, despite her expensive pixie haircut and Queen's English, had fallen for him right back. Her friends referred to him as 'Minnie's bit of rough', nevertheless wowed by the golden skin and dark ringlets that came courtesy of his long-gone Trinidadian grandmother. He'd once shown Sky a photo of a beaming woman in a tropical garden, hair in a red scarf, and Sky had envied him knowing a grandparent as much as she envied him the complexion that never went pink and freckled, like hers.

1

'We're as near siblings as either of us has,' Sky told Minnie crisply, and returned to making notes. Silence fell, but for the rumble of traffic outside in Cambridge Business Park and clattering keyboards from the admin office next door.

It gave Sky a hollow ache that Freddy didn't curb Minnie's snark. OK, she and Freddy had only shared a foster home for thirteen months – the happiest part of Sky's childhood – but then Freddy had let Sky sleep on his floor when, at sixteen, she had left her wayward, unreliable mother, Trish Murray, and dared anyone to make her return. She'd changed her name by deed poll and stuck with Terran – 'of the earth' – ever since. Now, Sky thirty-nine and Freddy forty-three, she helped him run Freddy Walker Acquisitions. Freddy *felt* like Sky's brother. She wished he'd stand up for their relationship when his girlfriend dismissed it.

She checked the time. The registration deadline for tomorrow's property auction was three p.m. and she planned to attend in person. She'd hung that on not wanting Freddy Walker Acquisitions to miss out if the internet connection failed at the crucial moment, but the pull was really about the property, The Corner House, being in Middledip – the village where Sky and Freddy had been cared for by a lovely foster mum known to 'her children' as Nan Heather.

At the same time, Minnie beamed at Freddy. 'Ready for lunch, Fred-fred?'

'Yep,' Freddy answered economically, but with a fond smile for his beloved.

Sky watched them pulling on coats, so incapable of taking their eyes from each other that they struggled with zips and buttons. As he exited, Freddy called back to Sky,

'See you later, mate.' He called everyone 'mate', regardless of gender. Freddy had risen from underprivileged kid to bricklayer, to foreman, to project manager, to making money hand over fist as a developer, but had never bothered to adjust his accent and vocabulary to go with his posh cars and smart clothes. Sky, in contrast, had listened to others to learn a more refined way to speak.

After a couple of minutes, Sky heard car doors slamming and the growl of Freddy's Lexus.

She rose, made coffee, then took out her sandwich to nibble as she clicked through her business emails, reading a couple of reports, then replying to a client who was ready to invest in a new project.

Next, she turned to her personal inbox. An October newsletter from a travel company reminded her that she'd yet to decide on her Christmas break. A festive Swiss skiing holiday was vying in her mind with a decidedly un-Christmassy Dubai beach, but she was leaning towards crisp white slopes and gluhwein. No doubt Freddy would be spending Christmas with Minnie so at least she didn't have another person champing at the bit for her decision. Other relationships and friendships had faded recently and she kept meaning to make time for new ones, but was too absorbed by her job. If the construction industry didn't shut down through Christmas and New Year, she'd have happily worked on The Corner House, co-ordinating a team of bricklayers, plumbers, electricians, tilers and decorators to bring Freddy's plans to life.

She grinned as she imagined the promotional blurb for that. *Set up a temporary office in a cosy cottage and spend Christmas implementing schemes of work and ensuring timely deliveries of materials! Marvel at the festive lights outside the village pub, join the carollers as they parade around our ten streets, then drink hot chocolate at the coffee shop.* She didn't remember a coffee shop from her childhood, but her research told her one existed now. And there were more than ten streets, of course – but not many more.

The Corner House, 1 Winter Street, occupied a large plot where the original village and the more 'contemporary and desirable' Bankside Estate met. Empty, swamped by its neglected garden, the property was ripe for redevelopment.

Sky sighed longingly. Her heart had reached out to The Corner House when Freddy had sent her its link in the auction catalogue, *exactly* when she was ready to buy another property for her private portfolio. If only she'd spotted it first . . . but no way would she try and snaffle it from under Freddy's nose.

While she dreamed fruitlessly of restoring the neglected but beautiful house, Freddy planned its conversion to two smart, compact town houses and two studio flats. His conversion would be more profitable than her fantasy restoration, Sky knew, having been the one to write the *Development and Performance Potential Analysis*. The Corner House was neither listed nor in a conservation area and at the pre-application site meeting, the planning officer had deemed Freddy's scheme to be in line with local neighbourhood planning. Young people struggled to get onto the property ladder in villages, and converting The Corner House would provide perfect starter homes.

Sky had highlighted Freddy's intention to cover swathes of the original soft grey stone with pre-coloured polymer render and replace the slates with a synthetic version but had been met with comments about good insulation. And what about the mature trees . . . ? Well, those of interest to the tree officer, like the stately white birch in the front

4

garden, weren't due for felling. Parking would be covered by a drive extended to take two or three cars and the handy pull-in outside. The Corner House Development, as it was now being referred to in the office, could make Freddy a handsome profit.

Sky had had no choice but to commission drawings and surveys for the pre-auction assessments. If the hammer came down in their favour, they'd have just twenty days to complete the purchase.

That Sky yearned for The Corner House was her secret, she thought, deleting another *Start your Christmas shopping now!* newsletter. If Freddy Walker Acquisitions got it, she'd project-manage the conversion, visiting Middledip regularly, maybe several times a week. Her heart trembled, swamped by memories of arriving at Nan Heather's as a scruffy ten-year-old in need of a home. Fourteen-year-old Freddy, already in Nan Heather's care, had introduced her to the village kids. Sky had known herself to be different, having a foster mother and getting free lunches at school, but Freddy had been that kind of different, too. That had begun their bond.

Her one Christmas in Middledip had been magical. A village hall party, the biggest, sparkliest Christmas tree Nan Heather could cram into her cottage, the most amazing dinner topped off with a Christmas pudding wreathed in flames . . . and *presents*. Presents! Drawing and painting things, a sparkly top and new trainers, books and mittens. Freddy had made her a mâché pencil box. To Sky, used to just a few Christmas treats at school and a mum washed away on a tide of alcohol, a cold flat, canned food and only the TV for company, it had seemed like a Hallmark movie. *A Proper Christmas for Sky* maybe, or *Christmas at Nan Heather's*.

She conjured up a vision of Nan Heather's beaming smile with a wistful tug at her heart. As well as hot meals and warm clothes that fit, Nan Heather had provided love and security.

Sky had been distraught when her time in Middledip ended just before her twelfth birthday. Trish had secured a flat in Bretton on the outskirts of Peterborough and declared herself able to look after Sky again. In fact, Sky reflected, deleting another email, Trish had probably got the flat *because* she felt able to look after Sky again. Possibly she'd done a moonlight from their old place in Bettsbrough owing rent, and then sofa-surfed or lived in a squat while Sky was fostered by Nan Heather. Or maybe she'd hooked up with someone who didn't want a kid around. Whatever, when Trish had eventually applied to be rehoused, she judged Sky to be a big tick in the right box.

Sky still ached at the memory of lying awake in that new flat, no warmer or less bare than the old, yearning to return to the comfort and love she'd found at Nan Heather's.

As the move had also meant swapping to a Peterborough school, only Hotmail and MSN via a public computer in the library kept her in contact with Freddy. That was how, when Sky was fourteen, he'd informed her that he'd passed his A levels and exchanged life in care for an apprenticeship and a room to lodge in. Nan, at sixty-five, was retiring from fostering. Sky had just discovered that Trish needed three months of rehab and, heart soaring, had been envisaging a joyful return to Nan Heather and Middledip. She'd gazed at Freddy's message, dumb with disappointment.

To a furious teen, it had felt as if Nan Heather had let her down.

Though placed with a perfectly nice family in Peterborough, Sky had stopped writing to Nan Heather, even if her new foster parents had provided stamps 'to keep in touch with your important people'. If Nan Heather had written to Sky while she'd been away from the Bretton flat for the three months of Trish's rehab that became four, then five, they weren't there when she reluctantly returned. Trish would have binned any letters. She'd never had much use for paper if you couldn't use it to roll a joint.

Unfortunately, while building his career with the single-mindedness of youth, Freddy too had let his relationship with Nan Heather slide. Now, twenty-seven years after Sky left Middledip, Nan Heather must surely be gone.

Sky clicked on the video on her laptop to watch the auction house's walk-through of The Corner House. Scant footage was devoted to the stone exterior, as trees almost smothered the property, but the interior was beautiful. Large, old-fashioned rooms sported dusty chandeliers; a cream-coloured range and a white porcelain sink nestled among wooden kitchen cupboards. Some rooms boasted exposed stone walls or curlicues of wrought iron at the windows, as in a Mediterranean villa.

Sky had also visited the property, a visit she hadn't told Freddy about in case he asked her to take Minnie along. Sky hadn't wanted Minnie looking down her nose and muttering that the village she came from was much posher – even if that was true.

Winter Street was half a mile from Nan Heather's cottage, but Sky had still revelled in being back in the village for a precious hour, though simultaneously laughing at herself. *Why are you so excited to breathe Middledip air again? You were here for just over a year of your childhood. Nobody will remember you.* Maybe someone from Nan Heather's family would still be around – she'd had a daughter, son-in-law and two grandkids a little younger than Sky – but, to them, Sky would just be one of a parade of kids for whom Nan Heather provided temporary refuge.

Sky watched the last few moments of the video, which ended with a last look around the high-ceilinged hallway, zooming in on its stained-glass door. Then she turned to completing her registration for tomorrow's auction before contacting a client to share with him her enthusiasm for the refurbishment of his latest investment property, a semi just outside Cambridge. She'd signed off its spruce-up yesterday – it had been transformed by new windows, doors and flooring, exactly as she'd promised – and she needed his confirmation that she could place it on the rental market.

She was noting the pleasing projected rental yield when Freddy burst into the office, clutching Minnie's hand.

Beaming and starry-eyed, his coat hung open. A damp brown patch marred the trousers of his silver-grey suit.

Pausing with her fingers over the keyboard, Sky stared at the muddy knee. 'Have you fallen over? Or did you need to change a tyre?' Then she noticed that Minnie's eyes were not just full of stars but glittering with . . . triumph? Her stomach swooped.

Minnie beamed. 'Fred-fred just proposed! He got down on one knee in the street, didn't you, darling? We're getting married. We just came to tell you we're going into Cambridge city centre to buy the ring. I'm fancying diamonds.'

Fingers still poised ridiculously in mid-air, Sky's heart turned to lead. 'Married?' she repeated stupidly.

Bashfully, Freddy swung Minnie's hand. 'It's gobsmacking, ain't it?' he demanded. 'Bet you never thought you'd see the day.' He gave Minnie a squeeze that almost lifted her from the floor.

Sky swallowed a sickly feeling of dismay. 'Congratulations,' she muttered.

'Thanks!' Freddy beamed, apparently unaware of the strangled nature of Sky's good wishes. 'Cracking, ain't it?' Then he said to Minnie, 'Didn't you want a wee? Isn't that what we came back for?' 'Wee' was Freddy's attempt at being polite in front of Minnie.

With bone-deep certainty, Sky knew that Minnie needing the ladies' room had been an excuse to call in at the office, so Minnie could see Sky's face as she heard the news.

'Oh. That's right.' Though looking disappointed at being obliged to leave the scene, Minnie turned her head to give Freddy a smacking kiss, then swished away, pausing at the doorway to the admin office to spread the glad tidings, if the cries of surprise were anything to go by.

Left gazing at Freddy, muddy knee and all, Sky felt misery creep over her like the October mist outside the office window. 'Wow,' she said. Then, 'Wow,' and 'congratulations,' again. She cleared her throat. 'This is a surprise.' An appalling one.

Freddy rocked on his heels and shoved his hands in his pockets. 'Yep.'

Sky realised she must take advantage of Minnie's brief absence. 'It's going to be interesting, isn't it? Minnie being my junior but marrying the boss.'

Freddy edged over to his desk and clicked his computer mouse aimlessly, looking at his screen. 'It's just a bit of an adjustment, mate.'

'Right.' Sky tried to calm her racing heart with a couple of long, slow breaths. Working with Freddy had been a joy until Minnie had arrived, unreliable but entitled, traits that seemed to whiz over Freddy's usually shrewd head.

Last month, Freddy had even empowered Minnie to buy at auction, which she'd stuffed up in spectacular style by accidentally buying a shop at a live-streamed event. The preceding lot had been withdrawn at the last minute but it beggared belief that Minnie hadn't noticed the auctioneer announcing lot thirty-two, a shop with flat over, rather than lot thirty-one, a vacant plot.

All this whirled in Sky's head as she answered through stiff lips. 'A lot of adjustment, I'd say. I presume Minnie's going to continue to work here?'

"Course.' Freddy squinted at his computer screen, which enabled him to avoid Sky's gaze. His muddy knee seemed to mock her, brown against the fine cloth. 'But not tomorrow. We're taking a long weekend to tell Minnie's family. See what they make of me, a rough diamond with a potty mouth.' He didn't need to say he wouldn't be bothering his own parents with the happy news, not knowing where to begin looking for his mum and barely able to remember there once being someone in his life called 'Dad'.

'Oh,' said Sky, hollowly. 'Freddy, I'm not sure if I—'

Minnie swirled back in time to interrupt. 'We're going to arrange Christmas with my people, too, Sky. Sorry we can't invite you, but you are only Fred-fred's foster sister, not a flesh-and-blood one.' She lowered her voice confidingly. 'We're looking forward, rather than back to unfortunate beginnings.'

Sky flushed. She and Freddy had been victims of those 'unfortunate beginnings' but Minnie made it sound as if Sky was somehow responsible. She tried to be pleasant, though. 'Freddy and I have spent some Christmases

10

together, but this year the subject hasn't even arisen. I'm going to book—'

But Minnie cut her off again. 'Must go. Have you offloaded that shop yet?'

Sky gaped. Had Minnie forgotten that Sky was Minnie's supervisor, not the other way around? And that it was Minnie's mess that Sky was clearing up? Freddy scratched his neck awkwardly but failed to put Minnie straight. Sky pointedly addressed her reply to him anyway. 'As agreed, the shop's on the open market. If it doesn't garner interest in eight weeks, I'll put it back in the auction.'

After an infinitesimal pause Freddy answered gruffly, 'See you do.'

He was enabling the fiction that it was Sky who'd messed up. Her heart scudded. Was this how things would be in the Freddy Walker offices from now on? Minnie queening it over Sky with her marrying-the-boss status, Freddy expecting Sky to put up with it instead of receiving her due respect as Freddy's right-hand person?

As if to reinforce this dread, Freddy went further. 'That auction for The Corner House is tomorrow. Remember what you're about?'

Blood began to thunder in Sky's ears. 'Bid no higher than three-fifty – though I think your ceiling should be four hundred,' she added.

That prompted Minnie to chime in. 'You know the rules. Don't exceed Freddy's limit.'

This obvious power play made Sky lift enquiring eyebrows. 'Has "don't buy a shop when you're told to buy a vacant plot" been added to the rules?'

Freddy eyes twinkled and for a moment Sky thought he'd laugh and acknowledge the hit. Instead, he let Minnie

11

tuck her arm through his and turn him for the door. 'No,' she said loftily. 'But "don't upset the boss's wife" has.'

Even Freddy looked unsure at that level of presumption, corkscrewing his neck to glance over his shoulder at Sky.

She jumped up in protest, inhaling sharply, thinking of all the sixteen-hour days and six- or seven-day weeks that her love for her job had prompted; the untaken annual leave, the directorship Freddy had often talked about but never bestowed. Before her eyes, her dream job was switching to a nightmarishly untenable position. 'I resign, Freddy,' she said steadily, not even raising her voice.

Freddy gave the kind of laugh that signalled he wasn't taking her seriously, sliding his arm around Minnie's waist. 'Yeah, right. See you Monday, mate. Text me tomorrow to say whether you got that place in good old Middledip, right?'

In fury and grief, Sky's voice failed her.

The newly engaged couple waltzed from the room. The door snapped shut.

She plummeted back into her chair, dizzy with shock. Freddy had let her down. She could live with him putting Minnie before Sky – but not standing by while Minnie trampled Sky's dignity in her croc-effect Christian Louboutins.

Woodenly, she turned back to her laptop and typed:

Dear Freddy Walker,

Just a note to formalise my verbal resignation. I have five weeks' holiday owing and as I've never had a contract, I'll take that in lieu of notice and consider my employment with Freddy Walker Acquisitions at an end with immediate effect from today, 27th October.

She printed and signed the single sheet with shaking hands and left it on Freddy's desk, then emailed him a copy in case he never found her resignation amongst the litter of his workspace.

She spent an hour on loose ends on this, her last day as development manager, including returning to the auction house website and marking potential properties for her portfolio. A new project of her own would provide a stopgap while she decided where she went from the job she'd thought would continue forever.

A tear quivered on her lashes. She blinked it away.

Then she positioned her work phone and laptop on the desk and left them there. Her own phone was in her bag and her computer at home in her smart apartment in an industrial conversion in Mill Park.

In a daze, she drove there now, going over her past as she battled traffic and cursed cyclists. Two years since she'd bought her apartment, after three years in a different apartment with smooth, blond boyfriend Blake. Two years before that, she'd left behind a house and garden when dark, sultry husband Marcel had had enough of her workaholic lifestyle which, he insisted, she hid behind because she was afraid relying on a real, live person might get her hurt. Sky had indulged in a cry on Freddy's shoulder and then buried herself even deeper in her work.

She'd been more successful at friendship than relationships, but, eventually, friends too had drifted away. Eloise had left for the States, Luisa had taken a job somewhere Sky couldn't remember, Marsha was a mum and the Christmas card Sky had sent a couple of years ago had been returned in January marked 'no longer at this address'.

These unpalatable consequences of her obsession with the metamorphosis of run-down properties into beautiful homes and profitable investments revolved in her mind as she parked at an electric-vehicle charging point outside her apartment building. After connecting the thick cable, she took the lift to the top floor. Slowly shedding her office clothes, she knew herself to be even more adrift now than when she'd walked out of her mother's life. Then, she'd at least had a plan – to sleep on Freddy's floor until she finished school and could generate enough money for a room of her own; to work hard and become self-sufficient so no one could let her down.

But now her busy, fulfilling job had evaporated, Freddy had hurt her, and she had nothing else.

She drifted into her kitchen area but couldn't eat or drink a thing. Her heart didn't know its usual measured beat but flung itself around her chest, chopping up her breath. Panicked and claustrophobic, she threw her coat back on and ran through the door and down the stairs, bursting into the pedestrian area. Like a demented jogger in jeans and a coat, she rushed along nearby streets as if synchronising the speed of her feet with her racing heartbeat would outdistance the awful events of the day.

It didn't work.

Freddy was marrying Minnie, who'd aimed to oust Sky in Freddy's affections from the first day she wiggled her bum his way.

She forced her feet to slow as people gave her odd looks. Her legs turned to washed string and she stumbled to a halt, pretending she'd stopped to gaze at a Halloween display of carved pumpkins in the window of a ground-floor apartment.

Freddy, and Freddy Walker Acquisitions, were gone from Sky's life. The fulfilment was over; the satisfaction of research, organisation, brain work and assembling good

14

teams of contractors. She'd shared *vision* with Freddy and been confident that the promised directorship would materialise eventually.

She hadn't foreseen Freddy finally conducting a relationship for more than six months, let alone going down on one knee in the street.

She *definitely* hadn't anticipated ever resigning from Freddy Walker Acquisitions and walking away from Freddy. From *Freddy*!

Chapter Two

Though spent, Sky knew she wouldn't be able to sleep. She dragged herself to bed and put the TV on. Her go-to comfort had never varied since a childhood of being left alone.

Wildlife programmes.

David Attenborough was her favourite – wasn't he everybody's? – but she could always find something that would transport her into another world and make her forget reality. Tonight, she sank herself in a show about nocturnal animals then a programme about polar bears. The shrinking polar ice cap made her cry. At least, that's what she blamed for the tears that blurred the TV screen.

Eventually, she slept, lulled by the hushed, soporific tones of Ralf Little narrating *Monkey Life*.

Her first waking thought on Friday morning was: *I resigned*. A horrified shiver shook through her. Lying back on her pillows, she checked her phone. No messages from Freddy. Maybe she could retract her resignation and . . .

And Freddy would still be marrying Minnie, who saw Sky as a barrier to erasing Freddy's past.

But guilt nibbled at her.

Should she have walked out? The admin office staff would have locked up last night and would carry on today. Freddy would return on Monday. But . . . no. Freddy would think he deserved better from her than to abandon her post. In her head she heard him say: *If you couldn't work with Minnie then you should have given me time to replace you, mate.*

She winced. Even if Freddy was marrying an entitled, possessive woman, he was *Freddy*. From beneath her crisp white duvet, she stared at her bedroom's smooth grey walls and white ceiling, her sense of injury wrestling with her conscience.

At least she'd registered for bidding on The Corner House today. She would still do that for Freddy.

She let out an enormous sigh, sat up in bed and reached for her phone to tap out an email.

Hi Freddy,
*   I overreacted yesterday. I hope you're having a fab celebration weekend. Let's talk on Monday. We must be able to work something out.*

She could suggest Minnie no longer be Sky's trainee. Freddy intended to give his new fiancée her own client portfolio eventually, so he could bring that forward and supervise her himself. Feeling better now she'd acted, she showered in her shiny, pristine bathroom before dressing in a rust-coloured suit with cream ankle boots.

Her present, comfortable lifestyle had once seemed a far-off dream. She dried her hair, gazing over the flat roof of a nearby apartment block towards the park, remembering how she'd set out to grow as a person, improving and diversifying herself like a property portfolio. Travel had been a notable absence in her upbringing, so she'd accepted invitations from colleagues at her first job, letting the friendly young women who'd experienced family holidays all their lives lead her wide-eyed through airports or show her how to get the train to music festivals with her backpack and tent. Clubs had been daunting, clothes shopping a skill to learn.

Looking back on it, that work-life balance had been healthy. Had the pursuit of success above all else only crept in when she went to work for Freddy?

Uncomfortably, she shifted her mind to the auction and the familiar, comforting role she was good at.

The Corner House would come up around lunchtime, but a couple of properties she was interested in for her own portfolio would go through earlier. The money was already in the bank, raised on other property she owned. She was a practitioner of the buy, restore, rent out, refinance cycle.

Just as she was threading her arms into her jacket, a notification popped up on her phone screen. *Email: Freddy.* A shiver ran over her as she opened it, and, in mounting disbelief read:

> *Actually I think you got a point there's prob not room in the company for minnie and you let's leave it that you've resigned mate x*

She gasped. Even with Freddy's customary disdain for capitals and the only punctuation applied by AutoCorrect, there could be no ambiguity. Really? *Really?* That was it for her and Freddy Walker Acquisitions? The end to thirteen years of joint success? Stomach churning, Sky shakily

18

touched Freddy's name on her contact list and waited for a call to connect. It was as if her life was tumbling around her shoulders.

The ringing tone sounded twice, then came Freddy's voice. He snapped, 'Not now, Sky, mate.'

Fresh shock and hurt lanced through her. 'I just want to talk—'

'I said not fucking *now*.' The line went dead.

Shaking, Sky dropped the phone to the bed. Like a sleepwalker she went to the open-plan kitchen with its trendy matt-grey units for a glass of water. After several minutes to compose herself, anger took over from pain.

So, that was that. Freddy could not have made it any clearer that the next phase of his life would not include a starring role for Sky. He'd found something better, even if Sky hadn't. The pain of betrayal made her stomach ache.

She gathered her things, slipped into her black wool coat and took the lift down to ground level. An hour later, she was parking outside the conference centre in Peterborough where the auction was to be held. She registered attendance, then entered the close atmosphere of the auction room, automatically selecting a seat where she'd be easily visible to the auctioneer.

None of the properties she was interested in had yet come under the hammer. She sat immobile on the red chair, half-listening to the rise and fall of the grey-haired auctioneer's patter, watching his spotters keeping eagle eyes on the bidders in case he missed a raised hand. It was as if Sky was floating, watching auction staff taking telephone or internet bids, in-person bidders nodding or shaking heads, holding up numbered paddles. The gavel banged the side of the lectern each time a property was sold.

The first of Sky's potential properties was lot forty, a 'walk-in', so well looked after it could only be the sad evidence of some poor buggers falling down on their mortgage payments. Buying it would mean little work before renting out to tenants, but also limited potential to add value. She'd once got such a good deal on a 'walk-in' in Cambridge that she'd literally only swept up before flipping the place with a sixty-grand gross profit, which had made it possible to convert a different property for multiple occupancy of vulnerable young people.

This time, the bidding went too high.

The auctioneer droned, the bidders shuffled and coughed.

Eventually, Sky heard: 'Lot fifty-eight. Four-bedroomed, detached property, on a generous corner plot, sought-after village location, needs complete modernisation.' The auctioneer's silver hair was beginning to flop forward in the overheated room. 'Who'll start me at two hundred thousand?'

The room slammed into full colour and crisp focus.

Lot fifty-eight was The Corner House. Freddy was expecting Sky to bid. Despite everything, if she could get it for him within his limit of three hundred and fifty thousand pounds, she would.

Bids began in a flurry. The opening bidder was a dark, glossy-haired man across the aisle, three rows forward. He was calm and composed, in contrast to a woman just in front of Sky who bid with jerky nods. Judging from the direction of the auctioneer's pointing hand, two further bidders were behind Sky and one of the auction house proxy bidders was bidding from the front.

The bidding climbed briskly to three hundred thousand. By the time it reached three hundred and forty thousand, everyone had dropped out apart from the jerky woman and the glossy man. Sky still sat motionless, prepared to swoop in on Freddy's behalf if she could.

At three-fifty, the woman shook her head instead of nodding. She'd had the same ceiling figure as Freddy.

'Three-five-one?' suggested the auctioneer.

The glossy man nodded. When he turned aside, Sky caught sight of light stubble and high cheekbones.

The auctioneer used his entire arm to point at him, like a Dalek with its ray gun. 'With you, sir, at three-five-one. Three hundred and fifty-one thousand pounds.' He scanned the room with his urgent, intense gaze and pointing arm, while his spotters alongside him performed scans of their own. 'All done? I'm going to sell. Going once . . .'

Sky wondered what the glossy-haired man's ceiling figure was.

'. . . twice . . .'

The glossy man hefted his white plastic paddle, ready to thrust it into the air.

A lust gripping her for the property, for the village, for something to cling to, Sky called clearly, 'Three-sixty,' and raised her right hand.

Glossy man turned in his seat to locate her with a dark, snappy gaze. She watched him try to compute why she'd come in just before the last bang of the gavel with a jump instead of a small step.

Silently, she enlightened him: *to surprise and destabilise you.*

'New bidder,' the auctioneer cried happily, swinging his outstretched arm towards Sky. 'Three-sixty I'm bid. Three-sixty, thank you, madam.' The arm swayed back towards glossy man. 'Three-sixty-one, sir?'

Glossy man glanced at Sky, clearly deliberating, then at

21

his catalogue as if the answer to whether he should take her on might be held there.

'Three-six-one, sir?' the auctioneer repeated coaxingly.

After a second, the glossy man nodded, but it was a quick, uncertain dip, nothing like his earlier calm confidence.

He's gone over his limit. He's probably wondering how much more he can scrape together, Sky thought dispassionately. She was well within four hundred thousand, which she'd considered the correct limit for The Corner House all along. 'Three-six-five,' she called, and held her paddle in the air to psych the auctioneer into dropping the hammer.

Her opponent shook his head.

Sky felt an exultant rush at the final crash of the gavel.

The auctioneer announced her paddle number. A grey-moustached member of the auction house staff ushered her to the contracts desk while the auctioneer's voice rose and fell as he moved on to the next lot. Sky went through the routine of providing her driving licence, proof of residency and the other details needed to carry out security checks. She paid the deposit and administration fee, which involved a call to her bank, then completed and signed the memorandum of sale. The man with the grey moustache reminded her that it was an unconditional sale and completion was required in twenty days. She nodded. It was all familiar, yet unreal.

Tucking her copy of the memorandum of sale in her bag she rose, knees like water. What would Freddy think of her buying The Corner House for herself, instead of for the company? She hadn't shafted him, but she'd never done anything that might be seen as poaching on his territory before.

Outside, in her car in the chilly grey car park, she paused to think, anxiety creeping over her in a sliding, sinking sensation of having no schedule and no one to meet.

Since the day she'd told a barely conscious Trish Murray, 'I'm leaving,' and abandoned the grotty flat, passing the broken lift and hefting her backpack down the dirty staircase, she'd known purpose. Get to Freddy's place. Get the best GCSE results she could – four A-stars, four As and two Bs. Get her apprenticeship, which proved to be with a housing association, study for qualifications, get on in her job. Work hard. Work all day. Work as many days as possible.

Now, it was only two in the afternoon, and it really didn't matter which way she turned out of the car park.

She hunted inside herself for something, anything, that didn't involve returning to her empty flat . . . and lit on the property she'd just bought. The Corner House wasn't yet legally hers, but she could look around the village. She was hungry. She'd try the coffee shop she'd seen mentioned on Middledip's Facebook page. Seizing on that spark of motivation, she started her car and pulled out of the car park.

The traffic was light on the parkways that seemed forever edged in traffic cones, and it took her only half an hour to drive around and out of the city, through Bettsbrough and into Middledip.

She pulled up outside The Corner House and gazed through her windscreen. The sky was steely, almost the same colour as the stone walls peeping between an explosion of trees and shrubs. What had once been a conifer hedge now erupted as wildly as Popeye's spinach when he squeezed the can.

As there was no one to mind, she got out, buttoning her coat, and approached the gate that sat diagonally where Winter Street and Great Hill Road met. Main Road ran nearby. Ignoring the protesting squeal, she opened the gate and shoved past the overhanging shrubs up the path to the oak front door with stained-glass apertures and oversized, rusty hinges.

Then she halted, feeling suddenly foolish. What was she doing? The house's only occupants were dust bunnies and she couldn't get in to clear them out until November 17th.

The wind wintry around her legs, she returned to the rusty, wrought-iron gate, and turned right into Winter Street, past the overgrown conifer hedge that rendered half the pavement unusable. A nearby clipped privet hedge seemed to be showing the conifers how a nice hedge ought to behave. She found herself at the beginning of the Bankside Estate. Built of either buff-coloured bricks or a dusky rose-pink, the houses followed a few basic designs, their gardens neat.

Winter Street segued into Top Farm Road and the properties became larger, some with porticoes, others with solar panels. Aiming for the centre of the village, she turned left, then crossed into New Street which, like Winter Street, had contemporary homes at one end but a couple of old stone places where it joined the old village at Ladies Lane.

Now she had her bearings. Left, past the village hall and the playing fields, to The Three Fishes pub on the corner. Right, and she was in Main Road, where the bus stop stood. It was where she'd caught the bus when she'd graduated to Bettsbrough Community College at age eleven, outside a brick cottage with a fountain in the front garden.

There was a garage. Had that been there? She frowned in thought, feet slowing. Her boot heels weren't great for walking, but she closed her mind to the burning spots on

24

her feet and checked out the village shop, opposite the garage. It had been called Crowthers. Now it was Booze & News.

She turned the corner into The Cross and gazed at the cottages of Rotten Row. She knew, as probably everyone in property did, that 'Rotten Row' was a corruption of 'Rue le Roi' or King's Street, but it must have been a tiny king that this row was named after. Nan Heather's place had been in the middle.

The cottage had barely changed. Same golden privet hedge, same cracked concrete path to the side door. Sky gazed up at the dormer windows, wondering who lived here now and if any neighbours remembered Nan Heather. Deciding that she could investigate once she owned The Corner House – she had to pinch herself at the thought – she moved on and turned right. And there stood The Angel Café, a red-brick Victorian set back from the road. Sky took a minute to admire the moulded bricks and the sliding sash windows. Then the lit windows beckoned her with the promise of steaming-hot coffee. She made for the door.

Inside, the furniture was painted sea green and the floor tiles formed a jolly multi-coloured mosaic. Just as she arrived at the shiny glass counter, grateful for the steamy warmth after the chill outside, a voice at her shoulder said stiffly, 'Congratulations on making the winning bid.'

Startled, she swung around.

The glossy-haired man who'd bid against her was gazing back, eyes as dark as coal. 'I have got the right person? You've just bought The Corner House?'

'I have.' Though he was frowning, she awarded him a polite smile. 'Sorry you missed out.' Generally, property auction bidders lost with no more than a grimace. Competitors rarely approached her – especially after she'd driven thirty minutes away from the auction house. 'You live in Middledip?' she asked, to check he hadn't stalked her here.

'I do. Buy you a coffee?' he offered, before adding less abruptly, 'Maybe a snack? I haven't eaten lunch.'

She hesitated. What she wanted to do was read her messages in case Freddy had tried to patch things up, in which case she'd explain why she'd bought The Corner House for herself. The glossy man was brusque in his disappointment at missing out, but she could only see one free table, so she'd probably end up sharing it with him anyway. 'Well . . . thanks.' To go with her coffee, she chose a brie and grape wrap, leaving him to carry the tray while she secured the table.

He joined her, bringing with him sachets of sugar and paper napkins. 'I'm Daz Moran,' he said, seating himself opposite her. 'Darragh, but I go by Daz.'

'I'm Sky Terran,' she replied, after thanking him for her wrap and ripping open its plastic covering. The mild, cheesy fragrance sharpened her appetite for the first time since Freddy had entered the office with one muddy knee. 'Is Darragh Irish?'

He nodded, tipping sugar into his coffee. 'My parents came to England as students.' He changed the subject. 'I was hoping to get The Corner House for a project with friends.'

'Sorry,' she repeated, without actual guilt. Anyone who got sore at being outbid shouldn't go to auctions. You put in a shedload of work and then someone came along with a higher bid, and it was all wasted. That's just how it was. 'What did you guys want it for?'

Daz unwrapped his tuna sandwich, pausing to lick a smear of mayonnaise from his finger. 'Dormitories. We

26

were calling it Adventure Accommodation. There are outdoor pursuits venues in the area, and they need places to sleep the kids with their teachers or youth leaders. We've been waiting for The Corner House to come on the market for ages. It's perfect. We'd planned five sleeping rooms with four double bunks in each, shower rooms and a dining room. We're completely stuck now.'

She felt sorry that he'd invested a lot of hope in the purchase but could think of only one reason why he might expend energy on this conversation when it was a done deal. She chewed a bite of the wrap, enjoying the creaminess of the brie and the tang of the red grapes. 'If you live in Middledip, I guess you bought me lunch to give yourself a chance to discover what I'm going to do with the property.'

He didn't deny it. The frown returned, hollowing his cheeks and making granite of his jaw. 'The Corner House stands on a big plot and there's anxiety in the village that some developer will knock it down to cram a modern apartment block on there. I live on Winter Street myself.' His gaze zeroed in on her.

'A property developer would have already performed a feasibility study,' she returned, prickled by the way he'd pronounced 'some developer' as if he'd meant 'some profit-mad, cold-hearted rat'. 'There's insufficient off-street parking to put many apartments on there, even if planning allowed the felling of trees. It's unlikely permission would be granted for a building of more than two storeys in such a rural location and the existing building's structurally sound, so permission to demolish is unlikely, too.'

He blinked under this onslaught of information. 'So, if you're not a developer . . . what are you going to do with the property?'

27

If she corrected his misapprehension about her being a developer, it would prompt a host more questions, so instead she paused to enjoy the moment, along with a rush of pleasure fierce enough to momentarily quell her uncertainty about the future and her hurt over Freddy.

'Not that it's anyone's concern,' she returned sweetly. 'But I'm going to live there.'

Chapter Three

It was early evening when Daz greeted Ismael and Vern at the door to his house in Winter Street. 'Well, as I told you in my message, I didn't get The Corner House. Sorry, boys. Some investor I am.' He ushered them in and closed the door before too much frigid October air swirled in behind them.

Ismael's eyes and hair were even darker than Daz's own, his skin the Mediterranean gold that went with Cypriot ancestry and, like Vern, he had contacts in activity centres. Heavily, he said, 'You were outbid. We knew the competition might have bigger budgets.'

Vern sighed gloomily. His blond hair went with his pale blue eyes. 'It would have been fantastic for our purpose, but we'll just have to keep looking.'

They followed Daz into the kitchen, slinging their coats over bar stools while Daz rummaged in the fridge for beers, sliding the cans across the white quartz top as his friends seated themselves at the breakfast bar. 'Thanks for coming here instead of meeting at the pub. Wilf's upstairs, gaming.' By 'upstairs' he meant the attic room where he

29

worked and where his gaming rig was, a magnet to eleven-year-old Wilford Brown. He dropped his voice. 'Since his dad went to prison and Wilf and his mum came to live in the village, he's here a lot. He's lost, poor kid. Discovering Lewis is a fraudster was shattering. He feels as if the whole village is talking about him.'

Vern pulled the ring tab on his beer. 'I've only met her through you, but his mum will reel Wilf in if you mention it, won't she? She seems a good sort.'

'Yeah, Courtney's great, but Wilf's fine here.' Daz took one of the white stools. 'She said he could stay till eight and I'm not going to kick him out early.' Daz had grown up with Wilf's dad, Lewis Brown, and the only letter Daz had received from him in prison had been a plea. *Whether Courtney remains my wife is in doubt, but she'll always be Wilf's mum, so please look out for her along with Wilf, if you can.* Though Daz hadn't really needed to be asked to support Courtney and Wilf, he'd fallen into the habit of downplaying his own shock and disappointment in Lewis to do so.

The past year had been a rollercoaster of change. Daz's pretty but capricious girlfriend Abi had left to live in London last November; Lewis had been incarcerated in January, causing Wilf and Courtney to move to Middledip in September. Courtney hadn't had a hope of keeping their enormous house in Bettsbrough without Lewis's salary.

Ismael and Vern were great blokes, but their history as Daz's mates was comparatively short. Both had come to Middledip as adults, whereas Daz had lived here all his life. They had wives, but Daz was single since Abi fluttered off to the bright lights of the city. Ismael was dad to a new baby, Vern had two kids at Middledip Primary School . . . and Daz had no parenting experience but was trying to 'be there' for a disorientated eleven-year-old boy. Nevertheless, throwing himself into plans for Adventure Accommodation with Vern and Ismael had helped distract him from knowing Lewis had been put away, and he couldn't shake the wretched feeling of disappointment that they'd missed out on The Corner House.

He hadn't realised how much he'd wanted the change the project would have brought him, until it had been denied.

Ismael looked pained. 'Poor Wilf. It's incredibly hard when someone you look up to lets you down.'

'I've found it hard enough, let alone an eleven-year-old,' Daz agreed gruffly. 'Lewis worked *in a bank*. He must have known his fraud would be found out sooner or later.' Like pressing a bruise, he had to keep testing how much it hurt that Lewis had abused a position of responsibility to target vulnerable customers.

Vern took a draught of beer. 'I'm not completely clear what he did. I read in the paper that there was a woman involved.'

Daz looked down, as if he bore some responsibility for his oldest mate's actions. 'She was an old uni mate. Very ill. She needed treatment abroad and he ran her GoFundMe page. He was manager of a small high street bank branch and when the money that was legitimately raised ran out, he identified an elderly, isolated customer with income and offered to oversee his account. Then he raised a loan in that customer's name, took the money and let the income service the repayments. He diverted statements to the branch so the customer "wouldn't be bothered by them". As more treatment was needed . . . he found more elderly, isolated customers to target. Then someone checked bank statements online. The truth came out. Lewis was prosecuted for confidence fraud and got four years.'

'Wow.' Vern shook his head, looking appalled. 'Have you been to see him . . . inside?' He said the last word as if he didn't want it in his mouth.

Daz had a practised reply to the question, which had the benefit of being true but disguised his unwillingness to see Lewis in his current circumstances. 'I'm on his list of prison-approved friends and family but don't want Lewis using up his prison visits on me. He needs them for his family.' He had other, similar, avoidance strategies: he didn't want to deplete Lewis's stash of private cash with phone calls and even emails cost forty pence to receive, as each had to be printed and taken to the prisoner. *The prisoner.* Just thinking the term put a lump in Daz's throat. Of course, he could have added funds to Lewis's prisoner account to fund contact between them. But he hadn't.

It made him feel guilty, but he wasn't the only one avoiding Lewis. Wilf had so far refused any contact at all.

Despite Lewis having brought her world crashing down around her, Courtney visited him every few weeks, and said he respected both Daz and Wilf's feelings.

Ismael seemed to realise it was time for a change of topic. 'What's the buyer aiming to do with The Corner House? Do you know?'

Daz propped his elbows on the cool white quartz, which Abi had made such a fuss about buying but had left behind a year ago, like everything else in the house, including him. 'Live in it, she said.'

Ismael's dark brows quirked. 'Does she have an enormous family? You could garrison an army in that place.'

Daz shrugged, then took a gulp of beer. 'I could hardly give her the third degree about her family. She did say she wouldn't demolish it and stick a crappy block of flats there.'

Ismael snorted. 'Think she'd have owned up to that? Maybe she recognised you as a concerned villager and told you what you wanted to hear.'

Though discomfort wriggled his stomach at this thought, Daz laughed it off. 'Aw, you're destroying my faith in humanity. And I bought her coffee and everything.' The glowing way she'd said, *I'm going to live here* had made him believe she had no plans to spoil their beautiful Cambridgeshire village. On the other hand, she could have meant: *I'm going to live here . . . until planning permission comes through. Then I'll cram the plot with nasty little rabbit-hutch houses and make a thundering profit.* Was Sky Terran that cold and designing?

He took out his phone and began a search. After trying various spellings of both Sky and Terran, he frowned. 'This looks like her on LinkedIn. Damn. She's a development manager for an acquisitions agency. That's a property developer by another name, isn't it?' He sighed heavily, trying to remember whether Sky Terran had stated that she *wasn't* a developer. 'Though I suppose developers need homes like anybody else.'

Ismael looked interested. 'What was she like, Daz?'

'Businesswoman, late thirties.' Daz took a reflective pull on his can of beer and enjoyed the zing of it on his taste buds.

'Pretty?' Ismael persisted shrewdly. 'Maybe her charms blinded you to her nefarious schemes.' His suggestive grin indicated that he was getting over the day's disappointment faster than Daz was.

Annoyingly, Daz felt his cheeks heat, recalling the trim figure, hair shining like clear honey and secured in a twist behind Sky's head. Though her self-possession and good looks were fresh in his memory, he lied. 'Didn't notice.'

33

A thumping of feet on stairs heralded movement above them and, seconds later, Wilf clattered noisily onto the wooden flooring in the hall. 'Mum texted. Gotta go,' he announced briefly, shoving his feet into dirty, unlaced trainers. His hazel eyes flicked to Vern and Ismael and belatedly he said, 'Hello.' He dragged a hoodie over his head and emerged with his untidy mouse-coloured hair spiking up around the quiff at the front.

Vern and Ismael smiled and returned his greeting. Daz rose. 'I'll walk you back, Wilf.'

'No need.' Wilf yanked his coat off the coatrack and perched the hood on his head, leaving the rest of the coat dangling down his back.

Good-naturedly, Daz winked. 'Yes need, because I promised your mum I would.' Daz's house was on the opposite side of Winter Street from where Wilf and Courtney now lived, and a bit further up. Middledip was the cosiest of little villages, but Courtney was nervous of the dark.

The other men rose and pulled on their coats, dumping their empty beer bottles in the recycling bin. Ismael said, 'We'll go to The Three Fishes. Coming later, Daz?'

Daz didn't want to say, 'Are you meeting your wives?' because that would only emphasise how odd he was still finding it not to be part of a couple or even suggest he didn't feel complete as a single man. Instead, he nodded. 'If I can. Don't wait for me, though.'

In another couple of minutes, he was locking his front door, Vern and Ismael receding down the street under the streetlamps, huddled into their coats as a clammy mist swirled along the street.

Wilf fell into step beside Daz, his laces still untied. 'So, that survival game I was playing,' he began, pulling his coat around himself against the bite of the wind but not threading his arms into the sleeves. 'It's one you're testing, right?'

'That's right. Quality-assurance testing. That game's age-appropriate for you,' he mentioned, to make sure Wilf knew Daz wouldn't let him play something like Resident Evil, in the eighteen-plus category.

He checked for traffic before they crossed the road to make the one-minute journey to the small house Wilf shared with Courtney. Most of Bankside's houses were between twenty-five and thirty years old, but theirs was a new build, squeezed between two of the original houses, bijou compared to their old house in Bettsbrough. The windows were small, and the roof only pitched one way. Daz thought it looked like a giant brick-built shed. When Courtney had moved back to the village, she'd hoped that Graham, Lewis's dad, would be supportive as she didn't get on with her own parents, who lived in Lancashire. Graham, however, had so far proved too trapped in his misery over Lewis to live up to those hopes. Nowadays, he hardly seemed to leave his cottage in Port Road and Wilf was reluctant to visit, declaring him grumpy. Still, Courtney liked the new house, perfect for someone with limited practical skills and modest income. It was OK on the inside, which was what mattered.

Wilf scuffed along the pavement, probably to keep the unlaced trainers on. 'That game's not for sale yet, is it?'

Daz zipped his coat to the top and hunched his shoulders. 'No, it's pre-release.'

The pavements glistened black as they passed houses with lit windows and cars parked outside. Wilf persisted, 'So, I can tell people that at school?'

'Absolutely.' Daz knew the transfer from primary to senior school hadn't gone smoothly for Wilf and rested a casual hand on the boy's shoulder, which was level with Daz's elbow. 'If you want to impress them, you can say it's a 2D sandbox game, due to be available on multiple platforms but the title wasn't disclosed to me because it's an industrial secret. Did you find any issues with it?'

They were approaching the shed-like house now. Courtney's car was drawn up in the drive and the front downstairs window was lit. Wilf frowned in thought. 'It wasn't smooth on level eighteen. I solved the problem of how to earn two nights' shelter but it kind of flickered.'

'You were on the PC, right? I'll see if it runs any better on Xbox.' Daz squeezed past the car on the drive.

Wilf tracked across the small lawn, opened the front door and shouted, 'I'm home,' kicked off his wet shoes, transferred his coat from his head to the newel post and set off up the stairs that led from the narrow hall.

Courtney appeared from the lounge, her straight black hair tucked behind her ears, gaze flying to her son in automatic maternal concern. 'Hi, Wilf. Everything OK?' Her forehead was frequently arranged in horizontal lines, these days. She was losing weight and the hems of her jeans trailed on the carpet because the waistband rode so low on her hips.

'Yeah, fine,' Wilf called back without pausing, though he threw his mum a smile. The firm click of a door a few seconds later suggested that he'd disappeared into his bedroom.

Courtney blew out her cheeks. 'I think Wilf meant, "Good evening, Mum. I'm fine, thanks, how are you? Goodbye, Daz. Thank you for letting me play on your computer. I'm going to my room, now."'

Daz chuckled. 'I don't remember being that gracious when I was eleven.'

She dimpled, smoothing her lines for a second. 'No. I think I spent most of my time sighing over the unreasonable demands of grown-ups. Got time for coffee?'

'Sure.' Aware that Courtney felt isolated in the new life thrust upon her, Daz didn't mention Vern and Ismael waiting at the pub. Now they weren't going to be converting The Corner House they'd no longer be pulled together by the excitement of the project. Newly aware of the casual level of their friendship – and that they weren't Lewis – he followed Courtney to what the sales details had termed 'an eat-in kitchen', which seemed to mean it was too small even to be termed a kitchen/diner. 'Pisser that I didn't get the property at the auction.' He'd texted to tell her.

She crossed to the shiny black coffee maker and pulled out a couple of pods from the drawer. 'Yes, sorry. Didn't get time to reply at work and then forgot. Shame.' But she sounded more listless than sympathetic, and the frown lines had returned. She handed him his steaming coffee mug after a few moments and plopped down onto one of the bistro chairs at the tiny table.

Daz took the other seat. 'How's everything?' It was a redundant question because everything with Courtney had been crap since the day Lewis had called to tell her, in a strained voice, that he was at the Bettsbrough police station and wasn't sure how long he'd be there. Poor Courtney. She'd assumed he was helping the police with some lowlife trying to defraud the bank . . . not Lewis defrauding customers.

She'd had trouble believing it, when Lewis had finally admitted that he'd been raising fraudulent loans in order to send his old infatuation Evira abroad for experimental treatment on her stomach cancer. Courtney had always

37

known about Evira, who'd lived in the same student house as Lewis – that Lewis had been mad about her but she'd friend-zoned him. It had been a shock that they were not only back in touch, but that he'd also risked everything to try to keep her alive. His desperate roll of the dice had failed on all counts. When the truth had finally sunk in, Courtney had been absolutely gutted. Daz didn't blame her.

All this Daz had discovered in retrospect, as Lewis and Courtney had hidden the whole horrible mess through the process of Lewis being suspended, investigated and then charged. Maybe Lewis had been hoping for leniency in view of his crime being a wild attempt to save another person. The judge, however, had noted that Evira had not been Lewis's wife or close family member and that, in any case, fraud and abuse of trust were not acceptable methods of supporting a cause. Furthermore, Lewis had allowed the dying woman to believe the money had come from fundraising, therefore dragging her unwittingly into a crime.

Courtney, stunned and betrayed but trying to keep up a façade of normality for Wilf, had gone along with hushing everything up at first. Then, one day, Daz had dropped by to leave a games controller for Wilf, a prototype he'd tested and wasn't required to return, and found Lewis at home instead of at work. His innocent enquiry as to why had caused Courtney to dissolve into roaring sobs and the ugly truth had sprung on Daz like a monster in a nightmare.

He couldn't erase the image of Lewis's hunted, guilty expression, the sweat that had gathered on his pale skin. *Lewis*. How could *Lewis* have been so misguided? Lewis had been a part of Daz's life for so long that he wouldn't have believed it if anyone other than Lewis had told him.

And now there was a big hole in Daz's life where Lewis used to be.

'Everything's OK, I s'pose,' Courtney answered unconvincingly, jolting Daz from his thoughts. 'Still hating the ghastly admin job.' Courtney now needed the income from full-time work instead of her former twenty hours a week, a need that had funnelled her into the 'ghastly admin job' at a hotel instead of the varied and friendly front-office position she'd enjoyed before. She'd recently interviewed for a role in the office of a Bettsbrough primary school and was awaiting the result. It would be less money, but she'd be eligible for family credit and able to spend school holidays with Wilf, making life easier.

She shifted to the subject that was never far from her mind. 'A lot of women would have cut ties with Lewis. But my focus is on Wilf. How can I encourage him to see or speak to his dad at the same time as dumping Lewis? Wilf's angry and confused enough.'

Daz sipped his coffee. He was angry and confused so goodness knew how Courtney and Wilf felt, but he knew his role in the conversation was to listen, and to respond neutrally. 'You don't have to make a decision yet.' He couldn't encourage Courtney to divorce Lewis but, at the same time, it was anathema to encourage her to stay.

She covered her face, and her next words were muffled. 'Lewis rang earlier, asking to talk to Wilf. I said Wilf was with you but also that he still hadn't agreed to take a phone call.' She curled her hands into fists. 'Lewis cried.' She gave an audible gulp. 'What happens when Lewis gets out? If Wilf starts talking to his dad, do I let Lewis live here, share my bed, for Wilf? Lewis betrayed me when he did what he did behind my back, for another woman. Why would he do that if he didn't have feelings for her?'

39

All Daz could do was pat her arm and murmur consolingly. He was supporting Courtney and Wilf because they were his friends, but that didn't mean he enjoyed these conversations. Evira *had* been 'another woman', but the term wasn't usually applied to a non-sexual relationship.

Courtney sat up, pulled a tissue from her pocket and blew her nose. 'Then Graham called me.' Angry colour leapt to her cheeks and her eyes glistened. 'We had a row.'

Daz frowned. 'It's easy to get into an argument with Graham, these days. He's a chippy little sod.'

She nodded, hurling her soggy tissue into the nearby bin – everything was nearby in a kitchen this small – and fishing out a clean one. 'He asked me what was going on.'

'Suppose he's worrying about Lewis. It's hard not to wonder what's happening to him in there.' Daz often said 'in there' instead of 'in prison'. 'Prison' was an ugly word.

Courtney blew her nose again, with an angry trumpeting noise. 'No,' she said with deadly calm. 'He wants to know what's *going on* between me and you. He all but accused us of having an affair.'

'*What?*' Daz's coffee cup slipped from his hand and sloshed half its contents over the tabletop before he caught it again. He gazed at Courtney aghast.

She snorted, her earlier listlessness vanquished by anger. 'With a liberal sprinkling of F-bombs I told him to get his mind out of the gutter, that you were being brilliant to me and Wilf, which is more than Graham is. He told me he's *embarrassed* by what Lewis has done. I told him that I know exactly how that feels, with a side order of "humiliated", "devastated" and "resentful".' Abruptly, the fight drained out of her. She slid her hand back over her eyes. 'The families are punished as much as the prisoner.'

'I know.' Not now daring to sling a friendly arm around

40

Courtney, who he'd never hesitated to greet with a hug and kiss to the cheek when Lewis was around, Daz crossed to the sink for a cloth to clear up the coffee spill. His hands shook with fury. Where had Graham been when Courtney had choked back the tears as she'd sold furniture to allow her involuntary downsizing? When she'd stuck her chin in the air as people had stared at her and Wilf, the visible evidence of the scandal? Graham lived only a ten-minute walk from his grandson and daughter-in-law, yet he hadn't visited once.

Courtney sniffed. 'Have you been in touch with him?'

Daz understood 'him' was Lewis, not Graham. She asked the same question a couple of times a week. 'Not since answering that first letter.' He tossed the cloth back in the sink and resumed his seat. With a huge effort, he offered, 'Would it make things easier for you if I tried to set up a phone call with Lewis?' He almost prayed aloud that she'd say 'no'.

'No.' She sighed. 'I just wondered.'

They sat on in silence, Daz feeling guilty because he was relieved to continue avoiding Lewis, who was exceptionally easy to avoid, being locked up in a Category C prison. Was the village rumour mill also remarking on his motives in helping Courtney and Wilf? Would it get back to his parents, who lived in the older part of the village, too?

A tear seeped from Courtney's eye and clung to an eyelash. 'I invited my sister for Christmas. She said we could go down to her but that she wouldn't come up here. She doesn't want to be here, with the pointing fingers. She asked why I didn't move right away, instead of coming to Middledip.' She reached for another fresh tissue and blotted her eyes. 'Perhaps I should have, but

I thought moving back here would provide a balanced path – get Wilf away from the immediate area we lived in but allow him to start the same senior school as his mates. But they don't know how to handle him. They make stupid jokes and they've nicknamed him "Criminal".' A tear splashed down onto her top. 'Of course, the village kids went to Middledip Primary rather than Oak Road in Bettsbrough. He doesn't know them and he's wary of what they might say.'

'Kids,' Daz growled, feeling as if he could cry for Wilf himself.

It was over an hour later that Daz felt free to leave. Thinking that a big, fat pint of beer might cheer him up, he strode away from his own house towards the pub, past the overgrown mess of a garden that surrounded The Corner House. He averted his gaze. This evening would have been so different if he'd been able to buy the old place. He, Ismael and Vern would have been making excited plans. He wondered if they'd ever find another property half so suitable. The huge rooms had lent themselves to dormitories so well.

In Great Hill Road, he marched beneath the as-yet-unlit Christmas lights on the lampposts, thinking about Sky, who'd so smoothly outbid him. Ismael had hinted that Daz had been distracted by a pretty face, but it had simply been a case of a bigger bank account.

He'd seen those TV programmes about property developers. They were rich. They were all about profit.

Chapter Four

Sky felt as antsy as a schoolkid who couldn't wait for the end of term.

She usually spent Sundays on domestic stuff or working, but she was too unsettled to clean or do her ironing. And she was unemployed.

Unemployed. That was taking some absorbing.

She had paperwork waiting but parked it for now, pulling on her coat before setting out into the early winter day. Enjoying the twinkle of ground frost, she strode past Fenner's Cricket Ground and around grassy Parker's Piece, where bare trees were encircled by fallen leaves as if their pants had dropped around their ankles.

Parents played ball with kids on muddy grass, making Sky feel conspicuously solitary. She liked children but had never yearned for her own. Marcel had accused her of being too used to not having blood relatives. She'd corrected him. 'I don't have blood relatives I *know* – apart from Mum, if she's still alive. Mum must have had parents and maybe other family members, but I haven't tried to find out. A family that produced Trish Murray . . . ? Dicey.'

Trish had only been sixteen when she'd become a mother, but it was doubtful she'd had other kids after Sky left, as her later relationships had been with women. Sky had always supposed she'd got pregnant while still exploring her sexuality. As for Sky's father, Trish had only ever said, 'I was tipsy. I went to a lot of parties in those days.'

Edifying – not.

Eventually, the fresh air made Sky hungry. She stopped at a cheery café where she demolished scrambled eggs on toast and two mugs of chocolate.

Finally, she'd walked her fidgets off and was ready to return home to work on the purchase of The Corner House, which would join the apartment she lived in, two houses and a house of multiple occupancy in her property portfolio.

Her breakfast bar doing duty as a desk, she scanned in the memorandum of sale and emailed it and the legal pack to her solicitors, ready for completion of sale on November 17th. She imagined herself moving to The Corner House, 1 Winter Street. It was an opportunity for a new life, and a more balanced one.

Ignoring the weight around her heart that Freddy hadn't tried again to contact her, she closed her laptop and arranged herself comfortably on a sofa to watch a documentary about langur monkeys racing across the rooftops of an Indian city.

She yawned as she arranged the cushions. This workaholic had resigned.

On Monday, she indulged in a lie-in, snuggling under her duvet as she listened to rain beating against the windows and wondered what was happening in the office.

Rising eventually, she ate breakfast and considered her move to Middledip. The decision about what furniture to take was simple: all of it. Her two sofas, bed, dressing table and a couple of side tables wouldn't fill a corner of one of the huge rooms of The Corner House. What else would she need for immediate occupancy? So much was built in at her apartment. She began a methodical perusal of the photos of The Corner House.

The kitchen boasted old-fashioned wooden cupboards, a range and a sink. She opened a new document and listed: *table, chairs, fridge-freezer, microwave.* She watched the video of the house's interior yet again, imagining it was herself pacing slowly through the rooms, and selected a bedroom overlooking the jungle-like back garden, with plaster roses around the light fittings and cornicing at the ceilings, then added: *wardrobes or clothes rail.* The floorboards might look fantastic if she sanded and polished them but would probably have shrunk with age, allowing draughts through the cracks. *Get a cheap carpet fitted for now.* The bathroom was cavernous, with an overhead toilet cistern and a monster-sized bath, but the boiler looked OK. *Electric shower over bath?* she tapped in on her laptop keyboard. It would mean spending on something she might change but filling that bath would take forever and would waste the world's energy.

At the foot of her screen, a red circle appeared, denoting the arrival of email. Unable to resist, she clicked on it. A column of unread emails looked back at her from her work inbox. Nothing from Freddy.

Blinking hard, she deleted her Freddy Walker Acquisitions email account from Outlook. Freddy would be able to access it from the work laptop she'd left behind.

Her personal inbox boasted just four emails, all of them from charities or holiday companies. It was a stark reminder of how few people emailed or called her on non-work matters. Her phone sat silently on the breakfast bar. Thoughtfully, she used one fingertip to set it spinning gently on the shiny countertop. Then she added to the list of things she needed when she moved to Middledip.

Friends.

It was nearly lunchtime when her intercom buzzed. She'd just hauled the mattress off her king-sized bed to access the storage beneath in search of collapsible boxes she'd used to move into her apartment. It took her ten seconds to disengage herself and cross the living space to the intercom by the front door. Breathlessly, she said, 'Hello?'

'Come to talk to you, mate.' Freddy sounded grim.

Her heart thumped against her chest wall. 'You know the way.' She pressed the door release, pleased her voice hadn't shaken, then opened the apartment door and awaited the sigh and ping of the lift. When it came, Freddy stepped out, his woollen coat well brushed, dark hair curling above his eyes, his expression both belligerent and defensive. She stepped back to let him in and soon they were seated on opposite sofas.

Sky's chest ached. Freddy looked so familiar, yet she felt almost as if he was no longer the boy who'd stepped in if anyone picked on her at school, and eventually offered her a role in his own business, working late into the evenings together, ideas coming one after the other, so exciting it hardly felt like work. If only there was no Minnie.

'What you playing at?' he demanded. 'I ain't accepting your resignation so you can forget it.'

Her smile quirked at his characteristic lack of ceremony. 'You've already accepted it,' she pointed out.

A dark frown knitted his brows. 'I ain't.'

Sky fetched her phone from the counter and pulled up Friday's email.

Actually I think you got a point there's prob not room in the company for minnie and you let's leave it that you've resigned mate x

Freddy snatched the phone from her hand and read, scowling. Pulling his own phone from his pocket he scrolled rapidly. Then his movements slowed. He slipped his phone away again. His gaze slithered away from Sky's.

Silence.

Sky's thoughts skittered around like mice in a box. Painfully, she swallowed. 'You'd never seen that email before, had you? It wasn't you who wrote it.' Minnie? Smart, if so, to replicate Freddy's 'voice' and disregard for punctuation.

Freddy scratched the back of his neck.

Softly, she said, 'My old role is no longer tenable.'

He stared at the windowpanes. The rain had turned to sleet and slid down the glass like broken stars. 'But it wasn't me who sent that email.' Obviously, he wasn't prepared to admit who had, though it was glaringly obvious.

'I called you to try and talk. You said, "Not fucking now!" That was definitely you,' she observed.

His shoulders drooped. 'Prospective father-in-law being tricky, right that second. Seems like he thinks Minnie's picked a bit of rough to annoy them, and he's appalled. Sorry. I meant to ring you back . . .' He tailed off. His face was more lined than she ever remembered seeing it. Sky held her breath, half-hoping he'd say, 'Leave it with me. I ain't having you shoved out, mate.' But he didn't.

'What about the projects you've been working on?' he asked huskily.

She hid a dart of pain at this confirmation that he was so in love with Minnie that he was going to sacrifice Sky. 'I've always reported to you, so you're up to speed. There are file notes for every job. Minnie can take over.'

She didn't miss the alarmed widening of his eyes as he switched his gaze from the sleety grey day to her. 'What about if you work from home? You've got your own client list.'

Sadly, she smiled. 'So I wouldn't be in the office, in the swim, part of things? I might as well set up on my own as do that.'

He waved that idea away. 'Not sure that would be ethical. Not unless you're moving away, I mean. You never start up in business close to your recent employer, now, do you?'

The injustice of this prickled. 'You did, when you began Freddy Walker Acquisitions. And there are no restrictive covenants in my contract . . . as I've never *had* a contract. Good job you didn't give me that directorship you used to talk about because then I would have responsibilities to the company that would prevent me from walking away.' She met his glare with one of her own. 'I haven't made up my mind what I'm going to do but if that's property development in Cambridgeshire then you'll have to suck it up.'

Freddy's gaze became appealing as he switched subjects. 'I know Minnie's a bit high-strung, but I love her. I ain't never loved no one—' He had to stop and swallow. 'And she loves me back.'

Sky melted.

Her anger and hurt drained away.

48

If there was one thing she wanted for Freddy, it was love. She softened her voice. 'That's why I'm trying to withdraw gracefully. It's best I go.'

Another long silence. Her heart thumped slowly, heavily, sadly. She didn't get up and make tea, which Freddy drank gallons of every day, the strong, milky brew he referred to as *builders'*. Shaky legs and a trembling hand would surely give away how hard she was finding this, how loudly a voice inside her was crying, 'No, Freddy! Dump Minnie and choose me . . .'

Abruptly, he asked, 'What did the Middledip property go for? Or didn't you attend the auction?'

'Three-six-five,' she answered. Shit. She should have emailed and told him before this. With a shrinking feeling of inevitability, she realised that things were about to go from bad to worse.

'Oh.' He blew out his cheeks and stretched his long legs out in front of him, seeming to relax. 'Shame we didn't get it.'

The words seemed to scour her throat when she admitted, 'I got it.'

Slowly, his eyes turned to flint. 'What?'

She met his gaze. 'Your ceiling was three-fifty. You wouldn't budge on that.' She didn't bother reminding him how he'd talked down to her on the subject. 'I didn't bid until it had gone over.'

He jumped up, chin jutting in the way she'd known for so long. 'You needn't think you can use my plans.'

'No, because they're your intellectual property. You know that I know that, and that I didn't like your plans,' she answered. 'I haven't decided what I'm going to do with the house, but it won't be to change it beyond recognition, like you were going to.'

They stared at each other. He shook his head. 'I'm disappointed in you, Sky.'

'Then we're disappointed in each other.' She paused to gather her thoughts. Though she didn't think the Princess and the Rough Diamond would last, she carefully filtered the snap out of her voice. 'You're looking for a way to provoke an argument so you can blame this upset on me. You'll feel better that way. But I want you to know that I want your relationship to work out for you. I love you like a brother.'

Despite her best efforts, her eyes swam with tears, and she never saw Freddy heading for the door. She just heard it close behind him.

Gone.

In books, damaged heroines sat dry-eyed, too hurt for tears. Sky, however, howled like a baby, mopping her tears and blowing her nose inelegantly on wodges of kitchen roll. There was no magic route back to how things had been with Freddy so long as Minnie the Minx was on the scene. She not only loved Freddy like a brother, but he was the only person she could think of who she did love, right now. Sky had softened and Freddy had met that with hardness. He'd rejected her and she was in pieces.

It wasn't lost on her that she was crying more violently for Freddy than ever she had for Marcel or Blake. It was Freddy who had the power to hurt her.

When the storm of tears had finally blown itself out, she sat down to think, her bed still in pieces and the packing boxes yet to be retrieved and filled. What was her long-term goal, once she'd done whatever she decided to do with The Corner House? Despite her brave words to her foster brother, she wasn't feeling crazy about setting up in property development alone.

Maybe she ought to try something entirely new. With rent coming in and no dependants, she could do what she wanted.

Could restore The Corner House, sell or let out and move on. That thought actually diminished her sense of purpose. Refurbish that gorgeous house for someone else? *Could restore The Corner House and live there, changing life in other ways.* That felt better. What other ways? *Education. Volunteering.*

A vision of the nature programmes she loved shimmered into her mind. She turned to her laptop and searched for 'ecology', soon becoming immersed in BSc courses that would allow her to study ecology or wildlife conservation.

She had oodles of UCAS points. During her employment at a housing association, she'd gained Level Three Business Administration and a Business Management and Marketing degree. She gazed dreamily at photos of students in a lecture theatre. Fancy her, Sky from the crappy apartment, with the mother who didn't come home some nights, as a full-time student. She could go to uni in Cambridge and drive to the campus from Middledip.

She frowned. Was that what she wanted?

No. Volunteering felt more her thing. She began fresh research. *Whoo.* Exciting opportunities. Critter Care Wildlife Society offered bed and board in return for hand raising rescued wildlife in British Columbia. Or, if she wanted to go to the subarctic, she could help look after polar bears unable to live in the wild. She imagined snowy landscapes and log cabins. People must strike up friendships in such close-knit pods – as long as she didn't get stuck with a Minnie type, always sucking up to those in charge and trying to appoint herself leader.

She browsed for a while without signing up to anything.

Instead, she made coffee, then returned to her list of things she'd need at The Corner House and amended *Friends* to *Lots of friends* and then added, whimsically, *Happiness*. Being happy was a goal unto itself, just the thing for a new Sky Terran.

Finally, she listed her flat to be rented out. At least for the foreseeable, she would be living in Middledip.

Chapter Five

The Corner House duly became Sky's on November 17th.
She arrived with the keys and, after battling her way
through the undergrowth to the front door, stepped into the
hall and breathed in the musty, dusty fustiness as if it were
Chanel. 'You're my new home,' she told the house, hearing
her voice ring with promise on its way up to the lofty ceilings.

The next week passed in a blur. She had to get the
utilities connected, a shower fitted, buy a shiny new microwave for the kitchen counter, arrange for the boiler to be
serviced and for a wallbox charger to be installed in the
barn. The chimneys were swept in the room that she'd
decided would be the sitting room and in the two ground-
floor rooms that opened into one another, which she had
no idea how she'd use.

Then she moved in, apologising to the removals men
who had to fight their way past shrubs that apparently
wanted to keep them out. Their van, like her white BMW,
had to stand on the road because the drive was completely
overgrown.

After the movers left, Sky stood in the sitting room.

Branches tapped at the windows as if to remind her how much work she had ahead of her just to allow light into the ground floor. The cornices were dusty, the floorboards faded, but Sky loved the feel of the room. It seemed to speak to her. A tiled, cast-iron fireplace cried out for an enormous, bevelled mirror above; the windows pleaded for soft, rose-coloured velvet curtains; ceramic and crystal light fittings demanded that Sky leave them exactly where they were. She tipped her head to gaze up at the old-fashioned grandeur, imagining the crystal carefully cleaned, picking up light from a Christmas tree in the corner and fairy lights along the mantel.

Her two sofas were, as she'd anticipated, lost in the lofty room, their contemporary ivory-coloured linen out of place in the faded splendour, like new kids in class wearing their old school uniform.

She moved on to the rear part of what she'd begun to think of as 'the big room', where French doors opened onto a patio – or they would, if the patio wasn't almost covered by drunkenly lolling shrubbery starved of light by overgrown trees. The front part of the big room, currently shut off from the rear with bifold doors, was similar to the sitting room, though more faded. Perhaps the last owner hadn't used it for a while.

Sky began to clean. First, she vacuumed up the dust bunnies and took the soft brush to the decorative plaster-work, before washing windows, floors and cupboards. In her bedroom, she hung the curtains from her apartment – more linen, but red this time – even if she could see no neighbouring houses from that window and would be sleeping and waking in the dark throughout winter. They'd minimise draughts until she assessed whether the windows needed to be replaced or repaired.

She paused to look out at the jungly rear garden. In the years of neglect, the trees had knitted into one another, deciduous trees insinuating their bare, twiggy arms into lush conifers as if trying to share their green clothes. Naked silver birch drooped, short-needled spruce forced its way past long-needled pine, and what she thought was a cherry tree glistened with brown buds as if already looking forward to bursting into pink blossom. She adored blossom.

She wasn't tempted to leave the garden completely wild, because that didn't chime in with her wish to see The Corner House emerge from its years of dilapidation. And what about any spring bulbs or flowering shrubs lurking below the trees? Smothered, they couldn't do their job in attracting bees and butterflies. It wasn't only that she couldn't see the wood for the trees – but that she couldn't see the house for the trees, or the trees for the other trees.

Love for her new home expanded Sky's heart. It was at least four times larger than she needed, but she couldn't think of a single place she'd lived – and, including foster homes, there had been twelve – that had made her feel so welcome.

Nan Heather's had come close, of course.

She worked on, cleaning the bathroom and kitchen, only pausing to snack on sandwiches, until, at nearly midnight, she made her bed and plummeted into it. It was the first night in the last month that she didn't have a single thought about Freddy, or Freddy Walker Acquisitions.

Sky woke with a thumping heart, not recognising the dim shapes of the room, the alcoves stacked with boxes.

Then she remembered that she was in The Corner House and stretched luxuriously, her hands brushing the cold, uneven plaster of the wall behind the bedhead. Her phone screen told her it was eight-thirty – later than she normally slept – and suddenly she couldn't *wait* to meet the day. She jumped out of bed and tiptoed across the chilly, bare boards to yank back her curtains.

It was a dry day. She was filled by the urge to start clearing the jungle, as she'd begun to think of it, to let The Corner House breathe and see daylight. Life had taught Sky not to waste things, and that included time. Furniture hunting could wait. Jumping into jeans and a thick jumper, she breakfasted on toast, standing at the plain wooden kitchen countertop, currently lacking table and chairs.

As she ate, she watched YouTube videos about pruning mature trees. By the time she was drinking her second cup of coffee from one of the elegant white porcelain mugs that didn't look as at home in this country kitchen as they had in her spiffy Cambridge apartment, she'd made a list of necessary tools. An hour on Gumtree and Facebook and she'd bought pre-owned loppers, secateurs, a chainsaw, a sabre saw, a hedge trimmer and a heavy-duty shredder. Except for the shredder, the power tools were rechargeable, relieving her of the worry of slicing trailing electrical leads. Another search yielded two configurable ladders and a piece of staging to go between them, which ought to be safe to work from.

It took her until past two o'clock to fetch all the items, making a separate trip for the shredder, which was, as the seller told her, 'chunky and ugly but will grind tree branches into a pile of chippings'. She was unloading the chainsaw, resolving that the first thing she'd clear was the path, when a woman in her forties came bowling along the pavement, red scarf flying and pom-pom hat bobbing over her long, dark hair.

'Well, hello!' she called.

Sky paused, wondering briefly why a stranger was beaming at her. Then she remembered she was in Middledip and smiled back. 'Hi.'

'Are you the new owner?' The woman arrived in a breathless rush. 'And getting straight on with things, I see. Do say that this lot's for the chop.' She waved an arm at the conifers that were hiding The Corner House as if to keep Prince Charming from Sleeping Beauty.

Sky's smile faded. 'I'm not felling these mature trees, if that's what you mean.'

Judging by the disappointed way the woman blew out her cheeks, that had been exactly what she'd meant. 'It's just that they make a mess of the whole street.' She sighed. Then, with the air of one remembering her manners: 'I'm Jessie, by the way. Or Jess. Winter Street's entering the Cambridgeshire Christmas Street Competition this year and I'm the organiser. We're taking over from Great Hill Road, which entered the past couple of years. We've all got the gardens neat and tidy, ready for the lights . . . and then there's yours.' She gave Sky a commiserating look, as if The Corner House's garden was an embarrassingly naughty child.

Sky's automatic reaction was to claim to be too busy for community stuff, but then she remembered she was no longer too busy for anything. And her intention was to make friends, wasn't it? She smiled again as she reached into her car boot for the hard hat, goggles, ear defenders and gloves she'd purchased from a DIY shop. 'What's this Christmas Street Competition about?'

Jess was eager to explain. 'It's run by the local paper and sponsored by Cambridgeshire businesses. The entrants go crazy, turning their street into a sparkly

Christmas grotto, and the judges choose a winner. Entries come from all over Cambridgeshire, of course, and the winner chooses a charity to benefit. This year it's ten thousand pounds.'

Sky was suitably impressed. 'Wow. What charity has Winter Street chosen?'

'Chester's House.' Jess moved closer, the wind picking up the ends of her hair to swirl out about her woollen hat. 'It's a Bettsbrough charity, providing help for homeless young people.'

Sky deposited her protective gear next to the chainsaw. 'OK. I'll cut my trees back and decorate them . . . in my own way.'

Jess's eyebrows shot up and her mouth opened delightedly – then the final words registered, and her eyes narrowed. 'In your own way?'

Sky turned her considering gaze on the trees crowding the public path like bullies in a playground. 'My lights will be solar. There should be enough daylight at this time of year to charge them. It would be great if you could encourage people to do the same, or at least use LED lights and not traditional, energy-gobbling, incandescent bulbs,' she added.

Jess nodded vigorously. 'Some of my lights are solar powered, because it's free. I'll put it on the WhatsApp group. Lots of people still have to buy their lights and might not have thought of solar power.'

'Then I'm in,' Sky said agreeably. She studied spiky brambles threading through the mass of vegetation. 'There's a single white birch in the middle of that lot. That would look great with twinkle lights, too.'

'Elisabetta loved that tree.' Jessie sighed. 'She loved her garden. She'd be heartbroken to see it as it is now.'

Sky hunched her shoulders against the chill that was creeping down the street as the afternoon drew on and the sky turned the clear blue that promised a frost. 'Elisabetta? You know the lady who lived here?'

Jess nodded, tugging her hat lower over her ears. 'Lovely lady. Italian originally but lived here for decades. Everyone was so sad when she passed away. The house wasn't sold for ages – hence the rainforest you're left to deal with.'

Sky grinned. 'Not quite a rainforest, but yeah. Overgrown.'

Jessie wrinkled her nose. 'I'd probably have the whole lot cut down and start all over again,' she confessed. 'Lots of nice decking and a more spacious drive.'

'I haven't found the drive yet.' Sky laughed. 'But cutting down these mature trees would be a crime. Think about the wildlife you'd make homeless. People are supposed to be planting trees, not disposing of them. You know they remove carbon from the air and give us our oxygen, right?'

Looking slightly alarmed, Jess stepped back. 'Gosh, you're quite green, aren't you? You're right. I was just thinking that the garden looks so small when it's all over-grown like this. It could be lovely.'

Sky gazed at the jungly mess. 'I'll make it lovely without destroying it. I want to get on with it, before the birds start nesting in February or March.'

'Well,' said Jessie in the kind of bright voice people use when they're not sure what to make of someone. 'Sounds fantastic. Thanks so much for joining in the Christmas Street Competition. Everyone will be pleased. The "Big Switch-On" of the lights is on December 1st at seven p.m., OK? We're going to have a bit of a street party with mulled wine and nibbles. Radio Bettsbrough's coming to cover it.' With a flurry of goodbyes, Jessie hurried back the way she'd come, the red of her hat and scarf standing out against the winter sky.

Sky hauled her purchases up the garden path, forcing back holly that wanted to snag her coat. Attached to the left side of the house was the barn, which had obviously been used as a workshop and boasted power outlets. From the plans, she knew there were steps from the rear to its flat roof, though they were currently obscured by rampaging shrubs. She opened the wooden door with difficulty and stored her purchases inside.

All that accomplished, she checked the time. There was probably an hour's light left of the short winter day. She could make a start on the shrubs beside the path. Secateurs in one hand and loppers in the other, she fought her way back to the black wrought-iron gate that would need a lick of paint sooner or later. Probably later.

First, she located the edges of the old stone flagstones, which were further back than she'd guessed. A job for the loppers. She regarded a red-berried holly bush, thinking that giving it a good haircut was going to leave all those berries to go to waste. She sighed. Being considerate of wildlife was always a balance and humans and animals had to coexist. She couldn't let the garden grow unchecked until the house was buried altogether. Thrusting the loppers into the bush, she began to snip. Soon she had a pile of spiky leaves and scarlet berries around her booted feet and was grimacing at the bare, spindly branches she'd exposed. She knew they'd leaf up again but for now they looked like a giant's hairbrush.

A voice came from the gateway. 'Hello, neighbour.' Behind her stood a small, beaming woman who looked to be in her seventies, bright turquoise cowboy boots peeping out beneath a cranberry-coloured coat.

60

'Hello,' answered Sky, half-dazzled by the cowboy boots as well as slightly envious of their glorious flamboyance.

Apparently seeing the exchange of greetings as an invitation, the woman stepped onto the flagstones. 'I'm Marietta Honey. I live next door.' She gurgled a laugh. 'I'm not calling you honey – it's my surname. Often causes confusion because I'm told I have a slight American accent.'

Sky found herself smiling back. The accent was more than slight. 'I'm Sky Terran. Are you American?'

Marietta shook her head, making her earrings twinkle in the fading afternoon light. 'Born and bred right here in Middledip but I married an American off one of the air force bases and went to live in Kansas. He left us five years ago, and I brought myself home.' She didn't pause for condolences. 'Why don't you come on over to my place for coffee and cookies? I think you've had the best of the light.'

As the sky had, indeed, acquired the pale luminosity that presaged winter's dusk and as she was happy to meet another resident of Winter Street, Sky said, 'Sounds great.' It was an enjoyable novelty not to rush through her day's tasks. No site visit awaited her as she cursed the traffic; no report demanded she write it – she just kicked the clippings aside and stowed her tools. She did lock the house, though she remembered that Nan Heather had never done so, as if it were a slur on neighbourhood honesty. She wondered if anyone in the village was still that trusting.

Marietta waited for her, her warm brown eyes twinkling. 'OK, let's roll.' The small figure turned right out of the gate onto Winter Street and pretended to fight her way through the overhanging conifer boughs, their dead needles and cones an inch thick on the path.

'I'm going to start cutting them back tomorrow,' Sky explained, feeling responsible that the encroaching greenery forced them into walking single file.

It turned out that the next-door, neatly clipped privet hedge was Marietta's and she stepped between its two sections onto a flagstone path just like the one Sky had begun to unearth at The Corner House.

Marietta slowed to let Sky catch her up. 'I guess your house and mine are the last of the original village. The rest of Winter Street is what folks call "The New Village" – Bankside Estate.'

'Love your place.' Sky paused to admire a bench facing the sunset and the wintry skeleton of a climbing plant around a rustic arch. The home itself was small, mostly stone but with a brick segment painted cream. Its roof was of the same tile as The Corner House. Diamond-paned windows blazed with the reflection of a last low winter sunray.

Marietta opened a wooden door on the side of the house. 'Come on in.' She threw her coat over the newel post of a tiny flight of stairs, revealing a purple-and-pink-striped sweater beneath, and then bustled into a kitchen that was little more than a widening of the hall itself. It was homely, Sky saw as she followed. Exposed beams were studded with hooks from which hung keys, scissors, a single horse brass and a roll of sticky tape. The overhead light was softened by a flowery cotton shade as dusk fell outside.

'When this place was built, it would have been a worker's cottage.' Marietta filled the kettle and took down mugs and plates from a rack, spooned coffee granules and plonked a canister of sugar and a bottle of milk on the table. 'It was left to me by my aunt. She had no kids of her own and it had been my grandma's before my aunt's. The village is a lot different to Kansas City, but it was what I needed.' Marietta deposited on the table a ceramic cookie jar in the shape of the head of a lugubrious dog, his dark red hat the lid. Motioning Sky to a chair, she pulled off the dog's hat and tilted the jar to display its contents. 'I know it's only November, but I've been practising my cinnamon cookies and gingerbread.'

'Mm, gorgeous.' Sky sniffed the spicy, aromatic smells wafting from the jar and took a gingerbread Christmas tree decorated with icing stars, and a cinnamon cookie that was iced to look like a snowman's head, complete with a jaunty red scarf.

Marietta beamed, choosing a gingerbread star and a cinnamon snowflake for herself. 'I can turn my hand to most things in a kitchen,' she said modestly. 'I've a young friend who loves to drop by for cookies and he needs cheering up right now. He lives with his mom – I mean, *mum* – just up Winter Street.' She indicated vaguely over her shoulder. 'I guess you have some gardening to do,' she went on.

'Just a little.' Sky laughed, when she'd finished a delicious mouthful of gingerbread. 'I'm looking forward to it. The house is liveable, but I can't arrange for a window to be replaced or gutters to be checked while the trees are smothering it.'

Marietta's grey eyebrows rose. 'On your own, pumpkin? No useful man? No team of landscapers?'

Sky picked up her snowman cookie. 'I'll get the trades in where I have to, but I intend to do everything I can – with the help of power tools,' she added. 'I'm fit, and a practical person.'

Dunking her second cookie in her coffee, Marietta ate

it messily. 'Do you not have a job to go to?' she asked, once she'd swallowed.

'Right now, my main job's The Corner House. I have rent from other property so I won't starve.' Sky took bites of her cookie between explaining how her last job had made it comparatively easy for her to become a landlord.

'And what are you going to do with your new home?' asked Marietta, leaning forward intently over her coffee cup.

Sky remembered her conversation with Daz Moran in The Angel. It seemed the residents of Winter Street really did care what happened to The Corner House, and she couldn't blame them. Any property developer worth her or his salt would transform it into several dwellings and get rid of what they could in the front garden in favour of off-street parking. Character would be sacrificed, a second storey added to the barn and, as Freddy had planned, great swathes of the original grey stone rendered to hide the joins between old and new. She didn't mention that she'd bought The Corner House on a wave of anger and want, an overwhelming urge to own the fine house and return to Middledip in the hopes of a happier life. Didn't want to admit that there had been no actual plan. Instead, choosing her phrasing carefully, Sky said, 'My urge is to restore it to a large and gracious family home.'

Marietta cupped her coffee in small, lined hands. 'It was once a farmhouse and belonged to the Carlysle Home Farm. They called it "the top farm", which is why Winter Street leads into Top Farm Road. I guess a farm manager lived in the farmhouse and someone more junior lived here, until the buildings were sold off. When I was a kid, your house and mine stood on the edge of the village. I used to walk from my parents' house to this little cottage.

It was Grandma's by then. I'd pick beans or knead dough with her.' She smiled reminiscently. 'She gave me shortbread and milk, too. I can't remember the family who lived in your big, grand house. Elisabetta bought it while I lived in the States. Then, later, Auntie May wrote me that the top farm had been sold to build a bunch of homes.'

Sky was fascinated. Some details had been made known to her during the purchase process, but Marietta brought the history to life. 'Did Elisabetta live alone?'

Marietta smiled as she offered Sky more cookies. 'Not originally. She had a husband and three or four kids. Well, the kids were her husband's nieces and nephews, but she raised them as if they were her own, after their parents died. But, one by one, they went back to Italy, where they'd been born, and then her husband passed on. The reason The Corner House took so long to sell was that those nephews and nieces had to be located in Italy and the necessary formalities gone through.'

Sky breathed out a small, 'Oh,' at this poignant picture. 'Did they visit her, after they returned to Italy? Or did she visit them?'

Marietta shrugged. 'Kids find their own lives, far away sometimes. They get involved, I guess.' After several beats, she added, 'Elisabetta died a couple of years after I got back, but I got to know her. She sure rattled around in that big place on her own, but she loved it. She and her husband had been happy there and she didn't want to leave. I'd say she was in that enormous garden every day.'

'The Corner House does kind of grab you by the heart,' Sky admitted. 'Did you leave family back in the US?'

The older lady sighed pensively. 'Well, not really. My son, Ira, lives in Indonesia. Once my husband Hal died, it seemed whether I was in the UK or the US didn't matter, so far as Ira was concerned. A Skype call is a Skype call, and airplane trip is an airplane trip.' She beamed. 'Ira and his wife and kids, they're coming here for Christmas, though. I can't wait.'

Though wondering where they'd all sleep in such a tiny cottage, Sky said, 'That sounds wonderful.'

'It is.' Marietta sighed happily. 'Hal's family is still in Kansas. Went there from Germany a couple of generations back. The family name then was spelled H–o–ë–n–e and pronounced "Hoyn", but Americans read it as "Honey", so the Anglicisation was adopted.' Marietta moved on again. 'How about you get to know a few people in Middledip? It's the pub quiz tonight and I need someone bright and young on my team.' She smiled hopefully.

This time, it wasn't just the reflex to say, 'Sorry. I'm too busy,' that caused Sky to hesitate. She *wasn't* too busy and was dismayed every time her impulses proved Blake and Marcel had been right that her life had revolved around work. It was the word 'pub'. Pubs weren't great when you hated the smell of alcohol. 'Thank you,' she replied carefully. 'At The Three Fishes?'

Marietta chortled. 'A pub quiz has to be in a pub, and that's the only one we have.'

And it was probably the centre of the Middledip activities that Sky genuinely wanted to be a part of. She could put up with a beery whiff. 'That sounds great.'

After arranging that Marietta would call at seven this evening so they could walk to The Three Fishes together, Sky said her goodbyes and opted to round off the afternoon with a stroll around the village. This leisure thing was growing on her all the time.

She strode into Main Road, turning right past The Three Fishes, where the quiz would be tonight. It was already

66

aglow with Christmas lights, as if the stone building had collided with a mini galaxy. Holly trees in pots glittered, windows and doors wore twinkling frames, and illuminated reindeer raced across windowsills.

A couple of hundred yards further on, an inflatable Santa stood sentry outside Booze & News, lit from within to become a beacon of light. Sky smiled as she passed, remembering Nan Heather sending Freddy or Sky shopping for odds and ends at the village shop, and where Sky had spent a new phenomenon in her life: pocket money. Nan had given her a pound a week, no fortune, but enough for sweets. Till then, Sky had only eaten sweets if a generous friend had shared, except for at a school Christmas party, or the amazing Christmas when Sky had won a box of Maltesers in the Year Five spelling competition. Maybe that was when it had clicked that education was the key to a better life, she thought, pulling up her hood because she hadn't brought a hat or scarf and the chilly breeze was diving straight down her neck.

In addition to the one-pound pocket money, it had been possible to earn an extra fifty pence from Nan Heather if you tidied your room on a Saturday morning. Sky had always succeeded in earning it. Sometimes Freddy would get her to tidy his room, too, and they went halves on the bonus fifty pence, which meant he netted twenty-five pence for doing nothing. It must have been a portent of Sky's place in Freddy's life – her work augmenting his income.

She smiled reminiscently, the pavement glittering with frost as she turned the corner. Her feet slowed as she drew level with Rotten Row, the small, terraced cottages cosy beneath the mellow glow of streetlamps and strings of Christmas lights dancing between them. Her head turned automatically towards Nan Heather's old house, just as when she'd passed it on the day of the auction.

Then her gaze zeroed in on a front window where a small, shrunken figure gazed out into the early darkness. A lamp behind the figure cast it mostly in silhouette, but Sky gained the distinct impression of a female in spectacles, shoulders bowed with age. It was as if one of the ropes of Christmas light had flown off its moorings to lasso her feet, because she stumbled and nearly fell.

The figure raised an arm and gave an amiable – if shaky – wave.

Sky's heart began a loud *boom, boom,* drowning out the sound of the wind and traffic behind her on Main Road. Slowly, she waved back.

It couldn't be. Could it . . . ?

Trembling, she raced up the narrow path leading to the side of the house. After a couple of steadying breaths, she knocked on the door, then cursed as she realised the person in the window might not be sufficiently mobile to answer. Sky could go around to the window, but might it scare the figure if a stranger – *possible* stranger – approached the glass and peered in? Damn. She should have asked around first, put out feelers at the pub tonight or with whoever was running the village shop—

Slowly, the door opened.

The woman who peered out at Sky leaned on a walking frame. Her curls were sparse and her face wrinkled like a walnut . . . but the smile was exactly as it ever was, filled with warmth and interest.

'Nan Heather,' Sky breathed, hardly able to believe the evidence of her eyes.

The old woman's smile widened, and her eyes lit up

behind the heavy spectacles. 'Do you mind coming inside?' she asked in a rusty voice. 'Only I'm not good at standing.'

'Of course,' Sky began, but Nan Heather was already shuffling her way to a plain table in the centre of the small, dated kitchen, a kitchen that brought memories raining down on Sky as she stepped in and closed the door behind her. The appliances had been updated but the white-painted cupboards were just the same. Even the worn wooden table looked to be the one where Sky and Freddy had sat to devour homemade casserole followed by apple crumble.

The old woman lowered herself into a kitchen chair that sported a jaunty yellow cushion. 'Sit down, duck.'

With a feeling of unreality, Sky sat. 'I don't know if you remember me,' she began.

Nan Heather laughed creakily. 'I think I do. At least, I know your voice. I don't see details very well, and you've grown up.' Her wrinkles changed angle as she smiled. 'You're one of my children.' It was a statement, not a question, and filled with joy. 'Sky?'

Sky's heart burned, not only because Nan Heather was still alive, not only that Nan remembered her but that she'd said 'my children' rather than 'my foster children'. 'Yes, I'm Sky,' she croaked.

Nan Heather slid a trembling hand over the tabletop and laid it on the sleeve of Sky's coat. 'Sky Murray,' she breathed. 'Little Sky Murray. Hello, my duck.'

'Hello, Nan Heather.' Sky gave a shaky laugh that broke with emotion. 'I'm Sky Terran now.' She blotted a tear that slipped from the corner of her eye.

Nan Heather grasped her other hand. 'You had the front bedroom, and Freddy Walker the back. It was hard to make you laugh, but when you did, it lit up your entire face. You made friends with the other kids, but you regarded adults with grave doubts. I can see you now, following Freddy onto the school bus when you started the big school in Bettsbrough. You were with me for over a year, till your mum got on her feet a bit.' Her smile faded, as if it needed a rest from lifting all those wrinkles. 'I retired from fostering. You and Freddy were the last of my children.' A tear began to follow the furrows of her face, pausing at the corner of her mouth.

'I know,' Sky whispered. Nan Heather's lined face blurred before her eyes. 'I'm sorry I didn't keep in touch.'

'You had your life to live,' Nan Heather declared hoarsely. 'I hoped things were looking up and you were too busy to write.'

Sky's conscience twanged. 'Life with Mum never got to the point of "looking up". I'm afraid . . . I'm sorry to say that I was upset with you because you couldn't take me in when I went back into foster care.' Her laugh was a strangled sound. 'I knew you were entitled to retire. I was just an angry kid.'

The small, papery fingers squeezed Sky's. 'You were entitled to mind. I'm sorry, duck.' The tear fell from Nan's cheek, and another slowly followed the same furrow, even as she creaked another laugh. 'I didn't know it was you when I waved. I wave whenever I glimpse passers-by. But tell me why you're in Middledip. I can't believe you're here. It's like Christmas come early. Get the shortbread tin out, duck. Do you remember where it is?'

Sky went automatically to the right cupboard and took out the scratched tartan tin. 'This reminds me of coming home after school to the smell of warm baking.' Taking only a small piece of the sweet, crumbly treat as she'd already eaten three cookies with Marietta, she told Nan

Heather about working with Freddy, skipping lightly over the trouble between them to dwell on her moving into The Corner House. 'I've already met a couple of neighbours. One collared me to join in this thing called the Christmas Street Competition.'

Nan Heather, her tears dried, beamed. 'Last year, my daughter Mo – do you remember Mo? – drove me round to see the lights. Like Blackpool Illuminations, it was.' Her smile dimmed, eyes enlarged by the lenses of her glasses. 'I'm ninety-two, now, and I don't walk well.' Then she laughed. 'You tell Freddy Walker that I'm glad he's thriving, won't you? Remember me to him.' Her smile wavered. 'I recall you both so well. Freddy was full of swagger but you, you were quiet and watchful.'

Then Nan sighed regretfully. 'Mo's coming to pick me up for dinner at six, so I'd better go change. We've made the sitting room into my bedroom with a wet room in the corner. It's ever so convenient not to have to climb those stairs. They're not suitable for a stairlift.'

Sky glanced at the kitchen clock, seeing that as it was five-forty-five, Nan Heather had given her every minute she could. 'Is there anything you'd like me to do for you before I go?' She wasn't sure whether to linger to say hello to Mo, but what if Mo got sick of the children Nan Heather had fostered, turning up, asking her to share her mother all over again? Maybe that was a meeting for another day.

'I'm fine, duck,' Nan Heather declared, breathless from pulling herself to her feet by dint of grabbing the table. 'But you'll come again, won't you, now you're back?'

Sky smiled through the burning of tears. 'You'll soon be sick of me.'

Nan Heather paused, one hand on the door that Sky remembered led to the dining room, which led in turn to the sitting room in one direction and the stairs in another. 'I doubt that very much,' she announced, with her creaking laugh. 'Write your phone number on that white pad by the telephone.' She nodded in the direction of a landline phone on the window ledge. 'Mo or my granddaughter Hannah will program it into speed dial for me.'

Sky did as bid, then, with a last, reluctant goodbye, feeling as if she might wake up and find the whole meeting had been a beautiful dream, she continued her journey up Port Road. She entered the Bankside Estate via New Street and Top Farm Road, joining Winter Street at the far end so she could check out how her neighbours were progressing with their decorations. Sure enough, once she attuned her eyes, Sky could see the ghostly outlines of icicles and snowflakes in the dark.

She'd be busy, cutting back her crazy, overgrown trees in order to catch up, but the idea gave her a cosy sense of community.

Chapter Six

A few hours before coming out this evening, Daz had received one of Abi's exuberant, chatty emails that made him newly aware of losing his girlfriend. An accompanying photo of her in a clinging pink dress made him equally aware that he hadn't lost his sexual impulse.

His few post-Abi adventures seemed a while ago. He'd set himself up on a dating app and found the whole process a shark tank. One woman knocked ten years off her age and paid him the back-handed compliment of saying his profile pic was so hot she'd presumed he'd been kitten-fishing – creating an artificially positive profile – which made him wonder why she'd 'super liked' him. Some women had been looking for love, others for sex. His preference was somewhere in between but he hadn't been drawn to the appropriate term of 'situationship'. With ghosting, benching, stashing and love bombing, dating apps didn't feel right for him.

He mulled over his situation as he headed for The Three Fishes past cosily lit cottages, pulling up his collar against a cutting evening breeze, pausing to let cars swish past,

73

their tyres leaving twin tracks through the frost. It was peaceful living alone, but he hadn't got used to sleeping alone. An amicable parting was an odd thing. It left a hole in your life but no anger or sense of injury with which to fill it. He hadn't had the decisive moment of discovering Abi in bed with someone else; she hadn't found him out in some unlawful behaviour – like Courtney had found Lewis.

The ending had simply evolved from Daz not loving Abi enough to radically change his life for her, especially with her butterfly tendency not to stick to things, and her not loving him enough to sacrifice a wonderful career opportunity. A vision of her indignant, incredulous face floated into his mind's eye. *But women are asked to relocate for men's careers all the time!* And his sad reply: *And some of them say 'no'.* The end point of their relationship had been decided by the dates on her new contract and the tenancy agreement for her flat slap-bang amongst the crowded, towering buildings of Borough.

London life was so incredibly not him, yet Abi now seemed as at home a short walk from London Bridge as she had in the village. Her email been almost poetic.

It's all clanking trains and roaring traffic and the Shard monopolising the skyline like a faceless glass giant – very buzzy. I still get lost in the multiple exits of London Bridge Station popping up between cafés and bars.

He was glad she was loving her new life but give him the clipped hedges and stone walls of village cottages any day – and definitely no 'faceless glass giants' marring the sky.

The Three Fishes hove into view, the epitome of a pretty country pub invitingly illuminated for Christmas.

74

He'd always find someone to chat to in its familiar community. Imagine exchanging that for the innumerable bars that came and went in London and the near-infinite combination of people filling them. Shortly after Abi's move, he'd visited her, and she'd taken him to a Victorian pub with flowers in window boxes. Though pretty on the outside, he'd been appalled by the crush of people inside, yelling their heads off to be heard at standing tables with only a lucky few getting uncomfortable pew-like seats at the edges of the room. And the basement toilets ought to have been condemned. The village pub was much more his style.

And it was Lewis, more than Abi, he missed seeing within its stone walls.

It had been brutal to have a horrible side of his best mate brandished in his face but it chilled Daz to think of him trapped in a bleak, alien world, caged in a warren of concrete rooms and scary strangers. Cut off. No privacy. No freedom. Long nights. Closing doors. What did prison smell like? Sound of?

To add to his gloomy mood, earlier today Vern and Ismael had let him know that they'd found premises for Adventure Accommodation. 'The place is ideal, hardly any conversion necessary,' Vern had enthused, when he'd called at Daz's house. Then his gaze had turned apprehensive. 'But . . . it's only available to rent. Sorry, buddy.' Renting premises excluded Daz, as there would be no role for an investor.

Daz had managed to summon a smile. 'I understand. Thanks for letting me know.' But he'd felt gut-punched, grasping anew just how great it would have been to work with Vern and Ismael on turning The Corner House's spacious rooms into dormitory rooms and converting the big bathroom into shower rooms. He'd hoped to establish a continuing role, rather than just be part of the start-up.

Because he hated his present job.

Hated it.

Whoever said 'be careful if you make your hobby into your business' was right. He'd known how rare it was to develop a game and then sell to a big concern, and it had seemed like a no-brainer to accept the employment that came along with the offer, sacrificing his old job in logistics and IT. How naïve he'd been not to recognise a standard move to 'bring him into the fold' for some strategic reason – weakening any future case he might bring against them, he supposed. Unfortunately, his role hadn't proved to be in development, as he'd assumed it would be. It was in quality assurance. 'Heading up a team' sounded OK, but it was donkey work, because QA testing computer games got samey and leading a team meant additional reporting.

He sighed. He was ready to get out, to chalk it up to experience and take comfort from the sum his game had earned him, which was what he'd been going to put into The Corner House.

If only his had been the winning bid.

He rounded the corner and crossed the frontage of The Three Fishes, its lights beaming a welcome to any villager in search of friendly faces and undemanding chat. Christmas trees and holly bushes stood sentry on either side of the door, a-sparkle with so many white lights it looked as if they'd been rolled in them.

He pushed open the heavy door – and his heart sank. Haden, one of the pub's managers, was at a microphone, his short hair neat and his black-rimmed glasses glinting. He boomed, 'Tonight's pub quiz will begin at eight!'

Daz stumbled to a halt. Crap. He didn't like pub quizzes and was *not* in the mood.

Every table was generously occupied, and Elvis, the other pub manager, was plonking down pens and registering quiz teams. Haden had bought out Elvis's previous partner in the pub and had begun the quiz – and fantasy football, and other noisy intrusions Daz tried to avoid. Elvis was more into the dining side, continuing the tradition of The Three Fishes putting on a Christmas lunch for any villager who didn't have a place to go. This year, the decoration of the pub had taken the theme 'A White Christmas' and as well as a million lights twinkling around the bar, faux snow had been painstakingly laid between the optics and along the windowsills. The ceiling of the dining area had somehow been lined with the stuff, as if it was a snow cave.

Daz was just debating backing out into the frosty evening when he heard his mother's voice. 'There's Darragh! Hello, my darling!'

He realised she was seated at a table near the fire with his father, Len, Marietta – who was friends with the elder Morans – and a much younger woman with long, rippling hair that poured over one shoulder of her sweater, her eyebrows arched in a way that lent her an expression of slight surprise. It was too late for Daz to escape. He began threading his way around the busy tables, calling hellos to Melanie from the shop; Carola from the café; Gabe who took in strays; Alexia, who, like Daz, had been brought up here. Both his parents rose to hug him, holding him fast in their arms for several moments before letting him go.

'Darragh,' his father rumbled, flicking back his brindled grey hair. 'You look cold. Come closer to the fire.'

Daz's mother, Sara, was still a good-looking woman, though her thick hair had faded from gold to silver, and she now wore glasses. Her eyes shone from behind the lenses. 'Your dad and I are waiting for a table in the dining room. Join us for dinner.' She lifted a hand to smooth his hair from his face, a habitual, motherly gesture, so familiar that it made him smile. The village pub atmosphere worked its magic, and he felt his mood lift.

'I've already eaten,' he said regretfully. 'Let's arrange dinner together soon, though.'

Marietta gave him a cheery, 'Hiya, pumpkin,' and he stooped to kiss her soft cheek.

Then he turned politely to the woman sitting quietly next to Marietta, intending to introduce himself, and recognised her with a jolt as the bloody woman who'd bought The Corner House out from under his nose. With loose hair and wearing a pale blue sweater with jeans, rather than severely upswept hair and a business suit, she looked a different person – still attractive and sexy, but different. And she was here, in his local, somewhere he'd come to relax.

'Hello again,' she said equably.

'Oh,' he said. 'Sky, right?' He heard the lack of enthusiasm in his voice.

She gave a small smile. 'Sky Terran. And you're Daz.'

Ignoring his mother's under-breath correction of, 'Darragh', he asked around the table, 'Anyone need a drink?' No one except him did, and when he returned from the bar, his parents had repositioned themselves so that the only empty stool was between them. He smothered a smile at their transparent desire to make sure they received plenty of his attention.

Sara opened the conversation. 'Abi emailed me today.' Her eyes on Daz's were soft, enquiring. His mum and dad

78

had been sad for him when Abi left, though unsurprised. Her parents passing away at the end of her teens had left her with few ties and probably they'd seen that Abi, unlike Daz, wasn't attached to the village. She'd only ever lived there because Daz had invited her to leave her flat in Peterborough and buy a house with him. They'd confessed to considering Abi high maintenance and changeable, and he'd found it hard to argue, because the terms were a negative version of 'quirky' and 'whimsical', which Abi was.

'She emailed me, too.' He took the first swig of his Guinness, black and glittering in the lights. 'Courtney's going to spend this weekend in London with her. I read Abi's email out and Courtney joked that it sounded absolute hell, all that enjoying yourself and having a good time, so I suggested the visit. It's happened quickly because this is the only weekend before Christmas that Abi could manage. Wilf's staying with me.' He swallowed more of the dark, heavy beer, feeling himself relax as it filtered through his system.

The frames of Sara's glasses were blue, which went well with the silver hair. She gave his arm a squeeze. 'You're a good man. It'll do poor Courtney good to get out. She can shop for Christmas goodies.'

Daz didn't argue, though he knew Courtney's budget was more aligned to Bettsbrough market than Borough Market. 'I'm running her to Peterborough to catch an early train tomorrow.'

He refrained from saying that he was being especially supportive because Courtney was at her wits' end about childcare over the Christmas holidays when Wilf had two weeks off and Courtney just a few days. 'Only three and a half weeks of term left, and I haven't heard about the school job or got childcare sorted,' she'd sniffed. 'If only

Wilf had been four or five years older when Lewis pulled his stunt and could have been left at home alone. I asked Graham to help but he was evasive. Wilf doesn't want to go there, really. Graham's so down, these days.'

Daz had known what he was going to say before he said it. 'Wilf can hang out at my place for at least some of the Christmas holidays.' He couldn't watch Courtney struggle so hard when he could help, though it would mean working long into the evening to meet his deadlines because he didn't get as much done with Wilf around as he needed to.

Unreasonably, this thought renewed his irritation with Sky Terran, the obstacle to him leaving his current role via Adventure Accommodation. He glanced her way, just as she broke off chatting to Marietta to cross her arms, grasp the hem of her blue sweater and pull it off over her head, displaying a plain white T-shirt beneath.

The act of her pulling off an item of clothing, even in such an innocent and casual manner, hit him in the groin. *Wow, she's hot.*

He looked away from a briefly exposed bra strap as fresh annoyance prickled. If you were irked with someone, you didn't want them to grab you by the libido. He scowled and slugged down more of his Guinness. *Bloody woman.*

One of the bar staff bustled over, hair in a neat ball behind her head and tied with tinsel. 'Sara? Len? Your table's ready now.'

Daz rose to hug both parents again and arranged to call on them during the week. When they'd gone, he glanced down at his pint. It was almost empty. He could swig the remainder and go home to watch Netflix. But then he realised that he'd missed Sky heading over to the bar. She was already being served, and another Guinness stood in front of her, along with drinks for her and Marietta. She paid, then managed to clutch all three drinks between her hands to carry them back to the table.

He eyed the Guinness balefully.

'Marietta bought. I just carried,' she said, giving him a quick smile as she deposited white wine before Marietta along with a fistful of change, and a clear liquid at her own place.

'Oh. You didn't need to do that, Marietta.' Awkwardly, Daz resumed his seat.

Her eyes twinkled. 'I have an ulterior motive. Jess and Ruth are usually on my pub quiz team, Marietta's Brain Bashers, but Jess texted to say they're stuck in a meeting about the Christmas Street Competition. I'm hoping you'll be on the team, instead.' She tilted her head and sent him a winning smile.

'Well . . .' he began dubiously, unsure how to say no to an elderly lady who was his neighbour and a family friend.

Evidently taking that as agreement, Marietta switched subjects. 'Sky was just telling me that she's lived in the village before.'

Daz felt a rush of surprise. 'Really?' He frowned at Sky, trying to place her in his encyclopaedic knowledge of villagers.

Marietta lifted her wine. 'Do you know Heather Elsworth, who lives in Rotten Row on Cross Street? She fostered Sky. I only know Heather by sight because she's very elderly now and doesn't get about much. I'm sure your mum will know her, though.'

'I know who you mean.' Daz sucked the froth off his fresh pint, gazing at Sky with renewed interest. 'When you told me you were going to live in Middledip, you didn't mention being a returnee.'

81

Sky shrugged. 'It was only a year or so, but I was happy here.'

'It's a happy village,' Daz murmured. Reddish lights glinted in her hair as the room brightened ready for the quiz. Her body was capable but curvy and another sharp jab of lust reminded Daz of his recent lack of sex. And why hadn't he noticed Sky's eyes before? They were a pale green, as beautiful as a winter sea. As they rested on him, for an instant he forgot she was his obstacle, forgot the noise of the pub around him, forgot about Netflix—

Sky turned away.

Marietta was introducing her to a bulky man who'd appeared at their table and Daz frowned to see that it was Bell, one of the Blokey Blokes usually known only by surnames, the barflies who swarmed around the dart-board and monopolised the big TV to watch sport. He was three years or so older than Daz, known at school as 'Bellend', a noisy, disruptive arse with embarrassingly heavy-handed chat-up lines. He'd mellowed since those days, but Bell was not exactly on Daz's Christmas card list because a couple of years ago he'd pressed Abi for an under-the-mistletoe kiss with the kind of insistence that would be unacceptable any time, let alone when her boyfriend was sitting beside her. Daz had jumped to his feet and Bell had backed off, but still. Rude.

Now Sky was smiling, her lips turning up at the corners and her eyebrows arching in that expression of cool surprise as Marietta said, 'Sky, this is Bell. He was fostered by Heather, too. Sit down, Bell.'

The man accepted the invitation with alacrity, not even glancing Daz's way. 'Hello, Sky.' Interest glinted in his eyes. 'Dear old Nan Heather, eh? Wonder how many kids she's helped. Wonderful woman.'

82

'Now Marietta's Brain Bashers can field a team of four,' Marietta crowed.

As Haden returned to the mic and called, 'Everyone ready?' Daz sighed, accepting the inevitability of becoming one of Marietta's Brain Bashers this evening, sufficiently familiar with pub quizzes to know that the role of spectator was even less entertaining than being in a team.

As Haden outlined the rules – '. . . if I see anyone with a phone then their team's disqualified . . .' – Daz watched Bell monopolise Sky.

Then Haden announced, 'Sorry, folks, bit of a glitch with the quiz questions,' and clicked off the mic while he frowned over his tablet, tapping and swiping the screen. It gave Daz the opportunity to listen in to Sky and Bell's conversation, learning that each had been fostered by Nan Heather at the age of ten, but six years apart. As Daz knew Bell to be about forty-five, that made Sky thirty-nine. Daz was forty-two.

He didn't remember Bell being fostered – Daz would have been only seven, after all – but it somehow fit in with the teenager he'd become, hiding uncertainty behind bluster. Daz was freshly grateful to have come from a fabulous family.

'It was just while me mum got away from me dad,' Bell was telling Sky. 'The old man had to be encouraged to clear off.'

Daz waited, wondering if Sky had a similar story. Apparently, she did. 'My mum was a perpetual irresponsible teenager. I was fostered twice – here and Peterborough. I used to think that when Mum fancied a break, she'd tell the social she was leaving me alone because she couldn't cope. Then she'd realise it was easier to get accommodation if you had a kid and ask for me back.' She made her tone jokey, but Daz felt as Marietta looked – horrified.

Bell made a grimace of fellow feeling, fondling the pint glass that seemed like an extension of his arm. 'Do you still see her?'

Sky shook her head. 'I left at sixteen. Slept on my foster brother Freddy's floor till I could afford a room of my own.'

A memory came back to Daz. 'Freddy – did he live at Nan Heather's?'

She turned those bright, stunning eyes back his way. 'That's right. Freddy Walker. Four years older than me.'

'He was the year above me. Would you have been on the bus to school, too?' Daz crinkled his brow as he tried to drag a memory from the caves of his mind, a small girl trailing Freddy onto the bus, looking barely old enough to be out of primary school. If that had been Sky, she'd certainly left that sticklike body behind.

She nodded, but just then Haden found a solution for whatever technical problem he'd encountered and tapped the mic to gain attention. Marietta took possession of the Marietta's Brain Bashers official answer sheet, depositing a spare pen on the sheet of scrap paper in the centre of the table provided for team members to scribble suggestions and avoid their answers being overheard.

Haden began. 'Question one. Which British football team is known as The Gunners?'

Bell grabbed the pen and scribbled, *Arsenal*.

'Question two. In the rock band Oasis, which of the Gallagher brothers is the eldest?'

Daz took the pen and wrote, *Noel*.

Marietta knew that in backgammon each player began with fifteen counters, Bell that Alan Jones won the 1980

84

Formula One Drivers' Championship and Daz that the simultaneous movement of two chess pieces was called castling. In each case, Marietta added the answer to the official sheet.

'As it's almost December,' Haden boomed through the mic, while Elvis and the young woman with the tinselly hair quietly served drinks from behind the polished wooden bar. 'What are the names of Santa's reindeers?'

While a side discussion began as to whether the plural of 'reindeer' was 'reindeer' or 'reindeers', Marietta wrote: *Rudolph, Dasher, Dancer, Prancer, Vixen, Comet, Cupid, Donner and Blitzen.*

Several culture questions were met with blank looks or hesitant guesses, then came a section headed 'nature' and Sky turned into a mastermind. She didn't just know most of the answers – she got *everything*.

Daz watched in bemusement as her round handwriting noted that Herdwick was a breed of sheep and Gloucestershire Old Spot a breed of pig, that the soft underside of a horse hoof was called the frog and that you'd never see a penguin and a polar bear together in the wild because they lived on opposite poles.

After the final question, Marietta exchanged answer sheets with the next table – a team from the village garage called Ratty's Garagistas. The marking disclosed that all of Sky's answers were correct.

'We won!' Marietta crowed, when each team had called out the score of the sheet it had marked. 'Twenty quid, please. I think I'll rechristen us Marietta's Dream Team.' They agreed that the twenty pounds would buy a round of drinks for the team, then they'd put the change in the charity box on the bar. Sky was drinking tap water, so the charity benefitted by quite a bit.

As Carola from the village hall and The Angel Café announced a competition for the Christmas tree made from the most unusual things – she held up a picture of one made entirely of stacked green books, as an example – Marietta unhooked her red coat from the back of her chair. 'Well, that was exciting, but now I'm going home to bed.'

Sky reached for her coat, too, and Bell jumped up. 'I'll walk you ladies home.'

'I can walk with them, as we all live in Winter Street,' Daz said quickly, never sure that Bell could be trusted.

After a quick farewell to Sara and Len through the arch to the dining room, the three of them let Bell join the rest of the Blokey Blokes and hurried along under the street-lamps of Main Road. 'Whoo,' cried Marietta, huddling into her oversized coat and pulling her scarf up around her ears. 'That wind's bringing snow or my name's not Marietta Honey.'

Sky tugged up her hood. 'I have outdoor work to do, so I hope not. Snow's not forecast on my phone.'

Marietta snorted. 'I can smell it coming.' She blew a white cloud onto the air, to prove how cold it was.

Daz found himself walking between the two women. Sweet old Marietta hooked a friendly arm through his and Sky walked carefully separate, hands in pockets. When they reached The Corner House, she turned into the gateway with a cheery, 'Goodnight.'

''Night,' Daz returned briefly, glancing wistfully at what could be seen of the big old house between the trees. He walked Marietta next door, following her between the hedges that kept her cottage private from the street. 'It's flaming dark here,' he complained, turning on the torch on his phone when the ground seemed to vanish into a black hole.

86

Marietta laughed. 'Happens every night.'

'That's because you have no lights and your hedge is about eight feet tall.' He held the phone higher so Marietta could see the lock she was trying to spear with her key.

'I'll have scads of light when I decorate the house for the Christmas Street Competition. I've ordered a truckload,' Marietta observed. She paused before adding with studied casualness, 'Though I'm kinda worried about climbing those ladders.'

Daz's hair stood on end at the idea of short and elderly Marietta scrambling up stepladders clutching strings of Christmas lights. 'Want me to help? Wilf probably will, too.'

'That would be fabulous,' drawled Marietta, sounding very American and very pleased. But she paused before going indoors. 'What do you think to my new neighbour?'

'Sky?' Daz queried, as if they had other new neighbours. 'She seems OK.'

'Only OK?' Marietta sounded reproving, as she shuffled a step over the threshold of her home. 'She's a stunningly beautiful woman with a bunch of brains. She's got more baggage than the luggage room of Kansas City Union Station, though.'

Then she vanished indoors, leaving Daz to stub his toe on the way back out of the dark garden, wondering how big the luggage room of Union Station might be and whether Marietta was talking about Sky's childhood, or if she knew of more baggage, or was just guessing.

Daz hadn't got off on the right foot with Sky but that hadn't stopped him seeing that, behind her jokey manner when she'd talked about her mother, darkness lurked in her green eyes. That childhood was enough baggage for anyone.

Chapter Seven

When it came to snow, Marietta's sense of smell proved more reliable than phone apps or the TV forecasters. After a chilly Saturday, Middledip woke on Sunday to a wintry scene, the cottages huddling under snow like frosted yule logs.

The first Daz knew about it was Wilf banging on his bedroom door and crowing, 'It's been snowing!'

Daz checked the time and groaned. 'What are you doing awake before eight on a Sunday?'

Wilf replied, as if he were talking to an idiot, 'Asking if I can go out in the snow.'

As he was responsible for entertaining Wilf this weekend, Daz shook himself to full wakefulness and wrapped his towelling robe around him before opening the bedroom door.

Wilf met him with a grin, his hair stuck up on one side as well as in his usual quiff at the front. His blue pyjama top bore a picture of a games controller and the words *Zzzz . . . recharging.* He hopped from bare foot to bare foot and gestured through the uncurtained landing window. '*Look.*'

Daz looked, and had to admit that the view was magical. A snowfield of soft white ridges cast shadows that looked almost blue in the early winter light. Each twig and leaf on the hawthorn hedge wore its own tiny white coat, and his lawn was a perfect blanket of cotton wool with only a few grass tips poking through, like little hands signalling for help.

It might be Sunday and he might have been up late working through a persistent bug in a game, but Daz remembered being eleven. Staying indoors when the first snowfall of winter was waiting to be played in? Not an option. 'Right,' he said, ruffling Wilf's hair so that it stuck up all over. 'Get dressed in properly warm things because your mum won't like it if I let you catch pneumonia. We'll have a bacon butty and go out.'

'Yeah!' Wilf disappeared into the bedroom he'd slept in, across the hall.

Daz dressed quickly before jogging down to start the bacon grilling and the kettle boiling. After a breakfast that Wilf seemed to dispose of in one gulp, they set out, Daz zipped firmly into his down jacket and Wilf skidding around, coat hanging open and hat askew as he made snowballs. Luckily, he was a rubbish shot and Daz was able to stride along without receiving a stinging snowball in the face. Above, pearl grey snow clouds were beginning to break apart and reveal a blue sky.

Wilf spoke breathlessly between running and skidding. 'There's not enough for a proper snowman, is there? I wish I had a toboggan.'

'We don't really have hills in the Fens,' Daz pointed out. 'Toboggans don't toboggan well on flat ground.'

'You could pull me along.' Wilf laughed, his cheeks red with the cold and eyes as sparkling as the snow.

Laughing, sparkling – that was how kids ought to look, rather than lost and insecure as Wilf so often did, Daz thought. Again, he cursed Lewis. But – live in the moment – Wilf was happy, Daz was enjoying the crunch of fresh, untrodden snow beneath his boots, and they were heading off the housing estate and onto the bridleways that encircled Middledip village.

But as they crunched onto the snowy footpath, Wilf, who'd been telling Daz he ought to develop a game set completely in the snow, halted. In silence he watched three people approach, two lads Wilf's age with a man they addressed as 'Dad', kicking snow at each other and laughing. Daz said, 'Good morning,' but Wilf didn't say a word.

Daz's heart bled as he watched the fun and joy leach from the boy's face and a scowl appear like storm clouds rolling over the landscape. The red cheeks turned dull and now sparks burned in his eyes rather than sparkles.

With jerky movements, Wilf returned to scraping up snow and then began to shy snowballs around wildly, accompanying each throw with an angry gasp. 'I can't hit anything,' he groused, flinging a snowball haphazardly at a tree stump with snow clinging to its side, where the wind had left it. The snowball broke harmlessly on the ground and Wilf growled as he scraped snow so violently that he dragged up dirt and leaves to besmirch its whiteness.

Daz watched helplessly, recognising the outward signs of inner conflict. The happy boys with their father had rubbed Wilf's wounds raw and he couldn't be blamed for finding an outlet for his emotions. He'd been uprooted not just from his big, luxurious home but also from his happy life – and it was all the fault of Lewis, who should be the one tramping through the snowfall with Wilf.

When Wilf had managed to slap a new snowball into shape, Daz spoke, making his voice even and easy. 'Turn your non-throwing shoulder towards your target.'

Wilf paused, panting. Sullenly, he followed Daz's suggestion, turning his left shoulder towards the tree stump.

'Now turn your top half towards your target and flick your wrist and elbow straight as you throw. Keep your hand pointing at your target as you let go,' Daz said, demonstrating with an empty hand.

Wilf rolled his eyes, but when he copied Daz's action exactly, gasped in disbelief. The snowball didn't travel far enough but it was dead on line for the stump. Unspeaking, but calmer, he gathered up more snow in his gloved hands, not complaining that the knitted rows were becoming sodden. After carefully compacting the shining white fluff between his hands, he stepped a little closer to the stump, turned his left shoulder, then rotated at the waist and let the stump have it with, a 'Yah' at the release. The snowball exploded on target in a glistening shower.

Daz clapped. 'Fantastic. You might have to take up baseball.'

Wilf's scowl gave way to a cautious smile, his hat more askew than ever as he shook his sodden hands. 'That was good,' he said wonderingly, then clapped his hands together, evidently succumbing to the hot/cold/numb/burning pain of wet hands.

As it didn't take a genius to have foreseen the soaked gloves scenario, Daz had stuffed a spare pair of his own in his pocket, stretchy ones he'd worn under ski gloves when he'd tried snowboarding one year. He waved them temptingly. 'Let me know when you've finished snowballing and you can change into these.'

'Finished,' Wilf declared immediately. 'My hands are freaking freezing.' He let his teeth chatter theatrically as he wrenched off the wet gloves from reddened hands and pulled on the luminous blue ones Daz supplied.

They set off once more, tramping side by side, screwing up their eyes against the glare from the sun bouncing off the snow. When Daz noticed that Wilf was trying to match his pace, he shortened his stride to make it possible. Wilf was small for his age, though he had the slight gangle that suggested a growth spurt wasn't far away.

After several minutes of crunching along the footpath, Wilf's feet slowed, and he screwed his head around to gaze towards a coppice of young trees. 'What's she doing?'

Daz shaded his eyes to look where Wilf pointed. In amongst the bare trees and whippy branches a figure crouched, motionless, her bulky coat black, her red-and-white hat a beacon on the monochrome landscape. A single line of snowy footprints stretched behind her, indicating her route to this quiet, still spot. 'I don't know.' Daz took an uncertain step off the path, feeling the springiness of grass beneath the snow. The figure didn't move. Her arms seemed to be clamped around her stomach. His mind raced over possibilities. Appendicitis? Miscarriage? Crap, he hoped not. 'We'd better check she's OK.' He glanced at his phone as he strode towards the coppice and was relieved to see he had a signal if he needed to call for medical aid.

But as they neared the woman, she turned her head to regard them, showing no sign of distress. In fact, she smiled, calm and lovely, a few freckles dotting her nose and pink roses blooming in her cheeks.

It was Sky Terran.

Daz's footsteps faltered. 'We thought you might be ill,' he called half-irritably and half-apologetically. He felt stupid to have ploughed so impetuously across the snowy landscape, only to discover the person he'd thought to help was the same one who'd upset all his plans.

'What are you doing?' demanded Wilf, before Daz could turn back and take the boy with him.

Sky's sea-glass eyes settled on him. 'I'm reading stories in the snow. They're invisible on an ordinary day. Look. Come round this way so you don't trample on it.' She beckoned him. Soon, Wilf crouched beside her, frowning in perplexity at the snowy ground.

'These marks here are made by birds,' she told him, pointing to tiny, spiky footprints of three toes forward and one back. 'See how they hopped this way, then that way? I think they might be blackbirds, who spend time on the floor, looking for worms or berries and seeds.' She indicated another place. 'A rabbit hopped along there. That's easy to recognise because of the two circles for its front paws and ovals for the back. You see how they're all close together? That's because rabbits put their back paws almost where their front paws went. Probably the rabbit was hoping to find some grass not covered by the snow. Then come the tracks of a fox, headed the same way, so I hope the rabbit got home safely.' She grinned, and Wilf grinned back, looking thoroughly engaged by her and the story. She tilted her head. 'It *could* be a dog who trotted along here without his human, of course. Which do you think? I think fox because of the shape of the toes.'

'Fox,' Wilf agreed promptly. 'I think it caught the rabbit and ate it.'

'Bloodthirsty,' Sky commented genially, 'but quite possibly right. All creatures must eat.' She straightened. Her attention remained on Wilf. Daz was unreasonably annoyed not to be included in the spell she was weaving.

93

She turned and waved towards her own footprints, which had meandered beside the hedge before turning towards this coppice. 'I saw badger tracks back there. They're so sweet, like little bear prints. That tells us that the snow fell before morning. Do you know why?'

Wilf gazed at Sky as if all he wanted in the world was for her to tell him. 'No. Why?'

'Because badgers are nocturnal. Mr or Ms Badger will have been snuffling along in the dark, trying to find burrows to dig up with big claws.' She made scraping motions; her fingers extended. Her lips were half-parted in a smile. Daz thought again of Marietta's description of Sky as stunningly beautiful. It wasn't just a surface-deep beauty, he thought grudgingly, but something that shone from within, something none of her 'baggage' had succeeded in dimming.

'Digging a new burrow for himself?' A small frown pinched a line at the bridge of Wilf's nose.

'More likely to be trying to dig a smaller animal out for his dinner,' Sky replied frankly. 'Though badgers do dig tunnels for themselves, too. Shall I show you the tracks?' It was only then that she glanced at Daz. 'If that's OK?'

'Of course. It's fascinating,' he replied politely, falling in behind as Sky and Wilf followed her footprints back to the hedge. Her coat was snowy at the hem from crouching, a fine white powder that melted as she swung along, a red tassel on her hat keeping time with her energetic stride. At the line of bare, spiky hawthorns she showed them the signs of a badger patrol – four toes, four claws almost as long, and a pad.

'Cool. Can we track a squirrel?' Wilf demanded, obviously enjoying this new activity.

Sky gave another considering tilt of her head. 'I think squirrels will be keeping warm in their nests in trees, or in the roofs of buildings. In winter, they only come out on fine days. I could show you deer tracks, but they're in my front garden and you might not be ready to head back into the village.'

'Yeah, we are; we've been out ages,' Wilf said, blithely not bothering to consult Daz.

Falling in behind again, Daz listened to Sky's clear voice entertaining Wilf with the information that deer prints looked like two commas, and that red deer and roe deer were both native to Britain. Wilf was unrecognisable from the angry child who'd hurled snowballs around in impotent fury only minutes before. Reading stories in the snow had grabbed his attention so thoroughly that it had – at least temporarily – lifted him out of the doldrums. Daz found himself mentally thanking Sky. He'd have to mention Wilf's tricky moment to Courtney later, but not yet. Courtney deserved her weekend away.

It occurred to him, as he trailed the animated chatterers, that he'd focused on Wilf this weekend, rather than where Courtney had gone – to be with Abi. Only two days earlier he'd thought quite a bit about Abi, and their past sex life. It flitted across his mind now that her blonde girliness was insipid compared to Sky. Then he felt disloyal. Pretty Abi had been his partner for several years. They'd shared plenty of good times.

The three of them followed the bridle path to Church Close, then crunched down Port Road and into the Bankside Estate. A few minutes later, Sky led Wilf through the scruffy wrought-iron gate on the corner of Winter Street. The cut edges of the shrubbery that had until recently tried to block the path showed through the snow.

Sky led Wilf beneath a tall, slender tree with white patches on its bark.

'Here,' Daz heard her say. 'See what I mean about the commas?'

Daz rose on tiptoe to peer over her bent figure. It was true. Each hoof print did look a little like two facing commas.

Wilf glanced around the garden. 'What have you done to those trees?' He pointed Daz's blue glove at three conical shapes that seemed to have been cut out of the hedge of pines running beside Winter Street.

Sky laughed. 'I've turned them into Christmas trees. Jessie, who lives along the road, came along to explain that Winter Street wants to win the Christmas Street Competition, and my garden was going to spoil the entry. She wanted me to cut the lot down, but that's not my plan at all. Wildlife needs trees and so do humans. I said I'd shape and decorate them instead. It's a job, though. I put up ladders around a tree, a bit like a scaffold, then I cut straight down between the tree and its neighbour and put the debris that falls down through my shredder. Then I cut the tree off at the height I want – one that will let a little of The Corner House be visible – and put all *that* through the shredder. Then I start on the hard work of shaping the tree.'

Wilf interrupted curiously. 'What's a shredder?'

Sky beckoned him towards the barn on the side of the house, which had been destined to become private quarters for the group chaperones, if Daz's bid had secured The Corner House. She said, 'I'll show you.' After opening the combination padlock with a few deft twists, she yanked one of the double doors open with an effort, piling up snow behind. Then she dragged out a large red machine on two wheels, paying out its electrical lead behind. 'Stand back,' she cried, once she had it on a firm piece of ground. She pulled on a pair of goggles that had dangled from a handle and started the machine with a beast-like roar.

Wilf beamed at the racket. 'Cool.'

Daz winced, wanting to stuff his fingers in his ears.

Sky picked up a handy branch lying beneath a tree and fed it into the beast, which angrily chewed it up and spat it out as a hail of wood chippings. 'There,' she said, switching off and letting the machine growl into silence. 'Usually, I collect the chippings into bags or spread them at the base of the trees – you can't see where now because of the snow. Then the worms will take them down and enrich the soil.'

Wilf's gleaming gaze was still on the rowdy machine. 'Give me a go,' he demanded eagerly, reaching out as if to try and get the correct combination of switches to bring the shredder back to life.

Sky slipped her hand over one of the buttons to prevent him. 'You'd need your dad's permission, and to put the goggles on.' She glanced questioningly at Daz.

In an instant, Wilf's smile turned to a scowl. 'My dad's in prison.' His hands dropped away from the shredder, and he glared at the ground.

'Oh.' Sky looked from Daz to Wilf and back again. 'I'm sorry to hear it.' She reddened, obviously realising that she'd put her foot in it by assuming Daz to be Wilf's father.

Daz slipped an arm along Wilf's shoulders. 'I'm a family friend. His mum's gone to London for a couple of days so Wilf's hanging out with me.' He gave the boy's small shoulders a comforting squeeze.

Sky switched her gaze to Daz. 'I heard you talking to your parents about someone going to London, last night, but I was talking to Marietta and didn't really take it in. Sorry I said the wrong thing, Will.' She looked genuinely sorry, her eyes round and her brows puckered.

'Wilf,' Wilf corrected her ungraciously.

She dimpled at him. 'I'm Sky.'

This got the boy's attention. 'Sky? Like . . . ?' He pointed up at the blue expanse above them, a few white clouds marching their way like the advance scouts of an army.

'Exactly,' she said, 'and my surname's Terran, which means "earth", so I'm sky and earth. I'm sorry about your dad.'

'Yeah. It sucks to have a shit dad. We had to move here to a crappy little house, and I don't know anyone on the bus to school.' Wilf scowled again, blinking fast in an obvious effort not to cry.

Although his instinct was to give Wilf a big hug and hurry him home, Daz held back. Wilf was quite capable of speaking up, if he wanted to go home. It was only a hundred yards away.

Sky edged closer, as if she wanted to radiate comfort Wilf's way because she didn't know him well enough for a hug. 'Haven't you lived in Winter Street very long? That's something we have in common, then. I only moved in on Thursday.' She hesitated. 'It must suck to be separated from your dad.'

Wilf shrugged one shoulder.

'I can only imagine,' she added, 'because I don't have a dad at all. At least, my mum never told me who he was.'

This brought Wilf's gaze up again, his eyebrows meeting in a puzzled line. 'How does that work? Like, she kept it a secret?'

Daz found himself smiling at this innocent view of the world. Wilf might have a lot of rubbish in his life but at least he wasn't yet so jaded that he'd drawn what to Daz was the obvious conclusion.

Sky laughed, her eyes crinkling at the corners, and took a hand from a pocket to pat Wilf's shoulder. 'I think it was that she had so many boyfriends she didn't know who was, er, responsible.'

'Oh. Right.' Judging from the blush that tinged Wilf's cheeks, the penny dropped. After a moment's thought he asked, 'Does not having a dad suck, too?'

Sky shrugged. 'I suppose so. I've never known anything else, after all. What sucked more was my mum not being good at taking care of me. If there had been a dad around, maybe he would have been better.' She began to wheel the shredder back into the barn, Wilf keeping pace as, without any sign of self-pity, she added, 'Other people looked after me, sometimes. Once was here in Middledip. I lived with a lady called Nan Heather. It was a happy time.' Parking the shredder neatly, she reached up to take some white items from a shelf.

'That why you came here to live in this house, now?' Wilf edged closer to inspect her finds.

'One of the reasons.' Sky showed him what she held. 'See these moulds? I got them to make fat cakes for the birds. I thought that if I made them in the shape of stars and snowmen, I could hang them on my trees as decorations for the Christmas Street Competition. What do you think?'

Wilf took two halves of a mould and fitted them together to make a snowman shape. 'Ace. Can I help you make them? What are fat cakes?'

Sky's eyes crinkled at Wilf ingenuously asking to be involved before he knew what fat cakes were. 'Birds need fat and seeds during the winter, so you make a mixture and squidge it all together into a cake. I should think you'd be great at it.' She examined the star mould, then her eyes twinkled. 'Look what we can do first, though.' She stepped outside and scraped one side of the mould along the floor until it captured a drift of snow then, with careful positioning, succeeded in clamping it around a whippy twig belonging to the tree with white bark. When, delicately, she parted the two halves, a star made of snow hung from the tree. 'There. A white birch with a white star.'

'Wowsers trousers,' Wilf breathed. Eagerly, he began piling snow into the snowman mould.

Sky turned to Daz with a grin, her unusual eyes blazing in the sunlight. 'I have one more in the shape of a Christmas tree. Fancy it?' She grabbed it from the barn and thrust it into his hands. He joined in readily. He wasn't such a churlish git as to turn up his nose at making snow baubles.

As they scraped together snow, cheering when the shapes successfully clung on, groaning when the snow decorations crumbled to the ground, Daz had the fleeting thought that this must be what it was like to be a parent. In happier times, he'd watched Lewis and Courtney sharing moments like this with Wilf and it was odd that he should be sharing with Sky Terran, of all people.

When they'd turned most of the snow in Sky's garden to slush, Wilf gave the blue gloves back to Daz. 'These are wet too, now.'

'Cheers,' Daz said sardonically. 'Sky, your gloves are soaked, too.'

Sky shrugged, peeling them off. 'Definitely time for a hot drink.' Almost shyly, she added, 'Either of you fancy it?'

'Not half,' cried Wilf, turning eagerly towards her tall stone house. 'Got hot chocolate?'

100

'I have,' Sky acknowledged with a grin. She glanced at Daz, lifting an eyebrow, looking hesitant, vulnerable almost.

'Coffee?' he asked, realising that her hesitation came from not knowing if he'd want to be invited.

She said, 'Sure.'

He thought he caught a flash of pleasure in her eyes.

After ushering them into the hall of The Corner House, she discarded her hat and coat on wall hooks, her pony-tail falling down her back as the hat came off.

Daz had viewed the house, of course, but being inside as a guest instead of an owner was tough. He looked about himself wistfully, admiring the staircase that rose in front of them and then branched in two. Sky led the way past the stairs and into the kitchen, which was pretty much as Daz remembered, apart from being clean instead of languishing under a patina of dust. A lingering smell of hot buttered toast provided a homely touch.

'Let's take our drinks into the sitting room. I don't have seats in here,' said Sky, shoving a biscuit tin into Wilf's hands as if aware how often a kid his age felt the urge to eat. With swift movements, she made hot chocolate for herself and Wilf and coffee for Daz. They followed her across the hall and through a tall door to one of the reception rooms where two sofas stood, stranded in the centre like the first awkward guests at a party. Sky took one sofa and Daz and Wilf the other.

Wilf showed no signs of being aware of there being anything unusual in the paucity of furniture and lack of photos or pictures on the walls, or that shrubs were squeaking and tapping at the windows. He began to regale Sky with a commentary on Minecraft, one of his favourite games.

Sky listened with every sign of interest, though she confessed that she'd never found time for computer games. 'Maybe when I've got the house and garden under control,' she said, with a 'try anything once' expression.

Wilf finally looked around. 'Do other people live here, too?'

Sky quirked an eyebrow. 'Just me.'

'Oh.' Wilf buried his nose contemplatively in his mug. 'We used to live in a big house like this, but there was three of us,' he said, when he emerged. 'If there's just you, you must have, like, loads of empty rooms.'

A succession of expressions rippled over Sky's face, each, it seemed to Daz, containing a separate emotion. Surprise. Regret. Maybe even dismay. 'That's true,' she said quietly. 'But I felt as if the house was waiting for someone to come and love it.'

Daz couldn't help a barbed reply. 'When you outbid me, you certainly seemed besotted.'

She flushed, and a note of – what? Despondency? – entered her voice. 'My job had sort of evaporated and I really wanted this place.' She frowned down into her mug. She, unlike Wilf, was managing to drink without growing a hot chocolate moustache.

Her wistful response made him sorry for his snark. More genially, he asked, 'What happens after the house is done?'

The corners of her mouth turned down. 'I wondered about returning to education, but I think maybe I should join a volunteer scheme.'

'What sort of scheme?' He envisaged her training for the Samaritans, listening with her peculiarly intent, thoughtful expression.

Absently, she combed her ponytail with her fingers,

102

forehead puckered thoughtfully. 'I could be a community warden at a nature reserve or volunteer at Wildlife Trust. I even read about a project working with rescue polar bears, if I felt like zooming off to Canada for three months.'

Wilf's eyes grew big and round. 'Polar bears for real?'

'For real,' she confirmed. As she went on to talk about the shrinking ice cap, she let her hair ripple over one shoulder and it lay there, catching the light. Daz found it almost too distracting to pay attention to her conversation.

He jolted out of his stupor when he heard Wilf say, 'Me and Daz are having pizza at his house tonight. Want to come?'

Daz blinked as he caught Sky's uncertain glance. 'That's really kind,' she murmured. 'But I don't eat meat, and not everyone is set up for that.'

It was the perfect opportunity for Daz to say, 'Oh, sorry. I only have pepperoni.' But Wilf . . . He met the eager gaze of his little friend, who'd had so much to put up with but had responded so positively to everything Sky had shown him this morning. Then he read the expectation in her eyes that he was going to sidestep having her around and before he knew it, he'd said, 'I have cheese and tomato pizza. Would that be safe?'

She regarded him searchingly for an instant. Then: 'Safe as houses. Thanks. What time should I arrive?'

Wilf grinned. 'Any time.'

Daz, more usefully, suggested, 'Seven?' And, as Sky gave him a flashing smile, he found it an effort to recall that this was the 'bloody woman' who'd spoiled all his plans.

Chapter Eight

Enough work faced Sky inside the house to keep her busy for a year, if only she knew what she was going to do with the place.

After Daz and Wilf had left, she stared through the sitting room window. Snow was melting from trees and shrubs, the drips pockmarking the white blanket on the ground, just like her conscience eroding her pleasure in The Corner House.

Empty rooms.

Wilf's remarks had got under her skin and lodged there, scratching against her sense of social and ecological responsibility. Should individuals occupy large houses, using energy to light and heat empty rooms? The average number of people in a UK household was two-point-four, a statistic central to Freddy's plans to carve The Corner House up into starter homes.

Her urge to return the house to its former glory grappled with whether it was right for one woman to take up all this space when she could have satisfied her lust for a life in Middledip by buying a small cottage, like Marietta's.

Yet it hurt just to think of refurbishing the house and selling it to a family.

Perhaps she should have let the brooding Daz and his mates buy the place for energetic youngsters on activity centre courses. That would have filled the rooms without wrecking the house's exterior appearance.

But she *wanted* The Corner House! She wanted it to be beautiful again, with a garden that could be enjoyed. Her heart cried out for it. Her mind had no right to nag at her with these doubts. She'd bought her new home fair and square.

Abruptly, she wheeled away from the snowy scene outside the window, needing to bury her misgivings under action.

Throwing herself down on the sofa, she took out her phone to scroll through Freecycle and Gumtree for a kitchen table and chairs. If she was guilty of taking up too much space on the planet, at least she could do an infinitesimal bit to safeguard it in other ways by upcycling some of the house's furnishings.

She paused. On her lock screen was a notification of an email from a company called Avenue Properties. What could they want? She was familiar with the company because they were based in Grantchester, just outside Cambridge, and competition for Freddy Walker Acquisitions. "'Ave a new property from Avenue Properties' was one of Freddy's favourite jokes. She tapped the notification and watched the email spring to life.

Dear Ms Terran,

Would you be interested in meeting myself and my fellow director Kris Mason for an informal discussion? Avenue Properties represents quality clients,

*and we'd welcome the opportunity to add a quality
staff member to our project development team.
     Kind regards,
     Alicia Sanders*

Sky read in astonishment. Well, that was direct. She'd
met Alicia Sanders a couple of times, a no-nonsense woman
in her sixties who evidently wasn't afraid to reach out for
what she wanted. She must have heard that Sky had left
Freddy's firm and tapped someone for her personal email
address. Judging from her designer clothes and the new
Mercedes every year, Alicia had made a success of her
business. Sky could just imagine Freddy's reaction if she
went to work for Avenue Properties . . .

Her eyes misted with sudden, unwanted tears. How
would Sky ever see that reaction? Since the confrontation
at her flat at the end of October, she and Freddy hadn't
exchanged so much as a text. The official procedure ending
her employment had been handled impersonally by the
admin office in sterile letters and emails that didn't even
wish her well for the future. Of course, Minnie might have
been behind that chilliness, but Sky knew Freddy had been
hurt that Sky had cut herself out of his beloved business.
He wouldn't take the blame for not putting Minnie straight
because he was in love.

Briefly, she considered reaching out to Minnie, then
dismissed it. Minnie not only wanted Freddy to herself,
but she also saw Sky as the living link to his past – a link
she wanted to sever.

Pain clutched her heart.

She missed being called 'mate', missed the buzz in the
office when a project was going well, Freddy's satisfaction
when she crafted a planning application that was approved,

his pleasure in their success. 'Not bad for two scruffy kids from Nothingsville, eh, mate? We show 'em all, don't we?' Sky knew that 'all' encompassed anyone who'd ever treated scruffy, underprivileged kids as if their situation was their own fault.

A memory floated back to her of Freddy, red and furious when a teacher had picked him out of a flood of students in the corridor and asked him why he never wore a school sweatshirt. 'I ain't got no sweatshirt,' Freddy had spat.

After a short lecture on the evils of the double negative, the teacher had gone on pompously, 'I'm still waiting for you to explain why you don't have a sweatshirt.'

His patronising lack of empathy had lit Freddy's – admittedly short – fuse. ''Cos no one ain't fucking bought me one.' Freddy had received detention because, obviously, you couldn't swear at a teacher.

But he'd also received a sweatshirt. The teacher had thrust it at Freddy with a gruff, 'Here. It was in lost property. I've put your name on it, so it doesn't get lost again.'

Both he and Freddy had known that the lost-property sweatshirt had never been Freddy's, but it was as near an apology as Freddy was going to get and Sky found herself smiling at the memory of the teacher's grudging attempt to make reparation for his thoughtlessness.

Then she wondered what Freddy would have had to say about little Wilf this morning, if he'd been there. 'Poor little bleeder,' probably, which Wilf certainly was. A poor little bleeder who'd made Sky feel as if someone had poked a sharp stick into her heart. How did the villagers of Middledip feel about Wilf's dad being in prison? Did everyone know at school? Wilf wore the air of aloneness that came from not finding a tribe. He'd blurted the truth out to her, a near-stranger. It had been prompted by her assumption that Daz was Wilf's dad, but he could have just muttered, 'He's not my dad.' Instead, his father's whereabouts seemed to burst out of him as if too big and awful to be kept in.

Poor little bleeder. Tears prickled her eyes, and she blinked. Jeez, she was getting emotional about a kid she barely knew. When Wilf had invited her for pizza, she'd read dismay on Daz Moran's face, but the hope on Wilf's had outweighed it. Daz seemed to be bearing a grudge about the house, but he was an adult. He'd get over it. Wilf was just a kid.

She shut down the email from Avenue Properties unanswered and opened Freecycle instead. Buying tables was easier than dealing with emotional stuff or planning a future when you were feeling battered by life.

In the evening, Sky set out to locate Daz's house, which he'd told her was 20 Winter Street. Wilf had added that he and his mum lived at 31a. She passed Marietta's hedge and followed the curve of the road, checking off numbers as she went. A stumpy cone of white in a neat front garden looked like the remains of a small snowman, and the occasional crevice or crack glowed white, as if someone had painted it. Otherwise, there was no evidence that Middledip had looked like a Christmas card this morning.

The roof of a smart semi-detached home caught her eye because a much thicker, artistically waved line of snow hung over the gutters as if poised to slip onto the next visitor. It took Sky a second to realise that it was fake, a decoration. She paused to gaze around herself. Various dark, sinuous shapes came into focus, and she remembered that every house was festooned with strings and clusters that, for the moment, only showed up in the streetlights if you looked for them. On one roof was the hint of a figure, and another beside a chimney. A row of icicles dangled from the edge of a roof like tiny mountaineers roped together. Lights had been carefully wound and tacked and twined everywhere, ready to blaze into life.

Ah. The Christmas Street Competition.

Dismay trickled through her. Jess had said something about a December 1st 'Big Switch-On' and today was . . . ? She took out her phone. Sunday, November 27th. Oh, hell. She'd promised decorations and solar lights and she so far had a big, fat nothing, apart from three vaguely Christmas-tree-shaped pines. She'd spent too much time on shredding her pruned material, wandering around snowy footpaths and dreaming about the house.

She raised her shoulders to her ears and let them drop on a big sigh. Well, she'd come to the village determined to become part of a community, so she mustn't fall at the first hurdle. Jess had said that local radio would be broadcasting from the event. It would be awful if their presenter called out the scruffy house on the corner, letting Winter Street down.

Frowning, she resumed her steps, finding number twenty on the opposite side of the street to her place. It was a large and modern detached house, built of buff-coloured brick. A feature panel of larch lapping covered the wall between the tiled roof and the canopy that spanned both porch and integral garage. And, *of course*, unlit strings of lights swamped the place like an industrial grade of bunting.

Sky trod up the paved drive and rapped the door-knocker. In moments, Daz stood framed in the open doorway. He wore a ribbed, round-neck top and black jeans. Both fit him snugly. She took a moment to absorb how well his solid body went with his dark, Jamie Dornan looks.

'Hey there, glad you could make it,' he said politely, stepping back to allow her in.

Wilf screeched into the hall, sliding on the laminate floor on his socks. 'Good. Now we can have pizza. I'm starving. We've been putting lights up. Daz let me use the staple gun. We haven't started Marietta's yet. We did some at our house, as well, but I've got to get Mum to get some more. She's coming home tonight but it'll be late so I'm sleeping here and going straight to school in the morning.' All this was delivered at top speed as Sky unzipped her coat.

Daz gave her a quick smile that seemed to say, *Wilf's excited. Can you enter into the spirit?*

Sky was happy to and gave Wilf her attention while Daz hung up her coat. 'Are you guys ready for the "Big Switch-On" already?' She groaned with exaggerated dismay. 'I haven't even bought my lights. I'll have to get myself in gear.'

Wilf's eyes widened hopefully. 'Shall I help you to order them? I can show you a site where Daz and Mum got theirs.'

'Sounds great.' Sky let herself be shepherded from the square hall. With a jolt, she realised that, wanting to enter into Wilf's excitement for his sake, she'd just accepted help – something she wasn't always good at. Maybe in close-knit communities, it was natural. In a spacious L-shaped living space, sofas and chairs gave way first to a dining area with a white quartz-topped table and black vinyl chairs and then a glossy kitchen with grey cabinets, copper-coloured handles and the same white quartz work surfaces. It was everything you'd find

110

under 'contemporary living' in a lifestyle magazine. 'Lovely home,' she commented politely.

Daz glanced around. 'More my ex's taste than mine, but comfy.'

'It's open plan,' Wilf put in, obviously intending to be part of the conversation.

'A pleasant living space divided by function and furniture,' Sky answered gravely, utilising the line she'd given clients when briefing a potential investment.

Wilf shrugged and homed in on the important stuff. 'Can we put the pizzas in now, Daz? Can I have Hawaiian?'

'Sure can.' Daz ruffled his hair as he headed for the kitchen area.

One adult satisfactorily occupied; Wilf turned to the other. 'Shall we order your lights now, Sky? Daz's laptop's here and the site we used is bookmarked.' He picked up a shiny silver laptop from the kitchen counter and situated himself at the dining table.

'Um . . . is that OK?' Sky sent Daz a questioning look, as his laptop was unceremoniously opened, and Wilf began to tap at it.

Daz gave a half-smile. It only curled one corner of his mouth, but it accentuated the hollows of his cheeks. 'It's fine, so long as you have your own credit card.'

Sky had a credit card tucked in her phone case, so she seated herself shoulder to shoulder with Wilf while he showered her with information about who had ordered what lights already.

Sky turned the machine so that she could see the screen. 'Let's look at eBay and Gumtree first in case we can get pre-owned.'

From the kitchen, Daz joined in. 'This competition's costing a fortune. Jess and her crowd are mad about winning but the only concession she's made towards cost so far is to post on the WhatsApp group about the benefits of using solar-powered lights.'

Sky glanced at him as he gathered plates and cutlery. 'That probably came from me. I'm always interested in conserving resources.'

But eBay, Gumtree and Facebook Marketplace disappointed her, having nothing to offer but new merchandise. 'Either they've all been bought up or it's in the terms that you can't sell them second-hand,' Sky observed. From Wilf's recommended site, Sky optimistically purchased twinkle-light curtains and icicle lights for the front left corner of the house, telling herself that she'd be able to reveal at least *that* much of the building by the judging date of December 23rd, then added everything she thought she'd need for the trees.

She was considerably poorer, but her shopping was complete by the time they gathered around the contemporary dining table, engulfed in the tastebud-tickling aroma of hot cheese and tomato with top notes of garlic bread. Daz had a bottle of beer, Wilf a glass of milk and Sky water. Wilf chattered between mouthfuls, scooping up strings of cheese from his chin as he told Sky how Daz had hung icicle lights around the roof once most of the snow had gone but let Wilf hang the star curtain over the porch canopy. 'Marietta's ordered a huge star for her roof,' he finished, reaching for another slice of thick-crust Hawaiian.

While Wilf reloaded his mouth, Daz took over the small talk. 'When Mum met you at the pub quiz, she didn't realise that you're the person who bought Elisabetta's house or she'd have asked your plans. They were friends.' His smile had warmed up a degree or two. His eyes were coffee-without-milk brown, to go with his dark, glossy hair. His eyebrows were straight, like lines dashed with a hasty pen, and he didn't look to have shaved today. Sky disliked beards, but she was a sucker for stubble.

A flutter low down in her belly took her by surprise.

'You did say that you're keeping the trees?' Daz went on.

Was that the faintest proprietorial note in his voice? A whiff of ready-to-be-righteous if she planned to cut many down because his project would have allowed them to remain? He was questioning the wrong woman on that. 'The only reason I'd fell any would be if they're unsafe. I want more trees on the planet, not fewer. I'm going to put up bird houses and bat boxes.'

'What are bat boxes?' Wilf mumbled through a mouthful of pizza, a comma of melted cheese beside his mouth.

'Places for bats to live,' Sky answered. 'Some British species are endangered as their habitats – the places they'd live naturally – are disappearing.'

'Why?' Wilf stopped eating to listen.

Sky picked up a fresh slice of pizza, curving it so the gloopy cheese couldn't slither off. 'Humans build over woods and fields or run a road through the middle. Bats are moving into people's gardens to get their own back.' She grinned at his rapt expression and summoned other facts that might interest an eleven-year-old boy. 'There should be squadrons of bugs in that crazy jungle around my house, so bats might live there already.'

She caught Daz's gaze on her and flushed. 'Saving the planet's a bit of a thing with me.'

His smile was warm, and she wondered if this was the first time he'd smiled at her and meant it. 'It's great. I suppose I thought that a property developer would garden with a bulldozer.' Daz took up his beer bottle and toasted her.

Surprised, and noting the sprinkling of acid on the phrase 'property developer', Sky took a mouthful of pizza and chewed slowly to give herself time to cast her mind back over their previous conversations. At the property auction she'd thought of him as 'the glossy man' but they hadn't exchanged a word until he'd introduced himself at The Angel. Apart from assuring him she didn't intend to erect a block of flats instead of The Corner House, all she'd told him was that she was coming to the village to live. The pub quiz . . . ? No, no career chat there. Nor in this morning's snow. 'How do you know whether I'm a property developer?' she asked.

Daz paused with his beer bottle halfway to his lips. 'I, um . . .' He cleared his throat and looked caught out. 'I looked you up on LinkedIn. It said you were a property developer in acquisitions management.'

'Development manager for an acquisitions agent,' she corrected softly. 'Or I was, for my foster brother's company. Why would you look me up? Were you and your mates thinking of expanding your budget and making me an offer for the property? But when you discovered I was a *property developer*—' she assumed a mock-scary voice '—you decided not to enter negotiations with such an unscrupulous specimen?' She pointed her slice of pizza at him. 'Just FYI, buying a run-down, neglected property and refurbishing it, incorporating modern energy-saving measures, is no bad thing. It helps the neighbourhood and creates a home where there may only have been an eyesore. If it makes a profit as well, then I'm comfortable with that.'

Wilf, his own pizza slice poised, looked from Daz to Sky, as if trying to work out the hail of long words.

Daz shrugged, the light reflecting off his hair. 'I was just

114

interested.' Then he halted. His eyes widened, as if realising that she could think he meant *interested* interested – as in *interested* – in her.

The idea created another of those flutters. She hadn't failed to notice the tension between them but had thought it the wrong kind. However, the right kind seemed unlikely, as Daz's dark gaze was anywhere but on her. She covered her uncertainty by turning to Wilf to tell him about 'tiny forests', the movement to cultivate pockets of fast-growing native trees. Wilf listened with polite interest as he munched down the rest of his pizza but was visibly less captivated by trees than by bats.

After the meal, he asked, 'Can I play on your PC for a bit, Daz?'

Daz checked his watch. 'Just for half an hour. Your mum said you had to be in bed, lights out by nine-thirty.'

Wilf disappeared upstairs while Daz made coffee for himself and Sky in grey mugs and carried them over to the sofas, waiting courteously for Sky to choose a seat so he could place her drink on a small glass table nearby.

As she hadn't looked him up on LinkedIn, she asked, 'What do you do for a living?' It was something good, judging by his comfortable home and the shiny newness of its contents.

He took a seat on the black couch and balanced his coffee mug on his thigh, steadying it by the handle. 'I head up a team of quality assurance testers of computer games. My workspace is upstairs in the attic.'

'Like a mad scientist?' She blew the steam from her drink.

'Totally bonkers,' he agreed affably. 'I often think so, when I'm playing the same level over and over on different platforms. There are advantages, though – flexible working hours, working on pre-releases, or being invited to the kind of conferences that are geek heaven.' He paused, before adding, 'I've developed my own games, too, and was lucky enough to have a success with a survivalist role-playing game.' Sky must have looked blank because he clarified, 'Humans trying to colonise an imaginary planet. It gained a cult following and my current employer bought me out for a nice lump sum, hence my potential role as investor in Ismael and Vern's accommodation centre.' A shadow crossed his face, and he sipped his drink for several moments. 'They've found somewhere to rent, now. Somewhere too good to pass up, apparently.'

Sky felt a pang of sympathy. Right from their first conversation, it had been obvious how much he'd pinned on The Corner House going to Adventure Accommodation. 'Sorry I beat you to the house, but there's always property around to invest in. Easier to do it without partners, in many ways. It's what I'm living on, while I decide what to do next.'

Her sympathy, genuine as it was, didn't seem to console him. Tautly, he said, 'The project with Ismael and Vern held attractions other than income.' Then his gaze sharpened. 'You have property of your own? Apart from The Corner House, I mean.'

She sank down further on her sofa. The suite was comfortable, as well as stylish. 'Two small, family homes in Peterborough, the apartment I've just vacated and a larger project.'

He cocked a sardonic eyebrow. 'Let me guess. It's one of those houses of multiple occupancy that people live in before they can even afford a studio flat. I've heard they're profitable. The residents live like students and piss the neighbours off with their partying.'

His comments could have been light-hearted, but Sky

felt the need to challenge his views. 'I don't know, because I've never been the kind of student with time for parties. All my qualifications were attained at the same time as I held down a full-time job. The property *is* an HMO, but I partner with a housing association to support adults with difficulties. It might be mild learning difficulties, mental health issues or someone who needs to get off the street. The average stay's two years. An onsite manager helps residents and encourages them towards more independent living.' Sky sipped her coffee, which was nice and creamy, just as she liked it. Seeing that Daz was looking discomfited, she added, 'HMOs are perfectly valid living arrangements. Not everyone can afford a big house.'

Daz shifted in his seat. 'Point taken. You've made me aware of my privilege. I'm healthy, I was brought up with loving parents in a nice, safe village. I didn't even get stuck with a student loan because my parents paid my way. I earn my living from the leisure industry.'

She smiled, interested that he'd been able to admit that he'd spoken thoughtlessly. 'Why shouldn't you have that life? You work hard, and you seem to be helping with Wilf, which you probably don't need to do.'

His expression relaxed. 'Hanging out with Wilf's not a problem. I've known and loved him since the day he was born. He's a fantastic kid, coping with a horrible situation.'

Sky couldn't help a spark of curiosity. She flicked a glance into the hall to check Wilf wasn't coming downstairs and lowered her voice. 'Is it OK to ask why his dad's where he is? Unless you'd prefer not, of course,' she added hastily.

Daz's expression shuttered. Tersely, he answered, 'You needn't be afraid of Lewis, if he returns to Middledip. It's what they call a "white collar crime". He abused his position in a bank. It was to help a friend, rather than himself.'

Sky turned this over in her mind. 'A female friend?' she asked delicately.

Daz scowled. 'Yes. But *only* a friend. She was ill and her only hope was treatment not available in the UK.'

Wow. That must have been some friendship. Sky gave herself a moment to try and imagine it. 'How shattering for Wilf. Courtney must be grateful for your help.'

Anger sparked in Daz's eyes. 'Lewis's dad, Graham, thinks I'm after Courtney. Well, I'm not. She's the wife of my oldest friend and we don't fancy each other. Graham should climb out of his pit of self-pity and do something helpful instead of setting himself up in judgement.' Then he rolled to his feet and went out to the foot of the stairs, raising his voice. 'Wilf. Time's up, mate. Get yourself to bed or your mum will get all scary.'

Wilf's laughter echoed down the stairwell. 'Mum's about as scary as jelly.'

Daz laughed too, then jogged up to say something else. Sky heard his voice, then Wilf's, muffled and distant. Conscious that she'd been invited by Wilf and not Daz, she finished her coffee. When Daz reappeared, she could retrieve her coat, thank him for his hospitality and say goodnight. She perched herself on the edge of her seat in readiness.

But Daz didn't come back downstairs. His voice seemed to retreat, and Sky could still hear it rising and falling, but it was faint. Bored, she checked her phone, finding a confirmatory email about the lights she'd just paid a packet for. On Instagram she spotted an old schoolfriend with her new baby and added, *Congrats! You're both beautiful.* She watched a YouTube video about nail guns versus staplers, then checked the time. Daz had been gone ages and still his voice was droning from somewhere. Did people read to eleven-year-olds? Must be *Lord of the Rings*, all three volumes, if so.

She wished she'd noticed where he'd stashed her coat, so she could slip away. Quailing at the thought of opening doors and poking around cupboards, however, she sighed but sat on until, finally, she heard Daz's footsteps returning.

'Sorry.' He thrust his fingers through his hair. 'One of my team called to say she's not going to be able to work on a project because she's had a bad diagnosis. I couldn't rush the call.'

Sky's irritation evaporated. 'Of course not. That would be awful. Shall I—' She'd been about to finish '—get my coat and leave you in peace', but she was interrupted by Daz's phone ringing again.

He answered it, with, 'I'll let you in,' and vanished back into the hallway.

Sky heard him talking quietly and a woman's voice answering. Sky sighed. Shit on a stick, if this was a booty call now Wilf was in bed she'd run home without her damned coat, if necessary.

But Daz reappeared with a small, slender woman. Her black hair was poker straight and when she saw Sky, she halted, looking apprehensive. 'If I'm interrupting—'

Simultaneously, Sky and Daz said, 'You're not.' Daz went on, 'Sky, this is Wilf's mum, Courtney. Courtney, this is Sky, the one who got The Corner House.'

Instantly, Courtney's eyes began to dance. 'Really?' she said to Sky. 'Your name's mud.' Grinning, she cast Daz such a laughing look that Sky couldn't take exception.

'He's called me a property developer. I think that's his worst insult,' Sky murmured.

Daz strode past them both towards the kitchen area. 'I'm going to have a whisky. What can I get you ladies?'

Courtney parked herself on the sofa. 'White wine, please. I've drunk so much with Abi this weekend that I might as well carry on. You'll join me, won't you, Sky?'

Seduced by Courtney's friendliness, Sky sank back in her seat, though she said, 'Water would be fine for me, thanks.'

Daz's voice floated from the kitchen. 'If you don't want alcohol, I have soft drinks or hot drinks.'

'Hot chocolate? Peppermint tea?' Sky didn't want more coffee because she soon got wired.

'Hang on.' Cupboard doors clicked open and shut before Daz called, 'I have sachets of hot chocolate with hazelnut. Any good?'

'Lovely, thanks,' she returned.

He clattered around and Sky turned back to Courtney and found herself under scrutiny. Sky smiled. 'You have a lovely son. It was Wilf who invited me for pizza, this evening. We got talking about animals when we came across each other on our snowy walks.'

Courtney looked pleased. 'Wilf WhatsApped me pictures of the snow. We didn't get it in London.'

Daz arrived, wine in one hand and hot chocolate in the other. 'Sky told Wilf about rabbits and blackbirds leaving footprints. He was entranced.' He returned for his own drink: a good tumbler of whisky. Sky could smell it as he passed her. He dropped down onto the sofa, the correct distance from Courtney to be friendly but not cuddly. His eyes rested on Sky. 'Don't you drink?'

She smiled and forbore to say, 'If I didn't drink, I'd die of dehydration, wouldn't I?' which was something she'd been known to utter in her less-patient moments. 'Not alcohol,' she answered, instead. 'My mum gave me an aversion.'

Courtney's brow furrowed. 'That sounds alarming.'

'It was.' Sky blew across the surface of her chocolate and inhaled the chocolatey, nutty fragrance.

'I don't know how I'd have got through the recent past without wine.' Courtney grimaced into her glass.

Sky didn't want this warm, weary-looking woman to feel criticised, because the world wasn't filled with Trish Murrays, who brought a life into the world only to push it to the back of a mind hazed by alcohol. 'I'm not suggesting you should try. I just don't want to be my mum and not dealing well with alcohol can be inherited.'

Courtney's smile reappeared. 'I can understand that. How is living in The Corner House? I'm surprised you can find it amongst the trees.'

Glad of the change of subject, Sky grinned. 'I love it. I'm going to do the garden up and check the building out while I decide what to do next.' That seemed a reasonable goal – decide not to decide.

But, as if able to read Sky's conflicts and uncertainties, Courtney said softly, 'If you love the house and the village, then stay,' and all at once, tears clogged Sky's throat. After Freddy and Minnie not wanting her around – nor Daz, really – it was balm to her damaged heart.

She swallowed down the emotion and moved on to the subject most parents welcomed – their offspring. 'Wilf's been helping me buy my lights for the Christmas Street Competition.'

Courtney rolled her eyes. 'He's crazy about it. If I wasn't hoping for greater community involvement, I'd tell Jess and her mates that the cost isn't what a newly single parent needs.' She grinned, but it wavered. 'It looks as if I'm going to have to find extra dosh for childcare for part of the school Christmas holidays.'

Sky was so aware of not being tied to a job at the moment that she spoke without really considering her words. 'If Wilf wants to hang out with me sometimes, he can.'

Courtney gasped, wearing an almost comical expression of shocked surprise. 'You must be joking!'

Sky registered shock on Daz's face, too and her cheeks boiled with mortification. For a moment, she'd forgotten that good parents wouldn't leave their kids with strangers. 'Sorry,' she blurted out in horror. 'You don't know anything about me – I'm just the crazy Corner House woman.' Then, when Courtney looked as if she might cry, she scrambled to her feet in confusion, pretending to check the time. 'Can you tell me where you hid my coat, Daz? I didn't mean to stay so late. Nice to meet you, Courtney. 'Night.'

She hurried from the room, aware of Daz at her heels. He extracted her coat from a cupboard several doors down the hall and held it up with old-fashioned courtesy for her to slip into. Even in her anxiety, her heart hiccupped at how close this brought them, her back almost brushing his front. His arms not around her but hovering.

His breath actually brushed her ear when he murmured, 'That was very nice of you. So few people offer to help Courtney that I think she was overcome.'

Slowly, Sky turned, not even stepping back out of the halo of his body heat in her shock. 'Really?' she whispered, searching his dark eyes. 'I thought she thought it was inappropriate for me to offer.'

The slightest smile touched his lips. 'You were generous. She's had a hard time and she gets tearful easily.'

'I see. I think,' she muttered, trying to reconstrue that incredulous: *You must be joking!* Sky had construed it as: *Don't be stupid* – but could Courtney have meant: *Are you sincere?*

In the same low murmur he asked, 'Would you really help?'

Awkwardly, she shrugged. 'If he didn't mind pottering in the garden or watching TV. I don't have computer games.' When Daz only gazed inscrutably at her, she yanked open the front door and hurried into a wind that carried sleet into her face, desperately sorry for Courtney if she was so fragile that even a casual offer of assistance could undo her.

Chapter Nine

Daz tried to avoid social engagements during working hours as a rule but, on Monday lunchtime, he made an exception for his mum's legendary homemade carrot-and-coriander soup. He was report writing today and deserved a break.

Sara had spent her working life in the rigid discipline of business and finance but, in retirement, found cooking relaxing. Daz slathered seedy bread with butter to dunk in the soup and relaxed at the oak table in the kitchen of the house he'd been brought up in, almost next door to Middledip Primary School. Lewis had lived just the other side of the school drive.

'I've made you apple cake, Darragh.' Sara smiled as Len cleared away the soup bowls. Apple cake was a recipe Sara had brought with her from Ireland, which she topped with a shake of cinnamon.

Len rubbed his stomach. 'My favourite.'

Sara looked at him severely. 'Not for you until you shave.'

Daz laughed. His father was growing a beard and his mother didn't like it. The back-and-forth on the subject had been going on for a few days. 'I'll eat yours, Dad,' he offered gravely.

Len assumed a beseeching expression but Sara sent him a stern look, though her eyes twinkled. Then she cut him a large slice of apple cake. Sara, Daz was certain, would soon have her clean-shaven husband back. Envious of their loving relationship, he watched them joking around and then left for his afternoon work session smiling, picturing them settling down for a nap together on the sofa after he'd gone.

He was about to cross Port Road and enter Bankside Estate when a hurrying figure caught his eye. He craned to see around the big red Santa standing sentry outside Middledip Primary School and caught the figure again, before it was hidden by a privet hedge so overgrown it would give The Corner House conifers a run for their money.

It was Graham.

Daz hesitated. He'd once known that house as well as he knew the childhood home he'd just left. Changing direction, he passed the big red Santa, strode up to the unruly hedge and turned in at the gate. In the previously pristine front garden, unpruned roses lolled raggedly in beds of weeds, browned and skeletonised by the freezing weather. Drifts of leaves half-covered grass that was so long it had lain down in surrender.

At the front door, its diamond-paned glass aperture obscured by a net curtain, he lifted the cast-iron door-knocker and let it fall with a clatter.

When a minute had passed without a response, he tried again.

He was about to turn away when the net curtain shifted, then the door opened with a bark of wood on wood. Graham peered out. His hair needed cutting and combing.

Daz summoned a smile. 'Hi, Graham. How are you?'

The older man let his hand fall from the door. 'Oh. It's you, Darragh.' Then, ungraciously: 'You can come in, if you want.'

'Thanks.' Daz followed him down the passageway, where junk mail had piled up against the skirting board. The air smelled like cooked cabbage. They went into the sitting room, where a TV was showing – ironically, Daz thought – a gardening show.

Graham switched it off. 'Something I can do for you?' He sounded harassed, as if he already had an endless list of tasks. He didn't offer Daz a seat or any refreshment, a reliable indicator that he wasn't in the mood for a long visit.

'No,' Daz replied, glad that Courtney wasn't pressing Graham to help with Wilf over the Christmas holidays. This sour house was no place for a grief-stricken boy. Graham might not feel up to arranging a twinkling Christmas tree in his window, but he did have plenty of time to dispose of junk mail and run the vacuum round the house. 'I had lunch with Mum and Dad, and I thought I'd see how you are.'

Graham shrugged. Daz took that to mean 'down and depressed', and decided that there was one point on which he could soothe Graham, at least. 'Apparently you suggested to Courtney that she and I might be cheating on Lewis. I just wanted to reassure you that it's not true. She needs support and I'm giving it.' He hoped Graham might catch the subtext, *because you're not.*

Graham's gaze slid away. 'I only asked about you and her, that's all. It's not like I made accusations. She took it the wrong way. I was just looking out for my son. It's bad enough he's locked up in that place—' He stopped to swallow hard. 'If his mother had been alive, she'd have broken her heart.'

'I know.' Daz took in the older man's slumped shoulders and unkempt clothes; his air of loneliness and grief. Part of him felt sympathetic, the other wanted to tell him to get a grip, to put on clean clothes, get up to Winter Street and spend a few hours with his grandson and daughter-in-law. Instead, he heard himself offer to trim Graham's hedge.

'Hedge?' Graham snorted. 'I can't worry about a bloody hedge when I have to see my lad sitting in prison.'

Daz left in a swirl of mixed emotions. Graham was able to visit Lewis, when Daz couldn't make himself do the same, but that seemed to be sapping all his energy. He'd let himself go.

On his way out, Daz paused to look at a photo in Graham's narrow hallway. It was from a family barbecue only a couple of years ago. Everyone – including Graham – was smiling, toasting the camera with their drinks. Wilf, beaming cheekily, also raised a half-eaten burger. Lewis's arms were around his wife and son.

Happy days.

Outside, the winter sky was pearly grey, as if it held more snow. Daz strode unhappily up Ladies Lane and into New Street, wondering if he should have been tougher with Graham – or softer. He took a left into Winter Street and noticed a figure in dark blue coveralls dragging branches along the muddy ground. Sky Terran. The big red shredder she'd demonstrated for Wilf stood alongside her. She looked up and waved a gloved hand at him. Daz nodded and waved back. It would have been friendlier to stop and chat, but he had feedback forms awaiting him.

He hated the reporting element of his job.

Cutting down a jungle looked as if it would suit his mood better, lopping off unwanted branches with the chainsaw and shoving them into the screaming shredder. Wouldn't it be great if he could cut out his negative emotions and destroy them like that?

Sky wished that winter days weren't so short. At best, daylight lasted from eight a.m. to four-thirty in the afternoon. Or she wished that she could work faster – but branches were heavy and unwieldy and so was the chainsaw.

It was getting towards dusk on Tuesday, and she was still toiling through reshaping the pines. Thursday, just two days away, was December 1st, the Big Switch-On. It would be a struggle even to get the trees on the Winter Street side of the garden threaded with lights.

Her legs trembled from climbing up and down ladders. Her arms ached as she fed the shredder's ever-hungry maw, yellow ear protectors defending against its deafening *neeeeooooowww* and goggles protecting her face from flying debris. *Neeeeooooowww. Neeeeooooowww. Neeeeooooowww.* Shredding had ceased to be entertaining. Even in heavy-duty gardening gloves, her hands felt scoured by pine needles. Her hair was bedecked with cobwebs and dust and dirt had crept inside her collar.

Neeeeooooowww.

Two figures entered her peripheral vision, startling her so that she involuntarily pulled back the frondy bough in her hands, making the shredder give a discontented burp. Her visitors were Jessie and another woman. Sky turned off the machine and let it rumble into silence.

'Hello, Sky.' Jessie beamed and stepped closer, looking as if she'd come straight from a Marks and Spencer window in a smart wool coat with tartan hat and scarf. Her tan leather ankle boots laughed at Sky's sensible green rubber ones. 'Are you busy?'

Sky pulled off her goggles and ear protectors, tempted to retort: *No, I'm just running this machine to mess with your head*. Instead, she dredged up a smile. 'Little bit.' She used a gardening-gloved finger and thumb to indicate a size of half an inch.

Jessie giggled as if Sky had made a huge joke. 'We thought we'd see how you're doing. This is my Christmas Street co-organiser, Ruth.'

Sky said a polite hello. Ruth was dumpy beside Jessie's slenderness and in her mid-fifties. Her grey, bushy hair fell past her determined chin.

Ruth cleared her throat and Jessie assumed a rueful expression, as if she knew what was coming and regretted the necessity. Bluntly, Ruth observed, 'You don't look likely to be ready in time for the Big Switch-On.'

Sky looked around at the tangled mass that was the three remaining unpruned trees on the Winter Street side, and the towering heap of branches awaiting ritual sacrifice to the shredder. The chippings the shredder produced had blown about to form dunes like a mini-Sahara. 'Doing my best,' she pointed out, politely, she thought, in the circumstances.

Ruth's lips thinned. 'Everybody else is ready. The Big Switch-On is on Thursday, you know. Two days away,' she added for emphasis.

Sky wasn't in the mood to apologise to Ruth, a stranger till this moment, for not having completed a monumental task when the deadline hadn't even been reached. She shook sawdust from her gloves. 'Feel free to pitch in. Would you rather climb the staging with the chainsaw – it makes your arms ache, though – or drag branches over to the shredder? Or you could collect the chippings into sacks.'

Ruth and Jessie exchanged looks that said: *Oh, dear. She's being difficult. She's going to let the entire street down.*

Sky wiped her goggles and prepared to start the shredder again. In a fractionally less confrontational tone, she suggested, 'Why don't I get back to work? It's only the switching on of lights that happens on Thursday and I'm sure I'll have some up by then.' She wasn't sure, but it was fruitless to prolong this meeting. 'The judging doesn't take place till nearly Christmas, which is plenty of time for me to finish what I've started.'

Ruth jutted out her chin as if in challenge, but Jess cut in hurriedly. 'Fair enough. We won't keep you.' She ushered the other woman away, though Ruth cast a lingering glance over her shoulder as if she still had plenty of opinions to share.

Sky restarted the shredder with a roar that made both women stumble as they navigated the twig-strewn path. The shrubs had been clipped to make the path accessible, but the stupid thing kept getting buried in fresh debris as Sky sawed and shredded.

An hour later, a smaller figure crunched up the path and Marietta grinned from the depths of her cranberry-coloured coat, its upturned collar framing her cheerful face. 'Hiya! I hear you had a visit from Jessie and Ruth,' she yelled over the racket from the shredder.

'Hiya.' Sky was happier to pause her shredding this time, partly because she'd reduced most of her pile of branches to wood chippings and was about to begin on another tree, partly because she liked Marietta more than Jessie or Ruth, but mostly because Marietta was clutching a tray of steaming hot chocolate and cookies. 'Food of the gods,' she said, dragging off her gloves to accept a mug and a cookie. 'Yes, Jessie and Ruth visited.' She took a blissful mouthful of double-chocolate-chip cookie.

Marietta gurgled a laugh. 'Ruth said you were obstinate.'

'That's true,' Sky agreed. 'And Ruth was overbearing.'

'There is that about her,' Marietta acknowledged. 'Don't you worry. Despite what the organisers think, the end of the world will not come if you don't have your correct quota of bling shining out on Thursday.'

Sky took another cookie. Amazing how much better one felt when surprised by something gooey and chocolatey. 'It's not as if I was sitting with my feet up, when they came calling like the Christmas police. There's a limit to how fast one person can work.'

'Sure,' Marietta agreed comfortably. 'But you're saving a little of your energy for the pub quiz, Friday, right?' She sent Sky a sidelong twinkle.

Sky couldn't help but smile back. 'I didn't realise I'd signed up to be one of Marietta's Brain Bashers again.'

'Well, of course.' Marietta switched on a faux-aghast expression. 'You know so much.' She held out the cookie plate invitingly, as if that might seal the deal.

Another of the sweet treats seemed to jump into Sky's hand. 'I scored well in the nature section. There might not be one this week.'

'There's one every week.' Marietta beamed.

Sky hesitated, remembering the interior of The Three Fishes – warm and welcoming, but also beery. 'Maybe. I want to see Nan Heather again.' But Marietta looked so disappointed that she added, 'I suppose I could do that on Saturday.'

Marietta's smile instantly returned. 'Thank you, pumpkin. I appreciate it.' They finished their afternoon snack and she stumped off with the empties, striding along in her cowboy boots. Sky hefted her chainsaw with renewed vigour.

When the light began to fail, she stowed her power tools in the barn. You weren't supposed to leave ladders and other staging around for burglars to find handy, but she was far too tired to dismantle it all, though she did move one ladder so she could clamber up onto the flat roof of the barn and lay out the solar panels, giving them Wednesday and Thursday to charge.

She paused to look around. A layer of brown leaves covered the flat roof but when she kicked some aside, she was delighted that it was substantial enough to have been paved. Close to the wall of the house, she spotted things that hadn't been visible from the windows – a wooden lounger and a charming wrought-iron table and chairs. The parapet formed a low wall around the three open sides of what, it now became obvious, was a sun terrace. 'Awesome,' she breathed, forgetting her tiredness in her delight.

Crossing to the back of the terrace, she inspected a flight of stone steps, the lower half of which was smothered by vegetation from Jack's beanstalk family. She pointed at it. 'You're for the chop as soon as I get the front garden sorted. This terrace is going to be fantastic in summer.' Her heart soared at the thought of bringing meals up to what she was sure would be a suntrap, as Elisabetta had obviously done. She stopped, realising that she'd just assumed she'd still be in this house when summer came.

Her gaze caught on a small mound against the wall, half-covered in leaves. She stepped closer to investigate and found a pair of green wellies, much like her own, evidently waiting for an owner who was never coming back. She had to swallow a lump in her throat, thinking of the unknown Elisabetta, who everyone said loved this house so much.

She shook off her earlier doubts. The house was in her custody, and she was going to make the sun terrace wonderful. And she'd find a way to make Elisabetta's boots into planters, so they could remain, a part of things.

When she climbed back down the ladder, she felt as if her recent decision not to decide had been the right one. By the time she'd had a long, hot shower and washed the day's tree debris from her hair, she was ready to pull on her favourite green sweatshirt and slightly clashing purple sweatpants and prepare dinner.

Rather wishing she had more of Marietta's cookies as dessert, she made omelette and salad, listening to music by Gayle and Adele, ate on her lap in the sitting room, and then washed up. She'd bought a kitchen table but the seller, though willing to deliver in his van for an extra tenner, wasn't able to do so until the weekend.

She'd just picked up her current read, a book about a Greek guy who'd fallen in love with an Irish tourist as a teenager and had just approached her on social media twenty years later, when somebody knocked on her front door. She paused, surprised. Maybe it was Marietta. She dropped the book face down on the sofa and hurried to answer.

It was Courtney, wrapped in a stylish black coat, a red beret perched rakishly on her dark hair, waiting on the doorstep when Sky opened the door. 'Are you busy? I made you a housewarming cake.' She extended an upside-down biscuit tin.

A tiny thrill of pleasure fizzing through her at this friendly overture, Sky stepped back. 'Fantastic. Come in.

I was about to make a cuppa and was sighing over not having much sweet stuff.'

Courtney nodded understandingly as she stepped inside, closing the door behind her. 'I must have heard your thoughts. Isn't your house beautiful?' She stroked the artfully turned newel cap before using it to hang her coat on.

Soon they were settled on a sofa, Sky with peppermint tea and Courtney with coal-black coffee. She inhaled the fragrant steam and let out a happy sigh. 'Gorgeous. I know it's meant to keep you awake but I'm always so tired that it doesn't.' She took an appreciative sip. 'Wilf tells me that you've lived in Middledip before. We have that in common. My first home with my husband was on the Bankside Estate, before we moved to Bettsbrough.' Courtney flicked Sky a glance. 'Wilf said that he's told you about Lewis.'

Sky hesitated. She didn't want to say, 'What, that your husband's inside?' and get Wilf in trouble for spilling the beans.

Perhaps seeing her hesitation, Courtney clarified. 'That Wilf's dad's in prison, I mean.' A shadow crossed her face. 'Poor Wilf feels incredibly let down and angry.'

'It must be difficult for you both,' Sky commiserated. She'd only met Courtney for two short periods but was having no trouble warming to her. It was great to relax into a feeling of companionship with a woman of similar age who seemed so lovely and straightforward – unlike Minnie, who brimmed with guile and hidden agendas. But Sky didn't want to think of Minnie tilting her nose in the air and considering herself a cut above ordinary folk – except Freddy, whose bank account and list of achievements were as handsome as he was – so she suggested, 'Shall we cut your lovely cake?'

'It's lemon drizzle,' Courtney said, as if that clinched it.

Once armed with the sugary treat, Courtney sent Sky a guilty look. 'I have an ulterior motive for bringing the cake. A Wilf reason.' She fidgeted. 'Were you serious when you said he could come to you sometimes over the school Christmas holidays?'

Sky finished a mouthful of delicious, lemony sweetness. ''Course. I wouldn't mess you around over something like that.'

Shoulders visibly relaxing, Courtney gave a tremulous smile. 'I'm sorry if my reaction on Sunday evening confused you. Daz said you shot off home because you were worried that you'd spoken out of turn. I wasn't horrified – quite the reverse. I couldn't believe my luck.'

Sky tried to put herself in Courtney's shoes. 'I thought I'd been presumptuous, offering to look after your son when you hardly know me. Parents must be incredibly careful.'

'But it often doesn't take long to get a feel for a person,' Courtney replied earnestly. 'Daz says Wilf likes you and that you were open with him about a problem in your own childhood – I hope it's OK to bring that up? Wilf talked as if you understood his feelings.'

Warmth spread up Sky's spine to think that she might have comforted a troubled child. 'If Wilf won't mind me being busy with the garden, he's very welcome.'

Courtney looked as if she might cry. '*Thank* you. I'll give you my contact details, of course, and Daz will be just up the road most of the time. He's offered too, so I thought maybe you could alternate? School ends on December 21st and goes back on the fourth of January.'

As Courtney listed which days she'd be off work and able to be with Wilf herself, Sky took out her phone and made calendar notes. 'Tell me which days you want me, nearer the time.'

Theatrically, Courtney clutched her chest in gratitude. 'You've no idea how you've relieved my mind. It should be much plainer sailing after these holidays because I heard today that I've got a job I applied for in the office of a primary school.'

Sky tried to congratulate her, but Courtney was plainly focused on her son. 'I've been at my wits' end. Poor Wilf doesn't want anything to do with Lewis – and I can't blame him.' She paused to find a tissue and blow her nose. Discreetly, Sky allowed her new friend a moment to compose herself. Courtney went on, 'I don't know if our marriage will survive.' She thrust her fingers through her hair, making it stand up, a bit like Wilf's. 'I know Daz told you why Lewis stole from the bank – to fund Evira's treatment. He was in love with her when he was young,' she added frankly. 'I believe him that she didn't reciprocate his feelings, so their relationship was always platonic, and I try and understand that she was in a terrible situation. But sacrificing *our* happiness . . . ? It feels like a hell of a betrayal, leaving us to pick up the pieces. I've even wondered if Wilf and I should move away and change our surname. Not that I know how you do it.'

'It's easy enough,' Sky observed. 'I did it.'

Courtney looked interested. 'Oh? You've been married, you mean? And went back to your maiden name?'

'No.' Sky snorted a laugh. 'I never took my ex-husband Marcel's name, Moynault. He'd say I wasn't committed enough. I didn't want Mum's name, so I chose Terran because it means "earth" and I liked the idea of being the sky and the earth.'

'That's lovely,' Courtney said, dreamily. 'Maybe I'll choose a name for myself too. Courtney Hoping-things-will-get-better. Courtney Not-wanting-to-be-a-prisoner's-wife.' She smiled without mirth. 'Are you single? Have you done any online dating? I'm thinking about it. Lewis isn't in a position to complain as what he did for Evira left me to deal with a broken-hearted son, downsizing, longer hours, little money and my dad-in-law being unable to look outside his own misery. Got to relieve stress somehow.'

Sky winced sympathetically. 'I haven't had time to think about dating, but a few dinners or trips to the cinema sound OK, now I'm less busy.' She explained the demands of her former role at Freddy Walker Acquisitions and how close she'd been with her foster brother until Minnie came along. 'I was too dependent on Freddy and work,' she admitted. 'Friends fell away without me really noticing.' Then, curiously, 'Will you put "married" on your dating profile?'

Courtney shrugged, scooping up cake crumbs with a dampened finger. 'Maybe "separated". You can't get much more separated than one of you being behind bars. Minnie sounds a piece of work,' she added, making Sky warm to her still more. Then she grimaced. 'I'm so not feeling Christmassy. My sister's invited us to Cornwall but I'm not trailing down there when I have such a short break. In fact, I wish we were in Narnia so it could be always winter but never Christmas—' She halted, a hand to her mouth. 'I've just realised I didn't ask about your Christmas arrangements when I was going on about you looking after Wilf.'

Sky wasn't worried. 'I don't have any. I'd intended to go away but that was before I bought the house. There's plenty here to keep me busy and there might be village celebrations to get involved with – as well as the Christmas Street stuff, that is.' She recounted Jessie and Ruth's visit today, making it funny instead of admitting she'd been feeling overwhelmed and that they'd made it worse. Clearing the garden didn't seem much of a problem, compared to a husband in prison and a broken-hearted son.

Courtney giggled. 'They have too much time on their hands. They're obsessed with this damned competition.' She checked the time regretfully. 'I need to get home for Wilf. Let me know if you discover any interesting village Christmas activities, won't you? Particularly if I could involve Wilf. He says the local kids already have friends, but I think he's keeping to himself rather than risk rejection.' She got to her feet.

Sky rose with her. 'I had to make those kind of changes a couple of times. It can take a while to fit in. My foster brother got in with kids by making them laugh with stupid jokes like being called Freddy because his mum was too poor to make it "Frederick".' Her laugh wobbled unexpectedly as she escorted her new friend down the long hall to the front door, so she changed the subject. 'Lewis won't get out for Christmas?'

Courtney's brows shot up. 'He began a four-year sentence in January. If everything goes well, he'll get release on temporary licence after two.' Indecision crossed her face. 'Or there's a chance of him being let out earlier than that wearing one of those tag things. In either case, he needs an address to come to. He asks about it when I visit him, hoping I'll say that *of course* he must come and rejoin his wife and son. When I refuse to decide, he says, "I do love you," and I think he does. I want to do what's best for my son, but there's so much to resolve, and I don't know if it's possible.' She paused, screwing up her face. 'Evira . . . the treatment wasn't ultimately successful. I'm so sorry about that, but in a way, it makes me angrier. That's cold, isn't it? As if I'd have been fine with it all if she'd lived – which I wouldn't.' She gave a sniff as she pulled on her coat and stepped outside. 'Your garden smells like fresh-cut wood. See you soon.' With a wave, she hurried down the path – or where it ought to be if not covered by twigs and chippings.

Sky watched her go, feeling helpless about the other woman's conflicts. They hadn't got around to exchanging phone numbers but that would come. Poor Courtney was stuck in a horrible situation, but there had been an openness and warmth that made Sky hopeful of a friendship to build on.

An hour later, another knock fell on Sky's door. She'd added a blue gilet to her lounging gear as the house cooled, but it wasn't until she answered the summons and saw Daz there that it occurred to her that green, blue and purple clashed, the sweatpants were baggy and the gilet too puffy.

Daz was enveloped in a fleece that was the dark green of the needles on her pine trees, and the streetlights behind him haloed his dark hair. 'Hi,' he said. 'Sorry to call unannounced but I don't have your phone number.'

Sky was thinking about the clean, glossy look of his hair and that he'd shaved tonight. It took her a moment to realise he was waiting for something. And then what it was. 'Oh!' she said. 'Come in.'

'Thanks.' He followed her to the big, bare sitting room, where the fire was burning and discarded his fleece, leaving him looking trim in jeans and a long-sleeved top. 'Marietta tells me you need some help with the garden.'

'Oh, it's OK. You work during the day,' she said, her default position still being to reject help. 'It won't be the end of the world if I don't have everything perfect for the Big Switch-On.' It would cause mild, soon-forgotten irritation in some of her new neighbours, that was all.

Daz fidgeted. 'If I don't come and help tomorrow, Marietta's going to ask Bell to do it.'

Sky tried and failed to see the import of this. 'But I'm fine.' She smiled in case she sounded ungrateful, but she had no wish to reinforce the myth that if a woman is struggling, a man should come along and save her. The woman just tried harder, that was all. Life had taught her early that self-reliance avoided disappointment.

Daz's gaze wandered around the room, pausing on the plaster roses and cornicing. Eventually, it returned to her. 'I don't know about Bell.'

She digested Daz's odd manner. 'Don't know what about him?'

His eyebrows formed a hard line. 'Maybe my opinion of him's coloured by him hitting on my ex-girlfriend Abi a couple of years ago in an unacceptably pushy way. Some people might think a Christmas kiss is an obligation, but I wasn't impressed.'

She arched her eyebrows. 'I wouldn't be, either. Thanks for the heads up, but I really am fine.'

He regarded her steadily. 'Courtney and Marietta say you're battling through, but Jessie and Ruth are hectoring you.'

She laughed. 'OK, I'm behind their schedule, but they'll have to understand that the front garden's taking longer than I'd hoped. It'll be ready for the judging, just before Christmas.'

He looked down and absently brushed something off his jeans. 'Courtney says you're helping her with Wilf. You probably don't realise what a massive relief that is to her.

140

It's an enormous favour, so why don't you let me do something for you in return?' He looked up at her then, dark gaze steady and persuasive.

Sky got an inkling of why a person might think there was something between Daz and Courtney. He was protective of her indeed, if he wanted to repay her perceived debt.

She took a moment to consider. Maybe the way to make friends in the village was not by shoving everyone away? There was still a massive amount of work to do; she was flagging. She imagined the effect of another pair of hands, particularly strong hands, by the look of Daz. Letting out a short breath, she said, 'Well . . . if you have an hour or two. Thank you.'

A smile flashed across his face. 'Great. I'll be along in the morning.' He stretched and then let his hands settle behind his head, one of his brows a fraction higher than the other as he scrutinised her.

Sky twiddled her hair. Perhaps he was wondering whether her outfit was a kaleidoscope stuck mid-turn. Or perhaps he was politely allowing her an opportunity to speak because he'd dominated the conversation so far. She asked, 'Wilf OK?'

His grin made his eyes sparkle. 'He is. He was at my place when Courtney came to collect him. She was a few minutes later than expected so he pretended to look at his watch and said, "What time do you call this?" I laughed and Courtney frowned at me.'

She found herself laughing, too. 'Great kid.'

'Yeah.' A pensive expression stole over his face. 'Sky,' he began. Then he paused to once again rub at a spot on his thigh. It drew Sky's attention to his long legs and the way he filled his jeans. 'Courtney told me you were talking about dating.'

'She seems to have told you just about everything we discussed,' she joked, but her heart put in an extra beat. Daz wasn't about to ask her out, was he? That wasn't the vibe she'd felt from him so far.

His brows lowered. 'I can see why Courtney's hurt enough to consider it.'

Ah. The ripples caused by Lewis's stay at Her Majesty's Pleasure were disturbing a big pond. When he'd said 'you' he hadn't meant Sky; he'd meant her and Courtney. She tried to will her cheeks not to flush an embarrassed pink.

His gaze levelled on her again and he grimaced. It pulled his lips to one side and skewed his nose, like a rabbit. 'I suppose I had some idea you could talk her out of having an affair. Now I've said it out loud, it sounds ridiculous.'

Yes, it was, partly because Sky didn't intend to talk Courtney out of it. It wasn't Sky's business, and neither was it up to Daz to decide whether Lewis deserved Courtney's loyalty. She decided to introduce another perspective. 'Maybe it's only an "affair" if she considers herself married? I know that she's married, in law, but emotionally . . . ?'

'Take your point.' He looked unhappy about it. 'She also said you'd told her about changing your name and she's thinking about doing the same. It's like she's leaving Lewis one step at a time. Lewis is my oldest friend.'

She resettled herself on the cushions, curling her legs beneath her. 'Then it's natural that you feel weird about standing by and watching, if Courtney decides to have . . . an adventure. Or two.'

'Two?' He closed his eyes, as if in pain. 'I suppose she's talking about online dating so she can keep it away from her doorstep. And Wilf.'

Sky thought that if Daz, who'd been mainly cool and

even offish with her, had lowered his guard sufficiently to discuss this with her, then Courtney and Wilf must matter to him a lot. She made her voice gentle. 'I don't know whether she's reasoned that deeply. People go on dates without going to bed.' Then, catching fresh dismay on his face, she realised he hadn't even mentioned bed, and coloured up again. 'Perhaps she's just looking for life outside her situation. I can see the attraction of a few exciting dates – escape the everyday, nothing too heavy.'

He stared at her for several moments. 'Life's thrown a lot of crap at her,' he acknowledged. 'Sorry I bothered you with all this.' He rose and began pulling on his fleece. 'See you tomorrow.' He headed for the hallway.

'As long as you're still sure about tomorrow,' she said, thrown by how abruptly he'd ended the conversation.

'Laters,' he called back. And Sky was left looking at the door closing behind him. It was a solid oak front door and it shut with a clunk, as if underlining how over this conversation was.

Chapter Ten

As he hurried away from The Corner House, still fastening his fleece, Daz knew he'd exited in an undignified rush like a dog called for its dinner.

It wasn't hunger for food that had hit him. It had been for Sky Terran.

He *wanted* Sky Terran – but didn't want her to notice the evidence.

Even in her odd get-up – was that multi-layered baggy stuff in fashion? – heat had washed over him. Her red-gold hair rippling loose over one shoulder, catching the light shed by the old-fashioned chandelier above. Eyes glowing, skin a translucent pink, that nervous lick of the lips . . . her blush when she mentioned bed.

Until that moment, he'd been focusing on managing the Courtney situation. When she'd arrived to fetch Wilf, she'd seemed the happiest he'd seen her since she'd moved into Winter Street, a laugh in her eyes, and 'What a nice woman Sky is!' on her lips. It had been great when she'd talked of the future – Christmas, the Big Switch-On, her relief to have help with Wilf's care.

Until . . . dating.

That was the point when his pleasure turned to dismay. Courtney wasn't *his* wife, but could he just say nothing?

As soon as Courtney and Wilf had headed home, he'd set off for the other end of Winter Street to see what could be gleaned from Sky, who he'd begun to think of as a bit like a hedgehog – soft and cute beneath her prickly armour. Dear old meddling Marietta's heavy hints that someone should help Sky with her trees had provided him with the perfect reason to call, especially as a spell outdoors wielding power tools appealed, after days of writing reports.

But he'd sounded like an idiot suggesting Sky might intercede with Courtney. He'd begun floundering, and when Sky had mentioned bed and dating in the same breath, he'd completely lost focus.

His house loomed out of the dark evening, the lighting cables glinting in the streetlights as if someone had wound loose threads all over it. Like the neighbouring houses, it was just awaiting the flick of a switch to transform an ordinary English street into a glittering bling-fest designed to outshine all other Christmas Street bling-fests.

Once indoors, he flopped onto the sofa and checked his phone. His attention was caught by a message in the WhatsApp group Adventure Accommodation, which he'd set up with Ismael and Vern when it had looked as if they might go into business together. Ismael: *Hey, Daz. Me and Vern are off tomorrow and meeting for a lunchtime pint at the 3 Fishes. Fancy it?*

Warmth spread through Daz at this friendly gesture. He tapped out a reply. *Will come if I can but, believe it or not, I'm helping Sky Terran trimming trees tomorrow. She's getting pressure from the Christmas Street Mafia re*

Thurs evening switch-on. Will try to join you for an hour, though.

He didn't have to wait long for another message, this time from Vern. *Need more hands? I don't mind helping.* Almost immediately, Ismael chimed in. *Same here. What time?*

Daz made the arrangements, pleased at this evidence that their camaraderie hadn't been entirely centred around The Corner House.

Next, he opened an email from Abi.

Wow, isn't it cold? London's lovely with all the lights, though. Oxford St and Piccadilly are ablaze. I walked all the way there and back last night, just enjoying the buzz.

Daz had no idea how far that was so checked on his map app. Two point three miles each way. Not as far as a complete circuit of the footpaths around Middledip, but it probably felt further with shoulder-to-shoulder people in your way and endless roads to cross. Abi went on:

Had a great time when Courtney came for the weekend. She's invited me back, sometime. That will feel weird! Not sure if I should stay on her sofa or with you. ☺

Daz felt sucker-punched. What? Abi wouldn't really feel entitled to stay with him, would she? When he replied, he'd skirt that question.

On Wednesday morning, he ate breakfast watching the day dawn, an apricot glow on the horizon as if a giant had awoken and switched on a light just out of sight.

Today, Daz was going to forget work and go and chop stuff up.

He found Sky already in her garden when he arrived at eight-fifteen, her hair swinging in a plait down the back of a battered khaki parka. He'd just started to explain about Vern and Ismael when they strolled through the gate, Vern fair and Ismael dark, both grinning. Ismael introduced himself to Sky. 'I hope you don't mind that we invited ourselves. We're interested in what you're doing here, seeing as we couldn't do it ourselves.'

'And no hard feelings about that,' added Vern, pulling on a blue-and-grey hat.

Daz felt a stirring of guilt. His friends were being gracious and mature over Sky getting the house. He knew that he hadn't been either.

Sky looked uncertain. 'Are you sure you don't mind helping me? You must be busy and—'

'Sure,' they chorused.

Sky hesitated and Daz wondered if he should have consulted her about Vern and Ismael, rather than just letting them turn up. Now he thought of it, she did seem the independent kind. But she raised no further objections, and so began an energetic morning with Daz wielding the chainsaw, Ismael the sabre saw and Vern feeding the shredder. Sky directed operations from the ground, from where she could identify which branches needed lopping. Daz had no idea how she'd managed that alone and could only assume she'd had to keep clambering up and down between the staging and the ground. It was amazing that she'd achieved as much as she had.

The morning wore on. Brush was shoved through the shredder. Larger branches were cut and stacked for next winter's fires. Sawdust was shovelled into builders' sacks that Sky found in the barn. They finished the last three trees bordering Winter Street in a couple of hours and moved on to the side bordering Great Hill Road.

When they stopped for coffee, Sky researched uses for sawdust. 'You can mix it with wax and make firelighters,' she said, between sips, her nose pink from the cold.

Ismael tucked his free hand into his pocket. 'Ratty and the other guys at the garage use sawdust to clear up oil spills, if you can spare some.'

Sky grinned, leaves and pine needles dusting her hair. 'The back garden's four times this size. I think I'll have plenty.' She turned back to her phone. 'Sawdust's good on icy paths, too, better than salt, because salt gets into the water and kills aquatic life.'

'She's concerned about the environment,' Daz explained to the others.

She nodded. 'You bet. I like our planet and all life on it.' Then she glanced down the path towards her gate and sighed. 'Well, most of it.'

Daz followed her gaze and saw Ruth staring into the garden. 'You'll never get the job done by standing around,' she called.

'Not true,' Sky called back. 'A break for refreshment will help us all work. Tired bodies and minds make mistakes.'

Ruth gave an irritable shrug and stumped off towards Main Road.

'I expect that's true, anyway,' Sky said cheerfully, taking their empty mugs. Soon she was dragging away one of the enormous bags of wood chippings, working as hard as everyone else with easy movements of her strong, lithe body.

Later, they ate lunch sitting on their coats on the kitchen floor. Sky made everyone cheese and tomato toasties and steaming-hot mugs of tea and served lemon drizzle cake, as if anxious to repay them in some small way for their labours.

'Courtney made the cake,' she said, licking her fingers when her slice had disappeared. 'And Marietta makes great cookies. I've obviously come to live in the right place.' She gave Daz a teasing smile, as if daring him to take the opportunity to complain about her buying The Corner House.

He didn't. He no longer wished she'd never come to Middledip.

When Wilf charged into the garden after school, Sky slung an arm around him as if he were her little brother. 'If you change out of your uniform, you can help. I saved a slice of cake in case you came.'

Wilf looked up at her with such adoration that Daz teased, 'Suck-up,' and Wilf laughed and ran off home to change. He returned at lightning speed, gobbled his cake and swigged down a can of Purdey's, an energy drink Daz had never heard of but Wilf greeted with greedily widened eyes. Then he slapped on goggles and fed the shredder for a few minutes. When it became obvious that he couldn't keep up the flow like Vern could, he fetched a shovel to scrape detritus from the old drive off Great Hill Road, the gate to which they'd just uncovered.

They all worked together in a cacophony of voices and power tool motors. It was past four-thirty and nearly dusk when they stopped, standing in the centre of the garden to survey the front of the house, which had emerged from the overgrown trees. Its tiled roof was mossy and lichened, the grey stone walls looking as if they'd stand forever. The frames to the casement windows were covered in once-white flaking paint, while flourishes and fluting ornamented rusty cast-iron downpipes and gutters.

149

'Wow,' Sky breathed, her green eyes luminous with pleasure. 'The trees look like they've been to the barber's for short back and sides.' She slipped off a glove and stroked the trunk of the big white tree in the centre of the garden, now freed from its prison of rampant brambles. 'Isn't the white birch beautiful? And I have a drive! *Thank* you, everybody.'

Daz, Vern and Ismael brushed down their work gear and told her, good-naturedly, that she was welcome, while Wilf demanded, 'Is there more cake?'

'Right here,' called a familiar voice, and Marietta toddled up the path with a box of homemade brownies and a big bottle of lemonade wearing a hat of paper cups. They stood around as darkness fell and only streetlights and the moon illuminated the scene, munching brownies and gulping lemonade, stamping their feet to keep warm now they were no longer busy.

Then Wilf said to Sky, 'Do you want Daz to help with your Christmas lights? Because you need them up for the Big Switch-On tomorrow night. There's going to be food and drink and stuff.'

Sky hid a grin. 'I'm sure Daz has something else he needs to do tomorrow,' she said patting Wilf's shoulder. 'He's been amazingly kind already considering—' She paused.

Daz wondered whether she'd been about to say, '—considering what an arse he's been about the house.'

But she continued smoothly, '—considering he has a busy job and a house to look after, and he helps your mum and you, too.'

'Yeah,' said Wilf, brushing these achievements aside. 'But—'

'I'll help,' Daz put in, before he knew he was going to say it. 'A shame to get this far and then miss the Big

Switch-On. You don't want to be left off Ruth's Christmas card list.'

Sky burst out laughing. It might have been the first time she'd really let go with him and laughed properly, her head back and that thick plait of hair swinging down her back. 'I won't argue, this time. If you can spare an hour, it will be great.' Then she turned to Ismael and Vern. 'And I think you've given up a day off to help me? You're both stars, honestly.'

The group dispersed with modest murmurings. Daz escorted a tired Wilf up Winter Street to see if his mum was home from work yet, and realised something. He hadn't had such a good day since Lewis went into prison.

Sky showered, watching pine needles flow down the drain. The day had passed in a flurry of hard work, but also with a feeling of camaraderie and community. She examined the thought that it had come about by her accepting help, which was not her default position. Apparently, if she wanted people in her life, she had to let them in. This community spirit thing would take some getting used to.

When she was out of the shower and seated cross-legged on the floor to blow-dry her hair, she returned to the website Wilf had shown her and bought more nets of lights, paying ten pounds for next-day delivery. It would be fun to see Ruth's face when Sky's garden sprang into so much glittering, light-encrusted life that it would probably be visible from the moon.

Hair dried, she decided on a tramp around the village before making supper. She still wasn't used to flaking out in front of the TV so early in the evening. Dressing in coat, hat and scarf against temperatures that were low even for the last day of November, she shoved her hands

151

into her pockets and set out to explore the rest of Bankside – Great Hill Road round to Top Farm Road, peeping into Hilary Close and touring Scott Road. In The Close, she spied a footpath back to Main Road, which brought her to where The Three Fishes shone like a beacon of fairy lights and Christmas trees.

She didn't stop. Her feet carried her further down Main Road, and soon she was outside Rotten Row, where she spotted, as before, Nan Heather's diminutive figure in the window. Heart giving a glad bounce, she hurried up the path and called through the glass, 'Nan Heather, it's Sky.'

Nan beamed, beckoning enthusiastically and pointing towards her side door. In moments, Sky was letting herself into the well-remembered kitchen, crossing the dining room and tapping at the door to the front room.

'Come in, duck,' she heard Nan Heather's rusty voice call, and turned the door handle. The elderly lady was pulling herself out of the chair with the aid of a walking frame. 'This is a lovely surprise,' she said, and opened her arms.

Throat tightening, Sky gently enveloped the slight, stooped figure in a hug. Her cheek pressed to the silver curls, and she breathed in the smell of shampoo and biscuits that seemed not to have changed in all the years since she'd lived in the little bedroom with the dormer window. Her eyes burned to remember Nan Heather being the very best person in Sky's younger self's world.

'It's lovely to see you,' she said, inadequately.

When they disengaged, Nan Heather's eyes looked as misty as Sky's. 'Let's sit there,' she suggested croakily, indicating armchairs facing one another. She made her way slowly, aided by the walking frame.

Seeing that Nan Heather embraced as much independence as possible, Sky didn't attempt to help, but took the vacant chair. 'What a lovely room,' she said, gazing around. A single bed stood in one corner, making the space a bedroom at one end and a sitting room at the other. The carpet was amber, toning with brown and gold velvet curtains at the window. A TV stood in a corner and a portable radio rested near Nan Heather's elbow. Sky couldn't remember the last time she'd seen a radio like that, a little silver box with a dial and an aerial.

'I told my daughter Mo all about you being back,' Nan Heather began. 'And my granddaughter, Hannah. They were ever so interested. Would you like a drink, dear? You could make us both some cocoa.'

'Lovely.' Sky jumped up and returned to the kitchen, discovering – when directed by Nan Heather – cocoa, milk and sugar. She even remembered that Nan Heather took it milky. Errand complete, she carried the mugs back into the front room in a haze of chocolatey steam.

'Did you talk to Freddy?' her hostess enquired eagerly.

Sky felt her stomach lurch and had to steady her cocoa to avoid spilling it. 'Not yet,' she said truthfully, sitting down. But she heard the tremor in her voice and a vision of Freddy sprang to her mind, first his usual self, bursting with ideas that spouted without pause, then his shuttered, granite expression when she'd seen him last at her Cambridge apartment, disappointment radiating from him.

Since then, silence.

Nan Heather sounded puzzled. 'No rush, duck. Just whenever you speak to him, you tell him how well I remember him, won't you?' Then she went on to tell Sky of Hannah living in the village with her Swedish husband Nico and two little stepdaughters. 'And my grandson, Rob, he lives in Bettsbrough with his wife, Leesa. They're expecting, you know,' Nan Heather enthused. 'Christmas is lovely with little ones. They get so excited, don't they?'

Sky said, 'Of course,' though her experience was largely limited to the nieces and nephews of Marcel and then Blake. It had been fun to see kids ripping into parcels and making boxes into garages for new cars or threatening furniture as they raced around on snazzy scooters, but she'd known those children only slightly. Her mind drifted back to Courtney's worries about what kind of Christmas she could give Wilf this year.

'My Mo and her husband, Jeremy, they put on a big Christmas dinner, every year. And they have the neighbours in for a Christmas Eve party.' Nan Heather paused to pick up her cocoa and sip. She held it in both hands. 'I can stay as long as I like, but it's good to have your own space, isn't it?'

'I've certainly got that.' Sky laughed. 'I don't think I realised how enormous The Corner House is.' Not strictly true. She'd known the exact dimensions on paper, but still there seemed a lot of space not occupied by herself or her furniture. She told Nan Heather about the working party that had turned up to complete the deforestation of the front garden today and showed her photos on her phone.

Nan Heather peered at them myopically. 'Tell me all your plans for the house.' Her eyes sparkled behind the magnifying lenses of her glasses.

Ruefully, Sky laughed. 'I think it's true to say my plans are fluid. I'm just enjoying it, right now.'

'And what does Freddy think?' Nan beamed in antici-pation.

The tightness returned to Sky's throat. 'He hasn't seen it since I moved in. He's busy with the business. He's getting married, you know. His fiancée's called Minnie.'

'Ooh! Do you have any photos of them?' Nan Heather's wrinkly cheeks rose with the eagerness of her smile.

'I have one of Freddy, I think.' Sky pored over her phone as she swiped through her camera roll, hiding her face until she could summon a smile. 'Here we are. This one's at the office, so you can see his business premises, too. I took it for his company newsletter.'

Freddy grinned from behind his desk. He held a set of plans in one hand and his phone in the other. His tie was on the desk beside him and his jacket hanging on his chair. Curls tumbled across his forehead.

Nan Heather peered at the screen again. 'What a man he's grown into,' she said wistfully. 'When he visits you, you will bring him to see me, duck, won't you?'

Sky's heart cracked, and she knew she had to establish contact with Freddy, to bring him to this wonderful woman who'd given them the love and care their flesh-and-blood families hadn't. 'I will,' she said firmly.

An hour later, when she'd washed the cocoa mugs and said goodbye, she texted Freddy as she walked. *Nan Heather is still alive and kicking. She's asking to see you.* She paused, then deleted the last sentence. That was doing things the wrong way around, creating a guilt trip. Instead, she wrote, *If you're ever Middledip way and call for coffee, she'd love to see you.* But she wasn't happy with that, either, because it was ambiguous. Delete, delete, delete. *I promised her that if you came to see me, I'd take you to visit her, too.*

It was nearly ten o'clock by the time her phone flashed with a reply. *Good to know she's still about thanks for the info.* Automatically applying her own punctuation, Sky saw that Freddy wasn't about to commit to anything. Despondently, she sighed, not sure who was most upset – her with Freddy or Freddy with her.

In bed, she lost herself in her novel, hearing the occasional sound of a car traversing Winter Street above the wind soughing through the trees. Gently, her eyes closed.

Her heart might be troubled, but Middledip was just the place to find peace.

Chapter Eleven

Thursday was the first day of December and once again involved scaling ladders, this time to attach icicle lights to gutters, and wind fairy lights through trees. Sky began early and Daz, true to his word, joined her soon after, business-like in blue jeans and tan work boots with a ski jacket. Greeting him, Sky found she was able to accept his help. Middledip was changing her.

The sky was the grey of ice on a puddle and their fingers became numb in the knife-like wind. 'Winter Street had better win this competition,' Sky grumbled, when they stopped for a warming lunch of soup.

From his position lounging on his coat on the kitchen floor, Daz snorted. 'I've done Courtney's house, mine and Marietta's already. You're a novice.'

She laughed. 'Or you're a mug.' Daz was nicer, now he no longer seemed to resent her so much for getting The Corner House.

They returned to work, flagging, freezing, grumbling, and then Wilf arrived, breathless from the run from the bus stop, to join in the last hour. They pretended that they hadn't been testing each skein of lights as they went, so he could have the pleasure of throwing switches and crowing when swags or nets or dangling icicles of lights sprang into life, even if dim in the daylight. Sky had left a special lamp for him to hang. It was the shape of a tilted watering can with a stream of twinkle lights pouring from the spout. He attached it to its hook with such a beaming smile that Sky had to gulp back tears and even Daz cleared his throat.

A smear of dirt decorating his cheek, Wilf told Sky, 'You'll see it every time you walk along your path.' He sounded so envious that Sky went on her phone and secretly ordered another watering can light, this time to be delivered to 31a, his and Courtney's house.

Eventually, they'd hung every possible icicle and twinkle. Even Wilf was content that Sky's garden was only slumbering until darkness fell and, when it was time for the Big Switch-On, the front of the house would awake in a blaze of light. Hovering at the gate, he reported gleefully on the activity further up Winter Street. 'Jessie and Ruth are already putting up tables for the drinks and food. That starts at six and the switch-on's at seven. Shall we call for you? Me and Mum and Daz are calling for Marietta, too.'

'That would be great,' Sky agreed, warmed that she'd been a Winter Street resident for only just over two weeks but was to be included in their group. She risked a glance at Daz to check for frowns, but discovered that he was smiling, too. He had a nice smile, now he was using it more.

Daz ruffled Wilf's quiff. 'C'mon, buddy. Bet you've got homework to do before the festivities.'

Wilf groaned, 'Bleurgh,' and sagged with exaggerated dismay, but went off to get the necessary evil over.

Sky spent a while organising wires so that all her switches were together on the floor near the barn door, then went indoors to warm up with a hot bath before the Big Switch-On excitement began.

Sky was ready before six. Once she'd dressed in thermals, jumper and jeans, zipped up her coat and added a cream Fair Isle hat and red scarf and gloves to the ensemble, she was too hot to wait for the others indoors.

She stepped out into the garden, the stark, newly shorn shapes of trees lit by the halos of light from the streetlamps and the air so cold it caught in her throat. Freed from clogging brambles, the ghostly arms of the glorious white birch rose into the darkness, its twiggy fingers level with the guttering of the house. It really was the most beautiful specimen, Sky thought. As she gazed up, a huge star suddenly flashed white, then red, then blue, and Sky realised Marietta must be checking a decoration on her roof. It flicked off again. Then Sky heard Wilf's giggle and guessed that he'd been behind the sudden vision appearing ahead of schedule.

Happy voices called down the street, probably from those manning the refreshment tables Wilf had been so excited about. The familiar strains of 'White Christmas' hit the air and, as if that were the signal, front doors opened everywhere and her neighbours shouted, 'Merry Christmas!' probably for the first time this year.

Sky could hold her own at any business meeting or cutthroat auction, but her tummy tossed now the moment had arrived for her to fully enter the Winter Street community. She hoped that more residents were like Marietta than like Ruth.

Then Wilf's breathless voice drifted her way. 'I'll get Sky.' His whippy little figure flashed past the recently created gaps between the conifers and then he burst through her gate. 'Good, you're ready,' he panted, beaming. 'Come on. There are sausage rolls.'

Sausage rolls weren't high on Sky's list of things to get excited about, but she laughed as he hustled her out onto the pavement of Winter Street where Marietta, Courtney and Daz were waiting.

Marietta awarded her a big hug. 'Let's get us some mulled wine.'

Courtney hugged Sky, too, then linked arms companionably. 'Lead on, Marietta.'

At the mid-point of Winter Street, quite close to Wilf and Courtney's house, the tables that had been set up wore skirts of red and white crêpe paper swagged with silver tinsel and a few people sang along to 'White Christmas' as they clustered around them. Daz bought plastic beakers of mulled wine for Marietta, Courtney and himself and spiced lemonade for Sky and Wilf from a tall woman with red wavy hair tumbling out from under an elf hat, complete with pointed ears.

'Evening,' said a cheerful voice, and Sky turned to see a grinning Ismael, a baby in a papoose on his front and a woman beside him. 'This is Linsey, my wife,' he told Sky.

Linsey gave Sky a big smile, 'Welcome to Middledip. And this is our baby, Leo, dribbling all down Ismael's jacket.'

'Awesome.' Ismael grimaced.

Sky gravely shook Leo's mittened hand. 'Hello, young man. You're gorgeous.'

Ismael pretended that she was referring to him, and Linsey gave him a friendly shove.

Daz bought Ismael mulled wine, too, but Linsey opted for lemonade. Marietta began chatting to Linsey about

160

the village school as the street filled up, the heaviest concentration of people around the refreshment stands.

At the table selling hot food, the redoubtable Ruth behind it, Sky got out her purse, not about to allow Daz to buy for a second time. She turned to Ruth with a smile. 'What is there?'

'Sausage rolls or soup,' Ruth answered, with a face like a grumpy puppet.

'Sausage roll for me,' Wilf cried. 'Please,' he added, when Courtney raised an eyebrow.

Courtney and Daz asked for sausage rolls, too, and Ruth slid each into a little white paper bag.

'What's the soup?' asked Sky, still determined to be pleasant.

'Chicken,' Ruth replied economically.

'Nothing for me, then,' Sky said, pulling out a note to pay for the sausage rolls.

Ruth looked grumpier than ever. 'We're raising money for charity, you know.'

Sky shrugged. 'Then you should sell something for vegetarians.'

Ruth rolled her eyes. She really did. Right in Sky's face. 'Give me a minute and I'll dig up a carrot.'

Slapping down the money, Sky sighed. 'Don't worry, I'll go to the next stand and buy cake instead.'

Wilf looked anxious. 'Can't I have cake now I've got this sausage roll?' He gazed at his half-eaten sausagey prize.

Courtney laughed. 'Let's all get cake. They look delicious.'

Leaving behind Ruth and her bad attitude, they crowded around the cake stall. Sky chose butter flapjack, Courtney and Wilf chocolate cupcakes and Daz a slice of Victoria sponge.

Munching her flapjack and sipping her lemonade, which

was delicious but icy enough to hurt her teeth, Sky spied a knot of people around a blond man pushing a wheelchair. 'Nan Heather,' Sky called in delight, as she spotted the wheelchair's occupant. Everyone in the group turned to regard her, while Nan Heather, done up like a parcel in coat and blankets, a fleecy hat that tied beneath her chin, waved a mitten.

Sky flushed as she realised Nan Heather was with her family. Sky was just one of the children Nan Heather had fostered. It wasn't really an option not to approach after yelling such an effusive greeting, though. Recognising Mo, Nan Heather's daughter, she gave a diffident smile. 'I don't suppose you'll remember—'

'Sky Murray.' Mo beamed. She looked as if she might even shake Sky's hand, except Sky held flapjack in one and lemonade in the other. 'Mum said you were back in the village, lovie. We must have coffee sometime and catch up.' She turned to the people hovering at her elbow. 'This is my husband, Jeremy, my daughter Hannah, who you must have met when she was a tot, her husband Nico and their kids, Maria and Josie.'

The girls smiled at the sounds of their names, and the elder, Josie, who looked about ten, peeped past Sky to where Wilf was standing. 'Hi,' she said. 'What are the sausage rolls like?'

Wilf looked startled to be addressed so chummily but managed a tentative smile. 'Awesome. The cupcakes are even better.'

Josie turned to her father, the blond man, Nico. 'Can I have a cupcake?'

'And me?' asked little Maria, who looked about four.

He smiled good-naturedly. 'Josie, you buy five cupcakes for us all, please.' He handed over some money.

As the girls ran over to the cake stand Hannah said to Sky, 'I'm afraid I don't remember you, but Nan was made up when you came back. She loves it when a foster child looks her up, and it hasn't happened for years.'

Sky felt a rush of pleasure. 'Really?' she squeaked. 'She was incredibly kind to me.'

'Was? Aren't I still?' demanded Nan Heather, making everyone laugh.

Josie and Maria returned. Several children of ages ranging from about nine to thirteen travelled in Josie's wake. She grabbed a cupcake and thrust the rest of the bag at her dad, then arrived in front of Wilf with a little jump. 'Are you allowed to hang out with us? Maria will have to stay with Hannah and Dad, but the rest of us are allowed to go off on our own if we don't leave Winter Street.'

After a moment's hesitation and a wary glance at the tallest, oldest boy behind Josie, Wilf said, 'Cool.' Then, 'OK, Mum?'

Courtney's face broke into a smile. 'Fine by me.' Like a school of fish, the children wheeled away and then darted up the street together.

Courtney beamed at Nico and Hannah. 'It's so kind of your daughter to include Wilf. He's finding it hard to get to know the village children. We've had a tricky time.'

'Children find their way in the end,' Nan Heather said wisely.

As the others fell into conversation about children and Daz drifted off to talk to someone Sky didn't know, she chatted to Nan Heather, who was managing to nibble her cupcake without shedding a mitten. Then, feeling that she didn't want to intrude on Nan Heather's family too much, though they'd all been incredibly nice, Sky wandered away, enjoying the babble from smiling faces all around. The music had changed to 'Let it Snow', booming out from a speaker on the corner of one of the tables, and she found her feet moving in time to its beat.

She'd just dumped her empty lemonade cup in a neighbour's conveniently situated recycling bin, and secured instead a beaker of instant coffee made with hot water from the urn and a slosh of milk from a carton, when Wilf appeared before her, trailing the gaggle of children behind.

'Are you still going to make fat cakes to decorate your trees?' he demanded. 'Can my friends help us make them?'

Sky couldn't help a beaming smile at how fast he'd gone from anxious isolation to referring to the group as 'my friends'. 'Of course. Not tonight, though, eh? At the weekend.'

'OK, cool,' answered Wilf, and the children turned away.

Then Sky froze as she heard the tallest boy ask Wilf, 'Is it true your dad's in prison?' His voice wasn't exactly hostile, but he sounded as if he expected an answer. On pins, Sky waited. Would Wilf clam up at the kind of inquisition that he'd been afraid of? She got ready to step in.

But then Wilf muttered, 'Yeah.' He scuffed one trainer on the edge of the pavement.

'For real?' demanded Josie, as if she thought it might be a joke.

'For real,' Wilf repeated, scuffing with the other foot.

Still Sky hesitated. She certainly wouldn't stand by if they gave him a hard time, but it would be better if he could handle this tricky moment himself.

'What for?' The tall boy frowned down at Wilf.

'Rude, Eiran,' Josie protested, sending her tall friend a daggers glare.

'Thieving,' Wilf answered nonetheless.

'Oh,' Eiran said. When he accepted the answer without probing, Sky relaxed a notch.

A girl who looked about the same age as the tall boy, sounded sympathetic. 'Crap for you.'

'Yeah.' Wilf looked up at her and nodded. With his hair poking out from under his beanie hat and his narrow shoulders drooping he looked so vulnerable that Sky held her breath, praying the village kids wouldn't be tricky. Kids could accept oddities that weren't your fault. Or, like animals, they could turn on a damaged one of their own kind.

But then Josie said, 'Do you know what you're getting for Christmas? I've asked for my own iPad and Dad's thinking about it. I asked my uncle Rob and aunt Leesa for a chalk comb.'

'What's a chalk comb?' Wilf demanded.

Josie earnestly explained the intricacies of combing a rainbow of chalk colours into your hair and the kids drifted away.

Sky breathed a sigh of relief that the prison conversation had apparently passed off without drama and swung around to look for Courtney. The person she found just behind her instead was Daz.

He was staring after Wilf. 'I didn't get all of that, but I could see you were listening in. Is Wilf OK?'

'Seems to be.' She passed on the gist of the conversation.

He frowned as he listened but, by the end, his face had cleared. 'It's natural for kids to be curious. Let's hope that tonight gives Wilf confidence that the village kids are OK.'

Then a deep voice said, 'Hi, Sky.'

Sky turned and saw Bell, thumbs hooked in his pockets. 'Hello.' She noticed Daz scowling and remembered what he'd said about Bell hitting on Abi.

'Buy you wine?' Bell said, nodding towards the mulled wine table.

Sky lifted her coffee. 'I'm sorted, thanks.'

'Cake?' Bell tried, looking disappointed.

'I've already had one,' Sky confessed. Then, not wanting to go through the rigamarole involving sausage rolls and chicken soup not being compatible with her lifestyle: 'Oh, look, is that local radio arriving?'

They all turned to look at a car with Radio Bettsbrough on the side. Instantly, Jess bounced forward to greet the occupant, a lone presenter with what looked like a satchel full of electronics and a microphone.

Marietta arrived, more mulled wine in hand. 'Several of Marietta's Brain Bashers in one place,' she cried. 'We're all OK for the pub quiz tomorrow evening, right, guys?'

'I'll be there,' Sky promised. 'I enjoyed it last time.' Much more than she'd expected. Another contrast to her old life and evenings at her laptop. She paused. Wow. Was that her – thinking negatively about the job she'd thought she adored?

Bell said, 'Yeah, right, I'm up for it.'

Daz was slower to reply. 'Count me in, at least for this week, Marietta.'

Then Jess halted a lusty rendition of 'Fairytale of New York' to plug a microphone into the PA. 'Hello, Winter Street,' she said, too close to the mic so that it squealed, drowning out the cheers she received in response.

'Right,' she continued breathlessly. 'Time for the Big Switch-On! I need everyone who's turning on the lights at their house to hurry into position. I'll count down from ten, then on "go" we'll all hit the switches at once, right? Then rush back to join the rest of us for more wine and cake, because there's loads left. All the funds raised go to the Chester's House charity.'

People detached themselves from the gathering to scurry back to their houses, Sky among them. It wasn't until she was well down towards her end of the street that she realised Bell was a step behind her. She turned to glance at him in surprise.

He shuffled awkwardly. 'Just thought I'd walk you home. It's dark.'

She laughed. 'It's not going to be in a moment, is it? I'm fine.'

He looked crestfallen. 'I just thought . . . woman on her own.'

'Well, OK,' she said. 'Thank you. It's a kind thought.'

By the time she made it to her gate and passing the soldierly rank of trees like a guard of honour at the border of the spacious garden, Jess was on the mic again, her voice rising in anticipation. 'Are we nearly ready?'

'Eek. Barely.' Sky ran up the path to the collection of switches beside the barn door, Bell still a step behind.

'Ten . . .' came Jess's voice, sharp on the freezing air. 'Nine . . . eight . . .' Others joined in, swelling, taking over, so that Jess had to hurry to keep up. 'Seven . . . six . . .' And then the voices thinned, began to exclaim and 'ooh' and 'ah' instead of count.

'Oh . . . it's snowing,' Sky breathed, blinking as a flake touched her face. 'What amazing timing.'

'Awesome,' agreed Bell, pulling up his coat collar and tugging out a hat to cover his stubbly head.

It seemed as if everyone paused to look up at the slow flakes floating down from the inky darkness, and then Jess's voice over the PA resumed. 'Even the snow's turned up to celebrate. Five . . . four . . . three . . . two . . .'

Sky hovered her fingers over the first four switches. 'One . . . GO!' shouted Jess, and Sky began frantically switching. Tiny points of light sprang to life in the trees nearest her as she fumbled with further control units. The next trees began to sparkle, and the next. Bell leant over and began flicking switches, too, so the white birch lit the bottom, then the middle, then the top.

'I could wire these into one switch for you, probably,' he said.

Sky pressed more switches, too. 'Darkness will bring them on automatically after tonight. Thanks, though.' Up the street, people began to cheer and clap. Marietta's star blazed above her roof, red, then white, then blue. Between the trees, lights blazed into life on other houses.

Sky got to the end of pressing switches and straightened up to look around. She laughed in delight. 'It's like a grotto. I may have overdone things.' There wasn't a shrub or tree that wasn't twinkling. Icicle lights dangled from the gutter and every windowsill, and the watering can Wilf had hung from a branch appeared to pour its stream of twinkle lights onto the ground. She was hardly able to see the snowflakes she could feel touching her face for the eyeball-aching blaze of white light around her. 'Let's go see the whole of Winter Street in all its glory.'

She jogged down the path and through the gate, then paused to drink in the majesty of a landscape that glittered as if the whole of Winter Street had been turned to diamonds and coloured jewels. White was brightest, but there were red Santas and blue icicles, green holly, golden stars, illuminated snowmen, Christmas stockings, sleighs, reindeer, snowflakes, candy canes, bells and wreaths. 'How beautiful,' she breathed, any resentments about the Christmas Street Competition forgotten.

'Awesome,' Bell agreed.

Slowly, people began to clap and whoop. The Radio Bettsbrough presenter took over the mic to stoke the mood. 'Yes, yes, give yourself that applause! You deserve it. *What* a coming together of community. *What* an example of neighbourly co-operation. You've transformed an ordinary Cambridgeshire road into Christmas Street.'

'I'll bet he's recording that for the segment he puts out,' observed Sky. 'And hoping to be quoted in the local paper. And there's the photographer, look, snapping away.'

Marietta popped from between her hedges, which now shimmered with silver and gold lights. 'See my star?' she crowed, walking backwards as she craned to get a better view. 'Look how that baby shines. I wanted something way up there because not much of my cottage can be seen from outside. The whole street looks like the Ice Queen's castle.' She took up station between Sky and Bell and linked their arms. 'Let's get mulled wine. Mulled wine in the snow – aren't we lucky?'

'I'll head for the coffee.' Sky grinned down at her diminutive neighbour, who was merry enough to have consumed several beakers of wine already.

'Coffee for me, too,' Bell said. 'I'm buying.'

Wilf came racing up. 'Isn't it amazing, Sky? Can I go look at your garden, seeing as I helped? I want to see the watering can in the dark. If it snows a lot, can we look at the stories in the snow again? Can my friends come?'

'Of course, of course.' Sky looked across at Bell, hovering. 'Thanks anyway.' Registering his disappointment, she added, 'Maybe another time?' Letting Wilf wheel her around by her arm, she headed back through her own gate, laughing as the youngster chatted like a runaway train about Daz's house and their house and Marietta's cottage. 'See Marietta's star? It's humungous.'

'Hard to miss.' As they stepped onto her path and Wilf paused to drink in the splendour, she became aware of someone else arriving beside her. Turning, she saw it was Daz. 'Come to admire your handiwork?' she asked.

He'd pulled a hat on over his dark hair, and it was speckled with snow, as were the shoulders of his jacket. 'Impressive.' Then Courtney arrived, and Marietta, and they banded together to tour the whole street, one sparkling house at a time. Everyone was doing the same and the radio presenter meandered between them, recording sound bites.

'We have bee lights,' Wilf boasted as they reached his and Courtney's house, showing Sky a bush crawling with illuminated bees.

She assumed a suitably impressed expression. 'Wish I'd seen them. I would have had them, too.'

At Daz's house, she listened while Wilf explained which icicles he'd hung and that the Santa and sleigh on the roof had been his idea. While he and Daz bickered in friendly fashion over who had hung the most lights, Courtney tugged Sky aside.

'I created a dating profile,' she whispered. 'Wow, it went crazy. There must be men just waiting for new profiles to go up.' Courtney pulled a face. 'I haven't responded to anyone, yet. I'm so used to being married. It's hard to detach from that, however ambivalent I feel about Lewis.' The snow was falling more thickly now, and she tightened her scarf as if the flakes were getting down her neck.

Before Sky could respond, Wilf broke away from Daz to join them. 'Please can I have another cupcake?'

Instantly, Courtney returned to Mum mode, slinging a friendly arm around her son's shoulders. 'I think you've had enough. Everybody's going home. The other kids have to get to bed, too, and I expect Daz is ready for a rest after putting up lights for half the street.'

The boy heaved an exaggerated sigh but bowed to the inevitable. 'I'll be able to see what the lights look like from my bedroom, I s'pose.'

Sky realised Courtney was right. Families were heading home, children trying to slide in the veil of snow that had fallen, the tiredest riding on adults' shoulders, a few munching a last treat. The figures still gathered around the tables of mulled wine, cake and coffee were mainly adults without children. Bell's bulky figure was easy to spot, half-turned, looking up the street towards them.

Sky hugged Wilf and Courtney goodnight and watched them cross the road to their own abode, then prepared to seek her own home. 'I'll just check on Marietta before I go. It's pretty slippery,' she said to Daz. The snow was heavier now, and she pulled her hood around her face.

He laughed. 'The more wine she drinks, the slippier it'll get.' To Sky's surprise, he fell into step beside her, rather than heading for his front door, as she'd expected.

As they approached, Marietta detached herself from the knot of people. 'You won't forget tomorrow's quiz night?' she demanded, as if worried they might have changed their minds from earlier in the evening.

They assured her they wouldn't. 'I'm going home,' Sky went on. 'Want to walk with me?'

'Sure, pumpkin.' Marietta waved to the last few people and shouted goodnight.

Sky was uncertain whether Marietta thought Sky needed company, rather than Sky worrying about the older woman falling as the snow began to settle, fluffy and white but treacherous underfoot. Whichever, Marietta chatted companionably as she led them into her half-hidden garden. 'You don't have to light the path for me this time, Daz,' she joked, gesturing to the strings of fairy lights twined around the arbour and the bench, then paused on her doorstep to fumble with her key.

Sky edged closer, expecting to follow Marietta in to check she was going to be all right. Then the lock turned, Marietta stepped over her threshold and pivoted to face them with a beaming smile. 'Need the bathroom, folks. Goodnight.'

'Will you be OK—' began Sky, but the door closed, and the key clicked audibly. Sky turned as she took a step back and bumped into the solid, warm bulk of Daz. 'Oh! Sorry.'

He apologised at the same moment and attempted to get out of her way. Both off balance, they ended up clutching each other's arms. Sky's breath caught in her throat at the *zing* that shot through her.

She glanced into Daz's face and found him staring back, brows quirked, lips parted. It was impossible to tell whether he'd felt something too or she'd just trodden on his toe. His hands tightened for an instant and then his arms dropped to his sides.

'Well, we're not needed here,' she managed.

He gave a faint smile and stood aside to let her precede him down Marietta's path, which now sparkled in the twinkling lights. 'How will your solar panels fare with snow on them?' he asked.

Sky halted. 'Damn. I never thought— Oof!' This time, Daz had cannoned into the back of her, nearly knocking her from her feet.

'Sorry. We're like a pair of toddlers.' He laughed, a rich, deep sound.

Her own giggle was a little breathless. 'I'm going to have to get up on that damned barn roof and change the

172

angle of the solar panels to make it harder for snow to stick. They're almost horizontal presently.'

'You can't get on the roof in the snow,' he objected, as they stepped out between the hedges.

'I can,' she corrected him. 'Although it would have been easier if I'd already cleared the steps up there from the patio. And the patio itself,' she added.

He turned left when she did. 'We should do it together, in case of accidents. It's dark.'

She halted and gazed around her at the sparkling, glittering, pulsing, twinkling Christmas lights on every cottage. 'Dark? I'm surprised a jet hasn't landed, thinking Winter Street's a runway.'

Again, he laughed. 'OK, not dark. But the DIY sites tell you not to use a ladder alone.'

'They do,' she admitted amiably. 'I generally ignore that advice, but it does seem sensible to be wary in this weather.'

Soon, they were tugging a ladder out of the barn and leaning it against the wall. Sky didn't give Daz a chance to make a chivalrous attempt to go up in her stead, but monkeyed up the rungs, clinging with her gloved hands and blinking at the sudden rush of snowflakes that met her as she hauled herself over the top.

Daz followed, and they quickly decided on a trellis against the wall as the spot to hang the panels. 'There's a little shelter from that windowsill above,' she said breathlessly, wiping snow from panels with gloves that quickly became sodden.

He wiped a different panel with his sleeve. 'Let's get this done. It's bloody horrible up here. The wind's spitting snow down my neck.'

'You're welcome to a hot drink, when we've done.' She caught a panel in mid-air as it fell from where she'd lodged it and tutted. 'I'll have to do something more permanent tomorrow.'

Eventually, the panels were up, Sky and Daz were down, and the ladder was back in the barn.

Sky found an empty box to invert over the huddle of light switches on the floor to protect them, then they bolted for the warmth of the house, teeth chattering. 'I'll light the open fire to augment the central heating.' Open fires didn't have good green credentials but neither did wasting electricity when there was a supply of dry wood left in the barn. She was a way off from transforming her new home into an eco-house.

They left their coats drying on the old-fashioned hall radiator. Sky ducked into the sitting room to set a match to the fire then went on into the kitchen.

Daz followed, hands tucked into his armpits. 'Everyone seemed to enjoy the evening.' His eyes followed Sky's movements as she filled the kettle and popped it on the hob.

She laughed, grabbing mugs and teaspoons. 'The best of it was Wilf hanging out with village kids. Courtney was stoked.'

'Let's hope it helps him feel more settled.' He held up crossed fingers. Whenever he talked about Wilf, a warmth glowed in his eyes that made him look a happier person – much happier than when he spoke of Wilf's father, Lewis. Maybe she'd been mistaken in assuming the shadows in his eyes had all come from him sulking over missing out on The Corner House. She wondered what it felt like to have a friend you'd known all your life, and then how it felt when that person let you down.

Then she realised that Freddy more or less fit that description, so she knew that Daz would be carrying around with him a hollow feeling of disbelief and confusion. She'd try to be more understanding.

When the coffee was ready, they carried their mugs into the sitting room, closing the door to the hall behind them. 'The fire soon warms the room,' Sky said, but they both sat on the same sofa, the one closest to the dancing flames.

Daz wrapped his hands around his coffee mug. His hair was tousled from when he'd pulled off his hat. Hesitantly, he asked, 'Presumably Bell behaved himself tonight? It's not my business,' he tacked on. 'But I don't like the guy and feel as if I ought to . . . check.'

She turned to regard him. 'He was fine. I know he hit on your girlfriend—'

'Ex-girlfriend,' he amended.

'—but he behaved perfectly. He kept trying to buy me coffee and he was being protective about the dark, that's all.' She turned her attention to her drink, wanting to enjoy it while it was still so warming.

For several moments, they sipped in silence. Then she sighed. 'You know, if we were all judged on how we were as kids, I'd be scruffy, snotty, angry, probably a bit whiffy. I'd drop F-bombs every other word.' She picked up on a sudden dancing of his eyes as she mentioned F-bombs and added severely, 'My role model was a woman who drank, smoked weed, neglected her kid and lied more than she told the truth. She cheated her benefits and pinched anything not nailed down.'

The laughter faded from Daz's eyes.

She sipped her coffee, trying to wash the nasty taste of the past from her mouth. 'After I got away from her, I copied how nice people acted and spoke. People like you. I tried to be the opposite of Mum in every way, and still do.' Her smile wobbled. 'I'm telling you this because Bell was fostered while his mum got away from his dad, which suggests his male role model left something to be desired and maybe hadn't considered women's wishes much. I'm not saying it's OK for Bell to try and kiss your girlfriend without her consent, of course I'm not. But if it was an isolated incident, maybe it was his roots showing for a moment – particularly if he'd had a few Christmas drinks.' She wrinkled her nose as she added, 'Alcohol has a bad effect on some people.'

The only sound was the crackling of the fire. Eventually, Daz sighed. 'Point taken. Food for thought. I'll try not to judge him. I'm sorry your mum wasn't the best,' he added. 'You've come a long way and it seems as if it was all down to you. You're pretty amazing.'

With an embarrassed laugh, Sky deposited her empty mug on the floor and curled her feet beneath her. She was warm now, and the heavy kind of relaxed that comes at the end of an active day. 'Nan Heather did a lot to send me the right way,' she said. 'And, later, my foster brother, Freddy. He was further along on the road from childhood, so I had his example to follow. Get educated. Work hard.'

Daz half turned to face her, one leg hooked up so that his knee almost touched her hip. 'He's obviously very important to you. Tell me about him.'

Although her heart ached whenever she thought of Freddy, she found that she did want to talk about him, and perhaps Daz was the perfect person to understand given that he'd been let down by an old friend, too. As well as being the nearest thing she had to a brother, Freddy was the nearest she had to a lifelong friend. 'Similar background to me,' she said. 'Fostered by Nan Heather. Got jobs with construction training and showed enough savvy to achieve supervisory positions. By the time he was twenty-eight he'd accrued money and contacts and, as the economy crashed, he began buying repossessed houses. When he was thirty and I was twenty-six, he offered me a job. I'd done my apprenticeship and degree with a housing association, so had relevant skills. I was doing fine at the housing association and there were several women my age who I socialised with, but it was nothing compared to what Freddy and I achieved together.' She glanced at Daz, to check there was still interest in his dark eyes before continuing. 'His core business is buying and refurbishing property on behalf of investors, who'll either flip them – that's sell them quickly and take the profit – or add them to their rental portfolio.'

While he listened, he'd propped an elbow on the sofa back and it pulled his top tight across his chest. As they'd both turned in their seats, they were facing one another. 'What was your role?' he queried.

'Same as Freddy in most ways. Finding projects, assessing them, taking suitable properties forward to development. I usually organised the finance. One of my exes, Blake, told me that I don't have a heart, I have a piggy bank.' She grinned, though Blake hadn't meant it as a joke.

He propped his head on his hand. 'Who were your clients?'

'I can't name names, of course,' she said. 'But some were professional sportspersons with lucrative but short careers, with no company pension. While they're earning well, they invest in a rental portfolio, which will provide income when they hang up their boots. That's where we come in. Where *Freddy* comes in, I mean,' she corrected herself tightly, punched anew with the realisation that there was no longer a 'we', when it came to Freddy.

Daz contemplated her for several moments. 'You sound so passionate about it. I'm wondering why you left.'

She laughed, but it emerged shakily. 'His girlfriend resented me. She was my trainee, and when Freddy proposed . . . well, my position became untenable.' A vision of Freddy's muddy knee swam in her vision. Minnie's triumphant pixie face.

Daz touched her arm, his gaze fixed on hers. 'Painful?'

'Yes,' she said, simply. And her eyes flooded with tears. 'The worst thing that ever happened.'

The room blurred as the tears began to slide down her face. 'Sorry,' she choked, horrified and embarrassed to be ambushed by her emotions like this. But it was as if the turmoil of the past five weeks broke over her in a new wave, and the reality of no longer having Freddy in her life threatened to suck her under. It was overwhelming. She couldn't breathe.

The sofa sank slightly, then warm arms came around her, holding her against a broad shoulder. A hand stroked her back. Her ribs relaxed enough to let breath flow back into her body and she hiccupped a sob. 'I texted him about Nan Heather earlier this week and he was still chilly. Minnie – his girlfriend – treats me as if I'm after Freddy, but to me he's a brother. He's all I have.'

The soothing hand continued to stroke her back and she felt a gentle pressure on her head. It was for all the world as if Daz had just kissed her hair.

She breathed her next sob away as she tried to decide whether she'd imagined it. Then, there, it happened again. Like a gift.

Slowly, she gained control of herself, pulling a tissue from her jeans pocket and sniffing. Then she straightened within the circle of his arms and looked into his face. His eyes were full of concern. 'I expect I look like hell,' she said frankly. 'My skin goes puffy and pink when I cry. I hardly ever cry. But thank you for the cuddle. And the kisses,' she added, unable to leave them unremarked.

His brows twitched, as if he was startled that the kisses had been noted. Then his eyes crinkled. 'I don't think a woman has ever thanked me for kissing her before.'

'It's been a while. I've forgotten the etiquette.' A combined sniff and laugh produced an embarrassing snort. 'Oh, *no*. Now I'm *oinking*.' She blew her nose.

A deep laugh rolled out of him, making his body shake against hers. 'Another first.'

His arms remained around her, warm and strong. Sky realised that now her breathing had accelerated. That must be what was making her giddy. It was *lovely* to be in a man's arms again. She savoured it, closing her eyes and breathing in the scent of him. Then a pair of warm, soft lips brushed over hers, and every hair on her body rose in response, tingling her skin – and several other places.

Her eyes flew open and she found herself staring into Daz's dark, bottomless eyes, stunned by her reaction. When had she last felt . . . *aroused*?

'Should I apologise?' he murmured.

When he'd just set her on fire with pleasure? Slowly, she leaned in and brushed her lips over his. 'Only if I should, too.'

His eyes glittered with amusement. 'This could be a fascinating game,' he drawled. His gaze dropped to her mouth.

The signal was too clear to ignore. She leaned in and kissed him again, this time slanting her lips across his. He pulled her closer. His lips parted and his tongue caressed her lips. With a tiny groan, she responded, and the kiss changed to something hotter, harder, deeper. She didn't want it to stop. Conscious thought fled as she struggled

179

closer, ending up half on Daz's lap, feeling his erection pressing.

He sucked in a breath so hard she was surprised he didn't swallow his tongue.

'Did I hurt you?' She tried to remove her weight, taking in his flushed face and glittering eyes.

'No,' he gasped, and pulled her close again. He nipped her neck, surprising a squeak from her. His hands slipped down to her buttocks, cupping her against him, giving her intimate knowledge of that impressive erection. She rubbed against him and took his mouth again, vaguely aware that she was disregarding things she ought to care about, like Daz being a neighbour and this constituting 'doing it on your own doorstep'. Until the last couple of days, he'd acted as if he didn't even like her.

Liking didn't *have* to go with lust, of course, but for her it was a minimum requirement.

Perhaps his mind was running along the same tracks as he gasped, 'I'd better leave.' But at the same time rubbing against her breasts. A groan rumbled deep inside his throat.

'OK.' But she couldn't resist diving into another kiss. She was on fire, on the outside; on the inside, her thoughts of neighbours and the like/lust thing jumbled in the face of overpowering need. All she knew for certain was that she wanted this man.

A voice said, 'Or you could stay.' And she realised the voice belonged to her.

Without another word, his hands found the bottom of her sweater and pulled, sweeping the soft knitted fabric over her head. The T-shirt beneath followed, carrying with it her ponytail tie, allowing her hair to slither down about her shoulders. He paused, breathing like a train. Then he settled himself more securely on the sofa and pulled her properly astride his lap while he drank her in. 'You're luscious,' he said, dipping his head and rubbing his cheeks softly against the part of her breasts that rose above her underwear.

She sprang the catch of her bra, aware how useless men were with those things when they were excited. And Daz was excited. It was in his movements, the heated breath that touched her skin just before his mouth did.

Time seemed to slow down.

She helped him with his top, then slid backwards from his lap so he could lift himself up and unfasten his jeans. When she tugged them down his boxers went too, and he sprang free with a sudden intake of breath. Somehow, they scrambled each other out of the rest of their clothes. His hands slipped over her nakedness, stroking, squeezing, trailing his fingertips over her erogenous zones, making her cling to his shoulders as her knees gave way.

They sank to the rug before the fire. Sky was aware of its heat playing over her skin, though most of her attention was on Daz, on his body, stroking the fine down over his taut buttocks, then sliding her hands around to take the velvety length of him in her hands.

Her phone began to ring.

'Fuck,' he said – appropriately.

'Forget it,' she breathed, trailing her thumbs over the smooth lines at his groin. The phone rang five more times, then stopped.

'Should you check—?' he whispered.

'Voicemail will get it.' She wriggled to feel his hardness against her stomach. 'Do you have—?'

'Yeah.' Breathing hard, he yanked his wallet from his discarded jeans and tumbled a condom onto the rug beside them.

She didn't help him roll it on because she liked watching him doing it.

Then he swept her down onto her back and entered her slowly, deeply. Completely. She was swept away by a tsunami of pleasure.

It was like waking up under the fireside rug. Daz's arms and legs, heavy in sleep, wrapped around her, while the remains of the fire gently toasted them both. Wiped out by the whirlwind of their lovemaking, they'd plummeted into sleep.

Daz stirred and made a sleepy '*Mm*', in his throat. 'That was awesome,' he murmured, curling more securely around her.

She agreed with her own '*Mm*', just as sated and relaxed.

His chest tightened and bunched under her cheek as he lifted his forearm to consult his Apple watch. 'It's after two a.m.,' he rumbled, before letting his arm fall again. He sighed.

'What?' she mumbled.

He sighed again. 'I was about to ask whether you'd like me to stay. Then I thought about doing the walk of shame up Winter Street under all those lights as people got up in the morning . . .'

'Oh.' She considered how many neighbours might glance out while opening their curtains. 'I'm not sure I'm sufficiently entrenched in the community to withstand the gossip.'

'S'what I thought.' He kissed her neck. 'I'll get dressed.'

It was a direct, grown-up way of handling the situation, she thought drowsily. No sneaking away while she was asleep. She dressed too, so she could see him to the front door.

He peeped out and whispered, 'The snow's mostly gone. No one will see my incriminating footprints.'

She snuffled a laugh. He pushed the door shut while they enjoyed one last kiss, warm, the scent of her on his skin, then he stepped into a garden floodlit by fairy lights and strode down the path and into the street.

The shape of his body flickered through the slots between the trees, then he was gone.

Sky yawned as she locked up, leaving clearing the coffee cups till morning but standing up the guard around the fire and retrieving her phone from the sitting room floor. Upstairs, she discarded her clothes in favour of a fleece dressing gown. A quick brush of her teeth and then she fell into bed, snuggling under the duvet to think back over the unexpected lust that had exploded between her and Daz.

Drowsily, she remembered her phone ringing and wondered who had been calling her late on a Thursday evening. Probably a wrong number.

Still, she slid the phone off the bedside table and checked the recent call log. It said:

Missed call: Freddy Walker.

Sky didn't sleep well after that. Though she'd rather revel in the afterglow of making love before the fire with Daz, her treacherous mind kept returning to why Freddy had telephoned.

Eight a.m. was a reasonable hour on a Friday to return a call, she decided. Curled on the sofa with the wintry sunlight streaming through the sitting room window and the white birch gleaming outside, she called him back. To her irritation, Minnie picked up.

Sky greeted her briefly before saying, 'I'm returning Freddy's call from last night.'

Minnie's voice was frosty. 'Must have been a pocket call. He didn't ring you.'

Damn. In all the hours she'd lain awake, Sky hadn't considered that possibility. But just as she was about to ring off, she heard Freddy's deep voice in the background. 'I did ring Sky, babe. Got to ask her something.'

'Oh.' Minnie's voice was full of astonished distaste, as if Freddy had requested a verruca for Christmas.

When Freddy came on, he wasted no words. 'You joining the opposition, then?'

If she'd harboured any shred of hope that her foster brother had been calling her with an olive branch, it vanished. She frowned. 'I don't know what you mean.'

'Alicia from Avenue Properties – she's interested in you, ain't she? I saw her at a networking brunch and that's what she said.'

'Oh.' Sky had forgotten all about Avenue Properties. She opened her mouth to say, 'I didn't even answer her email,' but Freddy hadn't finished.

'Don't even think about it,' he snapped. 'I ain't letting all that training go to the opposition.'

Training? Anger hit Sky so hard that her vision narrowed. 'I'd had years of experience when I joined Freddy Walker Acquisitions. I *brought* knowledge and contacts.' Silkily, she added, 'You don't need to concern yourself over what happens between Alicia and me.' And ended the call.

Then she went into her inbox and found Alicia's email. Furious that Freddy had let Minnie spoil everything, and now was trying to lay down the law, she almost agreed to a meeting. But that would be bloody-minded. After several deep breaths, she thanked Alicia for her interesting approach but said that she was still considering future plans.

Tucking away her phone, she grabbed her coat and boots and made for the barn, ready to start on the back garden with the chainsaw. Freddy was her old life. Her new life was calling.

Chapter Twelve

Daz awoke on Friday morning with that 'something's happened' feeling.

In a rush of heat, the hours on the floor in front of Sky's fire returned to him. Oh, *that* had happened. One minute they'd been talking, then she'd been crying, then they were kissing. And then . . .

'Amazing,' he murmured, stretching beneath the duvet, which alerted him to a carpet burn on his knee and a bruised elbow. There had never been a moment when he wanted to interrupt the flow by suggesting they move to her bed. Apart from slightly battered, he felt pleasantly drained – and, yeah, freshly horny as his memory supplied him with images of Sky, white skin glowing in the firelight, hair tumbling around her beautiful breasts.

A*maz*ing. From the first stirrings of lust through a thawing of resentment to mind-blowing sex in a week was rapid progress.

And Sky's heat level! She was a woman who knew what she wanted and wasn't afraid to ask. Or take. He'd experienced a blaze of excitement that left him feeling happier than for ages. He was single, so was she. A little 'adulting' could bring a lot of pleasure. *Had* brought a lot of pleasure, he corrected himself, contentedly.

He examined his feelings and decided that he liked Sky, now he knew her better, especially as she'd been nice to Wilf and Courtney.

Marietta had called Sky a stunningly beautiful woman with a bunch of brains, and she was. Her reaction to whether he should stay all night had been perfect: neither clinging nor booting him out. Nevertheless, as they would both continue to live in their glittering, light-encrusted street, it would be sensible to take things slowly.

As he rose and showered, Daz found himself singing 'All I want for Christmas is You' under his breath. The song had played over the PA last night as the residents of Winter Street had scarfed mulled wine and sausage rolls. It must have stuck in his brain.

His good mood continued as he ate breakfast then took his second coffee up to his lair in the attic. The feedback phase of the last project was complete, and his new project was a monster-tamer game, which was always fun, even though he had to follow stipulated patterns in order to produce the required data.

Mid-morning, he ran downstairs for coffee and biscuits. Some days, running up and down the stairs between the three storeys of his house was the only exercise he got. Maybe he'd coax Wilf out for a walk if he called in after school. They could watch the festive lights in Winter Street coming on. That made him think of Sky again, and the hours they'd put into decorating her garden. Damn, she was a hard worker. Never lost her cool. Good at problem solving. Looked cute in a woolly hat. Looked hot in just her own lovely skin . . .

As he crossed the hall, he caught sight of a white envelope on the doormat and paused to scoop it up. He threw it on the work surface of the kitchen, meaning to fill the kettle before looking at it, but froze as he noticed the annotation, top left:

Cell 4, E wing.

The handwriting was Lewis's.

Slowly, he picked it back up. He slipped his thumb under the flap and slit it open. The letter was written on a page from an A4 lined pad and was folded around a form. Daz smoothed them both out, heart trotting. The form said, *Visiting order.* His was the only name on it.

He took a breath, knowing both that he didn't want to read the letter and that he must.

Dear Daz, it said.

Hey, man, how are you doing? I've been thinking about you a lot.

Please will you use the enclosed VO and come and see me? Dad came recently, though he hates it (I'm not blaming him). Courtney visits every few weeks but there are things I can't discuss with her because there's tension between us.

Big shock, Daz thought, thinking of Courtney's bewildered resentment of the altered circumstances Lewis had catapulted her into.

I know this is an imposition, the letter continued, *but I'd be dead grateful. It is important. I have concerns about Courtney and Wilf. It would be great to see your ugly mug, too, and hear what's going on*

*in Middledip and beyond. Stuck in here is like being
in prison, LOL.*
Anyway, come if you can.
Here's hoping.
Lewis

Daz carefully refolded both letter and form. Appetite
and good mood both gone, he made his coffee on auto-
pilot, then stared sightlessly out of his window as he drank
it. The big hawthorn hedge looked beautiful on frosty
mornings and in spring it would froth with creamy blossom
but today it was just a mass of wintry, spiky twigs, plain
and dull.

A visiting order didn't mean he *had* to visit. He was free
to ignore both it and Lewis's letter. Free. Unlike his oldest
friend. His heartbeat hurried as he fought with himself.

From a selfish perspective, he didn't want to visit the
prison.

More generously, if Lewis needed him, he should go.

The contents of his coffee mug sank steadily as he
deliberated, struggling to apply logic to an emotional
matter – to reconcile the irreconcilable sides of his heart.
Eventually, he took out his phone and texted Courtney.

Can we have a chat, later, without Wilf around?

The reply arrived when he was back upstairs in his big,
black gaming chair, frowning at the screen where a brown,
hairy ball called a Rundschke refused to develop legs, even
when his character had successfully collected the growth
hormone that should have prompted it.

Courtney said, *Of course. After he's gone to bed.*

He settled down to see if the Parrybellums and Icyclops
would respond satisfactorily to the growth hormone, or

whether it was just the Rundschkes. Taming virtual monsters seemed a futile occupation compared to visiting his friend in prison to discover what was on his mind regarding his family, from whom he was estranged by more than walls and bars.

The thought weighed on him. When he checked his calendar and saw he was supposed to be at the pub quiz this evening, he knew it to be beyond him. He texted Marietta to apologise that he couldn't be a Brain Basher this evening after all. She replied that she understood. She still had Jessie, Ruth, Sky and Bell.

Fleetingly, he regretted missing out on seeing Sky and hoped Ruth wouldn't be unfriendly. Or Bell too friendly.

Daz lounged on Courtney's sofa, which was overlarge for her small living space as it had come from her previous, grander home. It was past ten p.m., but Wilf kept finding reasons to trail downstairs, as if he sensed that Daz wanted him out of the way and his inbuilt response was to try and discover why.

At last, when Courtney had hugged her son but told him firmly to stay in bed till morning, she got two glasses and a bottle of red wine, dropped down further up the sofa from Daz and demanded, 'What's up?' She looked tired and too thin, but managed a smile.

Daz had thought of little else today but this conversation. At one point he'd almost cancelled, when it had struck him that Lewis probably assumed Daz would keep the contents of the letter to himself.

He sighed. But was such secrecy fair to Courtney? Another of those bloody difficult questions.

Courtney had conducted herself with dignity throughout the whole Lewis shit show. Despite Wilf's blank refusals to speak to his dad in person, by phone or by letter, she'd continued to gently encourage him to do so. Her lifestyle had plummeted, people had gossiped, Wilf was upset and adrift, and Courtney had coped with it all. A lot of women would have cut Lewis from their lives forever.

No, Courtney did not deserve that Daz should visit Lewis behind her back. Deciding to tread a line between truth and the whole truth, he said, 'I've received a visiting order from Lewis. I didn't want to book a visit without letting you know first.'

Her light brown eyes widened. Her hair was messy and, even to his manly eye, looked as if it needed a good cut. It acted as a reminder of the reality of the kind of budget she needed to live within. 'You're going?' She sounded surprised, maybe shocked. 'You've avoided it till now.'

'True.' The red wine looked a clear, deep ruby in the glass but was cheap and vinegary on the tongue. Still, he took two mouthfuls while he considered his answer. 'He sounded down. Keen to hear about the wider world. I felt sorry for him.' None of these statements were lies but he was aware of the omissions between the truths. *He wants to talk to me about you* was definitely a betrayal of Lewis's confidence. These days, his conscience felt like a rat in a maze, circling ceaselessly to find right and too often feeling dangerously close to wrong.

'I see.' Courtney took her turn of sipping the cheap plonk and frowning thoughtfully.

'Do you mind?' Daz asked. 'Feel free to share your views.'

She rubbed her forehead. 'I don't have "views", anymore. All I have is confusion, fear and panic.'

He swore, his conscience jabbing him anew. 'If my going adds to any of that, perhaps I should continue to stay away.'

191

She smiled suddenly, looking more like the old Courtney, the one who'd fallen in love with Lewis and made him happy. The one Daz remembered laughing and smiling a lot more than she did now. 'Childishly, I want you up my end of the playground,' she admitted. 'But you're Lewis's best mate and if you want to go, go.'

Being Lewis's best mate was a problematic role, these days, but Daz strove for a neutral stance. 'I'm your friend, too, and I'm trying not to take sides.'

Just as neutrally, she answered, 'I know, and I'm not going to pressure you.' She drained her glass and unscrewed the cap on the wine bottle before filling the capacious wine glass almost to the brim. 'It might make you feel better to see Lewis again. Because he's behind bars, I think it's easy to mentally demonise him – which is Wilf's problem. When you see him in real life, scared and lonely in an alien environment, you realise that he's a man who's made a bad mistake. But he's still Lewis.'

For a moment, Daz could only gaze at her, a woman wronged yet trying valiantly to do the right thing. His voice became husky. 'That's one of the most incredibly generous things I've ever heard.' He hesitated. 'Lewis said his dad's visited. Have you seen Graham?'

'No,' she said, shortly. 'He seems to feel he has the monopoly on being affected by Lewis's actions.' She drank silently for a full minute.

When she spoke again, she'd changed the trajectory of the conversation. 'Speaking of people in alien environments, did you know that Abi shares her London flat?'

It took his brain a moment to make the leap from Lewis in prison to Abi living the London life. 'She has a boyfriend, do you mean? I suppose it's natural that she moves on.' He paused to check whether he was hurt and decided he wasn't. Sometime in the past year, his heart had got the message that he and Abi were over and once the initial hurt had healed, he enjoyed the calmer life he was left with. And last night he'd moved on pretty thoroughly himself. Heat pooled as he remembered how Sky had looked with her head thrown back as she'd ridden him.

Courtney shook her head. 'Not a boyfriend. A woman called Kremena owns the flat and Abi's her lodger.'

'Her lodger?' Abi didn't have her own place?

Courtney gave him a significant look. 'Abi was so keen I visited that specific weekend because Kremena was supposed to be away. Abi took over Kremena's room and put me in a shoebox-single – hers. She must have spent ages moving belongings about, presumably to create the façade that it's her pad . . . but then Kremena turned up. There was a row, which is why I came home early that night. Abi was embarrassed and Kremena was pissed off.'

Daz frowned. 'Why would Abi pretend?'

Courtney rolled her eyes at his failure to cotton on. 'She wanted me to think she's doing well enough to rent an entire flat. I think she's finding London tougher than she thought. After a few glasses of wine, she told me she's not making targets and therefore not earning bonuses. She chose to live in town so she didn't have commuting costs and hassle, but that means London prices for everything.'

'Wow. That's not good.' A butterfly by nature, Abi had fluttered prettily through his life, bringing colour and fun, and he felt cold now at the thought of her being unhappy.

'It's so Abi, though,' Courtney observed.

'Yeah,' Daz agreed with a sigh. 'It's her all over.' Image-obsessed Abi, seeing what she thought she wanted and determined to have it. Having made a big performance about her supposedly wonderful career opportunity and change of lifestyle, Abi would want to maintain the illusion.

Courtney looked apprehensive. 'You won't tell her I told you?'

'Not if you don't want me to.' He knew how uncomfortable torn loyalties felt. He placed his empty wine glass on the table and rose. 'I think I'll phone tomorrow and book the visit to Lewis.'

Courtney spoke into her wine glass. 'Let me know how it goes.'

Daz winced, because he knew he probably wouldn't – at least, not whatever Lewis wanted to discuss concerning Wilf and Courtney. He said goodnight and let himself out into the frozen night air, momentarily dazzled by the Christmas Street lights. Man, those things hurt your eyeballs. He glanced down Winter Street, squinting against the glare, wondering if Sky was back from the pub quiz. He hesitated, then took out his phone, texting with one thumb as he crossed the road on the approach to his own house. *Sorry I couldn't be at the pub quiz. OK to call you tomorrow? Xx*

He wasn't even in his front door before Sky texted back. *No problem about the quiz. Yes, call when you want. Xx*

OK. So that improved his mood. He let himself indoors, resisting the impulse to reply, *How about I come down now? Xx* That would sound like a booty call. If he was honest with himself, he thought, kicking off his boots and then hanging up his coat – he'd like it to be one.

On Saturday morning, Daz went to the prison's website and read the information for visitors, astonished to see that he was required to wear smart clothes – no shorts, vests or anything low-cut – bring photo ID and be prepared to have his fingerprints taken. Possessions would be stowed in a locker for the duration of the visit and there might be a sniffer dog checking for drugs. The visit would last not more than one hour but could be curtailed at the discretion of the prison.

'Serious shit,' he muttered. Reluctantly, he called the number, waiting in a queue for his turn to book a visit, which a brisk woman eventually set for two p.m. on Monday. The prison was a drive of about an hour and a half north of Middledip, but he needed to be there half an hour beforehand to go through formalities. Add another half an hour for adverse traffic and that meant leaving in the late morning.

The call took away some of his appetite for breakfast, but he toasted a slice of bread and made himself eat it, washed down with coffee.

To cheer himself up, he called Sky.

'Hiya,' she panted, just when he thought she wasn't going to answer. 'I was using the chainsaw and it took a moment to realise my phone was buzzing.'

He laughed, the weight of the call to the prison rolling from his shoulders. 'I don't think I've ever known a woman who could wield a chainsaw.'

'Sexist comment,' she said, her voice filled with laughter.

He thought about that. Sexist wasn't something he was used to being called. 'Nope,' he decided. 'It's a fact. How many other women have *you* known who used a chainsaw?'

She giggled. 'And your point is . . . ?'

The banter relaxed him. He wandered back into the kitchen area and dropped two more slices of bread into the toaster while holding the phone with his other hand. 'Are you busy later? Fancy a meal at the pub?' He wasn't exactly sure of their footing, yet. Maybe if things progressed, he'd suggest a proper date somewhere fancier outside the village. For now, pub grub at the local felt right. 'I mean, I know you don't drink, but you do go to the pub for the quiz so I thought—'

'The Three Fishes didn't feel too threatening,' she answered lightly. 'My table and chairs are arriving in the next hour, so I'll spend the afternoon stripping them, then I'll need time to clean up. How about eight o'clock?'

'Perfect.' As he'd need to walk past her front door, he added, 'Shall I call for you?'

'Fine,' she answered. Then she laughed, a soft, breathy laugh. 'My calendar's filling up, this weekend. Wilf and his new friends are coming tomorrow to make fat cakes to hang on the trees for the birds. I asked Courtney too because I thought she must want to spend weekends with Wilf, when she works all week.'

'Definitely. She's a great parent.' He smiled into the phone, taking sunflower spread out of the fridge and grabbing a knife and plate ready for when the toast popped up. He wanted to thank her for taking an interest in Wilf and his friends, which would help him form bridges in the community, but it seemed to be presuming on the territory of 'parent', so he just added, 'It's nice of you to give them your time.'

'But I like Wilf and Courtney so much,' she protested, sounding astonished. 'I'm not nice.'

He laughed. 'I think you're very nice. Didn't you notice?'

She laughed, a delighted, warm, intimate laugh.

His toast tasted a lot better after that call.

After a busy day taming computer-generated monsters, Daz was all set to enjoy his evening with Sky, watching her smile and chat over the table in the pub he'd known

196

ever since he'd been old enough to come in for meals with his parents.

The Three Fishes was full. The beams above their table were so laden with fake snow that he feared an avalanche and so illuminated with twinkle lights that the dining area gave Winter Street a run for its money. The buzz of conversation and laughter filled Daz with a feeling of well-being.

Vern was seated at a nearby table with his pretty blonde wife, Joanna, and when they came over to say hello, Joanna grinned at Sky. 'So, you're the one who upset all the men's plans for The Corner House?'

Though Sky grinned back as she said, 'Afraid so,' Daz thought he saw a shadow cross her face.

When the others had returned to their seats and Elvis from behind the bar had brought them a pint of beer for Daz and a lurid orange mocktail for Sky, he touched her hand. 'We're over missing out on The Corner House, really,' he told her. 'It's all yours.'

She brightened. 'I love it more every day,' she admitted. 'This morning, I cleared enough of the patio to reach the stone steps up to the sun terrace. Then, I stripped the old varnish off the table I bought.' She flexed an arm. 'Owning The Corner House is cheaper than joining a gym. I'm still not sure of my long-term plan, though. I'm kind of struggling with my conscience because no doubt there's a family somewhere that would fill every inch of it and love it as much as I do.'

They were interrupted by a female member of the wait staff coming to take their order. Sky chose a mushroom risotto and Daz steak and chips. When she'd gone, Daz said, 'Would you move out of the village, if you sold it on?' He was surprised by a sinking sensation at the thought.

She quirked her eyebrows. 'I thought you'd say, "If you're not going to live there, why the hell couldn't you let us have it?"'

He touched her hand. 'I've just told you that I'm over it.' And he was beginning to get an idea of how much Sky wanted to belong somewhere. 'Why are you so guilty over occupying the house alone? There's certainly room for more people in my house, yet it never crosses my mind – or the minds of millions like me, I should think – that I should downsize out of social conscience.' Before she could question whether that meant he didn't *have* a social conscience, he added, 'You could always have a big family of your own. Fill the place up.'

She blushed. 'When I was married, my husband wanted children. I was too career-orientated. He went back to France and found someone who made time for motherhood.'

He frowned, shifting over to let one of the wait staff squeeze between the busy tables. 'But you were entitled to want a career.'

She shrugged. 'I suppose he was entitled to want more of my attention.'

He thought about that. 'You could say it was like that with Abi and me, when she wanted to move to London,' he said honestly. 'We wanted different things and weren't prepared to sacrifice.'

Their meals arrived, steaming hot and fragrant. Daz watched Sky shake out her napkin and take up her cutlery. 'It's hard to reconcile the Sky I've got to know with the one you tell me was so career-minded. I see you working hard,' he added hastily, 'but you make time for Wilf and Courtney. And me.'

Her green eyes danced as she blew on a fork full of risotto. 'Maybe I've finally learned my lesson.'

'Do you still miss your old job?' Absently, he cut off a piece of steak, too busy watching Sky's graceful movements to really savour it.

One of her arched brows arched still further. 'I no longer wish my leaving had never happened.' She sounded surprised, almost as if she'd only just realised this. 'It was brutal, the way my life changed, but the worst of it was losing my relationship with my foster brother.' She glanced around as if taking in the happy faces and the tinsel in the cosy village pub. 'But look what I've got in exchange. Minnie's machinations had a silver lining. I'd let everyone but Freddy drift away and that's not healthy. I hadn't realised it was time for a change, but it was.'

'And fate sent you to Middledip,' he said, only half-joking. He addressed his chips before they went cold. After a few mouthfuls, he continued, 'It's time for change for me, too, because I'm not enjoying my job. Just don't know what I want to do about it.'

She looked regretful. 'Now the opportunity with Ismael and Vern's disappeared? But getting The Corner House would only have turned you into a *property developer*, like me.' Pronouncing 'property developer' with faux loathing, she made devil's horns with her fingers.

He laughed and almost choked. Wiping his watering eyes, he admitted, 'I've revised my opinion of property developers. Especially when they're hot and pretty.'

She began to smile and reply but then a gruff voice cut across them. 'Hello, Sky.'

Daz looked up and saw Bell beside their table. 'Hi, Bell,' Sky said easily, waving her fork in welcome.

'Hi,' Daz said, politely.

Bell acted as if Daz wasn't there. 'I really enjoyed last night.' He smiled into Sky's eyes.

'So did I.' Sky glanced at Daz, and explained, 'Marietta's Brain Bashers won again.'

'Great,' Daz said.

'We did. Enjoy your meal. See you next week.' Bell turned his bulky body sideways to edge away between the dining tables.

Daz tried to arch an eyebrow and emulate the expression of cool surprise that Sky did so well, but he knew his brows were uncompromisingly flat and he suspected he looked more like a pantomime villain. 'Is it my imagination or was he trying to sound as if you were out on a date with him last night? Maybe hoping I'll take the hint and vanish?'

Sky pushed her plate away with what sounded suspiciously like a sigh. 'No, I think that's all in your head.'

Oh-kay. He'd promised to try and be less judgemental about Bell. He cast about for a fresh subject. Sky wore her hair in a ponytail tonight, drawn up high on her head and rippling over one shoulder. 'Your hair's amazing. I loved seeing it loose.'

A small smile lifted a corner of her lovely mouth, because it had been loose when they'd made love. 'It didn't . . . get in your way?'

It was the first time they'd alluded to their naked encounter. A fire ignited inside him as he leaned in closer. 'I don't think either of us let anything get in our way, did we?'

Her winter-sea eyes smiled. 'Would you prefer something more . . .' she paused, as if selecting exactly the correct word, then ended softly: '. . . controlled?'

He almost growled. 'Out of control was fantastic. Though,' he added, after a moment for reflection, 'slow and sensuous would be just as good, if you'd like to try it.'

200

Her pupils dilated, and miniature reflections of the Christmas lights danced in them. 'For comparison purposes?'

He'd just begun to say, 'For any reason you want,' when someone else stopped beside their table. Daz sighed. Maybe the village pub hadn't been such a great idea.

This time their visitor was Carola, known to all of Middledip as the head of the village hall committee and of the singing group, organiser of anything that needed organising. As she worked at The Angel Café and was a regular at The Three Fishes, she was in a great position to nudge people to help with, donate to, attend, or buy something for her latest cause. 'Hello, you two,' she began gaily, apparently blithely unaware of interrupting a charged moment. 'Sky, have you given any more thought to entering the competition for the most unusual Christmas tree?'

Sky smiled, but protested, 'We only started discussing it at the quiz last night. I was going to ask a lad who lives near me if he wanted to be involved but I haven't seen him yet.'

Carola was eager to persuade. 'He'll have seen them on social media – people constructing Christmas trees out of books or bottles or gloves or whatever. It's five pounds an entry and the money's going to families who have a loved one affected by illness. It can be hard to find extra money for travel to hospitals or to stay nearby.'

Daz pulled out his wallet. 'Happy to donate.' He wouldn't bother putting together an entry, but he'd never known Carola fundraise for anything but an excellent cause. A thought came to him, and he added, 'Maybe one day the village could raise money for the families of prisoners? They suffer, even though they weren't the ones to commit the crime.'

Surprise leapt into Carola's eyes. Next came understanding, as if the words, *Oh, you mean Lewis?* had appeared in the air above her head. 'I hadn't thought of that, Daz. Thanks. Next time, OK?'

She whisked off to another table, her voice floating back to Daz and Sky. 'Hello, you three. Have you thought about entering the most unusual Christmas tree competition?'

When Daz glanced back at Sky, he saw her eyes were shining. 'That was nice of you,' she said softly. 'Big-hearted men are a favourite thing with me.'

Though he flushed at how obviously he'd drawn attention to what was constantly in his mind, he elected not to bring up his impending trip north to see Lewis. It had tormented him all day and who better than this gorgeous, unusual, warm woman to soothe his heart? He leant in towards her again. 'In that case – fancy coffee at my place?'

'I really do,' she said. And her voice was filled with promise.

Chapter Thirteen

It was cold out in the barn on Monday morning, but it was such a great space for doing messy jobs that Sky didn't care. Part of her mind was on stripping the varnish off the last of the six kitchen chairs. The rest was on Daz.

She'd had the best weekend she could remember. Saturday night had been as hot as the first time, their coffee abandoned half-drunk, Daz groaning at the sensation of her hair trailing across his naked skin, swiftly followed by her hands. She could still feel its texture, and his mouth on hers. Afterwards, she'd lain awake, watching him sleep, astounded at how they fit each other, enjoying the way his hair fell across his eyes, the shape of his mouth, his jaw.

When Sunday morning arrived, she'd left early to fulfil her promise to Wilf of making fat cakes, but it had been difficult to concentrate.

Wilf had brought two of his new friends, Josie, Nan Heather's great-granddaughter; and Eiran, the tall boy who'd quizzed Wilf on his dad's whereabouts. Sky had got them weighing out birdseed, peanuts, raisins and oats, then twice the weight in lard.

Courtney, who'd come along with Wilf, supervised them softening the lard in a pan to tip it into Sky's biggest bowl with the dry ingredients. 'Mush it all together with your fingers,' Sky had instructed them cheerfully, after checking it wasn't too hot.

Josie was a real live wire and Eiran obviously saw himself as the leader of the gang, but Wilf held his own, laughing at the others as their hands became clogged and coated with fat and birdseed. Then Sky and Courtney leant against the kitchen cupboards to watch them cramming it into the Christmas moulds Sky had brought in from the barn, or yoghurt pots that were roughly bell-shaped. After running string through the fatty mess, they tied in sticks to form perches for the birds.

Sky's fridge now hosted thirty fat cakes ready to release from the moulds. The kids were coming back after school today to tie the cakes to the trees. Approval had already been sought from the parents involved but there were no dark corners to worry about in Winter Street, with thousands of Christmas lights glowing into life as dusk stole across the sky.

Now, Sky removed her goggles, pulled off the old woollen hat that had been keeping the worst of the dust from her hair, then stood back to survey her work with satisfaction. She'd decided not to paint the furniture, but to finish it with wax and wire wool, which would give it a dull patina to match the old kitchen cupboards.

When her phone began to ring, she scrabbled for it beneath the layers of her coat, wondering if it might be Daz. She was surprised to read *Nan Heather* on the screen. Although she'd given the elderly lady her phone number, it was the first time she'd made use of it. Swiftly, she answered. 'Hello, Nan Heather. Is everything OK?'

Nan Heather sounded breathless. 'Are you at home? Are you busy, duck? Can you pop round to my house?'

Heart flipping, Sky threw down her cleaning rag and brushed off her coat, hurrying towards the barn door. 'I'm on my way. I'll be two minutes.' She sprinted towards the house. 'Are you ill?' Shoving open her front door, she raced up the hall to the kitchen, where her car keys hung on a hook. Her mind flew as fast as her feet. If Nan Heather was ill and had called Sky, her daughter Mo and grand-daughter Hannah must be out of the village. She would have to get hold of them as soon as possible—

'Why would I be ill?' Nan Heather demanded, in Sky's ear. 'I want you to come because Freddy's here. Isn't he big and smart, these days?'

Sky skidded to a halt. Her stomach lurched. 'Freddy's at your house? Now?' she asked stupidly.

'Yes, duck. Just turned up out of the blue. Lovely surprise! See you in a couple of minutes. Let yourself in when you arrive.' Nan Heather ended the call.

Sky stood on the flagstones of her kitchen, mind awhirl. Because she'd taken Nan Heather's breathlessness as illness, rather than excitement at an unexpected visitor, she'd committed to the visit. Freddy obviously hadn't apprised Nan Heather of the discord between them, any more than Sky had.

She returned her car keys to their hook. If there was no emergency, there was no reason she couldn't walk. In fact, she took time to change into less scruffy jeans, brush her hair and plait it before pulling on her hat and coat and opening the front door, loitering to admire her newly pruned trees and shrubs, all wearing a sheen of moisture from a winter mist that had just burned away. She wondered whether Freddy had driven by The

Corner House to see what impression she'd made on it in her weeks of ownership. Then she stuck her hands into her coat pockets and strolled, rather than hurried, to Rotten Row.

Minutes later, she was knocking and letting herself into Nan Heather's cottage. Heart in her mouth, she trod through the kitchen and turned towards the sitting room. There, Nan waited, her walking frame standing before her and her eyes almost disappearing under the wrinkles caused by a huge beaming smile. 'Did you know Freddy was coming?' she demanded, as soon as Sky stepped over the threshold.

Sky was able to say with perfect sincerity, 'Absolutely no idea.' She stooped to hug Nan Heather's thin shoulders then looked over to where Freddy sat in an armchair, hands clasped in his lap.

'Sky,' he said.

'Freddy,' she answered. 'This is a surprise.' Although she'd never felt so distant from him, their eyes exchanged a message. *We'll have to humour Nan Heather*. The old lady would be upset to know they were barely speaking. This very house was where she'd taught them what familial love could be, the concept of being brother and sister that had carried them through their adult lives . . . until the last few months. 'How are you?' Sky added, wishing with all her heart that she could rewind the clock a year, when they'd still laughed and joked with each other and driven Freddy's company forward every day. Minnie hadn't even been a name on an application form.

'Great,' he answered, neutrally. 'You? Enjoying living in Middledip?'

'Hugely. It's a complete change of pace. How's Minnie?' Sky watched apprehension flit across Freddy's face. His

206

hair was cropped shorter than usual, as if he – or someone – had tried to tame his curly mop.

'Great,' he repeated. 'Enjoying the wedding planning.'

Sky felt an enormous pang that she wouldn't receive an invitation. She pictured a huge, posh do, with Freddy stuck in the middle of it with the wrong accent, even if he had the right clothes. Were Minnie's friends his friends, now? Would they be pleased for him? Or did they wonder how Minnie had ever hooked up with someone like Freddy Walker? 'How are you getting on with your future in-laws?' she asked. 'Minnie's dad OK?'

'Fine,' he answered. A muscle flexed in his jaw.

'Had a few good chats with him?' Sky pressed. 'A good chat', usually uttered in a grim tone, was Freddy's term for a difficult conversation.

For the first time, humour gleamed in his eyes. 'Quite a few, yes.'

It was to be the last time they properly connected in the next hour. Freddy encouraged Nan Heather to talk about the old days, when her two spare bedrooms were always full of kids needing her wonderful brand of care. He told her all about his business and the areas where he and Minnie were looking for a house. Sky chatted about the village, mentioning Nan Heather's great-granddaughter Josie joining in the fat-cake making yesterday. Sky and Freddy hardly talked directly at all.

Nan Heather showed Sky a smart speaker her grandson Rob had bought her as an early Christmas present. 'That's how I telephoned you, duck. My Hannah's set up Alexa with her old mobile phone. Look.' Nan Heather cleared her throat. 'Alexa, call Sky Terran.'

Alexa's silky voice floated into the room. 'Calling Sky Terran.' And from her pocket, Sky's phone began to ring.

'Fantastic,' Sky said, admiringly, suddenly seeing how Freddy might have been cornered into Sky joining the meeting – Nan Heather instructing Alexa to call Sky without warning, and him having little choice but to sit there.

'Alexa, tell me a joke,' Sky tried, and Nan Heather creaked her laugh when Alexa told her two oceans never met but just waved to each other.

Wickedly, Freddy said, 'Alexa, play heavy metal,' and the sound of a heavily distorted guitar kerranged onto the air.

Nan Heather clapped her hands to her ears. 'Alexa, stop! You're not still listening to that row, are you, Freddy Walker?'

Sky laughed, remembering Nirvana and Slipknot blasting from a teenaged Freddy's bedroom and Nan Heather switching off his boombox at the mains if she wanted to speak to him. 'Alexa, play Christmas music,' she said, and the music switched suddenly to 'I Wish it Could be Christmas Every Day'.

It was a few minutes after that that Freddy 'noticed' the time, declared he'd be late for his next meeting, kissed Nan Heather's cheek, told her to look after herself, and hurried out with a brief, 'Catch you later, Sky.'

'Catch you later,' she echoed, wondering whether he'd left in a rush to prevent her leaving at the same time and trying to instigate a meaningful conversation.

She sat on with Nan Heather, agreeing how wonderful it had been to see Freddy, and amusing themselves with Alexa. 'Have you got one of these?' Nan Heather asked, patting the small black speaker fondly.

Sky shook her head. 'No. But I have Siri on my phone.' She took her phone out to demonstrate. 'It works in a similar way. Hey, Siri,' she said. 'Text Freddy Walker.'

Back came Siri's reply: 'Texting Freddy Walker. What would you like to say?'

'I'm not pursuing the opportunity with Alicia at present,' she dictated, deciding that one of them ought to show some generosity of spirit.

'Marvellous,' Nan Heather breathed. 'What did Freddy say in reply?'

'Nothing, he's probably driving,' Sky lied, watching a message pop up on her screen. Freddy's in-car system would have played her message to him and allowed him to dictate the reply as he drove. *Glad you came round to my way of thinking,* he'd said. Her hackles rose at the combative, abrasive retort. Evidently, Freddy's spirit hadn't got the memo about generosity.

Summoning a smile, she slipped her phone back in her pocket. 'Shall I get your lunch before I go, Nan Heather?' Burying her resentment and hurt in this small act of friendship, Sky heated the old lady's soup and buttered her bread, before returning home to work on her table.

Driving up the motorway, automatically checking his mirrors and dealing with traffic, Daz felt antsy about visiting prison, as if he was trying to smuggle contraband in or smuggle Lewis out.

Snowflakes began to fly into his windscreen as he headed north, suiting the wintry feeling in his heart. The traffic slowed. The verges began to turn white. By the time he passed the sign welcoming him to the prison – written by someone with a dark sense of humour, perhaps – he was about ready to turn about and drive home. Instead, he fed into the visitors' car park behind a train of other vehicles.

He switched off the engine and gazed at the towering fences, the barbed wire, floodlights and prison gates.

Despite the sprinkling of snow and the grassy areas surrounding the various blocks, the word that sprang to his mind was 'grim'. *Holy shit*. It gave him palpitations just to look at it.

Forcing himself from his car, he followed a procession of people to the visitor centre outside the gates, his visiting order to hand. Inside, a woman in black uniform directed him to a locker where he stowed his phone, keys and wallet, remembering to extract his driving licence for ID first. With only change in his pocket, he was passed through into the prison, where a male prison officer in the same dark uniform, checked the ID, ran a metal detector over him, patted him down, then took his fingerprints and a photo. A sniffer dog and its handler patrolled by with identical stern expressions. By then, Daz's jitters had jitters.

He joined a group of almost silent visitors. When two p.m. arrived, they were escorted down a corridor and through two gates into a big hall with a refreshments counter at one end. Fixed seating was arranged in groups – one red chair with three blue chairs facing. Sweat broke out on his forehead when he spotted Lewis sending him a weak smile. He was thinner. His hair was shorter and no longer smartly styled. His sweatshirt was plain blue, as were his jeans. It was, as Courtney said, alien to see him here, with prison officers standing around the walls, their gazes roving constantly over the assembly.

''Scuse.' A woman bustling past brought Daz back to himself and he realised he'd frozen, causing human traffic to swerve past him.

He made his feet move as, all around, greetings were exchanged. A child started to cry. Physical contact had to be kept to a minimum so when he finally reached Lewis's station, he gave his old friend a brief handshake. 'Hey.' Then his weak knees deposited him in one of the blue seats.

Lewis smiled self-consciously. 'Great to see you, Daz. Thanks for coming.'

Daz managed a smile, but it felt plastic.

Lewis looked sympathetic. 'Overwhelming, isn't it? I didn't think I'd ever get used to it.'

Daz tried to relax. 'How are you?'

Lewis made a movement as if brushing the words from the air. 'I'm OK apart from hating this place. There's two of us in a single cell and I keep out of it as much as jobs and courses will provide for. I'm mentoring inmates on managing money, too. Most face an altered financial landscape when they get out.'

'That's good of you.' Uncomfortable at the stark sketch of Lewis's life, Daz glanced around the room. Most visitors were leaning forwards, as if seeking to minimise the distance between those in the red chairs and those in the blue. Conversation flowed from everywhere, unceasing, some delivered with smiles and some decidedly not. Body odour mixed with the aromas of disinfectant and old food. Daz glanced at the refectory counter where people were beginning to queue. 'Want a coffee?'

Lewis shook his head. 'You'll waste half an hour waiting, if you go now. The queue will die down later.'

'Right.' Daz tried to behave normally and turned back to the familiar yet unfamiliar figure of Lewis. 'You said you had concerns about Courtney and Wilf. I think they're doing OK. Wilf's finally making friends in Middledip—'

'Yeah, Courtney told me on the phone,' Lewis broke in. He picked at his nails. 'I was hoping you could help me with other stuff about her.'

The back of Daz's neck prickled with the knowledge that he was about to be put on the spot. 'Oh?'

'Yes . . . well—' Lewis paused, fiddling with his wedding ring, gazing at Daz as if trying to read something in his eyes. 'Dad said he thinks there's something between Courtney and you.'

Fury boiled up inside Daz. 'I hope you shut him down. Your dad could spend his time supporting Courtney instead of making mischief.' He saw Lewis's gaze fly apprehensively to the nearest prison officer and lowered his voice. 'Have you brought me all the way up here to suggest I might be screwing your wife? If so, I'll go now.' The prison officer had begun watching them, but Daz didn't care. He'd be happy to leave.

Lewis's brows shot up. 'Hey, hey, I was about to say "but I don't believe that". Don't go—' He dropped his head, pressing his finger and thumb against his closed eyelids and his voice became muffled. 'You're not the worry, mate. It's her, with me being stuck in this place, not knowing what's going on in her life. She was fairly supportive at first, considering, but now I can feel her pulling away.' He wiped his eyes. 'Wilf won't have anything to do with me. She says she's encouraging him to talk to me by phone, but how do I know?'

Daz let his anger subside as he realised he'd jumped to conclusions. Gruffly, he said, 'Sorry if I got the wrong end of the stick. Courtney's being a bloody star, in my opinion, and I've heard her encouraging Wilf with my own ears. I'm trying to be a good friend to her, not because you wrote and asked me to, but because she deserves it.'

Needing a moment to regroup, Daz rose. 'I'll get us both a drink.'

Lewis didn't argue this time, but requested white tea. 'The coffee's piss,' he added succinctly.

Acting on this inside information, Daz ordered tea for himself too, carrying the paper cups by their rims as he crossed back to where Lewis waited. Daz had read on the website that prisoners would not be able to get up and move about, but it hadn't sunk in how vulnerable Lewis would look, glued to his chair like an obedient schoolkid.

He handed over the tea and resumed his seat, taking a deep breath and picking his words. 'You're hoping to keep your family unit intact, I take it?'

'Yes, I want my family unit intact. I want it *so much*, even if Courtney's not sure I deserve it.' Lewis sniffed, and his haunted eyes reddened. 'She feels betrayed, but I never slept with Evira. I was just trying to keep her alive because she was let down by the system. The treatment looked as if might work at first, but the money ran out too soon. It was tragic. Evira was a wonderful woman, who'd travelled to other countries doing charity work. She'd never made provision for herself. You met her when you came up to see me at uni, Daz.'

Daz remembered small, vibrant Evira, long brown hair swinging. Remembered how Lewis's eyes had followed her. 'You had a thing for her,' he said gently. 'Her friends called you Andy – 'andy for Evira if she needed a puncture fixed; 'andy if she needed to borrow money.'

Lewis flushed at this reminder of being the butt of a joke. 'Courtney said it was my old feelings coming out and that I became obsessed with helping Evira. If only the money hadn't run out . . .' He trailed off piteously.

Though Daz didn't feel entitled to weigh Evira's chance of life and say what it was worth, he agreed with Courtney's explanation for Lewis putting everything on the line, even if Lewis truly believed his actions had been justified. Madness might have gripped him when he knew his old infatuation's life was on a knife edge . . . but when the time had come to pay the price, Courtney had been dragged along with him. Awkwardly, he said, 'Only Courtney can say what matters to Courtney.' Once again, he felt sandwiched between man and wife, a position he loathed.

Lewis groaned, rubbing his forehead. 'I *did* used to have a thing for Evira but it was ages ago. I wasn't much more than a kid. There's never been anyone for me but Courtney since the moment we met.'

'I know.' Daz was beginning to steady now, to feel less engulfed by being inside a prison. He was about to say that it was Courtney who needed to be assured of Lewis's feelings, not Daz, when Lewis put a new angle on things.

He said, 'When I get release on temporary licence next year, I'll need a fixed address. If Courtney and Wilf won't have me back, I'll end up in some bloody hostel. I can't see Dad wanting me. He's ashamed.' Lewis's fingers dug into his legs.

Daz's own feelings concerning Lewis were disappointment and disillusionment. He wondered if he'd be able to step up and offer Lewis sanctuary himself, if it came to a straight choice between that or Lewis languishing in a hostel. He gazed at him, struggling to even see the Lewis he'd always known, the man who worked hard, loved his family and had been a great friend. He asked, 'But you hauled me all the way up here because you're concerned for your wife and child, right?'

Lewis's jaw quivered. Then heavy tears began to leak down his cheeks. 'Right. Sorry if I sounded self-centred. That's how you get, living like this. All you can think about is getting out. *Of course* I care about Courtney and Wilf. *Of course* I want them back. I want all my old life back. I dream about it. But Courtney—' He paused and felt in his pockets and, apparently coming up blank, wiped his eyes and his nose on his sleeve with an unattractive snort. 'Courtney's thinking about dating. She told me. A lot of people wouldn't blame her,' he muttered. 'But that doesn't stop me being desperate to keep her.'

Daz's heart began a long, slow, downwards slide. Courtney had gone so far as to mention dating to Lewis? That suggested more than idle speculation. Wordlessly, he got up and crossed to the bloke at the refectory counter to ask for a paper napkin. 'Best I can do is this,' the man said, offering a length torn from a blue roll.

'Thanks.' Holding it by one corner, so any watching prison officer could see nothing was being concealed, Daz carried it back for Lewis to wipe his face and blow his nose.

They finished their cups of tea, talking stiltedly about the village.

Daz considered telling him about Sky, then thought it might not be kind to talk to a man in prison about sleeping with a quirky, intelligent, hot-as-hell woman. Instead, he recounted what Courtney had said about Abi misrepresenting her life in London, but Lewis just answered glumly, 'I hope Courtney behaved herself when she visited Abi.'

Daz was glad when the hour was up. That was, until Lewis grasped his hand as they shook and murmured, 'I can count on you, Daz, can't I?'

Daz hesitated. 'For what?'

Lewis looked as if he was surprised that he had to put it into words. 'To persuade Courtney out of dating.' He gripped harder, his blunt fingers digging into the bones of

215

Daz's hand. '*Please*, Daz! You're going to, aren't you? Please? I'm begging you, man.'

Daz looked into the ravaged, desperate face of his oldest friend. 'If I can,' he mumbled reluctantly. Then a stunned Daz was obliged to join the herd of people funnelling back towards the gates, while the prisoners stayed in their seats. Emotions whirled inside him, making his heart thud. Lewis had no right to ask this of Daz . . . yet who could blame him for his fear of losing his wife and son?

And – unfortunately – what was more natural than pleading with his oldest friend for help?

He drove home, snow once again flying into his windscreen and turning the landscape white. He reflected on the human need for connection with loved ones that was presently consuming Lewis. What Daz felt a 'human need' for was a stiff drink.

Chapter Fourteen

Winter Street was glittering when Daz finally reached home. As if to celebrate the falling snow, some neighbours had turned their lights to 'flicker' and their pulsing ultra-blue icicles made it seem as if an ambulance had drawn up in the street.

Turning past a small car parked on the road, part-covered in snow, he pulled into his drive and saw that he must have left the kitchen light on. The glow reached him across the open-plan living space and through the front window. He let himself indoors, yanking off his coat. It was as he kicked off his boots that he heard a rustle and glanced up. And froze.

Abi stood in the hall, her blonde hair haloed by the light behind her. His mind flipped back to the car outside. He hadn't recognised it because of the snow, but now he realised it was Abi's. 'Hello, Daz,' she said. 'I let myself in. I hope you don't mind.'

It flashed through Daz's mind to say, 'Actually, I do. I've had a shit day and letting yourself in is a bloody imposition.' But something in Abi's voice stopped him and he remembered that this was the woman he'd once loved. Instead of her usual enthusiasm for life ringing in her voice, she sounded flat. And lost. 'It's rather a surprise,' he said woodenly, instead. 'What's up?'

She sighed. 'I might as well come clean. Things aren't working out for me in London. I've had a big falling-out with someone and I've— I've been suspended at work.'

Shock filtered through him. Suspended? *Abi?* What the hell could she have done? He could imagine her bigging herself up with a few fibs or sucking up to a boss, but nothing much worse. He found himself moving towards her familiar shape and touching her arm sympathetically. 'We'd better sit down. Want a drink?'

He drew the curtains to shut out the light show outside and soon they were each clutching a glass of whisky, sharing a sofa as they had so many times. 'What's been happening?' he asked.

Her lips moved in a parody of a smile, her pretty, elfin face pale. 'Did Courtney tell you I was sharing a flat?'

He nodded. 'More that you were someone's lodger.' She might as well know that he knew.

Woe crept into her blue eyes. 'Yes. London prices are ridiculous.' Her lips were almost bloodless as she sipped delicately at the amber liquid in her glass. 'The flat belongs to a colleague – Kremena. Sometimes, we clash.'

Daz recalled Courtney's account of Abi taking over Kremena's room without permission so she could pretend she was the flat's sole occupant. That could definitely prompt a 'clash'.

Gaze dropping to her whisky, aglitter in the light from a nearby lamp, she said, 'We had a drop-down, drag-out row at work. I let loose a string of swear words and my boss was with clients in a nearby meeting room and heard

218

every four-lettered word. I hadn't noticed the "in progress" sign on the meeting room door but, long story short, he had me suspended.'

He digested this. 'What was the row about?'

Her lip quivered. 'Kremena's boyfriend hit on me. Kremena found him trying to snuggle up. He said *I* hit on *him*.'

Helplessly, Daz patted her arm. Abi might be heedless and self-absorbed, but he'd never known her poach on another woman's territory before. 'What now?'

She shrugged. 'I'll have to negotiate with my boss to let me resign. I can't be sacked, Daz. How the hell would I get another job?' She gave a huge sniff, then shook back her hair. 'I haven't only come back because I've nowhere to go. I'd already planned to come back to see how the land lay.'

Her words rang in Daz's ears. He stared in amazement. 'What do you mean?'

'I made a mistake.' She wiped another tear. 'I was happier here with you than in my supposedly wonderful new life.'

'Abi—' he began awkwardly, conscious of all the good times they used to share but rocked by such an about-face.

She reached over and placed a well-manicured fingertip on his lips. 'Don't give me your answer yet. Just let me get my head back together, please?'

He gazed at her. She'd once meant a lot to him and she looked so forlorn and beaten that he couldn't find it in himself to send her away, or even make it plain that there would be no resurrecting their relationship. That conversation could wait for a day or two.

She tossed back the rest of her whisky just as Daz's phone began to ring. He checked the screen and saw *Al Silvester*. 'It's my line manager.' He debated whether to answer, but it was before six on a workday so Al calling wasn't unreasonable. He sighed and answered. 'Hey, Al.'

'Glad to get you, Daz,' Al's voice said in his ear. 'Can we talk about Samantha, from your team? She's asking for a team of her own and I'd appreciate your input.'

Daz smothered the impulse to say, 'She can have my team and welcome,' and made for the stairs with a polite, 'Happy to chat.' He climbed the flights of stairs to the attic, listening to Al lay out a team leader's role, as if Daz wasn't a team leader himself. Al liking the sound of his own voice did give Daz the opportunity to reach his computer room and open his laptop, scrolling to Samantha's feedback forms so he could discuss with Al how conscientious and thorough she was, certainly sufficiently organised to manage others.

He heard the doorbell ring. Al was still jawing about Samantha but seemed to be winding down, so Daz headed back downstairs. As he rounded the top of the second staircase, he saw Abi had answered the door. A pair of suitcases had appeared in the hall which, presumably, she'd brought in from her car during his call.

Sky was standing on the snowy doorstep, gazing at Abi with wide eyes. Oh, shit. 'Hang on,' he said to Al, speeding his feet.

'Oh,' he heard Abi say. 'I'm Abi. Was Daz expecting you? Only, we're . . . busy.' She spoke no untruths, but her tone and the delicate pause did a great job of creating the impression that Sky was an unwelcome intrusion.

Over Abi's shoulder, Sky's eyes met his for a long second, green and luminous, a hundred questions in their depths. Then she glanced at the suitcases before returning her gaze to Abi. 'It wasn't important.'

Abi shrugged and was closing the door almost before Sky turned away.

'Sky!' Daz called, trying to stop the door closing without barging Abi from her feet or dropping the phone.

Sky kept on walking. Daz could hardly broach the snow in his socks so, with a glare at Abi that earned him an injured look, he ended the call as soon as he could and turned to his ex. 'You don't live here. You don't hint my visitors away.'

Abi clapped her hand to her mouth. 'Oh, Daz. I'm sorry. I'm just such a mess.' And, brushing past him, she turned and, crying noisily, ran up the stairs. The flitty, excessive, mercurial side of Abi obviously hadn't changed and while he'd often enjoyed never knowing what she'd do next, this was not one of those occasions.

Gritting his teeth, he called after her, 'The bed in the spare room with the en suite is made up. Take that.' He wasn't going to have her holing up in his room, the room that used to be theirs, while he went after Sky. Swearing, he stamped his feet into his boots and pulled his coat back on, stepping out into a glittering world of snow and fairy lights. Somewhere in the street, children called to each other, voices muffled by the snow that had slowed to small, pretty flakes drifting gently through the still air.

Daz fastened his coat and hurried down Winter Street, crossing to The Corner House. Apart from the brightly illuminated garden reflecting in windows, no light showed. Footprints in the snow tracked from the house to the street, but not the other way. Still, he rang the bell and knocked. No answer. He pulled out his phone and dialled Sky, which went to voicemail, so he sent her a text. *Sorry Abi was chilly. She's upset over a problem in London. Please call me ASAP. Xx*

Lying in bed several hours later, with no call from Sky and still no answer when he tried calling her either, Daz reflected on how only a few weeks ago he'd been fondly remembering sex with Abi, yet now she was only a room away, he didn't want her at all.

He didn't want her here.

Sky had come along, vibrant and quirky, and turned his head.

Refusing to let herself feel hurt that Daz's ex had returned with suitcases and a possessive manner, Sky marched back down Winter Street, trying to distract herself by spotting inflatable Santas or snowmen her neighbours had added to their decorations.

Abi was back.

It would have been nice if Daz had mentioned it before Sky found out the hard way, but he hadn't. Life was full of disappointments, and this was just one more.

She shouldn't have turned up at his house unannounced. It had seemed a fun thing to do but had evidently been presumptuous.

He probably considered that, with nothing between them but a couple of hook-ups, they owed each other nothing.

At the end of Winter Street, she made for Main Road. Once past The Three Fishes, the cottages were more moderately decorated than in brash, flashing Winter Street. The real stars could even be seen, as if someone had poked the night sky and lodged diamonds in the holes. She stared up at their glittering perfection and let her steps slow as she enjoyed their simple beauty.

She loved the village, and she should concentrate on that.

Finding Abi with Daz had been a shock. But, hey. She was making other friends and being single was nothing new. She didn't need anybody else. Hadn't she proved that, over and over?

That's what she told herself all the way to Nan Heather's – and, later on, all the way back.

Her heart thudded so loudly she couldn't hear her own footsteps, though, and Daz's horrified, guilty face hung before her eyes.

On Tuesday, winter sun burned off a morning mist to leave behind a stunningly bright December day. Daz woke early, checked his phone for messages or calls from Sky – zero – then took a cup of coffee up to his computer rig in the attic with no enthusiasm for taming monsters. It seemed a futile occupation.

He must find another job.

He must sort his head out about Lewis.

He must get rid of Abi.

She hadn't emerged yet, though he could hear her moving around, the sound of drawers opening and shutting. Shit. She was unpacking. He heaved a sigh. He hadn't told her she could stay but neither had he told her she couldn't. Raising the subject last night had provoked a storm of tears and, bowing under the heaviness instilled in him by the visit to Lewis, he hadn't felt equal to one of Abi's scenes.

He left the house before ten o'clock to call on Sky. When she didn't answer his knock, he headed towards his parents' cottage, his haven whenever he was troubled. It had stopped snowing, but it looked as if someone had come along and iced the village like a cake. He made for Port Road, passing the school with its tissue-paper decorations in every window. Unfortunately, his need for a private chat was thwarted when he let himself into his parents' home to find them enjoying morning coffee with Marietta and another couple of their friends.

223

'Darragh,' exclaimed Sara, barrelling out of the sitting room to yank him into a warm hug. 'Carrot cake or flapjack? Look, everyone, here's Darragh.'

Len wandered out of the kitchen and clapped Daz on the shoulder. 'My new vanilla coffee will put a smile on your face. I'll get you a cup.'

Marietta swung her trademark turquoise cowboy boots. 'Daz put my star up on top of my cottage. You have a useful son, Sara. He's very good to me.'

'I should think so,' declared Sara, and ruffled Daz's hair fondly. Under their murmurs of approval Daz felt about ten.

So, though he enjoyed a large slice of carrot cake with a steaming mug of coffee and chatted pleasantly with his parents' cronies, he said nothing about Abi or Lewis. When he got away, he found that the fog had rolled back across the Fens and swallowed every last sunray. It was trying to swallow the cottages, too, cloaking the streets in grey. He decided to call on Graham, while he was so near. It would make his life easier if he could make sure Graham understood he wasn't at all interested in Courtney. He trod up the untouched snow of the path past the overgrown hedge, last year's plants piercing the snow.

It took Graham a full minute to answer Daz's knock, and then he stood in the doorway and didn't invite Daz in. 'Hello, young man,' he said dully.

Daz tried his warmest smile. 'I saw Lewis yesterday and thought you might like to hear how he is.'

'And how is he?' Graham asked, with no change of expression.

Daz hesitated. He'd been going to say, 'Fine,' but Lewis had been far from fine. He'd been frightened and confused and tearful. 'Physically OK,' he said, instead. 'The place is getting him down, of course. He was concerned about you, as well as Courtney and Wilf, so I thought I'd see how you are.'

'About what you'd expect,' said Graham. 'Thank you for calling, Darragh. Goodbye.' Daz was left staring at a closed door without having had the opportunity to say – again – that there was nothing to worry about between him and Courtney. He made his way home, dispirited and disquieted. How many lives had Lewis's crime affected for the worst?

Sky's car wasn't in her drive, and she hadn't responded to his attempts to contact her, so he didn't try her door again.

It was lunchtime by the time he arrived home, but he wasn't hungry and checked his phone to see a text from Courtney. *Can I see you later? Wilf's going home after school with one of his Bettsbrough mates. I don't have to pick him up till eight. Meet me at mine after work? X*

He hadn't made up his mind what to say to her when they met again, partly because Abi had cut the ground from his feet, turning up like that, but he returned, *Sure. X*

Then he noticed Abi's car had gone and felt a lurch of optimism that she'd left. A quick look around the spare room scattered with her hair straighteners and make-up told him that it had been a vain hope. It was hard to demand a leaving date when she wasn't there, so he went up into his computer room and tried Sky's phone again without success, then scrolled through a jobs site, looking for roles that interested him. Trouble was, he wasn't in the mood to be interested.

Abi still hadn't returned when it was time for him to go to Courtney's. The snow on the ground had turned to slush and the fog was thicker, making the street drab, despite the lights. Courtney answered the door looking tired, as she always seemed to, these days. The coffee was ready, and they sat in the kitchen to drink it. 'So,' she said. 'How did it go with Lewis?' Something in her expression told him that she already had an idea.

A sigh escaped him. 'Not especially well.'

Sympathy stole into her eyes. 'Prison's no holiday camp, is it?'

He shook his head. Words queued up in his throat, but he couldn't speak.

'Did he cry?' she asked softly.

He shot her a glance. 'Does he often?'

'Yes.' Her lip trembled.

Daz stared at her. 'Are all your visits to him like that? You never told me.'

She propped her head on her hand. 'It's hard to convey.' Then she sat up and fixed him with a gaze, not angry, but determined. 'I expect I know what he asked of you – to weigh in and try and influence any decisions I make about him, but I want you to leave it, Daz. I'm not going to be nudged or guilted into a particular decision.'

It obviously was not the time to hint that dating other men might do more harm than good. She'd headed him off at the pass, so he could do little but wait and see if a more opportune moment occurred. 'When did life get so hard, Courtney? How is it so difficult to know how to deal with him?' He waved a hand, as if that might scoop up the right words to express his dismay.

Very softly, Courtney said, 'Join the Lost and Confused Club, Daz.'

They talked for a while, but Daz decided not to mention that Abi had landed herself on him. The two were good friends and she'd rush across the road as soon as Abi turned up again, making it hard for Daz to have the frank discussion with Abi he intended.

When he eventually returned home, it was to find Abi cooking. She beamed when he came in. 'I tried to keep out of your way today, but we both have to eat, so . . .' She waved a hand at the pasta sauce in a pan. One of his favourite meals.

He drove his hands into his pockets. 'There was no need.'

Softly, she padded nearer, her feet in fluffy slippers, and laid her hand on his arm. 'We're going to have to get used to each other again, aren't we?' She tilted her head and peeped at him under her lashes in a way he'd once found pretty and cute.

Now, Daz was unaffected. 'Not really, because you need to decide on your next move. This can only be very temporary.'

Her smile faded. 'You won't throw me out for a few days, though, Daz?'

It was meant to make him feel mean, and it worked. 'Not for a few.' He left the room and tried Sky's phone again. When it went to voicemail, he texted her. *I would like to see you.* He didn't think adding a kiss would be welcome so sent it without.

After an uncomfortable dinner with Abi, where she chatted and he listened, his phone dinged. He checked it eagerly, only to see a message from Wilf. *You got your Christmas tree up yet? Because I can help you if you like.*

Despite his low mood, he grinned. Wilf was an amazing kid. He answered, *This weekend, OK?* His ex might be annoying, Sky might be avoiding him, Daz suffering for his confused loyalty to Lewis, but the very Wilfness of Wilf cheered him up.

Chapter Fifteen

In the morning, Sky read and reread Daz's texts and listened to his harassed voicemail telling her that he wanted to explain. She suspected that Daz had been there in person, too, because when she'd returned home from Nan Heather's last night, large footprints in the snow had trekked to and from her door.

She looked at her phone. She could return his call.

But something inside her wanted to see his face as she heard his explanation. It also felt safer to arrive unexpectedly once again and see how he reacted if Abi was still around. Embarrassed? Sheepish? Caught out? Or would he smile his usual, easy smile, and prove that there really was some acceptable explanation for his ex's presence?

She pulled on her outdoor things, determining to confront reality, yet give Daz a chance.

But she never knocked on his front door . . . because from the other side of the road she saw Abi, wrapped in a sexy negligee affair, gazing dreamily from Daz's bedroom window.

Sky turned away before she could be spotted, sweating

in humiliation, berating herself for thinking even for one tiny moment that the truth would be anything else.

Back in the safety of The Corner House, she spent the remainder of the day trying to work off her disappointment on her new dining set. When her phone rang in the afternoon as she was waxing the last kitchen chair, she almost ignored it, assuming it would be Daz again. She'd let his calls go to voicemail so far. She would have the Abi conversation, but not yet.

When she saw Freddy's name on her screen she still hesitated. Was she in the mood for his aggro? No. But curiosity got the better of her and she picked up.

Freddy's voice wasn't the clipped tone he'd taken to using with her recently. 'Some bloke's been here looking for you, mate,' he said.

'Who? Why?' It was so cold in the barn that her breath hung before her in a cloud.

He hesitated. 'He says his name's Ron Murray and he's your granddad.'

Sky froze.

When she didn't speak, Freddy said, 'I know. Stunner, ain't it?'

Sky tried to grasp the sense of his words. 'A guy called Ron Murray came looking for me and says he's my grandfather?' She'd never known her grandfather's name. Never known if her mother Trish knew it. It had crossed her mind sometimes to get a genealogist to discover whether she had family anywhere but had always rejected it, ruefully suspecting she'd learn of people just like Trish. She'd broken free and made herself something else.

'That's it,' Freddy confirmed.

Slumping down onto the chair she'd been working on, Sky said, 'What did he look like?'

'Santa bleedin' Claus. Bald on top and white beard.' He sounded almost like his old self, irreverent and jokey. 'Look, mate, I never told him nothing about you, but he left his phone number and asked me to pass it on. He said he'd very much like to hear from you.'

Sky tried to digest what she was hearing, gazing back over the years of her solitary, uncomfortable, insecure childhood. Why appear now? Where had this grandfather been then? Her phone pinged in her hand. 'I just texted you his number,' Freddy said. Then, curiously: 'Are you going to call him?'

'I don't know.' Sky found she was trembling. 'What do you think he wants?'

Freddy didn't need it spelling out what Sky meant. Like her, he knew it could be safer not to mix with your family. 'I dunno. He didn't look like an alkie or a stoner. Dressed well, so I shouldn't think he's trying to get dosh out of you.'

'Good,' she said faintly. A buzz began in her ears. It started far away and then became loud and dizzying. She had to bend forward and close her eyes. 'Ron Murray,' she managed. 'If he's for real, he's Mum's dad. Did he ask for Sky Murray or Sky Terran?'

'Terran,' Freddy confirmed, 'but he knew you was Murray.'

'How's he found me?' When she opened her eyes, the chairs and table she'd worked so hard on seemed to whirl about her, so she closed them again.

'I asked, but he got cagey.' Reflectively, Freddy added, 'Can't blame him, 'cos I was cagey with your contact details.'

'Thanks,' she said automatically. Then, with more warmth: 'Thanks, Freddy. I'll think about what to do.'

'Good plan.' He hesitated, before adding gruffly, 'Let me know what happens, if you like.'

A tiny seed of happiness sowed itself inside Sky at this first indication that there might be future contact. 'I will.'

For a long time after Freddy had rung off, she sat alone in the barn and wondered. Ron Murray. Granddad. Grandpa. Pops. Pappy. Names she'd never had cause to use.

After a while, she realised how cold she was. Unsteadily, she went indoors to curl up on the sofa and google Ron Murray.

It wasn't a particularly unusual name but the first few she found could be discounted via age or colouring. One Ron was a Veronica, so that was another off the list.

She found no Ron Murrays who looked remotely like Santa.

No Ron Murrays in whom she saw even the faintest echo of Trish Murray, gaunt and blonde.

She opened her text messages to gaze at the number Freddy had sent, scared by the knowledge that this Ron Murray could be anyone. Anything.

She thought about ringing Freddy back to talk it over, now she'd had time to absorb the news, but Minnie hadn't seemed to be around when he'd called earlier. If that had changed, she'd stick her oar in, perhaps making Freddy turn cold again.

Daz was . . . well, Daz was hardly a confidant with Abi in his bedroom, and Courtney would be at work. Anyway, neither of them knew what it felt like not to know your own history and be suspicious of stirring a hornets' nest by letting it in.

There was someone, though, someone who'd spent decades dealing with the dysfunctional, complex, far-flung families of children needing care. Sky threw on her coat and half-ran down Main Road to seek counsel she could trust. Nan Heather.

But when she reached Rotten Row, Nan Heather wasn't sitting in her window.

Sky paused, catching her breath. Should she knock? She didn't want to disturb the elderly lady if she was napping, or in the bathroom. As she hovered and havered, a car pulled up and Mo, Nan Heather's daughter, climbed out.

'Hello, Sky,' she called. 'Have you come to see Mum?'

'Well—' Sky was suddenly crippled with the old fear that Mo would think Sky was trying to steal her mother.

But Mo wore a cheerful grin. 'I'm taking her for her check-up. We've got ten minutes in hand, though. Come on in.'

'I could come another time.' Sky took a step back.

Probably Mo heard a wobble in Sky's voice because she gave her a shrewd look. 'Actually, it'll work out well if you sit with Mum for a few minutes while I clean her bathroom and smuggle her washing out. She tells me off if she sees me helping too much but, honestly, she *is* ninety-two.' This last was accompanied by an expressive eyeroll. Sky followed her into the cottage.

'Mum?' Mo called. 'Sky Murray's here. She's going to chat for a few minutes, OK? I'll just use your loo before we leave for Bettsbrough.' Sky didn't bother mentioning to Mo that she'd changed her surname to Terran.

Nan's voice wavered from the sitting room, 'Come in, duck, come in.' She waited in a chair close to the sitting room door, coat over the arm, obviously ready for Mo to take her out. With a conspiratorial glance, Mo slipped through into the bathroom and closed the door behind her.

232

Now Sky was here, all too aware of Mo in the next room, she didn't know where to start.

Nan Heather patted her hand, her skin soft and papery. 'What's wrong, duck? You look frightened. I used to see that on your face when you were a little girl. I thought you'd left all that behind you.'

Then Sky opened her mouth, and the words flooded out, describing the shock of Freddy's phone call. 'Ron Murray could be any kind of person,' she finished on a gasp. 'Mum was a scally, so won't he be? I've found peace, in Middledip. Do I want to risk that?'

Nan Heather stroked the back of Sky's hand with her thumb. 'Oh, my duck,' she whispered. For once she looked lost. 'Well. I don't know what to say. It could be lovely. Or it could open a can of worms. Well.' She sucked her teeth for a few minutes, while Sky waited hopefully for pearls of wisdom.

Nan Heather turned her head slowly, as if her neck was hurting, to gaze out of the window. Then she turned back. She sounded desolate, as if aware she was failing her foster daughter. 'Sky, the only thing I can tell you is that I don't think anyone can make this decision but you. I'm sorry.'

'Oh,' replied Sky, faintly. She tried not to sound too disappointed, but Nan Heather had always had answers before.

Mo emerged from the bathroom wearing an apologetic look and glancing at her watch.

Sky rose. 'You're right, Nan Heather. Thanks for the chat. Sorry to hold you up, Mo.'

She went back out into the cold having to accept the truth. Nan Heather was a kind, loving old lady who'd been a landmark in Sky's life, a beacon of love and hope to look up to and look back on. But not a magician.

* * *

Marietta hadn't reminded Daz about the pub quiz, but she hadn't sacked him from the team either, so he called for her on his way to The Three Fishes on Friday evening, feeling he should do something for himself rather than just being weighed down by the burdens thrust upon him by Lewis and Abi. It had been Monday when Abi arrived and he'd had an entire four days to catch Sky to explain, but had failed. He'd been equally unsuccessful in winkling Abi out of his home. Whenever he tried to corner her to make her contact her employer or find somewhere to go, she dissolved into tears. With a dramatic clutching of hair, she'd claimed to have seen a local doctor and been diagnosed with stress and given what she termed 'happy pills'. It had made Daz cautious.

She'd spent two evenings with Courtney, but Daz hadn't joined them, merely asking Abi to walk Wilf home, as she was going anyway, which meant he hadn't seen much of Courtney, either.

But enough was enough. Tonight he'd determined to use the pub quiz to bump into Sky. Freezing in Marietta's porch after ringing the doorbell, he began to think he'd missed her. When she finally appeared in her bright red coat and turquoise cowboy boots, she raised her grey eyebrows at him. 'So, you're a Brain Basher tonight, huh?'

'Is that OK?' he asked. 'I know I didn't make it last week, but something came up.'

'Sure,' Marietta said, sounding thoughtful.

He stepped back to allow her ahead of him down her garden path, the red, white and blue star flashing above them. At the pavement, she waited for him to fall in step. 'Is Sky coming?' he asked casually, crossing his fingers that the answer would be 'yes', because otherwise he'd let himself in for another damned quiz for no reason.

'Yes,' answered Marietta obligingly. Then she turned to regard him. 'She seems fragile right now. She came for cookies this afternoon and wasn't her usual self.'

His heart leapt as if trying to clear the light-bedecked trees into Sky's garden. 'Did she say why?'

Marietta shook her head. 'I'm just telling you what I saw, pumpkin.'

Daz wondered whether Marietta had also seen Abi coming and going from Daz's house and drawn her own conclusions.

Marietta huddled into her coat. 'Anyways, Sky's gone ahead to the pub.'

'Right.' Daz shortened his stride to match the older woman's as they made their way to Main Road, where sedate Christmas trees in windows or wreaths on doors were understated when compared to Winter Street's land of a million lights.

Christmas trees and holly trees at the door of The Three Fishes seemed to welcome them into the pub itself. The fake snow along every beam reflected the glow from the twinkle lights. Tables were crowded once again and, there being only just over two weeks to Christmas, festive jumpers, tinselly hairbands or Christmas pudding earrings were much in evidence.

'There's Sky,' called Marietta, raising her voice over the hum of conversation. Daz followed her pointing finger and saw Sky looking almost edible in a pale purple jumper that hugged her curves, her hair streaming down her back.

The only thing that spoiled the picture was that she was in earnest conversation with Bell, who looked as if he'd freshly trimmed his stubble and bought himself a new shirt.

Crap.

Daz had little alternative but to follow Marietta to the table. Sky and Bell broke off to greet them. Both had big grins for Marietta and Sky gave her a hug. Bell's smile for Daz was desultory and Sky's was wintry. Her green gaze seemed to skate over his face without making eye contact, although she did say, 'Daz.'

It was a long way from the way she'd said his name when naked in his lap.

Marietta seated herself next to Sky, who returned to her conversation with Bell, all but turning her back to Daz. A shapely back, curving to a narrow waist, with a river of hair gleaming reddish gold under the lights.

Then Jess and Ruth turned up and pulled up stools beside Daz, speaking across him to Marietta. Jess was bursting with news. 'We've had an email about the judging of the Christmas Street Competition on December 23rd. There'll be someone from the paper, one from the radio, and representatives from local business and the organisers.'

Ruth wore her usual grumpy expression and uncompressed her lips only to say, 'Everyone will have to be in their gardens, ready to talk about their decorations.'

Marietta bestowed upon Ruth a deceptively sweet smile. 'Say, you ever think about asking people instead of telling?'

Ruth's brows lowered ominously. 'You have to make people listen.'

'You catch more flies with honey than with vinegar,' Marietta retorted.

Jessie interrupted with an uncomfortable laugh. 'Well, we don't want flies, do we? We want to win the Christmas Street Competition! Ruth and I are going to run refreshment stands again.'

'Great idea.' Marietta looked more interested. 'I could roast chestnuts.'

Daz watched Sky talking earnestly to Bell and took comfort from the fact that theirs didn't seem to be a cosy, happy chat. Sky frowned and sighed; Bell shrugged or rubbed his stubbly jaw. Daz bought drinks for those who didn't have one, then settled back to be bored.

Just before the quiz kicked off, Carola came by, wearing an uncharacteristically glum expression. 'I don't suppose any of you know an alternative venue for the Quirky Christmas Tree competition, do you? I've had to let a funeral party have the village hall and the crafters have the back room at The Angel on Saturday afternoons.'

Briefly, Sky withdrew her attention from Bell. 'Isn't it tomorrow? I helped Wilf start a tree out of inflated disposable gloves. He and his mum are completing it tonight.' She didn't mention Abi. Daz wondered if the two had come across one another at Courtney's.

Carola gave a sad smile. 'Tomorrow, three p.m.'

Sky gazed at Carola meditatively for a few seconds. Then she glanced down, as if unsure of her own actions. 'Erm . . . The Corner House has two reception rooms that open out into one big room. It's only about half the size of the village hall, I'd guess, but how about that?'

Carola's face exploded into beaming pleasure. 'Oh, *please* can we try it? I hate to disappoint the kids. We've had twenty entries and I was worrying they'd be a bit lost in the village hall, so yours might be just right.'

'There are no Christmas decorations.' Sky looked unsure, now her offer had been fallen upon. 'I only moved in a few weeks ago and I've been concentrating on the outside, for the Christmas Street Competition.' She darted a look at Ruth, as if daring her to comment.

'We'll do it tomorrow morning,' Carola offered, instantly.

'I'll muster my daughters to help relocate decorations from the village hall. The funeral party won't miss them.'

'I'll help.' Marietta raised her hand.

'I will, too,' Daz said, scenting an opportunity to be around Sky.

Jess and Ruth declared themselves too busy and Bell said, 'I have to work tomorrow.'

Sky and Carola agreed to check out the big room at The Corner House as soon as the quiz was over.

Daz contributed little to the quiz, unable to concentrate. Even Sky didn't get all the nature questions correct and Marietta's Brain Bashers came third. Carola cruised up to collect Sky and the pair departed. For Daz, it felt as if the brightness had left the room, despite the multitude of lights twinkling around him.

As it would look stalkerish to follow too close behind them, he nursed the last of his beer while Marietta instructed Jess on the art of roasting chestnuts. Bell joined his cronies around the dartboard. When Daz judged a full ten minutes had elapsed since he'd watched Sky sashay through the door, barely bidding him goodnight, he felt he could leave.

A frozen wind keened over the village, and pavements and car windscreens had turned white with frost. He hunched into his coat. When he passed The Corner House and saw Sky, through a lit window, laughing with Carola, he felt even colder.

Chapter Sixteen

Sky rose early on Saturday. She hadn't slept well, plagued by the memory of Daz's gaze on her last night. She'd been rude and cowardly, not giving him a moment to tell her why he was living with his ex-girlfriend again, so soon after sleeping with Sky, when she knew from his messages that he wanted to explain. Sky felt queasy whenever she thought how she'd been opening her heart to him. Abi with her suitcases in his hall, then Abi in a slinky robe at Daz's bedroom window late the next morning, had been a stinging reminder that the only person Sky had ever been able to rely upon was herself.

She told herself she didn't want to know why Daz had been so sombre in The Three Fishes, or why Abi hadn't been alongside him. By far the easiest way to cope was to pretend his restored relationship didn't matter to her; pretend, as much as feasible, that neither Abi nor Daz existed. *Pretend that he hadn't been chipping away at the wall around her heart.* But as Daz was helping with the Christmas decorations today like the community-minded villager he was, Sky suspected she'd better brace herself for his company and, perhaps, his renewed attempts to explain.

Trying not to think of Daz, she ended up thinking about Ron Murray, or Grandfather Bombshell, as she'd begun to think of him – which only unleashed a different ball of emotions.

To drive them both from her mind, she threw herself into cleaning up the big room, ready for the Quirky Christmas Tree Competition. She pushed her vacuum cleaner over faded floral rugs, swept polished boards and dusted the bifold doors – Carola called them 'concertina' doors – and used a soft brush on the wrought iron at the windows and the intricate plasterwork above.

The room smelled musty, even after she'd cleaned the ledges with lemon furniture polish, but a sparkling frost outside dissuaded her from opening windows. No doubt the twenty groups expected would bring in fresh winter air.

Carola arrived punctually at nine with her adult daughters, Emily and Charlotte, lugging boxes of decorations hastily borrowed from the village hall. When the girls went off Christmas shopping, Carola surveyed the room. 'I did nothing but email, text and call people about the change of venue last night. Let's unpack everything, then we can see what will go where. I've brought tape, pins and Blu-Tack. I'll try not to spoil your décor, Sky.'

Carola's enthusiasm was cheering and Sky grinned. 'I'm not saving thirty-year-old wallpaper for anything special.'

Carola giggled. 'Perhaps we'll accidentally help strip it.'

Marietta arrived next, complete with a plate of mince pies to keep everyone's energy levels up. Then Courtney, Wilf and Daz arrived together. Sky managed to smile vaguely in Daz's direction, glad that, once again, Abi wasn't with him.

The morning passed in a blur of ladders, red balloons, green streamers, wreaths, silver tinsel, baubles, laughter and chatter. Wilf ran up stepladders at the least excuse, while Daz patiently handed up decorations to the excited boy.

Sky didn't let him catch her watching. Daz Moran was dangerous. She'd been falling for him and his explosive yet tender lovemaking, but she'd received a timely reminder of why she'd always found work more important than men – her mother had taught her early that she was easy to leave. Well, she wouldn't open herself up to Daz again. It would be like putting her heart in a mousetrap . . . the inhumane kind.

At lunchtime, Carola rang The Angel Café for snacks. At two-thirty the judges barrelled in, beaming and chatting. They were made up of Tubb who used to run the pub and his wife Janice; Gabe who lived in a smallholding filled with animals; Carola; and Daz's mate Ismael, who greeted both Sky and Daz as friends. Each tree would be scored for appearance, originality and quality of construction. Carola had made scoresheets.

Participating children would receive Christmas goodie bags containing a box of juice, an angel-shaped shortbread from The Angel, a chocolate Santa and a satsuma.

Carola had also brought a sign that said *Loo* for Sky to Blu-Tack to the door of the downstairs toilet at the end of the hall. Next, Carola produced disposable cups, a drum of Nescafé, a sack of teabags, sugar, milk and two kettles, then looked appealingly at Sky. 'Do you think you could possibly man the drinks? Mums and dads will happily pay a quid for a cuppa.' To prove it, she handed Sky a sign that said: *A quid for a cuppa.*

Sky groaned, 'Me? Holy sh—' then noticed Wilf in earshot and turned it into: 'Holy sugar.'

Daz had stayed away from Sky while they'd been decorating but now he materialised beside her. 'I'll help. It'll be easier with two.'

She wanted to snap, 'No! I don't want to be trapped in the kitchen with you.' She had no wish to be near his warmth and his clean-man smell, brushing against the body that had joined so gloriously with hers on the floor of the very next room.

But Carola clapped her hands and said, 'Thanks, Daz.'

So, Sky had to mutter ungraciously, 'You'd better help me carry the table in from the barn.' At least she'd get her table shifted indoors, something she'd been unable to accomplish alone.

Wilf danced out to the barn with them, his hair fluttering in the wind, telling them his form teacher had said they'd get a white Christmas for real because it always happened when a good bunch of mistletoe grew on his apple tree. His chatter saved Sky from having to say more to Daz than, 'OK your end?' and 'We'll have to turn it sideways to get in the front door.'

Excited children began to arrive, bearing bulky creations in bin bags and boxes.

Their parents greeted the *A quid for a cuppa* sign with cries of joy and soon Sky was busy setting out paper cups on her newly waxed table, which they'd positioned across the kitchen door like a counter. Daz refilled and boiled the kettles over and over, quietly efficient, and to Sky's relief he didn't initiate any more than necessary conversation.

Requests came for, 'Black tea, please, quite weak, no sugar, and a white coffee – can it be quite strong?' followed by: 'Three white coffees with sugar, just as they come . . . except not too strong and not too sugary and quite milky.'

The bowl Sky put out for the 'quids' filled with startling rapidity. Her eyes were fixed on what she was doing but she was excruciatingly aware whenever Daz passed behind her to place a freshly boiled kettle on the table and take an empty one.

Fulfilling the need for hot drinks seemed to go on forever.

Then Carola called everyone to the big room for the judging and Sky said, 'Let's shut up shop for five minutes to support Wilf.'

She didn't await Daz's reply, but shoved the money bowl into a cupboard, skirted the table and shot across the hall, passing under the staircase and into the big noisy room to join Courtney at the far end. Wilf crouched beside his tree of inflated green nitrile gloves secured to a wire cone, slipping silver foil between the fingers to look like baubles. 'Looks amazing,' Sky said to him admiringly.

Wilf flushed and glowed. 'Lots of others have been really clever, though.'

From behind Sky, Daz's voice said, 'Yours is clever, too.' Sky tried crossly to stop her spine tingling and wished Courtney and Wilf weren't his friends as well as hers.

Then everyone had to step back from their creations to allow the judges to parade slowly around, nodding and conducting low-voiced conversations, then fall in behind to suss out each other's entries.

First came a folded green paper tree with white poly-styrene balls stuck artfully along the branches; then stuffed fabric shapes, largest at the bottom and smallest at the top. Green-painted egg cartons had been punctuated with golden bows; green plastic bottles somehow clung to a central stem; Styrofoam shapes flowed with ribbons and baubles. The judges stopped for a long time to discuss a tabletop tree cunningly wrought of layers of white wax, melted then allowed to dry in fantastic shapes that made perfect, frondy, snowy branches. A camera tripod was strung with beads and baubles, followed by an edifice of wine corks and fir cones; and buttons studded a foam cone. Sky's favourite was a tree shaped from broccoli florets decorated with cherry tomato baubles and carrot sticks, created by Wilf's new buddy Josie.

Presently, Carola clapped her hands for attention. 'The judges will finalise their scores and aggregate them, so you have twenty minutes to take photos – do post them on the Middledip Facebook site – or to grab a cuppa.'

Sky scooted back to the kitchen. She knew, without looking, that the footsteps echoing behind hers on the floorboards belonged to Daz, and her neck hunched with renewed tension.

It was nearer half an hour than twenty minutes when Carola declared the judges ready. The money bowl was brimming, and Sky addressed Daz with the first non-essential remark of the day. 'I'm exhausted and the milk's finished. Let's close this kitchen.'

'Everybody's kidneys must be floating already,' Daz agreed.

They arrived in the big room in time to hear Wilf's glove tree announced as the runner-up and the broccoli tree as the winner. 'Yeah!' yelled a pink-faced Wilf, loudly. Amidst enthusiastic applause, he was presented with a box of chocolates and a proudly grinning Josie received a box of watercolour paints.

Courtney beamed all over her face. 'Fancy Wilf getting a prize. Thanks for your help, Sky.'

'Yeah, thanks, Sky,' agreed Wilf. 'Want a chocolate?'

Heroically, Sky said, 'Keep those for yourself, Wilf. If you open them in here, you'll have none left by the time you get home.'

244

Wilf looked horrified, and quickly made room for the box in his backpack.

For the next hour, people chatted and watched the quirky Christmas trees being dismantled to be taken home – and, in Josie's case, perhaps eaten. Sky had a chance to chat with Hannah, who was both Josie's stepmum and Nan Heather's granddaughter. She formed an instant liking for the woman who could apparently hold a sensible conversation with Sky and different ones simultaneously with Josie and the littlest sister, Maria. They were about to leave for Sweden. 'My husband's Swedish,' Hannah explained. 'He always visits his family in December.'

Finally, people began to drift off. Daz counted the bowl of money and found they'd taken over a hundred and fifty pounds. 'People consume their own weight in coffee at any village event,' Carola commented.

Wilf and Courtney went home, so it was left to Daz, Sky and Carola to clear up, then take down the Christmas decorations destined to be returned to the village hall tomorrow.

When the last was packed into Carola's capacious SUV, the big room looked forlorn. Carola gazed around it. 'Elisabetta used to teach little ones to dance in here, and sometimes hold dances for adult villagers, too.'

'I wondered what it was for.' Sky leaned her shoulders against a wall, suddenly shattered. 'Do you know everything about this village, Carola?'

Carola coloured but smiled. 'I try to. Elisabetta was a dear. She'd have liked you being the new owner because she was quirky, too.'

They laughed. Sky didn't mind 'quirky' and had enjoyed today. It had taken her mind off the Ron Murray question. It hadn't taken her mind off Daz, however, because he'd hung around all day, and was now gazing at her with the look of a man with something to say. She knew there was no point trying to get rid of him until he'd said it.

So, after Carola had said her goodbyes and Daz's dark eyes remained fixed on Sky, his hair falling across his forehead, she suggested, 'Coffee?' closing the front door as Carola backed out of the drive. 'I still have my own milk supply.'

Something like relief flashed across his features. 'Thanks. I don't think I got a cup for myself.'

She nodded. In the kitchen, her new-to-her table still waited for its chairs to be fetched from the barn, so they'd have to sit in the other room where, Sky was sure, the spectres of their earlier selves would roll around on the fireside rug in abandoned passion. She made the drinks, then, silently, Daz followed her to the sitting room.

The fire was unlit and would remain so. Dancing flames would be too much of a reminder. When Daz had gone, she might have a quick meal and go to bed to read.

After a hesitation, he sat on the opposite sofa. He didn't even take the first sip of coffee before his explanation began. 'Abi turned up unannounced. She's been chucked out of her flat by its owner and has a work issue, too. I'm sorry that you discovered her without warning, but I want you to know she wasn't invited. I wouldn't . . . What had happened between you and me . . .' He floundered to a halt.

She sank deeper into the sofa, despondent at being forced to contrast the two glorious nights with Daz and the horrible moment when Abi had opened the door. And the worse one when Sky saw her in his bedroom window. 'It's not just that she was in your *house*,' she began, tears beginning to burn at the memory of Abi in that sexy robe.

Daz cut in. 'She won't be staying, Sky. You matter to me. I can't get you out of my head.'

Since Sky being in his head didn't seem to have kept Abi out of his bedroom, anger flared. Presumably, he wasn't aware of what Sky had seen. Or did he just not feel it important? 'You're living with Abi.'

'I'm not *living with* Abi. She's staying with me until she gets sorted. Chucking her out without somewhere to go—'

'—is not very Daz,' Sky finished shortly. 'Please, don't say any more. Abi's there. I don't need details.' She didn't even feel she could contact Courtney so much, now she'd realised, through texts from Wilf, that Abi was calling in.

'That's not fair,' he said in a low voice.

She sighed. 'Life isn't.'

A minute's silence passed, as if they were in mourning for what was never to be.

Daz stirred. 'Marietta says something's troubling you.'

Sky sipped her coffee, trying to ease the ball of tears from her throat. 'It's nothing.' But her voice broke.

'Doesn't sound like nothing.' His gaze sharpened. 'No one's bothering you, are they?'

Oh, hell's bells, he was going to start harping on about Bell again. 'No. My foster brother says a bloke's looking for me,' she said abruptly. 'His name's Ron Murray and he claims he's my grandfather. Mum never told me he existed. I don't know if he's genuine. Freddy sent his phone number, but I can't decide whether to use it. He could be as crappy as my mum.'

Daz's mouth made a silent O.

Sky's fingers clenched around the coffee mug handle. The sitting room curtains were open and the million fairy lights in the front garden cast shimmering shapes on the floorboards, despite the chandelier shining from the high ceiling.

Daz swapped sofas, seating himself a good foot away from her. 'I can imagine that *would* be troubling.' Though he'd been freshly shaved when she'd first set eyes on him this morning, a sturdy five o'clock shadow now coated his jaw.

At his sympathy, despite everything, Sky's eyes heated. She pressed her finger and thumb to her eyelids to stop the tears leaking out. 'Yep.'

'Sweetheart,' Daz rumbled, as if their tetchy exchange about Abi hadn't happened. Sky felt his warm, comforting hand on her arm. 'If you're worried, don't call him. Block him.'

The muscles of her face twitched, as sobs threatened. 'But what if he's really my grandfather and he's OK? I've never had a family—' Then her voice began to shake. 'I asked Nan Heather and she said nobody could make the decision but me. Bell's deeply sceptical, sure that if my grandfather's taken this long to get in touch then he's doing it because there's something in it for him.' Then she realised she'd somehow found herself in Daz's arms. She gave a great sniff, pretty sure she should be pulling away, but unable to force herself to reject the comfort.

After a couple of minutes for Sky to gulp back the tears, Daz asked, unexpectedly, 'Do you have an A4 pad?'

She drew away to gaze into his face in confusion. 'I have printer paper.'

'Great. And pens?'

Mystified, she nodded, then went upstairs, blowing her nose. It took her a minute to find the box of paper stowed in her wardrobe. She took pens from her laptop bag and traipsed downstairs to find Daz in the kitchen. He'd fetched two chairs from the barn.

He took the paper and spread several sheets across the table. 'When I'm designing and developing a game, I make it all about decisions,' he said. 'I think of every alternative I can, all the consequences of each and where choices can be made. Then I drill down on whether a choice will lead somewhere or not.' At the top of the first sheet of paper he wrote: *Ron Murray is Sky's grandfather.* On the second: *Ron Murray is not Sky's grandfather.* On the next pair: *Sky wants to meet Ron* and then: *Sky does not want to meet Ron.*

On a surge of understanding, Sky snatched up a pen, too, adding to the first sheet: *How will Sky establish whether Ron's genuine? Or if he's a scally?*

Daz took it from her and added below her words: *Phone? Text? Private investigator?* Brow furrowed in concentration, he said, 'When I think the character's met a landmark goal, that's where I declare a change of level, but we're nowhere near that, yet.' Under *Phone?* he listed: *Take relationship no further* and then *Or further phone calls?*

It was dark outside the kitchen window. Sky hadn't completely cleared the patio yet and a shrub tapped the windowpane as if it was Ron Murray trying to get in. The fanciful thought made her shiver.

Daz took up a new piece of paper and wrote: *Sky is alone when she calls Ron.* Then: *Sky is not alone when she calls Ron.* Below that he wrote: *Possibly with? Courtney. Freddy. Bell. Nan Heather. Daz. Marietta. Someone else.* He paused and regarded Sky thoughtfully. 'About your grandfather being a scally, what would your specific fears be?' He headed a fresh sheet of paper: *Ron is a scally.*

Instantly, Sky's pulse quickened. 'He has a drink problem. He's after money. He's finding me on behalf of my mother — probably because *she* wants money.' This last was said in a small voice.

'Oh. Big fork in the path of character progress.' Daz began a whole new sheet. *Sky wants to be in contact with her mother.* Then: *Sky doesn't want to be in contact with her mother.*

They went on and on, littering the table and worktops with paper, pausing only for Daz to order takeaway from his favourite Thai restaurant in Bettsbrough and for them to eat it when it arrived.

It took a couple of hours for Sky to find her way through the 'game'. Finally, she clasped her head, which ached with concentration and apprehension. 'So, this is where I'm up to. Level one: phone Ron Murray – aka Grandfather Bombshell – and try to discover whether he's genuine. If I think he is, talk. Decide whether I want to prolong contact. If no, that's game over. If yes, level two will be to arrange a video call.' She glanced at Daz, her heart speeding so fast she felt sick. 'That may or may not lead to level three, meeting him on neutral ground. And level four, if it ever took place, meeting him at his home or mine.'

'And you can end the game at any stage,' Daz reminded her gently. He smiled and gave her a quick, friendly, one-armed hug. 'If I was really designing a game, I'd create weapons for your armoury . . . an extra skin of resilience and a measure of spirit of determination. Maybe a free pass or two for misunderstandings while you and Grandfather Bombshell get to know each other.'

She laughed shakily. 'How about a crystal ball? That's really what I need.' She slumped in her chair, surveying the litter of options and consequences. 'I'm going to call him now, before I second-guess, regardless of it being lateish.' And, for once, this was something she didn't want do alone. Awkwardly, she went on, 'Things are different now between you and me, but Courtney's tied up with Wilf. Marietta and Nan Heather both go to bed early. Would you . . . would you stay while I make the phone call?' It seemed right, when he'd been with her on tonight's mental journey, every step of the way.

A smile softened his voice. 'I absolutely would.'

She sucked in a long, shaking breath. 'Then let's hope he doesn't go to bed before ten.' Wiping her damp palms down her jeans, she hid her ID then dialled the phone number Freddy had texted. In her ear, the ring tone sounded once. Twice. Three times. Four. Five.

He wasn't going to answer.

She didn't know whether to feel disappointed or relieved.

Just as she expected to hear the robotic voice of voice-mail, the line opened. 'Hello,' said a man, in the tone of someone receiving a call from an unknown number and suspecting they were about to have their time wasted.

Sky swallowed. Daz covered her hand with his.

'Yes?' the voice said impatiently.

'Is that—' Sky's voice trembled and almost broke. 'Is that Ron Murray?'

An infinitesimal pause. Then the man's voice softened. 'Yes. Yes, it is.' When Sky found her throat had closed around any further words, he continued, 'Hello, there. This is Ron. Who am I talking to?'

She had to suck in a big breath before she could expel the words. 'I'm Sky Terran.'

A gasp escaped the man on the other end of the line. 'Oh!' he said huskily. 'Oh, Sky. Oh.' His voice wavered. 'I can't tell you how glad I am to hear from you. I believe I'm your grandfather.'

Her heart tried to bounce out between her ribs, making her feel faint. 'Why do you believe that?'

A smile stole into his voice. 'Because my daughter, Patricia Murray – Trish – told me so.' He hesitated. 'Were you born Sky Murray on May 23rd 1983?'

'Yes.' Sky closed her eyes, unsure what to think, to feel. Could this man be on the level? He sounded . . . nice. She licked her lips. Daz gently let go of her hand and moved away. She heard a cupboard opening, then a running tap. When she felt something cold touch her hand, she opened her eyes to see Daz proffering a glass of water. She smiled gratefully before taking several sips. 'Thing is,' she said, less shakily, 'my mother never spoke of her family.'

'Ah,' he said sadly. 'Our relationship with Trish deteriorated in her mid-teens.' His rumbling voice was soft and sad. 'My wife Stella and I were conservative, ordinary people, but Trish was out of control from the moment she hit puberty – smoking and drinking and sniffing and I don't know what. At sixteen, she stopped coming home.' He drew in a shuddering breath. 'We had her traced twice, but she just kept moving. In the end, we had to accept that she didn't want contact.'

The picture fit with the Trish Sky had known. It was striking that she'd left home at sixteen, just like Sky. Or no, maybe not just like Sky. Trish had rejected security and conservatism. Sky had fled from irresponsibility.

Ron began speaking again. 'A year ago, Trish popped up, out of the blue. Stella – your grandmother – had died several years earlier and I'd moved house. As I used to be a lawyer with high-profile cases, I'd removed my internet presence when I retired, but Trisha found my brother on LinkedIn.'

'Brother?' Sky's voice trembled again. She had a great-uncle?

'That's right. Perry.' Ron's voice was gentle, as if understanding that Sky was struggling to take everything in. 'Knowing Trish's absence was a great source of anguish, he gave her my number. She called and said, "Hi, Dad, it's me," as if the previous thirty-eight years hadn't happened. She's living in Thailand with a woman called Martha.'

'They're a couple?' Sky asked absently.

'They're in a relationship, yes,' Ron replied. 'Apparently, Martha was a teacher in Thailand when Trish was drifting there. They hooked up and Martha's helped her with substance abuse. She sounds like a good influence.'

Sky didn't censor her reaction. 'I wish her good luck. When she's put Mum to bed drunk a few hundred times, propping her on her side to make sure she doesn't choke if she vomits, cleaned up after her and then realised Mum's drunk all their money, Martha might think again.'

A long, slow silence. Then Ron groaned. 'Was that what it was like? You poor dear. I can't bear to think of it.'

Tears clogged Sky's throat, all the years of resilience and independence, undone by three words. *You poor dear.* She snorted back a sob.

'Sky,' said the soft voice in her ear. 'Sky, I didn't mean to upset you. It was a shock to know you existed, but I tracked you down because I want to know you. I'm not a threat. I never meant to make you cry.' He sounded close to tears himself.

Daz seized a clean sheet of paper and scribbled for several seconds. Then he held the paper so she could read it, which, when she'd scrubbed her eyes, she could just about do.

Sky continues the call.
Sky ends the call.

Sky arranges to speak again another day.

Blindly, she stabbed at the third option, tears slipping down her cheeks.

Gently, he took the phone. 'Good evening, Mr Murray. I'm Sky's friend, Darragh Moran. She'd like to call you again at another time, when she's had a chance to get used to things. Is that OK? Thanks. Yes, I will. Yes, of course.' He ended the call and slid an arm around her. 'He said to tell you he's thrilled to hear from you and very much hopes it will happen again.'

The only noise Sky could make was the *woo-hoo-oo* of overwhelming, uncontrollable sobs.

It took her twenty minutes of Daz holding her before she remembered Abi. Abi. Waiting for him in his home. In his bedroom again, perhaps. It took all her strength to rebuild the wall between them – the wall that would protect her heart. 'Thanks,' she said, sitting up and performing one last wipe of her eyes. 'I'll be OK, now.'

After a moment, Daz said gruffly, 'Time for me to leave?' Disappointment rang in every word.

She nodded, suddenly unable to meet his gaze. 'I'm exhausted.' Exhausted by the day, the emotion, the confusion. Daz's nearness. Their time in bed together was only a week ago but they'd flown too close to the sun too soon. Falling back into the cold waters of reality had hurt.

Summoning a watery smile, she moved out of touching distance. 'Thanks, Daz. You were a rock.'

'You've had an emotional time,' he said. 'And I'm so incredibly sorry about Abi—'

She waved this away. 'I think tonight's proved to me that friendship's more valuable than – than the other, anyway. We're friends. OK?' She was being ungracious and unappreciative, but was feeling too vulnerable to waver.

Daz stared at her for a long, unreadable moment. 'OK.' He rose. 'I'll leave you to your thoughts. Happy to help if you want someone around if you talk to Ron again. Or you decide you want to talk about Abi.'

'Yes. *No*. Thanks.' After seeing him out, she trailed upstairs to bed, head aching from her tears, to think about the man she was beginning to let herself believe was her grandfather, about the grandmother she'd lost without knowing, a great-uncle Perry – and maybe that meant a great-aunt and cousins? Also, about a Trish Murray who'd apparently cleaned up her act sufficiently to live in Thailand with a teacher called Martha.

Parking thoughts of Trish, she realised she hadn't asked Ron where he lived or whether he had anyone in his life to replace Stella.

She'd call him again.

But her last thought before falling asleep was about how great Daz had been, even when she'd shoved him away at the end. What might have happened between them if not for Abi?

Chapter Seventeen

Daz had walked home last night from Sky's house barely seeing the glitter of the Christmas Street decorations, his mind churning with disappointment that she flatly refused to talk about Abi. Mixed in was pleasure that, despite that, she'd wanted his support while she spoke to the grandfather she hadn't known existed. She'd let Daz in, even if she'd later regretted it. The contradictions and injustices of the situation had continued to keep him company while he tossed and turned through the night.

Then, suddenly, he jolted fully awake, an idea clanging into his brain.

It wasn't about Sky, because her stance couldn't be clearer.

It was something else about the emotional evening, something other than regrets – an idea for a game. And he hadn't had one of those for far too long. The hardest thing about developing a computer game was finding a fresh direction. He'd been lucky before, his survivalist game striking a chord with his YouTube following and word of mouth doing the rest.

He'd totally neglected YouTube since going into quality assurance. He could change that, but first he must experiment with his shiny new idea. He ran downstairs to grab breakfast but halted when he found Abi – lying in wait? – in her dressing gown, showing a lot of leg, and full of chat about Wilf's quirky Christmas tree success.

'He told me all about it when we had supper together last night. It's so lovely to see them whenever I want,' she told him gaily.

Daz frowned over the subtext. Far from making plans to move on, Abi was settling in. Distracted by his distress over visiting Lewis, he'd been sympathetic when she turned up. He'd believed her need for breathing space and lack of anywhere else to go and that sympathy had allowed him to give her the benefit of the doubt over the way she'd greeted Sky at the door and spoilt everything. Her claim of being medicated for depression had made him hesitant when he'd wanted a frank discussion. He didn't want to believe she'd pretend mental illness to manipulate him . . . but it wasn't hard to see that unhappiness only surfaced when he challenged her about future plans.

Sky had rejected him last night because of Abi.

Well, Abi wasn't the only one who could be manipulative. She'd been here six days now, and that was at least five too many. Abruptly, he said, 'I feel I've been neglecting you.' He watched the pretty face brighten, before clarifying, 'I haven't helped you make progress with your employer or find somewhere to live.'

She paled in tragic dismay. 'It's really tricky—'

Wordlessly, Daz made her a cup of coffee. In the old days, they'd have taken the coffee back to bed, but those desires were in the past. When she took the mug, he held on to it for a moment, looking into her eyes. 'It's Monday tomorrow. A week's long enough for the dust to settle. You should call your HR department or union. We need to get you sorted out.'

Abi's expression turned woeful. 'I'm not sure I'll feel up to it.'

He held her gaze. 'I'll help you. Tomorrow, right?'

He left for his computer room, feeling her gaze on his back. Upstairs, sinking into the office chair that, like his gaming chair, felt an extension of his body, he texted Sky. *How are you today?*

She replied straight away. *Fine, thanks. 'Relaxing' into a day with my chainsaw.*

It was the kind of superficial, jokey comment that friends exchanged. It pierced him like a thorn that the fire between them had been reduced to this.

Though his creative spark felt dimmed by the interactions with Abi and Sky – each unsatisfactory for differing reasons – Daz settled down to doodle and jot.

Since selling out – literally and figuratively – he'd been devoid of inspiration until this idea had hit for a role-playing game where the aim would be negotiating emotional pathways, and the 'setting' a dysfunctional family. He was damned sure that the dead ends, chasms and pitfalls of family dynamics could be as compelling as the dead ends, chasms and pitfalls of some fictitious planet. It could be the most fascinating life-simulation game since The Sims.

He'd call it Reimagined Families.

He paused and frowned. Oh-kay, he'd better check his contract. He was almost certain that it precluded him from developing new games, in some way. With a thumping heart, he scanned the clauses. *There.* He read anxiously to the end but, phew. Restriction ended with contract termination.

Right, then. Without second thoughts, he typed his resignation and emailed it to Al, his line manager. During his notice period, he'd work on the preliminary game framework in his own time. Then, boom, he'd be free to do a job he liked.

Swapping to his gaming rig, for the first time in a couple of years he illuminated his halo light and prepared to record for his YouTube channel, splitting the screen between his face and a still from his old game. 'Hey, guys, Daz here,' he plunged in. 'I've an idea for a new game, one that has me excited.' The word 'excited' made him think of Sky. He'd never seen her so jittery as when calling her grandfather last night. It had made him want to scoop her up and hug her. So, he had.

And she'd accepted it.

Until she hadn't.

Suddenly, concentrating on YouTube got harder, but it was something he could control, so he plunged on.

Monday. Daz knocked on the door to the spare room. Abi had avoided him for most of Sunday but now he could hear her moving around. *Knock, knock.* 'Hey, Abi.'

Pause. Querulous reply. 'I'm not decent and not feeling good. Can we talk later?'

Yeah, right. 'One hour,' he said sharply. 'I'll go up to work.'

In his computer room he texted Sky again.

I'm fine, she replied. *Sun terrace on top of barn now completely accessible. I'll invite you for a drink in summer.*

He turned to gaze over his garden where the hawthorn hedge was furred with frost. Icy puddles shone like silver. The scene glittered like a Christmas card.

Summer seemed an eon away.

259

His computer dinged as an email arrived. It was Al's reply to his resignation. His eyes ran rapidly over the lines. *Sorry to read you're considering resignation* – considering? He thought he'd already resigned. Blah, blah . . . *valued team leader* . . . bleurgh. *When can we discuss this on Teams?*

He replied, suggesting any time within normal working hours, and received another email. *Al Silvester invites you to a meeting.* Two p.m. today. He clicked *accept.*

He turned back to the monster-taming game he was heartily sick of QA testing. In a month he'd be free of this shit.

Noticing that an hour had passed, he went down to hammer on Abi's door again. Silence. With another knock, he thrust open the door. Her stuff was still there, but she wasn't. He even checked the en suite. Stalking to the window in his bedroom, he saw her car was absent from the drive. 'Fucking cheek,' he fumed. She must have crept out to avoid him.

Two o'clock rolled around and he joined the Teams meeting, the face of Al Silvester looming on his screen. 'Daz,' Al cried. 'Great to see you, buddy.'

'You, too,' Daz replied politely, not mentioning that Al looked more lined than last time they video-met.

Al grinned with a conspiratorial air. 'So, what I can do to retain you?' He winked, as if to say, 'I have sweeties in my pocket, if you're a good boy.'

Daz shrugged. 'Nothing, really.' As the fastest route to getting this over was with transparency, he added, 'I want to develop again. I was shunted into QA, but it's not for me and an idea's gnawing at me.'

Al's gaze sharpened. 'So, share your idea. If it has potential, I can talk to the rest of the leadership team about getting you a developmental role.'

'Really?' Daz stretched in his seat, looking out of the

window again. Frost still lay in shady hollows. 'When I requested that kind of role, I was told testing was my strong suit. Puzzling, as I was offered employment because I'd developed a game you wanted. A game that's still doing OK,' he added.

Al's expression became regretful. 'Everyone wants to be in development. Not enough posts to go around. But if you're so convinced of your idea—'

'I'm going independent,' Daz interrupted.

With a tug of his lower lip, Al assumed the expression of someone who regretted having bad news to impart. 'Don't think you can do that, under your contract, Daz.'

'Read it,' Daz advised him briefly. Then, with the ghost of a smile: 'I'll sell the game to you when it's ready, if the offer's right.'

'Hang on, hang on,' Al said jovially. 'Wouldn't you rather we worked together on this? All the resources of a big concern behind you?'

Daz didn't even have to think about that. 'But if I'm your employee, the organisation will own the intellectual property. If you own the IP, you control the rights and get the royalties.'

Al's smile became fixed. 'I see you've thought about this. Would you be interested in some kind of a co-op deal? Our resources, your idea, royalty split . . . ?'

This time, Daz paused. A co-op deal could mean continuing income instead of a flat fee. If the game did well, it would be an enormous income. 'If you come up with a split to interest me,' he said, making a mental note to find a lawyer or other expert in the field to make sure he didn't get shafted. 'But no rush. Early days.'

With a studiedly casual air, Al said, 'Ping me an outline, so I know what to put to the leadership.'

Daz laughed. 'You ping me your suggested terms of co-operation, contingent upon your approval of the idea if we ever come to an agreement.'

Al's turn to laugh. 'You can't expect me to go for that, Daz.'

'No,' he agreed easily. 'But I'm not giving you guys another idea without a better financial package than last time.' He checked the date. 'It's December 12th now, so could you ask HR to confirm my last day of work? I should imagine I have about a week's annual leave to come, taking into consideration the couple of days when I didn't log on last week.' There was a formula for 'days worked' based on a thirty-seven-hour week.

'You don't want to resign before the details are thrashed out, do you?' Al frowned.

'Yes.' Daz smiled.

After the call had ended, his lunch of a cheese toastie tasted particularly good. He didn't waste energy searching out intellectual property lawyers and advisers, because he didn't think Al would come back with a sufficiently tempting offer from 'leadership'.

Whistling, he shrugged into his coat and stepped outside, intending to visit Sky and see how she did. That's what friends did, right? When the frigid air pounced on him, he went back in and added hat, scarf and gloves to his ensemble.

It was too early for schoolkids to be home, so the street was quiet. He stopped to admire a glittering unicorn pawing the air on a lawn at number twelve, then crossed over to number one, The Corner House, following the roar of the shredder. There was no point knocking at the front door with that racket going on, so he continued to Great Hill Road, then clambered over the fence into the

262

back garden, falling into a mass of brambles that stuck through his jeans and almost took out his eye.

Directing several F-bombs at the clawing, spiny cables, he stamped them down and shook his jeans free of their thorny arms. Finally, he half-fell onto a patch of paving, landing painfully on one knee.

Sky and the shredder both let out a shriek.

'Sorry,' he shouted, straightening up and rubbing his throbbing knee. 'I knew you wouldn't hear the doorbell.'

Sky switched off the shredder and its moan descended into silence as she pulled off her goggles, ear protectors and hard hat. A pink, woolly beanie came off too, and her hair tumbled over her shoulders, blazing in the winter sun. Despite indentations left by the goggles, he thought she'd never looked more beautiful. 'So, you came via the back entrance?'

'More the back fence,' he admitted. 'I need to ask you something.'

She glanced at the sky. 'Well . . . there's only about an hour of full daylight left.' Evidently, she wasn't that fussed about hearing what he had to say. Probably, she thought he'd come to badger her about Abi again – which he would, if she gave him any encouragement. But he was trying to respect her boundaries, impossible though it felt when all he wanted to do was take her in his arms.

He looked at the stack of branches beside her and the space she'd cleared. Behind her stood a flight of stone steps to the barn roof and the chainsaw leaned against them as if waiting to be given a job. 'How about I cut the branches up for firewood while you shred the brush?'

She shrugged. 'Great, if you feel like it. Not working today?'

'That's part of what I'm here to talk about,' he said. 'Any spare goggles?'

263

She had, and he spent the next hour *neeeeowwww*ing through branches, throwing down brush for the yowling maw of the shredder and stacking logs.

Finally, the shredder decrescendoed for the last time and he powered down the chainsaw, realising how heavy his arms had become. Sky dusted chippings from her coat. 'Let's stick everything in the barn.'

Before they went indoors, she showed him her sun terrace. When they stood side by side on the paved roof of the barn, he gazed about, enjoying the unfamiliar vantage point. Christmas lights were just coming on up the street. Sky's front garden glowed as if sprinkled with fairy dust, contrasting with the back, where only a patch of tangled bare-branched trees and misshapen conifers had been cleared. 'What a fantastic spot,' he breathed, sucking in the frozen air and the smell of fresh wood.

Sky looked pleased. 'I love it.' She gave a theatrical shiver. 'But I'm so cold my nose is about to get frostbite. Let's go inside.'

Back at ground level, she showed him into the house through the back door to a small room he remembered from the plans. 'The mud room,' he said.

'Yes. You can tell it's been a farmhouse. It's such a functional building.' She hung up her hat, exchanged her coat for a fleece-lined hoodie and kicked off her wellies, slipping her feet into furry slippers in the shape of tiger's paws, instead.

'Scary lady,' he joked. 'Look at those claws.'

'Grr,' she answered, sounding more cute than scary, heading out of the mud room and turning left into the kitchen. She began to make coffee. 'What was it you wanted to discuss?'

He took a seat at the kitchen table, which somehow

looked new and old at the same time. 'I've had an idea for a new game, but as it came to me as a direct result of you picking your way through the decision as to whether to contact Ron Murray, I want to check it won't upset you.'

She brought him a mug, arching her eyebrows, which he took it as an invitation to explain. He also recounted his conversation with Al Silvester. She'd seated herself opposite him, long fingers wrapped around her coffee mug. 'I wouldn't mind in the least. Thanks for running it past me, though.'

He hadn't thought she would but asking put him in a good light and gave him an excuse to seek her out.

She looked suddenly shy. 'I rang Ron back this morning and I think that next time I'll suggest we FaceTime. Maybe at the weekend.' She screwed up her nose. 'I feel as if I should take it slow. Give myself time to absorb the change.'

His heart gave a leap of pleasure for her. 'Is it going well?'

Her hair danced as she nodded. 'He lives in Norfolk, right on the north coast in a village called Nelson's Bar, with a view of the sea and a pub only a stroll away. He was a criminal lawyer but retired ten years ago. The family used to live nearer Norwich, where Mum went to school, but he and my grandmother Stella moved to the coast. After she died, he moved to Nelson's Bar.'

Daz smiled. 'You sound as if you've accepted that he is who he says he is.'

Her eyes widened, as if she hardly dared believe it. 'I think so. He's offered a DNA test but I'm hoping that when I see him, even if it's just on-screen, I'll know, even though he says Mum took after Stella, not him. He's sent photos of Mum as a child and it's recognisably her. He's going to scan a load more family photos in for me.'

He smiled at her air of hardly daring to believe. 'I'm dead pleased for you.'

But then she sobered. 'Apparently, Mum's asked him to arrange a video call between her and me, too.'

'That's—' He wanted to say 'scary' or 'dangerous' but tried to put himself in her place and chose: '—got potential,' instead.

She grimaced. 'To blow up in my face, yeah. I haven't agreed, yet. But there's a new option for your game – once a relationship's established, it leads to another risky step.'

He debated using the opening to suggest a peril being a manipulative ex-girlfriend appearing out of the blue and clinging like a burr but decided it might freeze the present warmth between them.

They tossed around other ideas for Reimagined Families, laughing at the more ridiculous. When Daz eventually headed home, he felt happier – though rueful at their new relationship. Friendship.

Not what he wanted.

Nevertheless, and despite still not having sorted Abi out, he was happier, until he went in and found a letter from Lewis on the doormat, easy to identify from the cell and wing number on the envelope. Reluctantly, he opened it and read the terse sentences it contained.

Spoke to Courtney last night and she's still talking about dating. Can't think of anything else. It's killing me. Haven't you talked to her, Daz? Really, mate, I can't bear it.

Daz's heart sank like a stone. No, he hadn't talked to Courtney. Since Abi had turned up to disrupt his life, he'd hardly seen Courtney, and never alone. She'd indicated that what happened between her and Lewis wasn't Daz's business. With that, and in his dismay over Abi's intrusion and frustration over how to resolve the Sky situation, he'd managed to squash Lewis's request to the back of his mind.

Good mood blown, he stalked disconsolately into the kitchen. There was no sign of Abi yet, damn her. He opened the fridge and grabbed a tall can of beer. After ripping off the tab, he took a few good mouthfuls. Then he sat at the breakfast bar and, one-handed, texted Abi. *We need to talk. Stop avoiding me.*

He was just taking another swig of beer when the phone rang in his hand, startling him so much he lost his grip on the can, which executed a fine somersault, fizzing in a plume down his sweatshirt as it spun in the air. *Marvellous*, he fumed. When he saw it was Al Silvester calling again, he let the call go to voicemail.

He finished what was left of the beer and got a fresh can. He needed time to think.

Chapter Eighteen

On Tuesday lunchtime, Sky was just mulling over whether Abi had started a job locally and that's why her car was absent from Daz's drive so regularly, when she received a text from Courtney. *Any chance you could babysit tonight? My boss at the hotel, Clark, wants to buy his team Christmas drinks. I'm leaving them soon so would like to attend. Clark's paying for taxis to and from The Crown in Bettsbrough! Think we must have earned him a bonus. x*

Sky didn't hesitate. She hadn't seen much of Wilf, lately, cautious about calling in at Courtney's once she realised Courtney and Abi were friends. She returned, *Of course, so long as Wilf's happy with that. x* She felt unreasonably pleased that Courtney had reached out to her.

Courtney's reply flashed up on the screen. *Thank you! Wilf will love it.* ☺ *x*

Sky smiled. It would be great for Courtney to have a night out.

When she duly arrived at Courtney's little house in the early evening, the Christmas light in the shape of a watering can had arrived and Wilf was dying to show it off. 'Fantastic,' she said admiringly. 'I love the way you've positioned it, so it looks as if it's pouring water into that boot-shaped planter.'

'Good, isn't it?' he demanded immodestly. Then: 'I've done my homework.' Wilf had recently had a haircut and his cow's lick looked like a little rosette above his hopeful gaze.

The import of his pronouncement wasn't lost on Sky. 'That means we can do something fun.'

She found Courtney in the sitting room, checking her reflection in the over-mantel mirror while a Christmas tree twinkled with a rainbow of lights in the corner. Her black hair was caught up in a glittery clip and a grass-green tunic and black velvet jeans flattered her reed-thin figure. 'You look great,' Sky exclaimed.

Courtney looked relieved. 'Do I? I couldn't afford anything new.'

'You look perfect.' Sky hugged her and Courtney hugged her back, laughing and obviously excited at the treat ahead. Her taxi arrived ten minutes later, and she kissed Wilf before running out to jump inside.

Wilf looked at Sky hopefully. 'Do you game?'

Sky shook her head. 'Computer games? Not really. I thought we could look online for ideas for birdboxes. If we decorate them with holly and stuff, they can be added to my front garden for the Christmas Street Competition. I'm not sure birds will be moving in with my garden in its current state of blingdom, but they won't start nesting for a few weeks anyway. The Christmas lights will have gone by then.'

'Cool.' Wilf fetched his laptop, which was dated but functioning, and they sat side by side on the sofa, checking sites and discussing which garden birds they'd like to attract.

'I've got the tools,' Sky said. 'We'll need to order non-toxic paint.'

Wilf watched a YouTube video, where a bearded man was putting together a box for house sparrows. 'Can I use the drill? We'll use drills on stands next year at school.'

Sky hadn't a clue whether an eleven-year-old could be trusted with a hand-held electric drill, under supervision. 'Up to your mum.'

Wilf looked mutinous. 'If you don't have a dad, how come you know about drills and saws?'

'Foster brother showed me,' Sky replied, bookmarking a site that gave the dimensions for a house sparrow nesting box.

'Then why can't you show me? It's not like I've got a dad,' Wilf muttered. His cheeks flushed a dull red.

Tentatively, Sky observed, 'You do have a dad.'

The boy snorted. 'What good is he in prison?'

They watched the rest of the birdbox video in silence, while Sky's mind worked. 'You know,' she said carefully, when the bearded man was proudly displaying his completed house sparrow box, 'your dad did something wrong, but he didn't do it to hurt you. I'm sure he's very sorry you're affected.'

Wilf stuck out his bottom lip. 'He did it all for some woman I've never met, who was ill and died anyway. Mum says they were just good friends from the past, but she's sad. I know, even if she tries to hide it and visits Dad and everything.' He sounded close to tears.

Sky slipped an arm around his slight shoulders and hugged him. 'I know. He let a passion run away with him – like I did with my house. I wanted it, I didn't want someone else to develop it, but I didn't think about what I'd do with it myself, long term. Passion's a funny thing. It can make you act out of character.'

'Suppose.' Wilf sniffed.

Sky cast about for something comforting to say. 'I understand if you feel helpless. A bad thing happened. You can't change it. But there's always the future. We can usually have some say in that.' She stroked his hair. 'I used to feel helpless, when my mum was drunk or left me alone, but actually I *was* taking action, because I used to get money out of her and get the food shopping.' Better not to say she'd had to steal the money from Trish's purse.

In silence, Wilf began watching another YouTube video.

Sky hoped she hadn't said anything Courtney might object to. She'd report to her later, in case. Wow, parenting must be hard. Birds and bats were much easier than small human beings.

When the front doorbell rang a few minutes later, she looked up in surprise. Courtney hadn't told her to expect anyone.

Wilf thrust his laptop aside and ran to the window to check who was there. 'It's Daz.' He raced to open the front door. Sky heard Daz's deep voice and Wilf saying, 'Sky's here, 'cos Mum's out.'

Daz appeared in the doorway, his gaze warm when it rested on her. 'This is an unexpected pleasure. I saw Courtney's car outside so thought she'd be here.'

Wilf plumped himself back down on the sofa. 'Clark sent a taxi. They're going for drinks in The Crown in Bettsbrough.'

'Oh.' Daz plumped down into an armchair and regarded Sky with a frown.

271

She hesitated, trying to decode his odd expression. Was he annoyed with her that Courtney was out? Courtney didn't need to report to Daz.

Wilf rattled on happily. 'We've been looking how to make birdboxes. And Sky says I should think about Dad and the future.'

'Oh? And what does Sky recommend?' Daz asked.

Nettled by a sardonic note in his voice, Sky stepped in. 'I didn't recommend anything. It's not my call.'

'No,' Daz agreed slowly.

She frowned, mystified. He'd seemed OK when he came in but now was full of simmering tension, his brows drawn low like two dashes from a marker pen. What had altered his mood? They weren't sleeping together now Abi was back, but surely he shouldn't be glowering at her like that?

And then a whiff of alcohol reached her.

She tried not to stiffen but she'd long ago learned how to spot a drunk, and strange expressions and changeable moods were high on the list. The beery smell grew stronger in the warmth of the room. It made Sky's heart trot uncomfortably and she found it hard to join in Wilf's blithe chatter, particularly as Daz became increasingly morose. But he didn't leave.

When Wilf's weekday bedtime of nine p.m. came around, Sky went upstairs with him to remind him to clean his teeth. 'Your mum said you can read a book but your laptop has to stay downstairs.' He greeted this reminder with an expressive roll of the eyes that made her smother a smile.

Treading back downstairs after saying goodnight, she wondered whether Daz had got over his mouldy attitude because she'd rather curl up before the TV alone than be obliged to look at his moody mug.

But the moment she stepped back into the sitting room, Daz rose and closed the door softly behind her.

It made her jump. Now he was so close, the smell of beer was much stronger. Hell, he smelled as if he'd bathed in the stuff. Her breath got stuck behind her breastbone. 'What on earth's up with you?' she demanded, fighting the urge to back away.

His eyes were dark. 'I'm disappointed you'd babysit while Courtney dates.' Before Sky could reconsider whether to explain Courtney wasn't on a date, he swept on. 'Do you know I visited Lewis in prison last week? And it was an awful place. You've no idea.'

His low voice was probably designed not to reach Wilf's ears, but it was uncomfortably close to a growl. Still, sympathy swept over her, despite that and even despite the horrible beer fumes. She knew how bad he felt about his friend languishing behind bars, and the events that led him there. That was why he was so protective of Courtney, after all. 'I'm sure it is awful,' she began, trying to be gentle despite her nerves scuttling through her like mice. 'I didn't know you'd been on a visit.'

Daz shook his head. 'I didn't want to talk about it, or even think about it more than I had to. But I had to sit and watch Lewis crying because he thinks he's losing Courtney. You making it possible for her to see another man is not helpful, frankly.'

'Hang on,' she protested. The beery stink was making her feel sick and she had to take a step back. It was on his breath, too.

'Courtney's still married,' he interrupted.

Sky's breathing quickened. She tried to remind herself that Daz was only leaping to conclusions and that the alcohol was affecting his emotional state, but alcohol fumes filled her head. For an instant, her vision flickered. She knew it was Daz looming over her, but it felt like Trish, growling abuse, pushing Sky around. She took another step back. And another.

'Don't you think they deserve the opportunity to fix their marriage?' Daz demanded.

Her heart hammered. She couldn't think anything. Her mind had turned to fog.

'Lewis needs his family,' Daz said tightly. 'And I don't know what you've been telling Wilf about his dad. It's not something you can understand.'

Sky had to get away. To take a clean breath. The hammering moved into her head and she threw up her arms, coming up against Daz's big, heavy chest. She lost track of the conversation, couldn't think why he was going on about Courtney, and seized on his last remark. 'Because I've never had a father?' She pushed blindly, trying to shove him away. 'What do I know about families when I haven't really had one and had to borrow other people's families, like a little cuckoo in first this nest then that one?'

Daz fell back, his expression now one of ludicrous dismay. 'That didn't even cross my mind.'

'No, of *course* not.' Sky ducked, panicking, desperate to get away. Something snapped. 'Stop looming over me and venting. So arrogant and entitled, looking down on people without proper families, like Bell and me. Fuck off, you shitweasel! Get out!'

He took several more steps back. 'Sky?' He sounded horrified, astounded.

Her eyes burned. She was going to cry. She was going to vomit. She was going to pass out on the floor. '*Out. Out now.* Get out, get out, get *out.*'

In silence, he turned, took up his coat and opened the front door. In a second it had closed behind him.

Shaking, Sky sank onto the sofa, the tears finally spilling down her face, furious, queasy, breathless. Shit, she hadn't lost her temper for years. She wasn't even sure what had happened, except she knew she'd rediscovered the foul mouth of her youth.

She suspected she'd overreacted to Daz's attitude, but was hazy about exactly what he'd said that had made her flip. Jeez, he'd been drunk.

She wiped her eyes and checked the time. Courtney would be home in a couple of hours. She'd warn her that Daz thought she'd been dating and leave the rest to her.

By the time Courtney did creep in, kicking off her high heels, looking tired but cheerful, Sky had bathed her face in cold water, drunk a large mug of hot chocolate and was watching *Blue Planet* on TV.

'Everything OK? Wilf go to bed without trouble?' Courtney asked. 'Thanks so much, Sky. I really needed tonight.'

Switching off the on-screen image of sardines clustering into a shifting, silvery ball, Sky forced a smile. 'Wilf was great. But . . .' Swiftly, and as neutrally as she could manage, she summarised first her conversation with Wilf about Lewis and then as much as she could remember about the one with Daz – though she omitted the particulars of his disparagement of her lack of experience with family. 'We got snitty with each other and he charged off home with the idea that you were out on a date. Sorry,' she concluded repentantly.

Courtney flung herself on the sofa. 'Men! I suppose Lewis has been putting pressure on Daz to keep me out of trouble – as if it's any of his bloody business. Don't give it another thought.'

Despite that advice, Sky went home hardly able to think of anything else.

Daz lay in bed, shocked to the core.

Sky had *hit* him. Or shoved and windmilled him away, anyway. Nevertheless, he bitterly regretted his thoughtless remark, so easy to misconstrue. *And I don't know what you've been telling Wilf about his dad. It's not something you can understand.* He'd only meant she didn't know Lewis and had never seen the Brown family as a unit, in happy days. But she'd thought he was remarking on her upbringing and exploded.

Should he apologise and explain? He wasn't sure. Her attack had been shocking.

Sky had been *unstable*. Unreasonable. He thought of Abi, who'd at last come in, an hour ago, sobbing her way up the stairs. Daz had stayed under the duvet, listening, not sure if the tears were designed to bring him out to comfort her or to signal that she wanted to be alone.

He'd considered Abi the giddy, theatrical one, but tonight Sky had been every bit as irrational as Abi at her worst.

Did he even want another capricious woman – someone whose reactions could never be predicted? He realised that Abi, both past and present, had prompted a wish in him for a less volatile life.

In the darkness, his phone rang. After his disagreement with Sky, it wasn't the greatest shock to see Courtney's name on the screen. 'Hey,' he answered.

Down the line, Courtney's sigh was loud. 'Has Lewis asked you to try and stop me dating?'

He considered the best reply, caught in the same cycle of whether Lewis should have asked it of him but knowing the bro code was that he didn't admit it to Courtney.

'Your silence is answer enough,' she said. 'I'm sorry you were put in that position. I suggest you tell him it's not your business. However,' she said crisply, 'you should also know that I wasn't out on a date. It was Christmas drinks with a group of colleagues, OK?'

'Oh,' said Daz, blankly, wondering why on earth Sky couldn't just have told him that – although then he wouldn't have known that she blew up over small issues.

Courtney answered his unspoken question. 'Sky didn't owe you an explanation and neither do I. Goodnight, Daz.'

'Bye, Courtney.' Daz put his phone on 'do not disturb'.

Did he feel relieved? He wasn't sure. Courtney's disappointment in him and irritation with Lewis hadn't added to his comfort, that was for sure.

The Met Office issued warnings for snow, ice and freezing fog. Headlines shouted about 'Siberian snowstorms' and 'Arctic conditions' or joked about husky dogs. Schools issued contingency plans in the event of snowfall and bookies shortened the odds on a white Christmas.

Sky had battled grimly with her back garden all week but now it was Friday, she looked out on the wintry morning and decided on a day off. The bare trees were so frosty they all looked like the white birch. It had been a crap week anyway. Her disappointment in Daz hovered like a grey cloud above her head.

She'd just emailed Freddy to tell him all about her conversations with Ron Murray when her phone rang. Seeing Courtney's name, she answered. 'Shouldn't you be at work?'

'Work?' Courtney sounded as if she didn't know the meaning of the word. 'Our boiler's on the blink. It's like a freezer in here. Seriously, you buy a frigging new build to avoid this kind of crap.'

Sky commiserated. Then: 'Do you want me to wait in for the heating engineer while you go? I can wrap up warm.'

'Heating engineer?' Courtney yelped. 'I've rung four. Only two picked up and neither of them can come before Christmas.'

'Oh, dear.' Sky grimaced. 'I know someone who might come as a favour. Leave me a key and I'll try, anyway. Is Wilf going to Daz's after school, so at least he'll be warm there?' She hadn't seen Daz since they'd lost their tempers with one another. Abi continued to whiz up and down Winter Street in her little car. Courtney had told Sky that she'd explained the non-date to Daz. Daz had texted Sky to say he regretted getting the wrong end of the stick, but she'd misinterpreted his other remarks. She'd texted back, *Forget it.* That was three days ago, and they'd had no contact since.

'Daz is going to Birmingham to meet his line manager. They've invited him to talk about a new idea he had for a game.' Courtney sounded despondent. 'I called to ask whether Wilf could come to you after school. He doesn't want me to ask his granddad Graham because he's so gloomy. Unless you think your heating engineer might have it fixed by then?'

'Maybe. Of course Wilf can come, though.'

'Oh, Sky, I love you,' Courtney said impulsively.

With a rush of pleasure, Sky joked, 'You don't know if I can get your heating fixed yet.' She prepared to trade on an old relationship with a female engineer called Dee, who Sky had always made certain got her fair share of work.

Dee, however, didn't sound encouraging once she knew the details. 'I can swing by late morning, but that make and model of boiler has an ignition fault.'

Sky sighed. 'Oh, no. But could you come and see?'

At the appointed hour, feet slipping on the pavements as she strode up the road, Sky went to Courtney's to wait for Dee, her eyes straying to Daz's house as she passed. His car was missing from the drive and frost had coated the rectangle where it usually stood.

Dee duly arrived, a stocky woman in a red-striped hat and black coveralls, work boots on her feet. 'Whoo,' she said, hugging herself as Sky let her into Courtney's smart modern residence. 'Freezing, eh? Good to see you. Shame you left Freddy Walker's. That Minnie woman doesn't know her arse from her elbow.'

Sky grinned at this frank summation of Minnie's abilities. 'Thanks for coming out. My friend who owns the house is a single mum with a boy so . . .'

'I get it,' said Dee, briefly. But when she followed Sky into the kitchen and unclipped the boiler's front panel, she had no good news to share. 'As suspected, it's the electronic ignition.'

'Can you get the part?' Sky asked hopefully.

Dee was shaking her head before the words were out. 'We're all having trouble with these. Manufacturer should have recalled them. I'll order the ignition unit, but I'd be amazed if it came in before New Year. If your friend's got someone she can move in with over Christmas, I would recommend that she does that.'

'Oh. Thanks for making time, anyway,' Sky said hollowly, as Dee put through the parts order. But then an idea began to blossom, and she could hardly wait for Dee to hurry off to her next job, so she could text Courtney.

Heating engineer says it's the electronic ignition. Has ordered part but pessimistic about arrival before New Year. Why don't you and Wilf move in with me for Christmas? Her plans to get away for a festive break had never taken shape and she'd anticipated a quiet time – especially since Abi had reappeared. Now, the idea of sharing Christmas with Wilf and Courtney filled her with excitement.

In moments, her phone rang. 'Are you sure, about Christmas?' Courtney demanded, sounding close to tears. 'It's so incredibly kind.'

'Certain,' Sky returned, spirits soaring at the idea of sharing Christmas with Courtney and Wilf, imagining the laughter and presents and lovely meals. 'There's enough space here for you to have a bedroom each.'

Courtney burst into tears.

Wilf turned up at Sky's after school, a Peterborough United hat crammed over his ears, eyes watery from the wind, and she gave him the news that he was moving in with her and spending Christmas. 'Are you serious?' he demanded, eyes huge. 'Wowsers trousers, Sky. Wowsers *trousers.*'

'We might as well start getting your stuff,' she said, playfully pulling his hat down over his eyes. 'Christmas is going to be *fun.*'

It was when they were leaving Wilf's house, Sky carrying a bag of his clothes and Wilf bearing his PlayStation, that they saw Daz pull up in his drive across the road.

'We're moving in with Sky,' Wilf hollered as Daz emerged from the car.

Daz pulled up his collar against the wind that howled up the street and shook the Christmas lights. Wilf hurried across to impart details of the boiler story and Sky hovered uncomfortably in the background. Daz looked normal, today, she was glad to see – no sign of alcohol indulgence.

Wilf ended his story with: 'We've got to go back for my TV so I've got something to play PlayStation on.'

Daz looked at Sky, his expression inscrutable. 'Do you have enough beds?'

Sky hefted the bag of clothes currently making her arms ache. 'Courtney has airbeds.'

He nodded and turned to go indoors.

Miserable git, Sky thought in the direction of his stiffly held back.

By the time Courtney arrived home, Wilf's bed was inflated and made up and Sky was just tipping a bag of bedclothes over the airbed intended for Courtney.

Perilously close to a second bout of tears, Courtney wordlessly hugged Sky and returned home to pack her suitcase.

In a couple of hours, they were warm and toasty at The Corner House and ordering takeaway, which Courtney insisted on paying for to thank Sky for all she was doing for her and Wilf. Sky was intent on getting to the pub by eight for the quiz. 'I promised Marietta and it's the last quiz before Christmas because of the Christmas Street judging next Friday, and Bell can't be there because the darts team's playing an away fixture.' She wondered whether Daz would go. She hoped not, in case the combination of him and the smell of alcohol brought back the unpleasantness of Tuesday evening. She was glad this was the last quiz for a while, so she could steer clear of the pub.

'Of course,' said Courtney. 'Wilf, you get your weekend homework out of the way while I finish unpacking, then I'm going to try out Sky's huge, heavenly bath.'

Sky marched off to the pub, muffled up in her biggest, warmest outer garments. Wow, it was cold. She had to rub feeling into her ears, even through her hat. The village looked gorgeous, like a fairy tale, and she paused to admire a water feature that had created a free-form ice sculpture, like a wave as it broke. At least it was warm when she thrust the door open into to the crowded pub. She joined Marietta, who'd walked down with Jessie and Ruth earlier, pulling off her hat and explaining her tardiness.

'Poor Courtney,' commiserated Marietta. 'That girl just can't catch a break.'

Ruth stuck out her chin. 'I hope she's leaving her Christmas lights on. The judging is a week from tonight. We don't want one unlit house, like a missing tooth.'

'Did you see a house without lights when you came out?' Sky rolled her eyes and Ruth had the grace to look abashed. Sky glanced around. 'Doesn't the pub look Christmassy?'

A woman arrived at their table just as Sky finished her sentence. 'I'm glad to hear you're getting in the Christmas spirit,' she said shyly. 'Because I'm a total stranger and I've come to ask a favour. I'm Fallon, by the way. You're Sky, aren't you? Lovely name.' Fallon was young, only in her twenties, and currently blushing madly.

Sky blinked up at her, bemused. 'Hello. Ask away.'

Fallon fiddled nervously with her thin blonde ponytail. 'Carola said to ask you,' she went on in a rush. 'Like, is there any chance at all that I could borrow your big room for a birthday party? I've got twin girls, you see, and they'll be eight on Christmas Eve. I told them I'd try and save up for a party at a burger bar in Bettsbrough but with Christmas and everything . . .'

'Erm . . .' A stranger asking such a thing took her aback

for a moment. But then she saw the hope in Fallon's eyes and thought of community spirit, as well as Christmas spirit. Her heart melted at the anxiety and uncertainty on this young mum's face and she found it didn't feel too unnatural to say, 'OK.'

'Really? Oh, *thank* you. I'll bring the food and drink and everything,' Fallon gushed, looking as if she might cry. 'Would the 21st be OK, the day the schools break up? None of their friends will be able to come if it's on Christmas Eve itself.'

'Lovely,' Sky agreed. 'We'll have to think about seating, though, because I only have six kitchen chairs and a table.'

'You can have mine, too,' Marietta put in. 'It seats four.'

'I have a picnic set,' Jessie offered. 'How many kids will there be?'

Fallon's lip trembled. 'Oh, thank you all! Maybe ten, plus the twins, Zelda and Zara.'

'Invite more, if you can feed them,' Sky said recklessly. 'It's a big room.'

Fallon threw herself on Sky, which wasn't comfortable as she was standing and Sky was sitting. 'Thank you, thank you,' she sniffed. 'You're the best.'

Sky laughed off the effusive thanks. She didn't say she used to be the kid whose mum couldn't afford a party. At least, not as well as cider and wine.

Sky kept her end up in the quiz, but her mind was on when to get her Christmas food in. Good job that question asking to name a mammal that laid eggs was like ABC to her. *Duck-billed platypus,* she wrote on the answer sheet.

After the quiz – Marietta's Brain Bashers came third again – Jess and Ruth went into a huddle, before turning to Sky. 'I don't suppose we could borrow your room, too, could we?' Jess asked tentatively. 'There's a meeting about the Christmas Street judging – about a dozen of us. We planned to squeeze into Ruth's, but she's got her daughter's lot descending on her this weekend, and none of my rooms are big enough.' Ruth almost smiled at the mention of her daughter. It was only a slight rearrangement of her lips, but it was there.

'Erm . . .' Sky said again, picturing the Christmas Street Competition organisers invading her space. But she supposed she must take the rough with the smooth, when it came to developing community spirit. 'OK, it's nice the room's getting some use,' Sky said. Quickly, she added, 'So long as I don't have to join your committee.'

Jessie looked faintly disappointed. 'But you've been such an asset to the street since you came.'

Sky didn't mind being an asset but wasn't going to be part of any committee that contained Ruth. 'Wilf and I are making birdboxes,' she said firmly.

An hour later, she set off home again, trying to blow 'smoke' rings with her breath on the freezing air. For the first time, she was greeted by lights at the windows of The Corner House, telling her that her someone else was home, and was surprised by a sudden lightening of her heart. She turned up her path, admiring the illuminated watering can. It had a real dish of water under it now, for the wildlife, and she had to melt the ice every morning. The fat cakes in the trees were no longer recognisable as Christmas trees or bells, because the birds had been busily pecking. She made a mental note to make a fresh batch to hang for the Christmas Street judging a week from today.

She let herself in and found Courtney curled up on a sofa, the TV on and her phone in her hand. 'Wilf settle down OK in a strange bed?' Sky asked.

Courtney nodded. 'Surprisingly so – though he "forgot" to do his homework, so he'll have to do it in the morning. You're a star letting us move in. I can hardly believe we'll be spending Christmas here.'

'It'll be great.' Sky pulled off her coat and tossed it on the sofa. 'When I was in relationships, we always seemed to go to other people so it's fantastic to have friends at mine. A proper village Christmas! You'll have to cook your own turkey, though.'

'Mm. Of course.' Courtney's eyes had dropped to her phone. She coloured. 'Erm . . . would you mind babysitting on Monday evening? It's for a date, this time. I've been talking to a guy called Otis on the dating app and I'd quite like to meet him.'

'I don't mind,' Sky said, straight away, though aware what a big step her friend was taking. Then, after a moment to think: 'Are you going to tell Wilf it's a date? And . . . Daz?'

Courtney grimaced and dumped her phone on the table. 'Not Wilf,' she answered. 'But even if Lewis and I had officially split up, I wouldn't tell my son about a man I was seeing unless I thought the relationship was going to last. Daz, though . . .' She blew out her cheeks. 'Daz is a wonderful friend, but he can't decide my life for me. And neither can Lewis.'

Sky agreed. But she did hope Daz wouldn't turn up again while she was babysitting. 'Does . . . does Daz get drunk much?' she asked, trying to make it sound like a casual question.

Courtney stared at her. 'No more than anyone else, I shouldn't think. What an odd question.'

Sky wrinkled her nose. 'Yes. I don't know why I asked.' She hadn't told Courtney about the state of him when they'd had the spat. Daz had revealed himself to be a different man when he was drunk and, really, the best thing would be for Sky to forget that evening. And forget Daz.

Chapter Nineteen

On Saturday morning, Daz chanced upon Courtney and Sky outside Courtney's house.

Courtney waved a bag. 'We're clearing the contents of my fridge into Sky's.'

'Right,' he answered automatically. Sky was standing as frozen as if she'd been left outside all night and turned to ice, her gaze fixed on him. He hoped she wasn't going to kick off again and was about to carry on his errand to the village shop for a couple of things for his own fridge when Courtney's voice halted his steps.

She said, 'I should give you a heads up about something.'

'Oh?' He pushed his hands more deeply into his pockets. Sky was still regarding him unblinkingly. For some reason, her rabbit-in-the-headlights appearance annoyed him.

Courtney coloured. 'As there was tension around this subject before, I want to be transparent with you that I'm going on a date and Sky's agreed to babysit. I'll tell Lewis when I visit him on Sunday.'

Now Daz felt like the rabbit in the headlights. Or perhaps two pairs of headlights – Lewis's and Courtney's, leaving him with no idea how to hop out of the way.

Then suddenly Abi was flying up the drive, arriving in a flurry, throwing her arms about Courtney and hugging her with obvious relish. 'Courtney, I thought I heard your voice.' She'd been out of the house so much that Daz had barely seen her since he'd told her it was time to contact her HR department, and since the scene with Sky, he'd been too rocked by her unreasonable behaviour to push.

Now, over their heads, he saw Sky's expression was shuttered as her gaze moved from one person to another.

'Can I come in for coffee?' Abi demanded, as if Sky and Daz weren't there.

'We've moved in with Sky.' Courtney explained her boiler woes.

Abi swung on Daz. 'But they should spend Christmas with us, shouldn't they?'

With '*us*'? He glared at his ex in mixed irritation and astonishment. Then he saw dismay and shock flare in Sky's eyes, before the shutters came down again.

Courtney gave an uncomfortable laugh. 'Abi! We're already staying with Sky.'

'Oh. Oh, yes.' Abi giggled. For the first time, she looked at Sky. 'Hello, again.'

'Hello,' Sky returned colourlessly.

Abi and Courtney began to chat. Daz would have gone on his way, but Sky's expression made him pause. She looked so disappointed.

Daz was disappointed, too. Disappointed that Courtney was going to date after all and that Sky would enable it; disappointed in Abi for trying so blatantly to cut Sky out; disappointed that Sky was standing like a block of wood, avoiding his eye, when he felt she should have met his texted apologies with one of her own. But then he supposed Abi had never apologised for her excesses, either.

Then, Sky stirred. 'I'll go home, Courtney. Wilf will be impatient to begin those birdboxes.'

Courtney looked round. 'I'll be right behind you.' As Sky strode away, she gathered her bag to her chest and took a step or two after. 'I'll text you, Abi, and we can get together later. Maybe tonight, if Sky will babysit again.'

'That would be perfect.' Abi beamed.

Daz felt his scalp tighten at Abi acting as if she was once again at home in Winter Street. Then he spotted a green, chunky knit hat on the ground and swooped it up, knowing it was Sky's. It matched her eyes.

When Courtney had followed Sky, Daz abandoned his trip to the shop and followed Abi back across the road to his house.

Once indoors, Abi made to go upstairs but Daz stopped her. Quietly, he said, 'You couldn't have been more obvious if you'd carried a placard saying: *I'm here to reclaim my old boyfriend and my old friend.*'

Abi made as if to look injured and innocent. Then her expression changed. 'Is she something to you? Sky?'

'Not really,' he said, and his voice sounded bitter to his own ears, because that was only true because of Abi. Or maybe not, because presumably Sky would still have gone batshit crazy at him. He realised he was still holding Sky's hat and tossed it onto a table. 'But when you suggested Courtney and Wilf came for Christmas you trampled on her feelings. They're her guests. Not to mention,' he added, 'it's fucking presumptuous to invite people to *my* house, let alone ignore any Christmas plans I might have.' He didn't have many, but that wasn't the point.

She said, 'Sorry,' in a small voice. But he'd seen relief flicker in her eyes when he'd denied involvement with Sky.

'And it's time we talked,' he began. Behind him, the

letterbox clattered and the post pattered onto the doormat. Daz froze when he glanced down and saw an envelope bearing a cell and wing number. He sighed as he slit it open, aware of Abi slipping away up the stairs.

Dear Daz, Lewis had written.

> *Hope all's well etc.*
> *Hate to hassle you but Courtney's visiting on Sunday 18th. We're not allowed visits on Christmas Day, which is shitty. I'm going to ask her to let me come back when I'm released on licence – and NOT just to avoid being stuck in a hostel. I love her, even if I haven't shown that very well. So, if you get a chance to put in that good word for me, please do.*
> *I miss her and my little boy so much! It's killing me.*
> *Thanks millions,*
> *Lewis*

Daz stuck the letter in his pocket, feeling sick with sorrow for Lewis and his broken relationships. Courtney was indeed visiting on Sunday – tomorrow. Should he warn her what Lewis was going to ask of her?

Or should he register for the Email a Prisoner service as there was no time for a letter, and warn Lewis she planned to tell him she was going to date another man and had made it plain she was not going to listen to Daz?

He had no idea. And he was pretty sure he could hear Abi crying upstairs. Theatrics. Well, she was in luck. He was no longer in the mood to tackle her.

The Christmas Street committee had arrived at The Corner House, each carrying a chair, to use the big room. Marietta was among them, beaming and calling everybody 'pumpkin'.

Sky had retreated to the barn, watching Wilf painstakingly saw a rectangle from a piece of plywood. The template they'd downloaded and printed required five rectangles – two for the birdbox roof, two walls and a base – and two pentagons for the house ends. She had a small power saw and would start the first pentagon when she was happy that Wilf knew how to keep his fingers clear of the saw blade.

They wore coats and hats, even in the barn, in what the media was now terming 'the big freeze'. Sky had lost her favourite hat somewhere and had to wear her work-day one.

Wilf's face became red and perplexed whenever the saw caught in the plywood, or the blade deviated from the pencil mark. She'd shown him twice not to apply pressure on the up stroke, but it hadn't sunk in yet. You didn't learn by giving up, though.

As she watched him, a picture floated into her mind of Abi this morning. Had she reclaimed Daz as casually as she'd attempted to appropriate Courtney and Wilf? Abi was so girly and pretty, with her small frame and tiny rosebud mouth. Whenever she thought of her, Sky felt the most awful, bitter, green and bubbling jealousy, which made no sense when there could be nothing between herself and Daz, now. Not since he'd shown her tipsy Daz.

Courtney had arrived at The Corner House on Sky's heels, rolling her eyes. 'I'm imposing on you, Sky,' which had made Sky think, on an unpleasant shiver, that Courtney was about to declare that she and Wilf were accepting Abi's invitation to spend Christmas at Daz's house. Instead, Courtney had continued, 'You're already having Wilf tomorrow so I can visit Lewis, and Monday evening so I can go out with Otis. But is there any way you could have him tonight, too, so I can go out with Abi?' She'd given Sky a winning smile.

'Sure,' Sky had said, just relieved that it wasn't about Christmas arrangements. 'I'll be here, and Wilf will be here, so it's no trouble.'

Now, she said to Wilf, encouragingly, 'You're getting the hang of it. A long, slow stroke down. Good. That's almost a whole side cut out.'

Wilf puffed and panted over his task for another couple of minutes then gave a triumphant, 'There,' as a piece of plywood clattered to the floor and he held the remainder aloft. 'That's one wall done.'

'Fantastic.' Sky patted Wilf's narrow back. 'Do you want to do another? Or we could cut the pieces out with the jigsaw and then you can get involved with the gluing.'

'Jigsaw,' he decided promptly. His brown eyes danced. 'Isn't it funny that a power tool's called the same as a puzzle?'

She grinned. 'I suppose it is. Goggles on, if you're going to watch,' she ordered, and settled the plywood on the saw stool.

Then the barn door opened, and Daz walked in, mugs clutched in his hands. It was so unexpected that Sky jumped as if he'd prodded her with a pin.

He gave no signs of having noticed. 'Courtney sent out hot chocolate. You dropped your hat this morning, Sky.' He put down a mug each for Wilf and Courtney and, keeping one for himself, passed Sky her missing hat, her favourite green one.

'Thanks,' she said.

Wilf began to burble enthusiastically about the bird-boxes, explaining to Daz how the pieces would fit together. 'And we're going to paint them.'

Daz grinned at the excited boy. 'Amazing. By the way, I brought some chocolate digestives but left them on the kitchen table. Do you fancy fetching them?'

'Wowsers trousers, chocolate digestives,' Wilf enthused, and shot off through the barn door.

Daz turned to Sky. 'I'm sorry about Abi.'

Her neck bunched up. 'Trying to steal my Christmas you mean? Not your fault.'

'I know that,' he said, matching her short tone with his own.

Sky's stomach plunged as she remembered Abi at his bedroom window, and realised that he hadn't demurred when Abi had blithely issued her invitation. Was he finally making it plain that he was having ex sex? Or, more precisely, that Abi was no longer 'ex'?

It seemed she was destined never to know because Wilf powered back in, waving the biscuits, and when they'd eaten their share and the drinking chocolate had gone, Daz left with as little ceremony as he'd arrived. Sky set to cutting out rectangles and pentagons, beset with images of Daz making love to Abi in his bed, where he'd made love to Sky, too.

While Courtney was out with Abi that evening, Wilf played on his PlayStation, wearing his headset so he could talk to a friend he was playing remotely, shouting with excitement as his hands moved surely over the games controller.

Sky still felt unsettled about Daz getting back with Abi, and annoyed that she should care now she'd seen him in his true colours.

Would Courtney return tonight and explain awkwardly that she'd decided to spend Christmas with them after all? Sky would be alone again. In fact, she felt lonely already.

Marietta was visiting village friends and when Sky had called Nan Heather earlier, she'd been waiting to be picked up for dinner at Mo's house. Another name floated into her mind: Ron Murray. She'd said she'd FaceTime him – so why not now?

After texting first to check it was convenient, she propped up her phone on the kitchen table, sucked in a deep breath and prepared to set eyes on her grandfather for the first time.

And, with shocking speed, there he was, gazing back at her from the screen.

If any doubts lingered about their relationship, they vanished. His eyes were a pale wintry green, the eyes she saw in the mirror every day. He was balding with a trim white beard, and Freddy's Santa comment came back to her.

He beamed and Sky's eyes filled with tears. 'Hi,' she managed huskily, warmth stealing over her that there was someone so glad to see her.

Her grandfather had to harrumph before he could talk. 'You're a sight for sore eyes, Sky. What a beautiful woman, you are.' He leaned forward, peering at her in concentration. 'Much more like my side of the family than Trish. My hair was a bit like yours, when I had some.' He grinned as he stroked his shining head.

She laughed, drinking in his florid, good-natured face and his obvious excitement. 'It's good to see you, too,' she said, realising how much she meant it. They settled down to talk. He told her about the career he'd retired from, and how losing Stella had changed his retirement to a solitary thing. She thought his voice held a note of anticipation, as if he hoped she'd invite him to visit her, but she hesitated.

His next words made her warier still. 'I know you're not sure about speaking with your mother, but she asked me to pass on her contact details anyway,' he said, gruffly. 'She'd like to apologise for past behaviour, I think.'

Cynicism seeped into Sky's heart. 'Apologise? That's something new.'

Ron hesitated. 'All the more reason for you to give her the chance to do so, perhaps?'

'Perhaps. You can text me her number, I suppose.' She didn't say she'd use it.

Then she heard Wilf's feet thumping downstairs and he arrived, breathless, in the kitchen. 'Did Daz leave the rest of the biscuits? Who are you talking to?' With no regard for privacy, he squidged onto her chair beside her and peeped into the screen.

'It's my grandfather, Ron,' Sky said. 'I told you about him. This is the first time we've FaceTimed.'

'Cool,' answered Wilf. 'Hello, Ron.'

It was impossible not to fall for Wilf's untidy hair and puppy-like friendliness and Ron grinned. 'Good evening, young man. Hungry for biscuits, eh?'

'Always.' Wilf grinned back, then, turning to Sky, 'Can I have some?'

'Four,' Sky agreed, because that was what Courtney seemed to allow him. She explained to Ron who Wilf and Courtney were, then Wilf brought his biscuits back to munch as they all talked. Sky's heart gave a happy hop when the boy slipped an affectionate arm around her as he told Ron that they'd put five birdboxes together and would paint them soon.

When the call was eventually over, Wilf said, 'Your granddad seems cool. Why don't you go and meet him?' He cast a hopeful look at the rest of the digestives.

Sky, deciding she was in charge this evening, got him another. 'Why don't you go meet yours? He's only here in the village.'

Wilf looked surprised. 'But he's a misery guts. Though he didn't used to be,' he admitted.

She shrugged, taking a couple of biscuits for herself. 'He's upset about your dad.'

'Ha,' snorted Wilf. 'I will if you will.'

'What?' she said, more to give herself time than because she'd misunderstood.

'I'll see my granddad if you'll see yours. We could invite them both to the Christmas Street judging on Friday.'

Sky looked at Wilf's enquiring little face and thought how others had tried to get him to talk to his dad without any intention of doing anything half so scary themselves. 'OK,' she said with sudden resolution. 'We'll go to your granddad's cottage together tomorrow to invite him, if your mum's fine with it.' She pulled her big cardigan closer around herself, deciding she'd light the fire in the sitting room, even if it did make her think of Daz.

'OK, but he won't come,' Wilf declared. He glanced at the uncurtained kitchen window where the blackness had just begun to spot with white. 'Cool, it's snowing! Will you show me the animal tracks again tomorrow?'

Sky promised she would if they had time. 'We'll have a busy day, if we're also painting birdboxes. And I have to do some Christmas shopping.'

'Let's get it online now,' Wilf suggested, smothering a yawn. 'I'm looking forward to Christmas, now we're having it with you.'

Sky's throat closed up, so she just gave Wilf a big, silent hug. If she'd helped this sweet kid look forward to Christmas, then buying The Corner House had been worthwhile.

Chapter Twenty

Sky was getting used to other voices ringing out in The Corner House now, and people around the meal table. Wilf paused in spooning his porridge. 'When are we going out in the snow, Sky? It's Sunday, so no school.'

'Soon,' Sky promised.

Courtney, still in her dressing gown, stroked his hair. 'Are you sure you won't go with me to visit Dad?'

Mutinously, Wilf shook his head.

She sighed. 'At least I can tell him you're visiting Granddad, I suppose. How about you draw Dad a Christmas card?'

Another headshake.

Courtney produced a bought card. It showed a Christmas tree before a fire. 'OK. But I want you to put your name on this one, no arguing. I'll have to hand it in, but Dad will get it.'

Silently, Wilf wrote 'Wilf' on the card. No 'Merry Christmas' or 'love from'. Courtney grimaced but gave him a hug, nonetheless.

Leaving Courtney to dress, Sky and Wilf pulled on coats

and hats and stepped out into the snow, which squeaked beneath their boots. 'Cool,' breathed Wilf, gazing admiringly at the white edges to the trees. The snow had even settled on the wiring of the Christmas lights, as if someone had laced up the branches overnight. Then he giggled. 'Snow – cool. Geddit?'

They trudged up Winter Street, past Wilf's home on one side and Daz's on the other, Wilf skidding happily in the snow. Sky didn't look at Daz's house, not wanting to see his bedroom curtains closed and then speculate over what might be going on behind them.

Winter Street became Top Farm Road and in Hilary Close they picked up a footpath into the Carlysle Estate. Soon they became absorbed in spotting animal and bird tracks.

Wilf had remembered every track Sky had shown him before. 'No deer,' he sighed. 'I didn't see any in your garden, either.'

'They find sheltered spots in winter and hang out there,' Sky explained. 'They're probably in the wood around the lake.' She'd rediscovered the lake, but it would be too far to walk today if they were to call in on his grandfather.

Other villagers crunched along the footpaths, too, hurling snowballs or building snowmen. Wilf came across Eiran and another boy from school, rolling snow up like cotton wool and leaving a swathe of uncovered ground behind them. He helped for ten minutes, while Sky watched, happy he was with other kids. When the snowball was about three feet tall, it was too heavy to push, so Sky took pictures of the boys with it. Wilf tried to climb it but fell off with a loud, 'Oof!'

Giggling, he took the opportunity to make a snow angel, and even Sky participated, lying in the snow and feeling

298

the icy crystals trying to get between her scarf and hat. When they clambered up, Sky took photos of the angels and the boys' snowy backs.

When the other boys went home, Wilf let himself be herded towards Port Road, where his granddad Graham lived. 'Granddad's house is near the primary school,' Wilf said unenthusiastically. Then, brightening: 'There's Daz.'

Sky spotted the tall figure with the mixture of annoyance, jealousy and disappointment that was refusing to coalesce into acceptance of there being no future for them, not even for the friendship she'd tried to salvage from Abi's reappearance.

'Hey,' he greeted them, as they drew near. 'I've just had brunch with Mum and Dad. You look like walking snowmen.'

Sky brushed at her coat. 'Making snow angels,' she explained briefly, and let Wilf chatter about animal tracks and the giant snowball.

Then Wilf rolled his eyes. 'We're going to see Granddad. Me and Sky made a bargain that if I invited him to the Christmas Street judging, she'd invite hers.'

Daz sent her a quick look. 'Things still going well with Ron?' When she nodded, he gave Wilf's scarf a friendly tug. 'OK if I come along to Graham's?'

Sky thought he might have cleared it with her, too, but didn't argue after Wilf said, 'Yeah, great,' and looked relieved.

Graham's cottage boasted a small, square front garden and a squeaky gate. At the porch, Wilf hovered uncertainly.

Daz slipped an arm along his shoulders. 'Shall I knock?' Wilf nodded.

Knock, knock. Then, when there was no answer: *Knock, knock, knock.* Wilf looked hopeful. 'Maybe he's out.'

If he was, he'd gone before the snow began last night, Sky thought, as theirs were the only footprints on the snowy path. But then, slowly, the door opened. An elderly man peered out, his thinning hair sticking up, his eyes dull as they travelled from Daz to Wilf to Sky.

'Hiya, Graham,' Daz said jovially. 'Wilf wanted to see if you have everything you need in this weather.'

Graham smiled at Wilf, but it looked an effort. 'Hello, Wilford. I'm fine, thanks.' He paused, apparently at a loss for further conversation.

Wilf gave a small, polite 'Hello.'

It was Daz who kept things going, giving Sky sudden insight into why he'd invited himself along. 'This is Sky, who bought The Corner House. Courtney and Wilf are staying with her because their boiler's out of action.'

At least at this Graham's face creased in concern. 'No boiler? In that new house?'

Wilf joined in. 'It was freezing. They can't get the part for ages, so Sky invited us for Christmas. Mum's gone to see Dad today.' He paused and glanced at his grandfather and away. 'I didn't want to go.'

'No.' Graham sighed, evidently seeing Wilf's point of view.

Sky gave Wilf a tiny nudge. 'Didn't you want to invite your granddad somewhere?'

'Yeah.' Wilf cleared his throat. 'It's the Christmas Street Competition judging on Friday. Do you want to come? Me and Daz put up lights on our house, his house, Marietta's and Sky's, and me and Sky made birdboxes for her garden and we're going to decorate them this afternoon.'

Silently, Sky urged Graham to see what a fine grandson he had, and respond positively.

Graham gazed at Wilf. Finally, he cleared his throat. 'I'm not sure.'

Wilf began to turn away. 'It's OK. I know you're a mardy arse 'cos of Dad. I get it.'

Sky gaped at Wilf.

Daz looked away and coughed.

Graham's brows drew down. 'What did you just call me, young man?'

Slowly, Wilf's eyes grew round, as if he was realising what he'd said. Then he stuck out his chin. 'I called you mardy arse, Granddad. Sorry it's a swear word, but you are. You never used to be,' he added. 'But we're all sad, you know. Not just you.'

Graham gave a sudden snort. Sky looked at him carefully, trying to identify the emotion behind the strange sound. Then she saw the eyes were twinkling, and let her shoulders relax. He drew his brows down fiercely, though. 'Seeing as you asked so . . . nicely,' he said drily. 'What time?'

Wilf's face lit up, and he laughed. 'The judging starts at seven but there's going to be food and drink from six.'

For the first time, Graham gave his grandson a proper smile. 'I'll be there, lad.'

Graham didn't invite them in but catching a glimpse of piled up newspapers and dead plants in the hall behind him, Sky wasn't sorry. As they tramped back down the garden path, neither adult reprimanded Wilf for his language and Sky assumed that Daz, like her, was biting back laughter.

They trudged through the snow, Wilf chatting to both Sky and Daz but Sky and Daz not talking to each other. When they reached The Corner House, Daz carried on without hesitating, heading for whatever – or whoever –

301

awaited him at home. Wilf looked at Sky. 'Shall we check Marietta's OK in the snow?'

'Good idea,' Sky answered, suspecting Wilf was also interested in checking out Marietta's cookie tin.

Though she welcomed her visitors with cinnamon cookies and steaming mugs of hot chocolate, Marietta proved to be subdued. Even her cowboy boots stood facing the corner of the room, as if hiding their faces.

'Is everything OK?' Sky asked tentatively, when she noticed Marietta was doing more gazing into her mug than drinking from it.

Marietta sighed. 'I don't want to trouble you with it, pumpkin.' But her eyes began to look pink.

'It won't be a trouble,' Sky said softly.

Marietta sniffed miserably. 'Ira, my son, was supposed to bring his wife and kids over here for Christmas from Indonesia but the kids have gone and got measles. And the usual Christmas lunch at The Three Fishes for those alone is cancelled because Elvis's mum's sick and they're going to visit her.'

Sky took Marietta's hand, hating to think of the friendly little woman facing Christmas alone. 'Then come and join us at The Corner House. Wilf and Courtney are there already. A big Christmas will be so much fun.'

Marietta glanced up uncertainly. 'Oh, my, I wasn't trying to invite myself.'

'You didn't. Please come,' Sky assured her promptly. 'We'd love it. Nothing swanky, you know – just festive food, Christmas movies and good company.'

'And presents,' Wilf put in invitingly, reaching for another cookie.

A small smile lifted the corners of Marietta's mouth. 'Really?'

'*Really*,' Sky declared. 'You were my first friend here in Winter Street. If not for you, I wouldn't have settled back into Middledip half so quickly.'

When they left an hour later, Marietta looked much more her usual self.

Sky felt happy, too, until she spotted Abi whizzing up Winter Street in her little car, and wondered if she was rushing back to see Daz.

Wilf proved a welcome distraction. 'Shall we go in so you can invite your granddad to the Christmas Street judging?'

Sky shoved Daz and Abi from her mind. 'Yes, let's.'

Abi was in the kitchen, cooking. As Daz crossed the hall, he could hear her music blaring from her smart speaker, and wondered why he'd never noticed before that she filled the air with her choice of music without wondering whether others shared her wish to hear it.

But at least she was here in the house, so he could finally tell her that it was time she left. He'd lock her in and make her listen, if he had to. Then a flicker of movement on the other side of the front door glass alerted him to an approaching figure. As he was only two strides away, he reached out and opened the door. 'Courtney,' he said, when he saw his visitor. 'Come in.'

'Thanks.' She smiled as she stepped in, but then her gaze flicked in the direction of the kitchen where Abi's singing, along to Ariana Grande, wasn't quite reaching the high notes. 'Ah. I forgot she'd be here.'

'Let's go up to my computer room,' he suggested, aggravated that he couldn't have a private conversation in his own house.

'Thanks.' Courtney went ahead up the stairs, tugging off her coat.

In the attic, she took the office chair, sitting on her hands and twirling pensively. 'I saw Lewis,' she said, without preamble. 'I told him I'm going on a date.'

Daz flumped into the gaming chair, feeling the familiar chill when he thought of Lewis, locked up and miserable. And now more miserable, surely. 'Right.'

A sigh escaped Courtney and her light brown eyes fastened on his. 'Daz, I don't want this to be an issue between you and me. Lewis had no right to try and involve you. He's determined to hold out hope for the future but all I promised was that I'd continue to encourage Wilf to allow contact. I think he understands my position,' she added softly.

Daz tried to reconcile this 'understanding' with his memory of Lewis's tears; the letters begging for help. Had his friend bravely maintained his composure for the duration of Courtney's visit? Had he returned to his cell and only allowed his heart to break there?

Courtney gave Daz's leg a nudge with her foot, as if aware of his thoughts. 'It's truly between me and Lewis.'

His chest ached. 'I understand. I'll butt out.'

Her whole body seemed to relax. 'Thanks. You've been a star and I feel bad that you were stuck in the middle.' After a few moments, she cocked her head as if she could hear the music from down in the kitchen. 'Abi's still here. You know she's hoping . . . ?'

'I won't be revisiting our relationship,' he said, guessing that's what she meant. 'I felt I had no choice but to give her time to sort herself out, but she's pushing her luck.'

Musingly, Courtney said, 'Last night, when we were out, she kept asking about what was going on between you and Sky.'

His heart twisted. Sky had looked gorgeous when he'd seen her with Wilf this morning, though she'd talked to

304

Daz as little as possible. He told himself it was better that way, if she was so . . . well, unbalanced, the way she'd yelled and shoved him out of the door that night. He winked at Courtney. 'Ah,' he said. 'That's where *you* have to butt out.'

On Monday, Daz left the door to his attic computer room open while he wrote handover notes for whoever would take his role, so he could hear when Abi opened the spare room door and trod softly downstairs. Determined not to let her race off somewhere and avoid him again, Daz padded downstairs after her.

He found her grabbing a cereal bar. Her coat was over her arm, as if she had indeed planned yet another speedy exit. 'Hey,' he said, putting out two mugs beside the kettle, a silent signal that he expected her to stay. 'You're going to talk to your boss today.'

Visibly, she jumped. 'No, I don't think—'

'It's time, Abi.' Daz glanced at her phone in her hand, just as it lit up with a call notification. The phone must have been silenced but the caller ID said *Kremena*. 'And it looks like your flatmate's calling,' he observed. 'You can talk to her, too.'

Abi looked away, bottom lip jutting. 'Not sure I want to talk to her.'

Daz knew this Abi, when her cheeks flushed, and she couldn't meet his gaze. His bullshit detector pinged. 'But you need to.' Meanly, disregarding all the rules of privacy, he positioned himself to block the only way out of the kitchen area and leant on the wall.

With a great show of reluctance, red flags burning in both cheeks, Abi picked up the call. 'Kremena,' she said crisply.

Though Abi held her phone to her ear and Daz was several paces distant, he had no trouble hearing Kremena's end of the conversation. 'Abi,' she wailed. 'Why haven't you been taking my calls? I caught Spiros hitting on someone else. He's obviously slime. I should never have believed him over you, and I feel so guilty. I've explained to Andrew at work, and I don't think he wants you to resign. I don't, either. What about Christmas? We had so many plans together. Come home, and we can get everything sorted. I'm so sorry, Abs.'

Daz raised one quizzical eyebrow.

Abi's entire face became one giant blush. 'I don't know . . .'

Daz folded his arms and raised the other eyebrow, too, leaving her in no doubt that he was hearing every word. If he'd ever harboured doubts about the wisdom of this confrontation, they evaporated. She'd so obviously seized on the spat with Kremena as an excuse to throw herself onto his mercy and hope for developments. She'd probably even invented the depression and happy pills, which was *so* not on, on every level.

Abi glanced his way and seemed to deflate. 'Um, OK,' she said resignedly. 'I'll call Andrew. If that goes well, then I'll be back later today.' Her shoulders drooped still further. 'I suppose London's where my life is now.'

While Abi finished up the call, Daz made the coffee. When she put down the phone, he handed her a mug. 'All sorted, then,' he said quietly, too relieved to call her on the fact that she'd obviously been taking him for a fool for far too long. Shame her getting between Sky and him had become moot.

'Yeah.' Obviously mortified, her gaze slid to the window and the snow that glittered fiercely beneath a blue sky.

He couldn't resist underlining that he was on to her and all her crap about having nowhere to go. 'I hope you have a happy Christmas with your friends.'

'Yeah,' she repeated. 'You, too.'

Daz thought that this festive season would prove more to be got through than enjoyed, but he said, 'Thanks.'

Chapter Twenty-One

On Monday, Sky spent the day in Bettsbrough, finishing her Christmas shopping, listening to the Salvation Army band on the square and admiring the strings of giant silver baubles that criss-crossed the streets and reflected the Christmas shoppers below.

Reaching home, though tired by the crowds and the different carols playing in every shop, she wrapped her presents in snowman-bestrewn paper. The Corner House was looking as festive inside as it did out, thanks to swags of greenery wound with baubles everywhere. Sky had bought a Christmas tree in a pot so she could plant it outdoors after the festive season, and it had almost vanished under an avalanche of tinsel because Wilf had dressed it. He'd coaxed Courtney to help him retrieve their tree from their house and put that up in Sky's hallway, too.

In the evening, Courtney went on her date with Otis, the man from the dating app, meeting him at a pub off the A14 and texting Sky *All OK* and *leaving for home now* messages.

Sky stayed up until she got home but Courtney was quiet, saying only, 'He was nice enough, I suppose,' before she yawned and drifted off to bed. Sky's heart ached for her friend, who was so obviously struggling to find a way to live her life after her husband's imprisonment. It didn't sound as if Otis would be the magic ingredient.

Wednesday's kiddies' party in the big room passed off with a lot of noise. Finishing school early for the Christmas holidays, Wilf volunteered to 'help', which involved him lording it over eight-year-olds and assisting in the eating of party food.

Nan Heather spent Thursday at The Corner House with Sky and Wilf – Courtney being at work – because Rotten Row's water was off owing to a broken main. Mo was committed elsewhere and Sky enjoyed Nan's company. Wilf formed an instant alliance with her, as every kid seemed to, and they raided the Christmas biscuits and played card games that Wilf would normally eschew in favour of PlayStation.

In the afternoon, Wilf went up Winter Street to play Daz's PC, and Sky was glad that, at eleven years of age, he was well old enough to go alone.

All week, snow showers topped up the lying snow, like a decorator giving the world a fresh coat of white paint. Everyone was aware that other Christmas Streets were being judged elsewhere in Cambridgeshire and Jessie WhatsApped everyone urging them to cross their fingers that the snow remained, as she was sure the streets judged in snow would fare better than any judged in horrible brown slush. Local radio presenter Chatty Charlie would be one of their judges, along with Janette Meredith-Parker from the local paper. An organiser plus a representative from the business sector would complete the judging posse. *We need to win this, team!* she signed off.

Sky's birdboxes were up, and on the Friday of the judging she, Wilf, Eiran and Josie tied the new bell-shaped or Christmas-tree-shaped fat cakes to the trees in place of the heavily pecked ones. They used different coloured foil ribbons, to reflect the lights when they came on, and Sky kept going up to the terrace to brush snow from the solar panels, ensuring they'd be properly charged.

The snow floated to earth like white feathers, turning the treetops into judges' wigs, and also muffled sound so it was a surprise to look up Winter Street and see that refreshment stands had already appeared outside houses. Daz was helping Marietta set up her roasted chestnut stand and Wilf and Eiran joined in, making the canopy supports look like candy canes with red and white ribbons.

Throughout the day, Sky's heart put in an extra beat. Her grandfather would soon be arriving. It was still surreal to know he existed, let alone that he'd soon be here, flesh and blood.

Courtney arrived home having finished work for her Christmas break, pink-cheeked with cold after leaving her car on Main Road and walking the last bit. 'I hardly dared leave footprints in the snow in case the Christmas Street committee told me off.' She laughed, throwing off her coat. 'Doesn't Winter Street look splendid? I need to change into warm things.' Wilf had returned from Marietta's and she grabbed him for a big hug. 'Put two pairs of socks on and your big boots.'

Wilf's eyes shone with excitement. 'Doesn't Sky's garden look awesome? And it's still snowing. It's like being in Switzerland.' He scampered upstairs.

Sky, too, followed Courtney's suggestion of extra socks,

though she had snow boots. Back downstairs, she'd just found a mitten that had lost itself behind the radiator when the front door knocker sounded. A thrill shot through her so sharp it was almost painful. Taking a deep breath, she answered the door.

On the doorstep stood a man with a white beard and a fleece hat, looking apprehensive and excited. 'Sky,' he said hoarsely.

They stood perfectly still, drinking each other in. Ron Murray. Her grandfather, green eyes glinting with the hint of tears. Then, somehow, she was in his arms, feeling wanted and loved – and a bit squashed – while he wordlessly patted her back.

Then Wilf's voice behind her said, 'I always get in trouble for leaving the door opened like that. It lets the heat out.'

Laughing, Sky ushered Ron inside. 'Thank you for coming.'

Ron's voice was tight with emotion. 'This is like all my Christmases come at once.'

Wilf, having FaceTimed with Ron and discussed biscuits, treated him like an old friend and when Courtney came downstairs, she followed suit.

At six o'clock, they hurried out into Winter Street to join neighbours as bundled up as they could possibly be in scarves, hats, mittens, coats and boots. 'It's *freezing*,' cried Wilf, cuddling himself dramatically. But then Josie and Eiran came up and the children wandered up the road to construct a slide on the pavement.

Courtney danced about on her tiptoes to keep warm. 'I suppose I ought to stop them, in case someone slips and hurts themselves, but I don't want to be a spoilsport. And look at how many other kids are joining in. It's good for Wilf.'

Sky laughed. 'I made slides when I was a kid. Any free entertainment was good entertainment.' She tugged her hat down more snugly, then peered at an approaching figure. 'Isn't this your father-in-law?'

Courtney started. 'Hell's bells. I never thought he'd really come when you said Wilf had invited him.' She visibly squared her shoulders. 'I ought to make him welcome, hadn't I?'

'It might pave the way for a better relationship,' Sky agreed. Then a lovely vision of the big Christmas that she was allowing to evolve came to her and, daringly, she added, 'You can invite him to The Corner House on Christmas Day, if you want. Tell him Marietta's coming, too.'

Courtney looked astonished. 'Seriously?'

Sky shrugged, enjoying slowly becoming accustomed to the feeling of being a part of things. 'Don't let him be alone.' She watched Courtney shuffle through the snow to intercept Graham, who wore a woolly cap with a scarf tied over it. Feeling suddenly shy, Sky turned to Ron. 'How about you? You've probably got loads of Christmas Day plans, but you'd be welcome, if not.'

Ron's green eyes glowed. 'I'd love to,' he said. 'Friends have invited me but I'm sure they won't mind.' Then, as if frightened the emotion would overcome him, he said gruffly, 'Looks as if there's a barney going on over there.'

They headed to Marietta's chestnut stand, where Marietta was in animated discussion with Ruth.

'Don't be stupid,' Marietta said flatly.

Ruth glared. 'It's important—'

'What's up?' Sky demanded. Then a chill that was nothing to do with the snow climbed her spine as Daz stepped out of Marietta's garden, no doubt also drawn by the debate.

312

Marietta blinked away tears. 'Ruth doesn't want me to light the chestnut brazier in case it melts the snow.'

Before Sky could echo Marietta's declaration that Ruth was being stupid, Daz told Ruth casually, 'According to the WhatsApp group, the judges have arrived in Top Farm Road, ready to progress down the street with the photographer.'

Abruptly forgetting all about the chestnuts, Ruth turned and scurried away.

Sky tilted her head as she regarded Daz. If it wasn't for how he was when he was drunk, Daz would be such a great guy. But . . . *in vino veritas*. A drunk showed their true personality.

Still, as he'd been helpful when she hadn't known what to do about Ron, she introduced him. The men regarded each other keenly as they shook hands.

Courtney arrived with her father-in-law in tow, who trailed a step behind as if unsure of his welcome. 'Graham would love to join the Christmas Day gathering at The Corner House.' Then, seeing Daz, 'How about you? You'll come, won't you?'

Courtney inviting someone to her house on Christmas Day without consulting her wrong-footed Sky, but it would be awkward to rescind the invitation so, politely, she said, 'I expect you already have Christmas Day planned but Marietta, Ron and maybe Graham are joining Courtney and Wilf and me, and you and Abi would be welcome to drop by. I think we've bought enough to feed an army.'

A guarded look entered Daz's eyes. 'Abi and I won't—' Then a loud bang interrupted whatever he'd been about to say.

Marietta leapt back from her brazier. 'Oh, my. I think I let the gas run too long before I pressed the ignition.'

While Daz checked that the brazier was burning safely now, Sky was glad to chat to Graham, though smarting that Daz had obviously been about to brush the invitation off.

She and Ron, Courtney and Graham, moved up the street to find spiced lemonade and mulled wine. Sipping the warming brews, they paused to watch the children enjoying their pavement ice slide, squealing with triumph if they achieved the whole slippery journey on their feet.

An older gentleman snuggled into his scarf and grumbled that the slide was a danger to unwary pedestrians.

Another echoed Sky, earlier, when he pointed out, 'I used to do the same. Didn't you?'

'But we're older and wiser, now,' the first man said. 'We ought to stop it.'

It was Graham, unexpectedly, who chimed in, 'They're only kids. Let them have some fun. It's not often we get a white Christmas.' And nobody else complained.

While Courtney reminisced with Graham about a snowy family holiday in Scotland when Wilf had been young enough to be pulled along on a toboggan, Ron chatted animatedly to Sky about how pleased he was to be invited to the Christmas Street Competition, repeating, 'Absolutely delightful. How wonderful. Can't believe I'm here,' until Sky began to believe he meant it, and relaxed.

She even managed to open up to him sufficiently to murmur shyly, 'Thirty-nine years is a long time to wait to meet your grandfather, but I think the wait was worth it.' Ron clutched both her gloved hands in his, and beamed as brightly as the lights around them, and Sky thought her heart would burst.

Presently, a knot of people progressed down the street, Jess on one side and Ruth on the other, while a young

314

woman took photos of the flickering, pulsing Christmas lights. 'This must be the judging panel,' Sky remarked. 'Jessie asked me to stand by in my garden, ready to explain the solar lights, fat balls and birdboxes. As it's at the end of the street, it'll provide a sort of full stop to the judges' tour.'

Ron, part way through a conversation with Graham, waved her on her way. 'I'll be fine chatting to your delightful friends.'

Sky set off, grabbing a bag of hot chestnuts from Marietta en route to keep her hands warm as she waited beside her open gate, which she and Wilf had wound around with greenery.

Daz was standing near the mulled wine stand.

She sighed. Their two nights together had been incredible, but he'd been horrible when boozed up. Angry. Towering over her. Stinking. She shuddered, glad he'd refused her Christmas invitation, no matter how ungraciously. If he liked getting drunk, Christmas would be the ideal time. Imagine if he got like that again.

The procession of judges hove nearer. Vaguely, she recognised the local radio presenter, Chatty Charlie, popular for a morning show filled with innuendo he somehow got away with because it was funny. Janette Meredith-Parker, the reporter, was beside him. A couple were part of the group, too, the woman clinging to the man's arm. Then the man halted. 'Hello, Sky.'

Sky snapped out of her thoughts of Daz and focused. 'Freddy?' The woman – Minnie, naturally – was staring Sky's way. Sky gazed back, bemused. Freddy and Minnie knew she lived in Winter Street, of course, but their appearance had taken her entirely by surprise.

Jessie fluttered closer. 'Do you folks know each other? Freddy's representing the business group that's sponsored the competition, Sky. He told me he lived in Middledip as a child.'

Minnie looked po-faced. 'Sky's an ex-employee.' Somehow, she made it sound as if Sky had been caught dipping into the company's bank account.

She flushed, but said calmly, 'Freddy and I have known each other since we were kids. He's my foster brother. We were both cared for by Heather Elsworth and visited her together recently.'

Minnie looked at her fiancé in evident surprise. No doubt that didn't fit with her aim of coaxing Freddy it was best to forget his roots.

Freddy kept his gaze trained politely on Jess. 'It was coincidence that I was allocated Middledip. I didn't know until this afternoon.'

Chatty Charlie redirected the conversation by turning to Sky. 'We understand there's something special about your garden, erm . . .'

'Sky Terran,' she supplied. 'I wanted to be part of the Winter Street entry, of course, but I'm interested in wild-life and ecological issues, too.' She went on to speak about the solar-powered lights, the water left out for the wildlife and the Christmas-themed fat balls for the birds: '—which feed squirrels, too, if they venture into the cold, because they don't know the fat balls aren't really for them,' she finished. All the time she was speaking, both Janette Meredith-Parker and Chatty Charlie held mics towards her. The photographer asked for a shot of her holding up a Christmas-tree-shaped fat ball.

Sky was aware of Minnie, looking put out, on the fringes of things. Mentally, she shrugged. If Minnie couldn't cope with Sky in the neighbourhood limelight, it was her problem.

Then Jessie leapt in. 'Well, judges, shall I show you to my home for the warming coffee and cake I promised you?'

The attention was removed from Sky as if by a switch.

Minnie began talking to the journalist. Jessie and Ruth herded their VIP guests like sheepdogs, one fawning and the other grumpy. Marietta gave out paper bags of chestnuts as they passed.

All at once, Sky was tired. It had been a shock, seeing Freddy, and the easy way he and Minnie had turned away saddened her. The delightful, feathery snow was giving way to tiny, hard little flakes that stung. The spiced lemonade had left her with a funny taste and hot chocolate appealed more. Stepping back, she began up her path.

'Sky, mate. Got a minute?' It was Freddy's voice, unusually tentative and unsure.

Surprised, she spun around. There he was, in her garden, bulky in the long woollen coat he usually wore over a suit, hands buried in its pockets. 'Sure,' she said cautiously, wondering what he'd come back to say this time.

He huddled into his coat. 'I was just thinking of when we lived in Middledip.'

She smiled. 'Happy days.' This was firm ground. They'd both been happy at Nan Heather's.

He grinned, looking suddenly boyish. 'Minnie weren't that pleased when we found out our judging patch was Middledip, but I was. It feels good to be back here.' He cleared his throat. 'It made me see why you did what you did to get The Corner House.'

Her forehead felt as if it might crack in the cold as she furrowed it in a frown. 'What I did?' Her mind flew back to the auction and how heavy with misery she'd felt. 'All I did was buy a property that had gone above your ceiling

317

price. If I hadn't bought it, someone else would have.' Someone like Daz.

Freddy looked wrong-footed, as if he'd forgotten that vital detail. 'S'pose. But you knew how much I wanted it. You could have rung me and asked to go higher.'

A snort escaped her. 'To be told "not fucking now", like when I rang to discuss my resignation? Anyway, the interval between bids lasts seconds, as you well know. You'd have had to be on the line, ready, and you weren't, because you were meeting Minnie's family.' But something about the conversation, about the way he was trying to allocate blame, his reaction to her buying The Corner House, was escaping her. For the first time, she looked beneath the discord that Minnie had artfully created. Slowly, light dawned. 'Oh, Freddy, you wanted the house more than I realised. Were you looking for a return to Middledip, too?'

'Well . . . S'pose.' He banged his gloved hands together and looked away. 'I shouldn't have let Minnie talk me into setting the ceiling price so low.'

That was the last piece of the puzzle to slot into place. 'Ah.' Cautiously, she said, 'Minnie's never keen on reminders of your childhood.'

He sighed. 'No. She doesn't think it's good for me.'

Sky hoped that Minnie's unfortunate attitude did spring from love. Behind the trees, the noise and merriment in Winter Street continued, Sky half-listening to Marietta chatting to someone and the sounds of kids playing further up the street. Snatches of conversation floated to her about mulled wine, conjecture about whether any of their sound bites would be used when the results of the Christmas Street Competition were announced on Chatty Charlie's Christmas Eve show, tomorrow. Whether Winter Street could possibly have *won*.

Then an impatient but well-spoken little voice emerged over the chatter. 'Where on earth did Fred-fred get to? He was just behind me and then he disappeared.'

Next came Ruth's voice. 'Maybe he's in Sky's house, as he's her brother?'

Minnie gave a sigh. 'He's not her brother. They were in the same foster home briefly, that's all. She was a brat with an alkie mother and he was kind enough to look out for her.'

'Really?' demanded Ruth, sounding fascinated at this gossip.

'Really,' Minnie confirmed. 'She latched on to Fred-fred and he found her a job.' Sky stood, frozen in more ways than one, unable to even look at Freddy as Minnie's dismissive discourse ran on. 'She left the business quite suddenly. I had no idea Fred-fred had seen her since.' Minnie's cultured tones lowered. 'Nor that he'd seen the funny old woman who looked after them. I suppose he felt he had to drop in and give her money for Christmas or something.'

Sky jumped as Freddy's roar almost split her ear. '*Minnie!*'

From the other side of the trees came a crystal silence.

Freddy stomped down the path and rounded the trees. 'What the bleedin' 'ell, Minnie? Everything you just said was either bullshit or spin.'

'Oh,' said Minnie in a small voice.

Hurriedly, Ruth said, 'Well, I'll leave you two to your conversation.'

Through a gap in the trees, Sky watched Freddy and Minnie retreating up Winter Street towards Top Farm Road, backs stiff and faces turned crossly towards one another. 'Wow,' she said aloud. She ought to be feeling triumphant that Freddy had heard Minnie at her worst, but she hoped Freddy would be OK. He'd looked winded.

Ron came down the street, the lights illuminating his beard. 'My word. Was there a fracas?'

She summoned a smile. 'A bit of a falling-out.'

He stamped his feet. 'I'll leave now, darling. It will be a slow journey in the snow. I'll make it back for Christmas Day, though.'

The word 'darling' warmed her more than any hot chocolate could have, and – spontaneously – she gave him a hug. 'Will you be all right? There's one bedroom left free here if you want to stay.'

Ron grinned. 'I'll be fine, dear. I'm too old for camping out with no toothbrush or fresh clothes.' He returned her hug with interest and vanished into the night.

All Sky wanted was a hot bath before the others came home, time to herself to get used to the idea of a warm and loving granddad in her life. Alongside that hovered the skin-crawling knowledge that Sky's very existence, and a background she couldn't help, made Minnie, who'd been brought up in a comfortable home with every advantage, describe her so distastefully to someone she'd just met.

Experiencing such contrasting emotions was exhausting.

Chapter Twenty-Two

The news broke on the Chatty Charlie Christmas Eve show, immediately after the eleven o'clock weather and travel.

All morning, the chatty voice of Charlie had been foreshadowing the announcement. 'Which Cambridgeshire street has won the Christmas Street Competition? Which charity will receive ten thousand pounds? Stay tuned . . .' Sound bites played in from every street that had entered. Courtney, Marietta and Sky listened as they made mince pies and delicious-smelling cinnamon stars in Sky's warm, sugar-laden kitchen. Thawing towards his granddad, Wilf had gone to Graham's to rescue his Christmas tree from a dusty cupboard and decorate it.

'I wish Chatty Charlie would get on with the announcement,' Marietta grumbled, shaking icing sugar over her latest batch of cinnamon stars.

Then, just as the eleven o'clock news approached, a sound bite played and Courtney squealed. 'That's you, Sky!'

Sky paused, mincemeat jar in hand, neck prickling at the odd sensation of hearing herself say, 'I'm interested in wildlife and ecology,' then going on about fat cakes and birdboxes. 'Wow,' she breathed, appalled. 'Don't I sound an insufferable smartarse?'

The others roared with laughter. 'You do not,' Courtney said, giving her a squeeze that left flour all over Sky's Christmas jumper. 'You sound interesting and caring.'

News items followed. Snow was still coating Cambridgeshire's roads. Christmas shopping was rocking the high street. Then came travel news and the weather forecast – freezing temperatures that would make conditions slippery, in view of the already fallen snow – and finally Chatty Charlie got to the point.

'My guest today is Janette Meredith-Parker from the paper, who, as you know, has been part of the Christmas Street Competition every bit as much as our wonderful radio station.' And they went all over the whole Christmas Street Competition scenario as if they hadn't been talking about it all day.

'Blabbermouths,' Marietta groused, setting the cinnamon stars to cool.

'I hadn't realised there had been so many entries,' said Courtney. 'It sounds like dozens. Winter Street doesn't stand a chance.'

Then, finally, Chatty Charlie cried, 'So, Janette, put us out of our misery. Tell us which Cambridgeshire street has won the Christmas Street Competition and *ten . . . thousand . . . pounds* for its nominated charity.'

A theatrical rustling of paper. Janette Meredith-Parker cleared her throat. Then, finally, she cried, 'Well, Charlie and lovely listeners, the winner *is*—' a theatrical pause '—Winter Street from Middledip village!'

Sky, Courtney and Marietta stopped and stared at each other. Then, as one, roared, 'We *won!*' And threw their arms around each other, flour and icing sugar flying.

Janette Meredith-Parker went on. 'Their charity is Chester's House in Bettsbrough, a haven for young adults who need somewhere to stay. Well, well, well, congratulations to Winter Street and the residents who worked so hard. For me, that eco garden swung it, Charlie.'

'It was so different,' Charlie agreed. 'It brings awareness to things we should all think about more.'

Marietta and Courtney swung around on Sky with huge eyes and excited grins.

Sky clapped her hands to her cheeks. 'It's just a good story within a good story, that's all. But we *won*, right?' Then their phones began to ping with excited messages from the Winter Street Christmas Comp WhatsApp group, and it was ten minutes before Sky remembered the mince pies in the oven.

In a couple of minutes, Wilf burst in, Graham following more sedately behind. 'We won!' Wilf hollered. 'We heard it on Granddad's radio. Isn't that awesome? Shame we don't get any of the money. Ooh, can I have a cookie?'

Courtney gave him a hug. 'I can see I'll have to explain the meaning of the word "charity",' she said with mock severity. 'But you can certainly have a cookie because you helped with the lights on at least four houses, so you deserve it.'

Then they all dragged on their coats and went outside, where Winter Street was alive with people congratulating each other and exchanging jubilant high fives. Jessie appeared with a stunned expression and boxes of Roses chocolates to pass round. Marietta fetched cookies and Sky mince pies while Ruth brought out the tea urn, and proved that even she could smile, sometimes.

The residents of Winter Street were becoming adept at mini street parties.

* * *

On Christmas Day, Sky awoke before the others – surprising as Wilf was in the house and presents waited, piled beneath the tree. Snuggled in her robe, she stood at her bedroom window and watched the winter sun dress the sky in a coloured coat of misty mulberry, apricot and blue. Beneath, the snow twinkled as if with a million lights.

Beautiful.

How lucky she was to be back in Middledip. It had been good to her once before, and now she had neighbours and friends with whom to spend Christmas. No luxury festive break could compare.

Hearing Wilf's excited voice, she pulled back her hair into a messy topknot and hurried down to light the fire she'd lain ready last night, and switched on the tree lights to glow gently.

Wilf burst into the sitting room, his dressing gown flying open over red pyjamas. 'Mum's coming down and we can open our presents.' He grabbed a gift and then shoved it hastily back in the pile. 'But she said not to touch them before she got here or I'd have to wait till Boxing Day,' he whispered.

Sky laughed at his round-eyed trepidation. 'Let's make hot chocolate,' she whispered back. 'That will bring her down.'

'Cool.' Wilf sprang up and raced across the hall.

The smell of chocolate worked, and Courtney soon appeared, yawning. 'Merry Christmas.' She hugged Sky and then tied Wilf's dressing gown belt.

Soon they were tearing at wrapping paper. Wilf had bought Sky new gardening gloves and Courtney a box of lavender-scented toiletries. 'Aw, thank you, darling,' Courtney said, kissing the end of his nose.

Sky hugged him. 'You shouldn't have spent your pocket money on me. I didn't expect a lovely gift like that.'

Wilf looked bemused by her naïvety. 'I didn't. Daz gave me present-buying money, like Dad used to.'

'How kind of him.' Sky's heart ached that Daz couldn't be so nice all the time.

Courtney had bought Sky a new coffee maker, which Sky was sure she couldn't really afford. Courtney waved her reservations away. 'You're worth it. Look what a lovely friend you are to Wilf and me.'

'Aw.' Sky gulped, and presented her with a luxury spa gift set, in return.

After seeking Courtney's advice, she'd bought Wilf a voucher for a computer game store, but as that was boring, had also made him a wooden bug house filled with cones and cut-up bamboo tubes, to attract insects into his garden in spring.

Wilf greeted every present with, 'Wowsers trousers, thank you,' and looked as joyful and delighted as a child should look on Christmas morning. Eventually, though, all the presents had been opened. Wilf went to his room to play a PlayStation game Courtney had bought him. Courtney put the turkey in the oven while Sky showered and blow-dried her hair, then began on the vegetables.

When Marietta arrived, Wilf hurled himself downstairs to collect his gifts of a selection box, a jumper and a box of double-chocolate cookies. 'Cool, thanks,' he breathed.

When the doorbell rang again, Sky opened the door to a spruced-up Graham. 'If you meant it about joining you,' he said diffidently, 'I do have a weakness for turkey.'

Sky ushered him in. 'Merry Christmas! Of course, we meant it.'

He presented each of them with family-sized boxes of chocolates, which Sky thought he'd probably bought hastily from the village shop, but as he produced cards with money in for Wilf and Courtney, too, she felt he'd made more effort than anyone would have anticipated a few days before.

She glanced at her watch. No Ron, yet, and no message. But then, just when the vulnerable patch in her heart was wondering if he'd decided not to spend Christmas with her after all, he appeared at the door declaring, 'Bloody roads are atrocious. I haven't missed lunch, have I?' And Sky found herself once again buried in her grandfather's hug. It was almost beginning to feel . . . well, normal.

Ron had brought six boxes of chocolates. 'Didn't really know how many of us there would be,' he observed cheerfully.

Gleefully, Wilf added another box of chocolates to his stash.

Ron turned to Sky. 'I have something else for you, dear.' Bashfully, he held out a square parcel wrapped in red paper.

'Oh, thank you,' Sky breathed, taking it with wonder. 'It's quite heavy.' She unwrapped the parcel, conscious of several gazes fixed on her. To her absolute shock, she found a worn wooden box full of jewellery that gleamed dully in the light. Most of it was gold, heavy, and old-fashioned. Wordlessly, she gazed at Ron.

His smile wavered. 'It's your grandmother's jewellery. I hope it makes up for all the Christmases we've missed.'

Sky found herself in another huge hug, one that went on and on. In a muffled voice, she said, 'This beats what I got you by a mile.'

But when he opened the two thick sweaters she'd bought for him, he beamed. 'Splendid! My wardrobe is missing a woman's touch – since I lost your grandmother,' he added gruffly.

Sky went off to make the nut roast, leaving the others to chat around the fire. Setting the kitchen table, she reflected that it was a good job Daz hadn't wanted to bring Abi. There were only six chairs and that would have made eight people.

Lunch was the traditional mix of delicious, rich festive fare, pulling crackers and reading out weak jokes, paper hats sliding drunkenly over eyes. Sky got a green plastic ring, and Wilf a yellow plastic frog. 'Don't touch it,' Sky cried in mock horror. 'It's a golden poison dart frog and you'll end up spending Christmas in hospital.'

Wilf looked impressed. 'You get poisonous frogs?'

Ron and Graham shook puzzles of metal interlocking rings from their crackers and began a competition to see who could get the rings apart fastest, while Marietta's cracker yielded a red plastic heart, which she clipped to her Christmas cardigan that bore reindeer galloping around the hem.

Mid-afternoon, after Christmas pudding had been eaten and the dishwasher stacked, Courtney checked the time. 'I've arranged a call from Lewis.'

Graham grew suddenly pink around the eyes. 'I'd like to join that, please.'

They both looked hopefully at Wilf.

Instantly, Wilf's smile vanished. Sky's heart ached for him. But it also ached when she thought of Lewis, who she'd never met and who had done reprehensible things, but who was spending Christmas in an inhospitable place, apart from his family, and she found it in her heart to be glad when Wilf said, ungraciously, 'Oh-*kay*. I'll speak to him.'

Courtney gave Wilf the biggest, tightest, squeeziest hug that Sky thought she'd ever seen. She had to swallow hard before saying, 'You guys go upstairs to take the call. I'll make coffee when you get back.'

Once they'd gone, she explained to Ron who Lewis was, and how Wilf had been feeling.

'Dear, dear,' said Ron, sombrely. 'There are no winners in those situations.' He relapsed into silence for a minute.

Remembering he'd been a lawyer and wondering how many 'situations' he'd seen, she said, 'Certainly, none of it is the fault of Lewis's poor family. It's good of Wilf to reach out to his dad on Christmas Day. He's got a big heart, hasn't he, Marietta?'

'Oh, my, that boy's a joy,' Marietta agreed sleepily. She looked as if she'd like a nap.

Ron rubbed his beard and cocked an eye in Sky's direction. 'You know, it's only just past ten in Thailand.'

It took a moment, but then his meaning rushed in on her. She swallowed. Ron was thinking that if Wilf could talk to his dad, then Sky could talk to her mother. Her stomach whirled.

Her grandfather took her hand in his lined but warm and strong one. 'It will mean a lot if you talk to Trish.'

Sky studied him. 'Mean a lot to you? Or to her?'

He looked pensive. 'To me, certainly. And I assume her, too, as she asked me to see if I could arrange it.'

Marietta climbed to her feet. 'And you folks are reminding me that I need to Skype my Ira and his family. It's about the same in Jakarta. Shall I go into the kitchen, Sky?'

Sky sighed and bowed to the expectations of others. 'You stay in here. My laptop's already in the kitchen and Ron and I can sit at the table and talk to my mother together.' If she was going to have to do this thing, she was going to have her grandfather – now beaming – at her side.

It took only a couple of minutes to get settled and open FaceTime. Stiffly, Sky typed in the contact details and sat back, gazing apprehensively at the screen. Her fingers twitched with the need to slam the laptop shut, assailed by old images of thin, furious Trish, hurling things, venting scorn and venom, hair pulled back but never cut.

Ron took her hand, as if her thoughts had shown on her face.

The screen flashed.

Sky gripped Ron's fingers, fighting fresh anxiety.

Then all at once there was the image of a woman staring at her through the screen and Sky shrank back. She couldn't swallow or even lick her lips. The woman's hollow cheeks had filled out and her bobbed hair was brushed, streaked and highlighted. Her eyes were nicely made up. Beside her sat another woman, one with a smart, short, silver cut. They all stared at each other.

It was like a disturbing dream, one where you didn't really understand what was going on, except that it was threatening. Sky wanted to wake up and end it.

Ron cleared his throat. 'Trish, Martha, Merry Christmas.'

Then the well-remembered voice reached Sky's ears. 'Merry Christmas, Dad.' Then, breathily: 'Sky. It's great to see you.'

Paralysed, Sky's heart felt as if it were fighting her ribcage to get out.

Ron squeezed her hand again. 'She's grown up beautiful, as I told you, Trish. She's a wonderful, warm human being.' When no one responded to his hearty encouragement, he added, 'Trish, I think you had something to tell Sky, didn't you?'

Sky watched Trish's expression. Hunted. Scared. Sky knew how she felt.

Then Martha slipped her arm around Trish and kissed her temple. It was odd to witness Trish being treated so tenderly and Sky realised she'd never before seen it. Trish cleared her throat. 'I'm sorry, Sky,' she said. 'I was the cruddiest mother on the planet. I was selfish and negligent. I feel terrible. I don't expect your forgiveness, but I want you to know that I've faced up to my behaviour. I'm an alcoholic.' She directed a smile at Martha. 'It's only in the last couple of years, when we got together, that I began to clean up my act. Martha's my partner, by the way.'

Martha gave a gentle smile. 'Hello, Sky.'

Stiffly, Sky nodded.

Trish's lips twisted. 'I'd love to tell you that I'm totally sober and together, but that would be overstating. I'll just say I've improved.'

Martha gazed into the screen, as near to meeting Sky's gaze as a video call allowed. 'Trish very much wanted to make contact, Sky.'

As something was obviously expected of her, Sky croaked with an effort, 'Merry Christmas.'

Everyone echoed, 'Merry Christmas,' as if they hadn't already said it. Sky saw disappointment in her mother's face, but the settled-looking, well-nourished woman kept fading, being overlaid with the too-well-remembered snarling, yelling Trish. Sky still wanted to close the laptop. Close out the past.

While she fought her inner battle, Ron told Trish and Martha about their white Christmas in Winter Street and Trish and Martha described their barbecued snapper on the beach. Martha spoke of her life as a teacher in Thailand at a language school. Ron described his drive out of Norfolk in the snow. Martha said the sea had been a beautiful twenty-eight degrees Celsius this morning, when they swam.

Mother and daughter stared at one another, wordless.

Sky took in the wooden walls of the building her mother and partner occupied, their ease with one another, the happiness in Trish's eyes.

Then, with relief, she heard voices from her sitting room: Wilf's high piping, Graham's deeper rumble. The others must have come back downstairs after their call to Lewis.

Ron must have heard it too, as he wound up the call as if it had been no more than a warm family chat. 'Well, I know Christmas is almost over for you, in Thailand, but Sky still has guests. We must let her join them.'

Martha said something just as friendly and polite. Trish said, 'Bye, Dad. Bye, Sky.' And, after a hesitation. 'I hope we can speak again.'

Sky just said, 'Bye.'

And finally, thankfully, she reached out and shut the laptop lid.

Ron slipped his arm around her. 'That was tough, I know, darling. Thank you for trying. I hope it wasn't too much for me to ask.'

Sky was too relieved it was over to do more than hug him back. 'I never made that coffee.'

Ron looked suddenly drawn, but if he was disappointed that Sky had nothing to say about her mother, he didn't say so. 'It'll be one for the road for me. I have a bit of a journey.'

When they joined the others, passing around coffee and hot chocolate, it seemed that the other calls had gone well. Marietta chatted happily about what she called 'the grand-babies' and even if Courtney, Wilf and Graham all looked as if they'd shed a tear, they were smiling now.

Wilf said to Sky in a low voice, 'Dad sounded just the same.' It was said so much as if Sky alone would understand that he'd expected Lewis to be changed, that she hugged him hard, wanting to reassure him that she understood the experience of being damaged by the one who was meant to keep you safe.

'I spoke to my mum,' she whispered. 'She didn't sound the same.' She thought of the rages. 'She sounded better.'

Wilf looked wise beyond his years. 'Weird, huh?'

Sky could only nod.

Wilf wriggled out of the hug. 'Daz came, while you were in the kitchen. He brought me headphones on a stand and Mum and Marietta perfume. And he left something for you.'

'For me?' Shocked, Sky took a soft floppy parcel from Wilf's hands. Daz hadn't been on her Christmas shopping list. Since the night he'd got drunk, she hadn't thought they were on those terms. Realising that everybody was waiting expectantly, she opened the parcel, pulling from the paper the softest sweater in pale blue. On the front was embroidered, *Bee happy, bee friendly*, and buzzing around the words were black and gold felted bees with silver wings. 'Oh,' she murmured. 'I must thank him.'

'Can I come?' demanded Wilf, jumping up.

Sky was taken aback. She meant she'd thank Daz *sometime*, not this instant. 'We can't interrupt his Christmas. He had plans.'

Courtney spoke up. 'He was going home from here. He's spent most of the day with his parents, but they've gone to friends this evening.'

'I wouldn't want to barge in on him and Abi.' Sky smoothed the sweater, feeling the softness against her skin. 'I'll call him tomorrow or the next day.' She pictured him and Abi snuggled up on one of those big sofas, watching movies and eating chocolates. Maybe Abi was in that silky robe.

Wilf picked up the last box of chocolates that Ron had brought, the one that remained unallocated. 'Well, I'm going. I'll take these and tell him that they're from you. It won't be Christmas tomorrow or the next day.' He sounded disappointed in Sky.

Courtney wrinkled her nose. 'I'd rather Sky went with you. It's dark.'

Sky frowned at her. Why didn't Courtney go with Wilf if she was so concerned?

But then Courtney went on, 'I want to walk Graham home and have a little chat.'

Ah. She must want to discuss Lewis. Sky suppressed a sigh. The jumper, so unexpected, could be an olive branch. They had friends in common, after all, and if they went on hardly talking to each other in company, it would affect everyone else. She could 'bee friendly' in response. 'OK, Wilf. You wrap the chocolates for me while I see everyone out, then we'll go. You're right. Christmas presents should be given on Christmas Day.'

Ron had already buttoned his jacket and was holding Marietta's cranberry-coloured coat for her. At the door, Sky gave Ron a big hug. 'Sorry if that call didn't go as you'd hoped.'

His big arms hugged her back. 'I know it was hard. I'm proud of you for letting her reach out. See you soon, I hope.'

This last would have been such a normal, grandfatherly phrase for most people, but it made Sky's eyes boil and she could only wave and smile as Ron gave Marietta his arm along the slippery path, calling their thanks for a lovely day and renewed Christmas wishes as they went.

Courtney and Graham left next, Graham looking happier and more relaxed than Sky had ever seen him.

She closed the door behind them and, for a moment, felt alone . . . until Wilf boinged into the hall with apparently boundless energy. 'Here's your coat. I'll carry the chocolates.'

Chapter Twenty-Three

Sky made Wilf wait while she changed into boots, added mittens, hat and scarf to her ensemble and made him find his hat, too. The village looked like an ice sculpture, and she wasn't braving the iron chill until they were both properly dressed.

Winter Street was eerily quiet, apart from the crunch of snow beneath their boots. Everyone must be indoors, eating Christmas goodies and enjoying their gifts. Only Santas and snowmen grinned from gardens that were lit up like . . . well, like Christmas Day.

Wilf raced ahead, the chocolates, now wrapped in starry blue paper, rattling. 'I'll bet our slide's crazy slippery.'

'Be careful,' Sky warned, almost losing her footing herself because half her mind was on which Daz they'd meet – the nice one, the moody one or the loved-up-with-Abi one. She didn't let herself think about the drunk one. Something blue caught her eye and she stooped to retrieve Wilf's thick woollen hat from the icy ground. 'Your ears will get frostbite,' she called, waving it at his departing back.

But Wilf was racing towards the ice slide that glistened like a strip of metal on the pavement. He yelled, 'Watch, 'cos this is going to be awesome.' His hair blew back and his feet scrabbled furiously for grip. With a whoop, he leapt into the air and landed on the polished ice. But . . . 'Whoa!' Instead of coasting along the slide on his feet, somehow Wilf's legs flipped out from under him.

As if in slow motion, his young body began to backflip. The crack of his head meeting the ice reached Sky over the hushed street.

'*Wilf*,' Sky gasped, scrabbling for purchase on the slippery snow as she tried to break into a run. 'Wilf, are you OK?'

Wilf was not OK. Wilf lay perfectly still on his back, mouth half-open and one arm outflung. His face was white.

'Wilf?' Sky cried, falling to her knees. She patted his face, praying he was only stunned and would open his eyes with a faint, 'Wowsers trousers.' But it was as if Wilf had become part of the village ice sculpture, frozen and white.

'Wilf, wake up, darling, oh, holy shit, Wilf please, please, *please* wake up. Don't be hurt, Wilf, *please*,' she begged.

Then suddenly someone was scrambling across the icy road, skidding to a halt by their side. 'What happened?' demanded Daz's voice.

'He slipped and banged his head,' Sky sobbed. She dragged out her phone. 'Courtney's gone to Graham's.'

Daz breathed hard, his breath hanging before him in a white cloud. 'You get her here. I'll call the ambulance, then run and get a quilt to cover him up. You know not to move him, right?'

She nodded distractedly, most of her attention on her

phone as Courtney's voice said brightly in her ear, 'Hey, Sky. Everything OK?'

'No,' Sky howled. 'Wilf slipped and hit his head. He's unconscious. Daz's calling the ambulance.'

The next half-hour passed in a blur. Courtney's panicked arrival, grey with anxiety. Daz piling a quilt over Wilf. Sky apologising, explaining, retelling, hearing herself say piteously, 'If only he hadn't dropped his hat. It might have cushioned him a bit.'

Courtney crying, pleading with Wilf to wake up. Wilf not waking up. Neighbours emerging from houses, asking if they could do anything. Sky feeling sure her tears would freeze on her cheeks but powerless to stop them falling.

Finally, a flashing blue light brighter than all the Christmas lights, a man and a woman wearing coats over their green paramedic uniforms, asking questions, reassuring. Getting Wilf onto a stretcher.

Courtney stumbling in the ambulance.

Daz saying, 'I'll follow in my car.'

Sky running beside him, so stunned she could hardly feel the snow beneath her feet, jumping into the passenger side of his car without asking and him not saying she couldn't. Catching up with the ambulance on the Bettsbrough road, still flashing its lights but unhurried. *Like it's carrying a cargo of eggs*, she thought despairingly.

Through Bettsbrough, under the jolly lights that paled in the flashing blue from the ambulance.

Out again towards Peterborough, along the parkway and finally to the hospital. Daz parking, taking her hand across the car park, not with tenderness but probably because he didn't want to have to attend to her if she fell too.

Into Accident and Emergency. Sky realising that she still held Wilf's blue hat and dissolving into fresh tears. Daz slipping an arm around her while he talked to the receptionist. Listening. Nodding. Saying, 'OK. We'll wait over here.' Pulling Sky along. 'Sit here.' Leaving her for a moment then returning with paper towels for her to soak up her tears.

He gave her hand a comforting squeeze, then let go. 'Courtney's with him.'

Sky nodded. 'It happened so quickly,' she whispered.

The hand took hers again and stayed there, this time. 'It wasn't your fault. It was an accident.'

But it felt like Sky's fault.

They waited. People came and went, seeking treatment or seeking their loved ones who'd been brought in. Inappropriately cheery tinsel twirled around the reception desk and a TV on the wall silently showed a Christmas movie, subtitles flashing across the foot of the screen.

The waiting area smelled of vomit and, after a woman arrived who'd had an accident with a carving knife, of blood. Two ambulances passed the doors, blue lights flashing.

Eventually, a nurse approached. 'Darragh Moran?'

'Yes.' Daz leapt up, and Sky tried to do the same, but her legs had turned to string.

'You're here for Wilford Brown? His mother wants you to know that he's regained consciousness and he's to have a scan.'

'Oh, *thank* you,' they chorused, although the news she'd given them was only partly positive.

'What's the scan for, exactly?' Daz demanded.

The nurse smiled. 'That's all I know, I'm afraid.'

The darkness outside matched that in Sky's heart as they resumed their seats. She shivered, though she still wore her coat. Daz's lay beside him on a chair. A memory flashed of him flying over the snow towards her and Wilf. 'How did you know to come out?'

He hadn't taken her hand again. 'I was closing the curtains upstairs and saw you kneeling beside him in the snow.'

'Thanks. It was a big relief.' She wondered how he'd left things at home. 'Sorry if it's spoilt your evening.'

'I wasn't doing much,' he replied tonelessly.

She couldn't not ask. 'Did Abi mind you coming?'

She sensed, rather than saw, his head turn towards her. 'Abi went back to London on Monday.'

Sky turned this over in her mind and realised she hadn't seen Abi whizzing down Winter Street in her car in the last few days. 'Not in a snit because Courtney and Wilf were spending Christmas with me?'

He barked a laugh. 'Because it was time for her to return to her real life.' He glanced at her. 'She turned up saying she was in a jam. That's the only reason I let her stay. We didn't get back together.'

She arched a brow at him. 'I saw her in your bedroom window, wearing a sexy little robe. And I know which is your bedroom,' she reminded him pointedly.

Shock flickered in his eyes, but he countered emphatically. 'Then it must have been while I was elsewhere, because at no time did she enter my bedroom while I occupied it.' He paused before adding, 'I don't want to speak badly of her, so I'll just say that it eventually became clear that she had an agenda.'

Sky's heart leapt. 'And you were on it?' At his nod, she wondered if this could be true, if Abi had been creating the appearance of intimacy while she tried to get Daz back . . . but then she recalled Daz's unacceptable behaviour when drunk and her heart resumed its normal position. Her mother's face as she'd seen this afternoon swam into her imagination. She'd improved a lot since the growling, swearing, drunk of Sky's childhood, but Sky had been unable to trust her, wanting to back away, even though there were two computer screens and several thousand miles between them.

She sighed.

After another hour of nothing to do but watch TV subtitles or patients filling up the rows of chairs, Sky needed the loo. 'Got to find the ladies',' she murmured.

After visiting the facilities, she found a vending machine and bought two coffees, carrying the squashy plastic cups into the waiting area. Her attention was so focused on not letting them slip or slop that she barely noticed a group of men milling before reception until one backed up and dashed both cups from Sky's hands, all over the legs of some poor woman sitting quietly nearby.

'Ow,' cried the woman.

'I'm so sorry,' Sky gasped. 'I just—' She looked at the man, expecting him to apologise, too. He'd backed into her, after all.

But what she saw was a swaying, weaving group of sullen expressions. The man who'd knocked her, sneered. 'Fuck off.'

Sweat broke out over all of Sky's body.

The man waved a hand in her face. 'I said, fuck off! You shouldn't be so pissing clumsy, you stupid cow.'

Sky trembled. He glowered. As if her paralysis was a threat, he loomed nearer, getting in her face, a deliberate intimidation tactic. 'I *said*—'

The smell of alcohol stinging her nostrils, her arms flew up of their own volition and batted wildly. 'Get off me! Stop! Get out! Go away.'

'Ouch.' The man stumbled back into two of his mates,

who instantly shoved him back in Sky's direction. Her hands were already out, fending him off, fighting back against his towering, unsteady aggression and the stink of beer. 'No! Don't,' she cried.

Then Daz was there, getting between her and the drunk, nudging her backwards, encircling her with gentle arms. 'It's OK, Sky,' he murmured. 'You're OK. You're OK. I'm here and you're OK. Just breathe.'

Then other people clattered onto the scene. Security, Sky thought shakily, seeing men in dark uniform. They told the drunken group to sit down quietly or leave. 'We don't want to call the police because they always get here in a bad mood if you drag them away from their Christmas pud,' one security guard said with false bonhomie.

The men fell back, grousing and grumbling like a pack of dogs.

A security guard approached Sky, who was quaking in the circle of Daz's arms. 'Can you tell me what happened, love?'

Sky couldn't. She was too busy trying to control her choppy breathing and galloping heart. It was Daz who explained about the man knocking into Sky and panicking her with his aggression. The woman who'd been the unlucky recipient of two flying cups of coffee backed him up.

With a bit of shouting about 'the fucking National Health', the men decided that whatever had brought them to the hospital wasn't urgent enough to keep them there and careened out through the sliding glass doors.

The room relaxed.

Sky collapsed into a seat. Some kind person went to the vending machine and replaced her coffee, but she shook too much to lift it to her lips. Daz had to cup his hand around hers and hold it steady.

When she'd managed several mouthfuls he murmured, 'That was a full-blown panic attack.'

Her teeth chattered. 'I suppose.' She felt stupid and conspicuous now, miserable at losing it when all that mattered this evening was Wilf.

Daz stroked her back. 'You were . . . like you were with me that night at Courtney's.'

Her hand trembled anew, and her voice almost dried up. 'The night you were drunk, you mean?'

'I wasn't drunk.' He met her eyes when she glared up in naked disbelief. 'I wasn't, Sky,' he insisted gently. 'I hadn't even had two beers. I spilled most of one down my sweatshirt, and drank one other.' Understanding flashed into his eyes. 'But you thought I was drunk, right? I smelled of beer.'

Jerkily, she nodded. 'You *acted* drunk. You closed the door and backed me against a wall. You towered over me—'

'No,' he contradicted her slowly, his voice filled with compassion. 'I acted *angry*. I did close the door, so Wilf wouldn't hear us, and then *you* backed away from *me*. As for "towering", well, I'm taller than you, that's all. I'm sorry if that felt intimidating.' His hand continued its soothing stroking of her back. 'I was upset after seeing Lewis, and also because I thought you were babysitting while Courtney dated. Lewis had begged me to talk Courtney out of it and I was torn and unhappy. I was angry, but I smelled of beer and you translated that as drunk.'

Trembling, she managed to get her coffee to her lips herself this time, trying his hypothesis on for size. 'Perhaps,' she admitted waveringly. 'I was certain you were drunk. People behave true to type when they're drunk. Some get affectionate . . . and others are aggressive.'

He took her cup and placed it along with his between his feet, so he could take her hands and examine her face. 'You thought you'd seen me in my true colours – aggressive – and you had to defend yourself.'

'Yes,' she whispered, trying to re-see the scene in her mind to assess whether his version of events could possibly be true. 'Mum got verbally abusive when she was drunk. And she was always drunk. I was a child. Ranting and screaming was frightening. Perhaps—' She paused for a deep breath. 'Perhaps in similar situations, those feelings of fear and anxiety return. I—I thought you were a threat.'

He swore, then brought his arms up to cradle her softly against him. 'I wasn't drunk but I'm sorry I frightened you. I'm sorry I let my temper show. I didn't realise you were having a panic attack. I thought you were trying to attack me. I didn't understand. I thought it was an unreasonable overreaction.'

Her head somehow found its way onto his shoulder. 'I didn't attack you. I was just pushing you away.'

Quietly he said, 'It *felt* like an attack.' Sombrely, he added, 'Abi was what Mum calls "high maintenance". I didn't want to get involved with another unpredictable woman.'

'Oh.' She digested this. 'Sorry,' she said awkwardly. 'I've always overreacted to drunks, but no one else has ever put two and two together.'

'I think it's called being triggered.' He kissed her hair, and they sat on in silence.

Though the room was cold and filled with unhappy, ill or injured people; though she was still terrified for Wilf, Sky was filled with peace.

Finally, her eyes closed.

Then suddenly she realised that Courtney was crouching before them, wan, tear-stained, but smiling. 'Wilf came round in the ambulance, but I couldn't leave him till he'd had a scan. He's concussed, but no fracture.' She stopped to wipe her eyes. 'He's staying in for twenty-four hours because there are things that can happen after a bang like that. I'll stay with him.' She gave a strangled laugh. 'To think that I was the one saying kids ought to be allowed to have fun when people said the slide was dangerous.'

An enormous pang of guilt speared through Sky. 'So did I.' She had to wipe her eyes. 'Shall we fetch you an overnight bag?'

Courtney straightened up, shaking her head. 'It's nearly two a.m. I'm only going to nap in the chair alongside his bed and you look exhausted. It would be great if you could bring it in the morning, though.'

Drained by trauma and emotion, Sky didn't argue. After Courtney had returned to her son, Sky trailed across the icy car park holding Daz's hand. She'd lost her mittens somewhere, but his skin was hot against hers.

He told her to get in while he scraped the windscreen, and she was too washed out to protest. When he finally climbed in beside her, he again gathered her up in his arms. 'I truly didn't understand.'

'That's OK, because I didn't either,' she said, kissing the side of his face.

His arms tightened. Gruffly he said, 'It's not OK . . . unless we can take up where we left off.'

A whoosh of joy raced through her, sweeping away the fatigue that until a moment ago had felt as if it were consuming her. 'Where did we leave off?' she asked, needing to be sure she wasn't harbouring false hope.

His stubble was rough as it brushed her cheek. 'Before bloody Abi turned up and before our confrontation, I was about to try and start something real with you. Move us past the amazing sex into a fuller relationship.' He disentangled himself enough to draw back, questions in his eyes.

She beamed in reply, stupidly happy. 'You don't want the amazing sex?'

'I *do*,' he declared. 'As well.' He kissed the tip of her nose. 'But all I want to do in bed tonight is hold you close and be thankful that we're together, and that Wilf's going to be OK.'

'That,' said Sky, nuzzling his neck, 'sounds perfect.' Then, on reflection: 'But are you sure about the "all"?'

His laughter was low and warm. 'You can wake me whenever you want.'

Chapter Twenty-Four

It was still dark when Sky became aware of Daz moving about her bedroom. She lifted her head and squinted at the clock. 'It's not even seven. Are you sneaking off on the walk of shame?' she joked drowsily.

Daz arrived back on the bed with a bounce, nuzzling her neck and slipping his hand into the warmth beneath the duvet to stroke her back. 'I was trying not to wake you. I want to sprinkle something over that slide before anyone else hurts themselves. I don't think I'll ever forget the sight of Wilf lying there, so still.'

Sky shuddered at the vision his words conjured up. 'Me, neither. Hang on. I'll come with you. I have heaps of sawdust that will be just the job.'

They were used to piling on every item of outdoor clothing they could in this cold snap but even so, they both sucked their breath in with a 'Whoo!' as they stepped out into the frozen morning. The mass of fairy lights embroidering the trees and shrubs were just beginning to fade in the face of the steely dawn.

From the barn they took shovels and buckets and in

the back garden scraped away snow to hack at the frozen crust on the sawdust pile to reach the powdery stuff. They filled both buckets and soon were slithering their way up Winter Street.

When they reached the kids' slide, they spread the sawdust with long, even swings of the shovels until what had looked gleaming and pretty under a fresh coat of frost turned to brown, ugly slush. Ugly, but safe. They didn't stop until the buckets were empty.

Sky hunched into her coat. 'Ruth will complain we've spoiled the snow.'

'Let her try,' Daz said balefully.

When they popped over to Daz's house, they found the chocolates Wilf had wrapped for Daz on his doorstep. Sky had to blink tears away as she read the label, *To Daz from Sky* in Wilf's immature handwriting. 'Someone must have found it where he dropped it and delivered it. Aren't people in Winter Street lovely?'

Once indoors and out of the cold, they texted Courtney for news of Wilf. Her reply read: *Seems OK this morning apart from headache and big egg on his head. Got to be alert and eating before release. Xx*

'Phew,' breathed Sky.

Back at The Corner House, they packed a change of clothes and toiletries for Courtney and Sky drove them to the hospital. Courtney came down off the ward to meet them, wan and tired. 'I've been keeping Graham in the loop and he's coming to see for himself that his grandson's OK, but Wilf should be out this evening, if all's well. They've given me an information sheet about head injury and what to look out for.'

'Call us when you want fetching.' Daz gave Courtney a hug.

Sky and Daz went home to spend a quiet Boxing Day together. When they returned in the evening, Wilf was discharged but subdued, his unnatural pallor and careful movements heightened by wearing yesterday's rumpled clothes. He managed to smile for them but climbed into Sky's car with a sigh of relief. Courtney got into the back seat with the battered boy.

Once home, Courtney emailed Lewis to tell him what had happened, then rang the prison to ask for the email to be printed out and taken to him without delay, in the circumstances. When she came off the phone, she was frowning. 'It was only fair to tell Lewis that Wilf's been in hospital, but I've asked him not to phone today. Wilf doesn't need the anxiety. I'll try and get him to agree to talk to his dad again soon, though. Lewis will be worried to death.'

Then her lip wobbled, and Sky scooped her friend up into a big hug. 'Why don't you and Wilf have something to eat and go to bed?'

Courtney's head was heavy on Sky's shoulder. 'I think I could sleep here, standing up, to be honest.' But she managed a smile and said, 'Bedtime, Wilfie.' He didn't even argue.

As they'd all effectively missed Boxing Day, Sky declared Boxing Day to be the 27th instead. 'After all, we have plenty still to eat.'

Wilf was brighter, but happy to take it easy on the sofa with one of his many boxes of chocolates until summoned to the table for meals.

It was after lunch when Sky heard a car draw up outside and glanced out, starting when she recognised a familiar profile with short curly hair and a determined chin. 'It's

Freddy,' she murmured to Daz, as Courtney was napping on the sofa and Wilf glued to the whizzing, whooshing action of a Star Wars film.

Daz raised his eyebrows. 'Really?' They both watched as Freddy slammed his car door and strode through Sky's garden gate.

She went to the door, wondering, but offered genially, 'Hi, want to come in for coffee?' rather than demanding answers from him on the doorstep.

Freddy's eyebrow quirked, as if surprised at his welcome. 'Thanks, mate.'

As the others were in the sitting room, she settled him at the kitchen table while she made hot drinks. 'Nice to see you.'

Freddy rubbed his nose sheepishly. 'After Minnie being out of order on Friday?'

That seemed ages ago, now. 'Minnie said it, not you. And you expressed your displeasure,' she added, smiling faintly at the memory of his furious roar.

He sipped in silence for several seconds. Then, gruffly: 'I came yesterday evening, but you weren't in.'

'We had a mishap here.' She recounted the details of Wilf's accident. Then, because it was Freddy and he'd struggled out of the same kind of unpleasant hellhole she had, told him about the drunken men at the hospital, and how she'd realised she had issues with anger plus alcohol.

He nodded along, frowning, but also sympathetic. 'Makes sense.'

She grimaced. 'It caused a misunderstanding.' She explained how differently she and Daz had interpreted the same angry scene.

Freddy listened intently. 'It's down to Daz I came yesterday.'

She stared at him. He'd hung his coat on the chair and his grey jeans and red sweatshirt suited him. She hadn't seen him in anything other than office clothes for ages. 'Daz?'

'Yep.' He sipped his coffee. 'Me and Minnie had a bleedin' great row, after we'd had sherry with them women, Jessie and Ruth. Minnie stomped off to my car while I cooled off a bit. Turns out it was outside Daz's house, and he came out to chat. Said he knew you and had worked out who I was. Said you were settled in Winter Street but—' A bashful look stole over his face. 'He said you missed me. Said I should call in.'

Heat flooded Sky's face. 'Daz said that on Friday?' At that point, they'd still been stiff and tricky with each other – she'd thought he was a mean drunk and he'd thought she was the one with anger issues – yet he'd done something nice for her. She had to swallow a lump in her throat. 'I hope you patched things up with Minnie.'

'No, you don't.' He grinned. 'And I ain't going to.' He sighed. 'When she hooked up with me I just thought some posh birds like a bit of rough. I was OK with that.' He waggled his eyebrows. 'I like posh birds. But she wanted to erase my past, and even if she truly thought it was for my sake, it didn't work.' He blew out his lips. 'I'm sorry I took her side against you, Sky. I guess I was besotted. You're a good mate and I was a bad one. That's what I came round to say. And 'cos I never had nowhere to go for Christmas,' he added with a laugh, as if signalling that they'd been serious for long enough.

Sky gave a wobbly grin. 'We missed Boxing Day because of Wilf, so we're having it today. Why don't you stay?'

He rubbed his hand through his dark, curly hair. 'Even though I ain't been much of a brother?'

She squeezed his shoulder. 'A brother isn't always perfect. But he's always your brother.'

After checking Courtney had woken from her nap, Sky took Freddy into the sitting room to be introduced to everyone, saying to Daz, 'I understand you've already met.' Softly, she added, 'Thank you.'

The film had finished, and Wilf felt well enough to fetch the biscuits and pass them around.

Freddy said to Sky, 'Any chance you'll come back to work with me? There might be a directorship going.' He grinned.

She snorted. 'That directorship's a myth.' Before he could reply, she added more seriously, 'Maybe. But not yet, Freddy. I'm going to do something with The Corner House first. I've been torn, wanting to stay but knowing it was too big for one person. I've let other people use it for a few things, recently, especially the double reception room on the other side of the house.' She indicated the direction with a chocolate biscuit.

'Is that the big room?' Wilf asked.

Sky nodded. 'I'd like to do something with the place that's for more than me, but with me in it.'

'Give parties?' Wilf asked hopefully.

She laughed. 'I'm not sure there are enough people in Middledip to want parties here all the time.' She turned back to Freddy. 'I could convert the upper floor into a flat for myself, opening out onto the sun terrace over the barn, and divide the ground floor and barn into three self-contained units, maybe for supported living.'

'Vulnerable adults again?' Freddy asked through a custard cream.

'I don't think so,' Sky said slowly, thinking about what she'd observed in Middledip over the past months. 'What the village needs more is small units for the elderly. People like Nan Heather. It's OK for her to live on the ground floor of her house, but the doorways won't be wide enough if she needs a wheelchair full-time. She could go and live with her daughter, but if she wants proper, suitable, purpose-built sheltered accommodation, she has to leave the village.'

'And she'll never leave Middledip,' Freddy said immediately. 'Sounds like a brilliant plan, mate. You could do a bit of consultancy work for me while that's going on though, eh?'

'I'm not working your hours again,' she joked. 'I've got more in my life than work, now.' And more in her life than Freddy. Her gaze strayed to Daz.

He caught her glance and blew her a tiny kiss.

'Bleurgh,' protested Wilf. 'Are you being kissy with Sky, Daz?'

Daz grinned, and reached out to ruffle Wilf's hair, but then withdrew in deference to the egg on his head. 'Every chance I get,' he confirmed.

'Oh, good.' Courtney beamed.

'I guessed as much,' said Freddy.

In the evening, Sky and Freddy walked through a Narnia-like Middledip to Mo's house in Main Road to say Merry Christmas to Nan Heather, who was spending Christmas there. Each had a present for their old foster mum – a warm cardi, gaily wrapped, from Sky; chocolates in a carrier bag from Freddy. Mo and her family wouldn't hear of them just dropping off the gifts and dragged them in to ply them with mince pies.

Then they left them alone in the sitting room with Nan Heather, claiming it would give them a chance to clear up the kitchen. *How understanding,* Sky thought. *What a family.* And she felt ashamed for every time she'd felt sure

Mo must hate having to share Nan with the children she fostered. The truth was, Mo was as kind and big-hearted as her mother.

Sky told Nan Heather her plan to convert the ground floor of The Corner House for what she diplomatically termed 'the over sixties'.

Nan looked delighted. 'There's a need for that,' she declared, squeezing Sky's hand with her shaky, papery one. 'I'm proud of you, duck.'

Sky didn't know whether Nan would ever move into The Corner House because planning permission took forever and then there was the actual conversion works, but, mentally, she reserved one for her, just in case.

Then they said their goodbyes and returned to The Corner House, lit up as brightly as the trees encircling it, to find that Courtney and Daz had realised no one had eaten much proper food today and had made two curries, one turkey and one veggie.

'Smells delish,' proclaimed Freddy, happily discarding his coat on the newel post.

But before they could even start cooking the rice, Sky's FaceTime alert sounded.

'Wonder if that's Ron,' she mused, fishing out her phone. '*Oh*.' The name on the screen was Trish Murray.

Daz checked the screen over her shoulder and abandoned the cooking to others so he could usher her into the empty sitting room. 'It's up to you whether you take the call,' he reminded her as they sank down on the sofa. His eyes were filled with compassion and love.

'I know.' But Sky took a deep breath and touched the green button. When Daz made as if to go, she grabbed his hand and pulled him down again. Trish's face swam onto the screen. She was alone today, apparently on a gorgeous beach of endless white sand edged with swaying palm trees. It seemed a long way from a white Christmas in Winter Street.

Trish smiled. 'Hi,' she said awkwardly. 'I didn't know if you'd answer.'

'Hi,' said Sky, cautiously.

Trish's hair blew around her face and she hooked it behind one ear. She still looked clear-eyed and sun-tanned, as she had on Christmas Day. Was that only two days ago? So much had happened. Trish cleared her throat. 'I was useless last time. I didn't know what to say.'

Sky swallowed. 'Same.'

Trish gave the ghost of a smile. 'I was overwhelmed with guilt. Dad's right, though. You've grown into a beautiful woman.' She cleared her throat. 'To be honest, I mostly looked up my family because Martha thought I should, and I love her. She hasn't caught on yet to what a sleaze I am,' she added, with a painful smile. 'But now I've seen you again . . . I want to know how you are. Will you tell me something about your life? Who you are now and what you do?'

Sky blew out her cheeks, caught unawares by such raw – and rare – honesty from her mother. To refuse seemed harsh in view of the effort it had probably cost Trish, so she embarked on her potted history. It was a lot more about coming back to Middledip than about the years of work-plus-study and then working for Freddy, or past relationships with Marcel and Blake.

Trish listened, a line between her eyes. When Sky wound down, she said, 'You'd never have become a successful person, if you'd stayed with me. You did the right thing by leaving.'

Sky nodded. There was no point in pretending. She'd

abandoned her childhood as firmly as she'd shut the door of their flat on Trish's drunken snores. She'd experienced no guilt as she'd shucked off any responsibility for Trish and concentrated on making a life as different from hers as possible, and she felt none now. For the first time, she was curious though. 'Did you ever wonder what became of me?'

'I did,' Trish answered unexpectedly. 'I used to walk around Peterborough city centre, looking for you. I asked kids of your age if they'd seen you. If they had, they never admitted it. I even wrote down the names of kids I'd heard you mention, so I wouldn't forget. Like Freddy Walker. That was how Dad tracked you down, in the end.'

'I know.' She strived to view those days through her mother's eyes. 'Were you angry?' She felt Daz's hand tighten around hers.

'Of course.' Trish sighed. 'Nothing was my fault, in my eyes, and I saw you as a deserter. We'd been in a shitty life together, and you'd got out and left me to it.' She screwed up her face. 'Alcohol can make you feel like you're a saint and everyone else is a sinner. It was a big part of my rehab to understand that it's not true, to get sober enough to realise that I'd *created* that shitty life.' She cleared her throat. 'I hope you're OK, like I am with Martha.'

'I am.' Then Sky found herself struck by the urge to share something important with the woman who was her mother, at least genetically, yet no longer the mother she'd known. She altered the angle of the screen, so that Daz was in view. 'This is Daz.'

He smiled. 'Hello, Trish.' Then, as if to give Trish some indication of how things were, he lifted Sky's hand and kissed it.

Smile lines appeared beside Trish's eyes. 'Good to meet you, Daz. Martha's more my cup of tea, but you look very nice.'

Sky laughed.

They ended the call with no promises to stay in touch. Sky hadn't decided whether she wanted to. It took more than a couple of calls to erase a lifetime of distrust and disappointment.

Daz tugged her into a warm, tingly hug. 'OK?'

She nodded against his chest. 'At least I have one positive picture of my mother to go along with all the negative memories.' She lay against him for several minutes, listening to the bumping of his heart, trying to sort out her feelings about friends and family. Most people automatically classified family above friends but family hadn't figured large in her life. Ron was more likely to be close to her than Trish was.

She knew she was quiet during dinner, which they served themselves directly from the saucepans Courtney set in the middle of the oak table. Freddy left after the meal, dropping a careless pat on Sky's shoulder with, 'See you soon, mate. Thanks for . . . everything.'

But Sky jumped up and gave him a long, wordless hug, that she hoped conveyed, *I'm so glad you're back in my life.*

Courtney sent Wilf to bed early again, though said he could watch Netflix on his laptop till he was sleepy. Sky looked at Courtney's tired face and said, 'We'll wash up. You need an early night, too. Have a hot bath.'

'That would be awesome,' Courtney replied thankfully.

After clearing up, Sky and Daz flopped onto the sofa. Sky checked the time. 'It's only nine o'clock.' She yawned as she snuggled into him, fitting herself against the lines of his body.

Daz nuzzled her hair. 'I can leave, if you're tired.'

Sky turned her face up to brush her lips against his two-day stubble, letting her mouth drift to a point behind his ear that she'd already discovered made him shiver with pleasure. 'Do you want to leave?'

'No,' he rumbled. 'I want to stay. I was giving you the option.' His mouth set out to follow the curve of her throat.

The rush of pleasure was so intense that her head fell back against the sofa. 'Stay,' she whispered.

'I want to make love with you in front of the fire, again.' His hand slid inside her jumper, leaving what felt like a trail of sparks across her skin. 'But, with Wilf here—'

Arching her back so his questing, caressing hand could access the fastening of her bra, she murmured, 'The beauty of these old doors is that they have locks with keys.' In an instant, she found herself in sole possession of the sofa as Daz strode across the room. A grinding click of the door lock, then he was back, swooping her off the sofa and onto the rug, throwing wood on the fire to make it blaze before pulling off her sweater, taking the band from her hair and shaking it free.

'I don't think I ever thanked you for the beautiful sweater, with the bees,' she murmured, slipping her hands into his clothes to follow the ridges and planes of his back, feeling the downy hair of his body stroke her skin as his top rode up. 'It was a big surprise.'

'I suppose I was still fighting with myself about what our relationship was going to be,' he admitted. 'Reluctant to accept "nothing" as the answer.'

She sighed, the cool air of the room touching her naked top half on one side while the fire gently toasted the other. 'I'm sorry I didn't do the same.'

He drew her against him, tilting her chin so he could

look into her eyes. 'There's nothing I want more than this,' he said. 'You.'

She lifted one hand to stroke his face. 'Consider me yours. I've found it hard to give all my love to anyone in the past. I think I've been saving it up for you.'

Epilogue

One year later

Compared to last year, Christmas Eve in Winter Street was a quiet affair. Not many had wanted to enter the Christmas Street competition again. Some cited the expense, others the effort – it had been all very well putting the lights up in a flush of enthusiasm but taking them down and finding somewhere to store them had proved a pain. Someone said flickering lights gave her daughter migraines. Winter Street had done its bit for charity and now the residents wanted a more relaxed festive season.

'Well,' Sky said, holding Daz's hand as they approached Graham's little house near the school. 'I've never attended a "coming-out party".'

Daz chuckled. 'It has echoes of a debutante's ball, doesn't it? Graham's obviously got his sense of humour back if that's what he calls Lewis's welcome-home lunch.'

Lewis had returned to the village the day before with a tag on his leg, gaining early release on a scheme called Home Detention Curfew.

After a lot of soul searching, Courtney had ended their marriage and it had been Graham to offer the required permanent abode. Courtney hadn't replaced Lewis in her life but enjoyed occasional dates, happy in her little house and firmly part of the village.

Wilf was speaking to his dad again, though Courtney had confided to Sky that there wasn't complete trust. However, they were all sufficiently friendly that she and Wilf had spent this morning at Graham's helping prepare the lunch buffet.

Sky and Daz were living at Daz's house because work had begun on the conversion of The Corner House. Completion was scheduled for February – which, even with Sky's project management skills, probably meant March. The grounds were to be a wildlife garden, with suitable space for people to sit out and enjoy the fresh air, and Sky and Daz couldn't wait to move into the apartment on the top floor, with its sun terrace. Sky hadn't found herself able to sacrifice the sun terrace to solar panels, but power was to come from carbon-friendly air source heat pumps.

Daz was in talks with a computer games company – not his old one – and was expecting a good offer for Reimagined Families in the New Year. The strain of hating his job was gone.

She swung his hand, wondering how he was feeling. This would be the first time he and Lewis had met since prison visits, which Daz had forced himself to make every couple of months in the past year. Sky herself was in a bit of a funk about Lewis being around. Her second-hand knowledge of him was that his actions had thrown the lives of her loved ones into disarray, yet he'd been important to Daz for so long. He might be expecting Sky to like Lewis, as Abi had . . . but what if Sky didn't?

It was a big worry, because last night they'd exchanged engagement rings, an intimate moment in the gentle glow of the Christmas tree, before they plunged into Christmas itself, which would involve so many other people. Daz had asked her the week before, as they'd curled up together on his big sofa. The village group, The Middletones, had been singing 'White Christmas' outside and he'd kissed her and said, 'I'm so incredibly happy living in Winter Street with you. Marry me, Sky? I want it to go on forever.'

For once in her life, Sky hadn't had a single doubt that she was loved. 'I want that too. Yes let's,' had felt like the only possible reply. No showily romantic proposal could have meant more to either of them. A row of chunky sapphires now felt unfamiliar against Sky's skin, but pleasure shimmered through her every time she wriggled her fingers and felt her ring there. It was a symbol of Daz's love, just like every touch and glance he sent her way.

Sky resolved that even if she disliked Lewis, she'd pretend, for Daz's sake.

They were met at Graham's cottage door by Wilf, a taller, more confident boy, now, who flattened his quiff with hair clay. 'Hey, guys,' he said breezily. 'The others are all here.'

'Hey, Wilf,' they chorused, stepping into the warm – and now tidy – house.

'The others' proved to be Daz's parents, Len and Sara, who Daz greeted with hugs, and Marietta, whose friendship with Graham had grown as she'd encouraged him to believe that the village didn't judge him for Lewis's crimes.

Daz let go of Sky's hand to step forward and hug a man Sky had only seen in photographs. 'Lewis,' he cried, clapping his shoulder. 'I want you to meet Sky.'

'Hi,' Sky said, being sure to sound friendly.

But then she was claimed by Sara and Len, who'd known about the engagement but hadn't seen her ring. 'Welcome to the family,' cried Sara, hugging Sky hard.

Sky had to swallow a lump in her throat. 'Thank you,' she said huskily, returning the hugs.

'Darragh,' Sara cried more loudly. 'Congratulations, our wonderful son. Do you have a ring, too?'

With a grin, Daz let his parents examine the titanium band, plain but for a tiny inset stone to match Sky's more flamboyant sapphires haloed with tiny diamonds. A hail of exclamations and congratulations followed, as everyone else clustered round to see the rings.

Though she joined in the joy, hugs and kisses, Sky was ever conscious of Lewis hovering nearby.

Then Courtney, Graham and Wilf brought out a finger buffet, and everyone grabbed plates and tucked into the delicious food, perching on chair arms where there weren't enough seats to go around. Daz ended up beside Lewis and was soon talking about events from before Sky had returned to the village. She had the opportunity to study Lewis. He looked an OK guy, but also, like a plant deprived of light, thin and pale, his shirt hanging on him. It must be a double adjustment for him to be in a normal home again, but that home not be his own.

Sky noticed that Daz used 'we' when referring to himself and Sky and 'you' when he talked to Lewis. She didn't know whether Lewis noted the fine distinction but soon found herself feeling half-sorry for him. She, too, had endured unwanted changes and found herself on the fringes of things. Whether it was a man coming out of prison to live in his dad's house or a child moving into foster care, a seismic change was a seismic change.

And weren't decent people meant to help prisoners out

on licence look forward, rather than back? She took a breath. 'We're meeting for drinks at the pub, tonight, if you fancy joining us,' she said, adding, 'Lewis,' when she saw he wasn't sure if the invitation was for him. 'My foster brother Freddy will be there, too.'

Awkwardly, he smiled. 'Um, thanks. Not sure.'

Perhaps he was aware that braving the pub, when the whole village would know he'd been in prison, might be tough. Or maybe, Sky thought suddenly, the tag on his leg as a condition of Home Detention Curfew restricted him to his registered address in the evenings.

Marietta obviously hadn't considered this either, as she chimed in, 'After Christmas you can join Marietta's Brain Bashers, our pub quiz team. We're nearly always first or second.'

Daz laughed, moving over to pick Sky up from her seat and sit down with her on his lap. 'We won't be if they take out the nature section, as Haden's threatening to. Sky smashes that segment.'

'Bell's really good at sport, too,' she protested, snuggling into Daz's arms. Daz had adjusted his attitude to Bell, once he'd seen that Bell never tried to be more than a friend to Sky. Also, Daz was more understanding now that a tricky childhood was never completely left behind.

'Aren't I good at anything?' Marietta demanded, affecting an injured air.

'Cookies,' said Wilf, through a mouthful of one.

As everyone laughed, Lewis looked wistful, and Sky could imagine he was realising how much he'd missed out on: two years of Wilf's life, Courtney striking out alone, Daz falling in love. Even the success of Marietta's Brain Bashers.

Marietta must have noticed, too, as she tried again to include him. 'Did you know that Sky's making units for the elderly at The Corner House? Elisabetta, who lived there before, she'd have been pleased, because it was hard for her living there on her own, in the end. And Heather, who fostered Sky when she was a child, she's taking one of them.'

Sky's heart warmed, as it did every time she thought of this. 'She gave me a home when I was a kid. It feels good that I'm giving her one, now.'

'Great,' said Lewis. 'No place like home.' And his gaze strayed to Courtney, who was talking to Wilf across the room. The wistful light in his eye suggested he knew his home and theirs would always now be separate. Sky had to swallow a lump in her throat.

Later, after the party, and before joining the others at The Three Fishes, Sky and Daz wandered hand in hand to say Merry Christmas to Nan Heather, who was with Mo and family for the festive break. As they walked, Sky said, 'I've never really understood that inmates "pay" for their crimes while in prison, but the cost to Lewis has been high.'

Daz sighed heavily. 'I'm afraid you're right.' Then he smiled, his dark eyes reflecting the Christmas lights weaving above the village streets in the winter wind. 'But that's the past. It's up to him to make the best of things, now. Let's go show Nan Heather your ring and update her on progress at The Corner House. That's our future. The house that brought us together.'

Sky stopped to drag him into her biggest, gladdest hug. 'I hope you didn't only propose so you got The Corner House after all?' she demanded teasingly.

Daz smiled, but he didn't enter the joke. He just gazed at her with his dark, intent eyes. 'I already told you – I want you here forever.'

And they kissed to seal the deal, while fairy lights twinkled down from lampposts and Christmas trees shone from every cottage window.

At home in Middledip. Together.

Loved *A White Christmas on Winter Street*?
Then why not try one of Sue's other cosy Christmas stories or sizzling summer reads?

The perfect way to escape the everyday.

Curl up with these
feel-good festive romances . . .

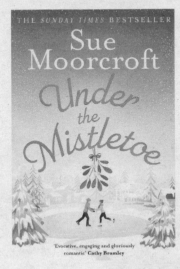

Available from all good bookstores now.

More heartwarming stories of love, friendship and Christmas magic!

Available from all good bookstores now.

Grab your sun hat, a cool glass
of wine, and escape with these
gloriously uplifting summer reads. . .

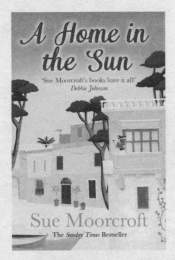

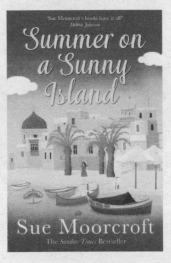

Available from all good bookstores now.

Dive into the summer holiday
that you'll never want to end . . .

Available from all good bookstores now.